FULL FRONTAL FICTION

ALSO FROM THE EDITORS OF NERVE.COM

Nerve: Literate Smut
(edited by Genevieve Field and Rufus Griscom)

Full Frontal Fiction

The Best of Nerve.com

EDITED BY
Jack Murnighan
AND
Genevieve Field

THREE RIVERS PRESS • NEW YORK

Grateful acknowledgment is made to the following for permission to reprint previously published material:

Excerpt from *Perv: A Love Story,* by Jerry Stahl. Copyright © 1999 by Jerry Stahl. Reprinted by permission of HarperCollins Publishers, Inc. Excerpt from *Music for Torching,* by A. M. Homes. Copyright © 1999 by A. M. Homes. Reprinted by permission of HarperCollins Publishers, Inc.

W. W. Norton & Company, Inc.: "A Caring Rescue," by Andre Dubus III. From *House of Sand and Fog* by Andre Dubus. Copyright © 1999 by Andre Dubus. Used by permission of W. W. Norton & Company, Inc.

Published by Three Rivers Press, New York, New York. Member of the Crown Publishing Group.

All stories originally appeared on Nerve.com and, unless otherwise specified, are reprinted by permission of the author.

Random House, Inc., New York, Toronto, London, Sydney, Auckland
www.randomhouse.com

Printed in the United States of America

Design by Paula Kelly

Library of Congress Cataloging-in-Publication Data
Full frontal fiction : the best of Nerve.com / edited by Jack Murnighan and Genevieve Field.
p. cm.
1. Erotic stories, American. I. Murnighan, Jack. II. Field, Genevieve. III. Nerve.com (computer file)
PS648.E7 F85 2000
813'.01083538—dc21 00-030218

ISBN 0-609-80658-0

10 9 8 7 6 5 4 3 2 1

First Edition

CONTENTS

INTRODUCTION

ONE BODY BUMPING AGAINST ANOTHER: in this act, lives are made, minds are derailed, souls are bared and human beings are exposed at their most animal—and thus most human. Nine out of ten bipeds surveyed will tell you it's the most fun thing in the world, but sex still remains a mystery, the thing we will do the most in our lives without ever having a solid grasp of what it means.

If consciousness is the defining characteristic of humanity, then those things that elude our minds' grasp allow us to see our limits, help us understand who we are. Sex, by denying comprehension, catches us in its mirror, if we bother to look. For the fiction writer seeking to represent human experience as we know it, the challenge to depict and delimit sex is as alluring as it is daunting.

Few writers make the attempt—those who do find themselves at the end of language's tether, seeking to find words and phrases to circumvent the pat clichés of erotica and pornography. You are unlikely to think that English is short on adjectives until you start trying to describe what sweat on skin tastes like, or what is seen in the flash of emotions as you enter someone or someone enters you. A million components of sex are taken for granted; when you try to recover them in language, their immediacy becomes distant, their familiarity strange. The pen falters.

What's more, most every relationship has a sexual dynamic, and the relationship affects the sex no less than the sex affects the relationship. And thus the problem with both erotica and pornography: They remove sex from its real human context and, in doing so, erase much of what makes the sexual experience what it is. Both genres idealize our positions and performance (in different ways, of course), but in their attention to physiology they tend to leave out the psychology. Like playing notes without chords, they make a kind of melody, but miss much of the poignancy and resonance of music.

The authors in *Full Frontal Fiction* play both sad and happy songs. Some address sex head-on, bringing bodies into visible and poignant collision; others approach it obliquely, exploring the impact of sexuality on characters caught in its throes. Though each of the stories may be erotic, there is no sugarcoating of experience: in one, a Siamese twin helps set up her other half; in another, a man gets a call from his girlfriend's husband; in a third, two mentally handicapped men have a covert wedding. This is not sex writing as we normally think of it, not what I expected to find when I signed on as editor of Nerve. This is sex seen as a microcosm for life as a whole, painted in the full spectrum of its complexity. I often say that a Nerve story should be stimulating above *and* below the neck; the reality is that, working in unison, each half helps facilitate the other.

—*Jack Murnighan*

I am never inclined to fault those who look for sex in literature; looking for sex, they may find something else.

—*Anthony Burgess*

FULL FRONTAL FICTION

ReBecca

BY VICKI HENDRICKS

AS HER SIAMESE TWIN joined at the skull, I know Becca wants to fuck Remus as soon as she says she's going to dye our hair. I don't say anything—yet. I'm not sure she's even admitting it to herself. The idea doesn't sit well with me, but I decide to wait and see just how she plans to go about it.

It's a warm, clear night, and not a bad walk to Payless Drugs. Becca picks out a light magenta hair-color that to me suggests heavy drug addiction. "No, siree," I tell her. "I know my complexion colors. I'm a fall, and that's definitely a spring." No spring that ever existed in nature, I might add.

"Oh, stop it, Rebby. We'll do a middle part and you can keep your flat brown and I'll just liven up my side. I want to get it shaped too—something that falls around my face."

"It better not fall anywhere near my face."

When we get home from the drugstore, she reads the instructions aloud and there are about fifty steps to this process by the time you do the lightening and the toning. Then she starts telling me which hairs are hers and which are mine. We've gone around on this before. It's a tough problem because our faces aren't set exactly even:

I look left and down while she faces straight ahead and up. For walking we've managed a workable system where I watch for curbs and ground objects and she spots branches and low-flying aircraft. She claims to have saved our life numerous times.

"Oh, yeah? And for what?" I always ask her. And she always laughs. But now I know—so she can fuck Remus, the pale scrawny clerk with the goatee who works at A Different Fish down the corner. Now it's clear why Becca didn't laugh when I pointed out his resemblance to the suckermouth catfish. Also her sudden decision to raise crayfish. Those bastards are mean, ugly sons of bitches, but they suit Becca just fine. They're always climbing out of the tank to dehydrate under the couch, so we have to go back to the store for new ones. Fuck—I'd rather die a virgin. We entertain ourself just fine.

It's two A.M. when she finishes drying that magenta haystack and we finally get into bed. Then she stays awake mooning about Remus while I put a beanbag lizard over my eyes and try to turn off her side of the brain. I know where she's got her fingers. There's a tingle and that certain haziness in our head.

We barely make it to work on time in the morning. Then Becca talks one of our coworkers into giving her a haircut during lunch. The woman is a beautician, but she developed allergies to the chemicals, so now she works at the hospital lab with us.

They're snipping and flipping hair in the break-room to beat shit while I'm trying to eat my tuna fish. "Yes!" Becca says, when she looks in the mirror. Her side is blunt-cut into a sort of swinging pageboy. She tweaks the wave over her eye, making sure we'll be clobbered by a branch in the near future.

We get home from work that evening and—surprise—she counts the crayfish and reports another missing. I try to scramble down to look under the couch in case the thing hasn't dried out yet, but she braces her legs and I can't get the leverage.

"You know how much trouble it is for us to get back up," she says. "Anyway, it'd be covered with dust-bunnies and hair."

At that moment I get a flash of guilt from her section of the brain—she's lying. There is no fucking arthropod under the couch. She wants badly to get back to that aquarium store.

I catch Becca smiling sweetly at me in the hall mirror. I forgive her.

She insists on changing into "sleisure wear"—that's what I call it—to walk down the street. The frock's a short fresh pink number with cut-in shoulders. I'm wearing my "Dead Babies" tour T-shirt and the cutoffs I wore all last weekend. Becca has long given up trying to get me to dress in tandem.

We see Remus through the glass door when we get there. He has his back to us dipping out feeders for a customer. His shaved white neck almost glows. The little bell rings as we step in. Becca tugs me toward the tank where the crayfish are, and I can tell she's nervous.

Remus turns. Straining my peripheral vision, I catch the smile he throws her. I can feel this mutual energy between them that I missed before. He's not too bad-looking with a smile. I start to imagine what it's going to be like. What kind of posture they'll get me into. Maybe I should buy earplugs and a blindfold.

Becca heads toward the crayfish, but I halt in front of a saltwater tank of neon-bright fish and corals. A goby pops its round pearly head out of a mounded hole in the sandy bottom and stares at us. "Look," I say, "he's like a little bald-headed man," but she just keeps trudging on to the crayfish tank, where she pretends to look for a healthy specimen. Remus comes back with his dipper and a plastic bag.

"What can I do for you two lovely ladies tonight?"

Becca blushes and giggles. Remus reddens. I know he's thinking about his use of the number *two*. He's got it right, but he's self-conscious...like everybody.

She points to the largest, meanest-looking crawdad in sight. "This guy," she says. I figure she's after the upper-body strength, the easier he can knock the plastic lid off our tank and boost himself out over the edge. "Think you can snag him?" she asks Remus.

He takes it as a test. "You bet. Anything for my best customer—s." He stands on tiptoe so the metal edge of the tank is in his armpit and some dark hair curls from his scrunched short sleeve. He dunks the sleeve completely as he swoops and chases that devil around the corners of the tank.

Remus is no fool. He's noticed Becca's new haircut and color. I'm thinking, get your mind outta the gutter, buster—but I'm softening. I'm tuned to Becca's feelings, and I'm curious about this thing—although, it's frightening. Not so much the sex, but the idea of three. I'm used to an evenly divided opinion, positive and negative, side by side, give and take. We might be strange to the world, but we've developed an effective system. Even his skinny bones on her side of the balance could throw it all off.

Remus catches the renegade and flips him into the plastic bag, filling it halfway with water. He pulls a twist-tie from his pocket and secures the bag. "You have plenty of food and everything?" Remus asks.

Becca nods slowly and pokes at the bag. I know she's trying to think of a way to start something without seeming too forward. Remus looks like he's fishing for a thought.

My portion of the gray matter takes the lead. "Hey," I say, "Becca and I were thinking we'd try a new brownie recipe and rent a video. Wanna stop by on your way home?"

Becca twitches. I feel a thrill run through her, then apprehension. She turns our head further to Remus. "Want to?" she says.

"Sure. I don't get out of here till nine. Is that too late?"

"That's fine," I say. I feel her excitement as she gives him the directions to the house and we head out.

When we get outside she shoots into instant panic. "What brownie recipe? We don't even have flour!"

"Calm down," I tell her. "All he's thinking about is that brownie between your legs."

"Geez, Reb, you're so crude."

"Chances are he won't even remember what we invited him for." Suddenly, it hits me that he could be thinking about what's between my legs too—a natural ménage à trois. I rethink—no way, Remus wouldn't know what to do with it.

Becca insists that we make brownies. She pulls me double-time the four blocks to the Quickie Mart to pick up a box mix. I grab a pack of M&M's and a bag of nuts. "Look, we'll throw these in and it'll be a new recipe."

She brightens and nods our head, I can feel her warmth rush into me because she knows I'm on her side—in more ways than one, for a change.

We circle the block to hit the video store and Becca agrees to rent *What Ever Happened to Baby Jane?* She hates it, but it's my favorite, and she's not in the mood to care. I pick it off the shelf and do my best Southern Bette Davis: "But Blanche, you are in that wheelchair."

It's eight o'clock when we get home and the first thing Becca wants to do is hop in the shower. I'd rather start the brownies. We both make a move in opposite directions, like when we were little girls. She fastens on to the love seat and I get a grip on the closet doorknob. Neither of us is going anywhere. "Reb, please, let go!" she hollers.

After a few seconds of growling, I realize we're having a case of nerves. I let go and race Becca into the bathroom. "Thanks, Rebelle," she says.

At 9:10 we slide the brownies into the oven and hear a knock. Remus made good time. I notice Becca's quick intake of breath and a zinging in our brain.

Remus has a smile that covers his whole face. I feel Becca's cheek pushing my scalp and can figure a big grin on her too. I hold back my wiseass grumbling. So this is love.

Becca asks Remus in and we get him a Bud. He's perched on the love seat. Our only choice is the couch, which puts me between them, so I slump into my "invisible" posture, chin on chest, and suck my beer. I know that way Becca is looking at him straight on.

"The brownies will be ready in a little while. Want to see the movie?" she asks.

"Sure."

Becca starts to get up, but I'm slow to respond.

Remus jumps up and heads for the VCR. "Let me," he says.

"Relax," I whisper to Becca. I'm thinking, thank God I've got Baby Jane for amusement.

The movie comes on and neither of them speaks. Maybe the video wasn't such a good idea. I start spouting dialogue just ahead of Bette whenever there's a pause. Becca shushes me.

The oven timer goes off. "The brownies," I say. "We'll be right back." We hustle into the kitchen and I get them out. Becca tests them with the knife in the middle. "Okay," I tell her. "I'm going to get you laid."

"Shh, Reb!" I feel her consternation, but she doesn't object.

The brownies are too hot to cut, so Becca picks up the pan with the hot pad and I grab dessert plates, napkins and the knife. "Just keep his balls out of my face," I say.

That takes the wind out of her, but I charge for the living room.

Remus has moved to the right end of the couch. Hmm. My respect for him is growing.

We watch and eat. Remus comments on how good the brownies are. Becca giggles and fidgets. Remus offers to get us another beer from the fridge. Becca says no thanks. He brings me one.

"Ever had a beer milkshake?" I ask him.

"Nope."

"How 'bout a Siamese twin?"

His mouth falls open and I'm thinking suckermouth catfish all the way, but his eyes have taken on focus.

I tilt my face up. "Becca would shoot me for saying this—if she could do it and survive—but I know why you're here, and I know she finds you attractive, so I don't see a reason to waste any more time."

The silence is heavy and all of a sudden the TV blares—"You wouldn't talk to me like that if I wasn't in this chair" — "But Blanche, you are in that chair, you are in that chair."

"Shut that off," I tell Remus.

He breaks from his paralysis and does it.

I feel Becca's face tightening into a knot, but there are sparks behind it.

I suggest moving into the bedroom. Remus gawks.

I'm named Rebelle so Mom could call both of us at once—she got a kick out of her cleverness—and I take pride in being rebellious. I drag Becca up.

She's got the posture of a hound dog on a leash, but her secret thrill runs down my backbone. I think our bodies work like the phantom-limb sensation of amputees. We get impulses from the brain, even when our own physical parts aren't directly stimulated. I'm determined to do what her body wants and not give her mind a chance to stop it. She follows along. We get into the bedroom and I set us down. Remus sits next to Becca. Without a word, he bends forward and kisses her, puts his arms around her and between our bodies. I watch.

It's an intense feeling, waves of heat rushing over me, heading down to my crotch. We've been kissed before, but not like this. He works at her mouth and his tongue goes inside.

The kissing stops. Remus looks at me, then turns back to Becca. He takes her face in his hands and puts his lips on her neck. I can smell him and hear soft kisses. My breathing speeds up. Becca starts to gasp.

He stops and I hear the zipper on the back of her dress. She stiffens, but he takes her face to his again and we slide back into warm fuzzies. This Remus has some style. He pulls the dress down to her waist and unhooks her bra. She shrugs it off.

"You're beautiful," he tells her.

"Thanks," I say. I get a jolt of Becca's annoyance.

My eyes are about a foot from her nipples, which are up like gobies, and he gets his face right down in them, takes the shining pink nubs into his mouth and suckles. I feel myself edging toward the warm moist touch of his lips, but the movement is mostly in my mind.

Remus pushes Becca onto the pillow and I fall along and lie there, my arms to my side. He lifts her hips and slides the dress down and off, exposing a pair of white lace panties that I never knew Becca had, never even saw her put on.

He nuzzles the perfect V between her legs and licks those thighs, pale as cave fish. Becca reaches up and starts unbuttoning his shirt. He helps her, then speedily slips his jeans down to the floor, taking his underwear with them. I stare. This is the first time we've seen one live. I feel a tinge of fear and I don't know if it's from Becca or me.

"Got a condom?" I ask him.

"Oh, yeah," he says. He reaches for his pants and pulls a round gold package out of the pocket. Becca puts her hand on my arm while he's opening it, and I turn my chin to her side and kiss her shoulder. We both watch while he places the condom flat on the tip of his penis and slowly smoothes it down.

He gets to his knees, strips down the lace panties and puts his mouth straight on her. His tongue works in and I can feel the juices seeping out of me in response. Becca starts cooing like those cockatiels we used to have, and I bite my lip not to make a noise. Remus moves up and guides himself in, and I swear I can feel the stretching and burning. I'm clutching my vaginal muscles rigid against nothing, but it's the fullest, most intense feeling I've ever had.

Becca starts with sound effects from *The Exorcist,* and I join right in because I know she can't hear me over her own voice, and Remus is puffing and grunting enough not to give a fuck about anything but the fucking. His hip bumps mine in fast rhythm, as the two of them locked together pound the bed. I clench and rock my pelvis skyward and groan with the need, stretching tighter and harder, until I feel a letting-down as if an eternal dam has broken. I'm flooded with a current that lays me into the mattress and brings out a long, thready weep. It's like the eerie love song of a sperm whale. I sink into the blue and listen to my breathing and theirs settles down.

I wake up later and look to my side. Remus has curled up next to Becca with one arm over her chest and a lock of the magenta hair spread across his forehead. His fingers are touching my ribs through my shirt, but I know he doesn't realize it. I have tears in my eyes. I want to be closer, held tight in the little world of his arms, protected, loved—but I know he is hers now, and she is his. I'm an invisible attachment of nerves, muscles, organs and bones.

It's after one when we walk Remus to the door, and he tells Becca he'll call her at work the next day. He gives her a long, gentle kiss, and I feel her melting into sweet cream inside.

"Good night—I mean good morning," Remus says to me. He gives me a salute. Comrades, it means. It's not a feeling I can return, but I salute back. I know he sees the worry in my eyes. I try to take my mind out of the funk, before Becca gets a twinge.

Remus calls her twice that afternoon, and a pattern takes shape over the next three days: whispered calls at work, a walk down the street after dinner, a 9:10 Remus visitation. I act gruff and uninterested.

When we go to bed I try not to get involved. You'd think once I'd seen it, I could block it out, catch up on some sleep. But the caresses are turning more sure and more tender, the sounds more varied—delicate but strong with passion, unearthly. My heart is cut in two—like Becca and I should be. I'm happy for her, but I'm miserably lonely.

On the third day, I can't hold back my feelings anymore. Of course, Becca knows already. It's time to compromise.

"I think we should limit Remus's visits to twice a week. I'm tired every day at work and I can't take this routine every night. Besides," I tell her, "you shouldn't get too serious. This can't last."

Becca sighs with relief. "I thought you were going to ask me to share."

I don't say anything. It had crossed my mind.

"Just give us a few more nights," she says. "He's bound to need sleep sometime too." I notice her use of the pronoun *us,* that it doesn't refer to Becca and me anymore.

She puts her arm around my shoulder and squeezes. "I know it's hard, but—"

"Seems to me that's your only interest—how hard it is."

I feel the heat of her anger spread across into my scalp. I've hit a nerve. She's like a stranger.

"You can't undermine this, Reb. It's my dream."

"We've been taking care of each other all our lives. Now you're treating me like a tumor. What am I supposed to do?"

"What can I do? It's not fair!" she screams. Her body is shaking.

"It's not my fault, for Christ's sake!" I turn toward her, which makes her head turn away. She starts to sob.

I take my hand to her far cheek. I wipe the tears. I can't cause her more pain.

"I'm sorry. I know I'm cynical and obnoxious. But if I don't have a right to be, who does?" I stop for a second. "Well I guess you do... So how come you're not?"

"Nobody could stand us," she sniffs.

I smooth her hair till she stops crying. "I love you, Becca... Fuck—I'll get earplugs and a blindfold."

That night we take our walk down the street. There's nobody in the store but Remus. He walks up and I feel Becca radiating pleasure just on sight. He gives her a peck on the cheek.

I smell his scent. I'm accustomed to it. I try to act cheerful. I've pledged to let this thing happen, but I can almost feel him inside of her already, and the overwhelming gloom that follows. I put a finger in my ear and start humming "You Can't Always Get What You Want" to block them out. Then it hits me.

"Headphones—that's what I need. I can immerse myself in music."

"What?" asks Remus.

"Oh, nothing," I say, and then whisper to Becca, "I've found a solution." I give her a hug. I can do this.

The little bell on the door rings. Remus turns to see behind us. "Hey there, Rom," he calls, "how was the cichlid convention?" He looks back at us. "Did I mention my brother? He's just home from L.A."

Becca and I turn and do a double-take. In the last dusky rays of sunset stands a mirror image of Remus—identical, but a tad more attractive. A zing runs through my brain. I know Becca feels it too.

Girls

BY JOSEPH MONNINGER

FRANCIE USED TO TALK about the Wailing Wall, Israel, life on the kibbutz. She had gone there once and picked weeds for a summer. She showed me a slide show her parents had put together of a family trip to Jerusalem. She shot the slides against the white wall of the playroom, bright squares of light and desert, and afterward let me work through the zipper of her jeans, gold teeth clawing the back of my hand. This was in New Jersey, a long way from Israel.

Marie cocked her thumbs in the sides of her panties and stepped out of them. Beside her bed, on a rainy afternoon, she lay down and spread her legs, her right knee propped on a Kermit the Frog doll. Other dolls spilled to the floor and the white, puffy curtains breathed in and out with the damp wind. When I stood to go to the bathroom afterward the dolls stared up at me. Later, she made tea and loaded it with cream and sugar. She sat on the backyard lawn furniture, though it was April and chilly, and watched leaves collect in the corner by the patio door.

* * *

You'd go to Friendly's, order a milkshake, park around the back. Three or four guys in the car with you, waiting. Then the girls showed up, their cars smaller somehow, gum, cigarettes, barrettes scattered on the dash, birch inchworms coating their windshield. "Hey," you'd say. Then out in the darkness leaning against the car, the engine warm, the painted lines on the parking lot smooth under your bare feet, and you'd notice she has painted her toenails, maybe for you.

Up and down, up and down, faster, faster, her hand yanking and swirling your penis, her head against your shoulder, her eyes closed against this courtesy. "Hmmmm?" she asks and when you say "nnnnnnn" she works her hand faster, her face somewhere else, thinking about her outfit, about her mom, about the slow steady beat of the Beatles' "Norwegian Wood." When it starts she steps away and holds your penis out, introducing it to the large maple you had been leaning against, letting you finish anywhere, anyplace, as long as not near her.

In the eighth grade Chris Lambla played the same song five times on the turntable, "Never My Love," by The Association, and we danced in the basement of her parents' house. Her breasts lived in the soft wool pouch of her angora sweater. She told me that her mom had gone with her to pick out the sweater, the skirt, too, and that she hated shopping with her mom. Once, she said, she had gone shopping with her mom, had fallen asleep on the way home, and had come awake, hours later, in the vault of the garage. She thought she had been buried alive, something she had been learning about in Tuesday afternoon catechism. The saints, she meant, they had sometimes been buried alive. And she danced against me, the lights dim, the music syrup, and I moved my hand to her bra strap, to her waist, and once, at the end of the night, to the round hump of her ass, weighing it like a farmer judging soil.

Cindy: "If you love me then you won't ask me to do anything I'm not comfortable doing. Do you really like me? Do you? Because I like you, I do, but it's not all about what we do right here. I mean, in a car like this. I mean, what do you really think of me?" She chewed cinnamon gum, the kind with the liquid center. "Cum gum," she said, laughing at the way the gum squirted when she bit into it. That was when she wasn't talking about love and respect.

In the school hallway, we tried to spot Jane Ritzo, who supposedly went on the pill her sophomore year. She went on the pill for Grady Whittle, lead guitarist in The Balloon Farm. The Balloon Farm played at every high school dance, every Teen Canteen, every backyard Sweet Sixteen. Jane Ritzo went on the pill as a gift to Grady is what we heard. She put a bow on the pill packet and gave it to him. Now they were seniors. We had never heard of anything so fine and generous. When we managed to spot her in the hallway, we speculated about those pills. We pictured them, one by one, on her tongue, going down.

Snack bar cook, you grill hamburgers at Echo Lake Swim Club. Mrs. Staub has a plain piece of lettuce with cottage cheese glopped on top. A slice of pineapple, if one is available. She wears a white visor and comes to the snack bar in her bathing suit, bends to rub her foot free of sand or bark bits. You peek down the top of her suit, feel you must keep your distance from the counter. She pays with red nails, her purse snapping primly when she puts the change inside. "Thanks," she says. She walks to the picnic table and sits, eats with knife and fork balanced carefully in her hands. She is brown as pine ship tar, her lipstick pale pink. You see her legs sometimes under the table, watch as they live what seems a life separate from the one her hands live. At the end of the summer, at the pool dance, you kiss her daughter, Sally, who is small and timid, a ghost of Mrs. Staub. You put your hand on Sally's breast fast, faster than you should, and she lets you. She knows she is a ghost, a daughter ghost, and finally you dry hump on a pool pad in the towel room at the back of the men's locker room. Through movement, she becomes her new self, is no longer a ghost, and you kiss a lot, kiss like crazy, Sally becoming a new Mrs. Staub.

She left a note in my locker, slipped it through the vents, the note all curlicues, circle-dotted-I's, red paper. Hi! it said. I had a great time last night!!!!!! See you in Chemistry, 3rd period!!!!!!!!

I rode Sarah on the bar of my English racer bicycle, my arms braced on either side of her. She sat sideways to me, her hair smelling of Prell, my thighs stropping against her body as I pedaled. She turned to me and kissed me and closed her eyes. She closed her eyes while I pedaled and steered.

Skip and I once took this girl Carol out and we had her sit between us in his truck, and we both fiddled around with her crotch, our hands touching sometimes. She let us. She put her hands on our crotches, too, arms out like she was flying, like she was holding our wankers as handles and leaning away, a hood ornament, a bowsprit. Even then, I wasn't sure what she got out of it.

Janie smelled like something sweet, something made up, like a candy store with the door closed too long. Claire smelled like a lawn product, hazy, aerosol, capped. Only Molly smelled of the outdoors. She kept crickets in the top drawer of her desk all winter. It became a ritual with her: in Autumn, before the first frost, she captured a dozen crickets, carrying them to a Hellmann's mayonnaise jar with hollow hands. She dumped them in, screwed on the top, and later put them to graze in the top drawer of her desk. They lived in grass clippings and cedar and maybe that's why Molly smelled so good. At night, after we had turned to spoons, I put my nose against her hair. The crickets rubbed from the desk, summer, winter, spring, and cedar baked into the air at every breath.

Coach B said girls can drain you. Before the game, for a few days, he said stay away from them. Keep your head on the game, he said. I used to meet Sue at the 7-Eleven in Mountainside. She wasn't my girlfriend so it really wasn't against Coach B's rules. We stood on either side of the comic kiosk and spun it back and forth. I liked Silver Surfer, she liked Spider-Man. In the buggy fluorescent light outside she smoked cigarettes and told me about her boyfriends. We pretended we were friends, that I was just listening, but we always ended up kissing in a group of beeches a block from the store. I used to put my hand on her breast and let it rest there, afraid to go further, afraid I wouldn't keep my head in the game. Her nipples, though, felt like buttons to some place I wanted to go.

They would place the rubber on the tip of your penis, check it for size like a mechanic checking a nut, then roll it forward. They did it while they looked up, or kissed, or did anything in the world except look at what they were doing. Some of them made you do it yourself, so you felt like a fireman suiting up or a surgeon fitting on gloves. The slow wrap of the thing squashed your penis like the muscle movement that lets a boa slowly swallow a rat. Afterward, when you saw your mom put shelf paper in the cupboards above the washing machine, you understood: no unsightly rings, no mess, always spongeable, always hygienic.

In the Lido Diner on Route 22, Paula reached her bare foot under the table and put it squarely on my crotch. She gazed at me and let her eyes go slack. We both pretended that was the first time anyone had done that to me, pretended, too, that she had never done that to anybody else.

One summer night, in the heart of heat, you walk with your best girl out onto the Echo Lake golf course. You don't dodge the sprinklers at all. You let them go over you and see her skin showing through her shirt, the hint of her skin, and you get water on your hair. You start kissing and you pull her down, or she pulls you down, and you get her out of her clothes fast. You too. Naked, with the water whipping you once every twenty or thirty seconds, you screw like mad, like wild things, grunt, shove, dig into the dirt, grass, sky, the sprinkler, her, shove shove, and kisses, kisses like maniacs kiss, like dying people kiss, you love her, love everything, love that she likes the sky above you and the sprinkler, and you keep going. Then she says she's cold so you lead her to a tall bank of grass, both of you carrying your clothes, and under a tree, out of the sprinkler whips, you make love, kiss more, talk to each other, say you love one another, and when you come it starts somewhere down deep, far away, and it arrives like a sound you have been waiting for, like a key in the door. You feel like crying and she holds you, and that starts you again. This time more simply, more gentle, and you kiss until you know it is late, very late, and then together you gather your things, dress, cut through Wittingham Place, over to Baldwin, and you can't stop kissing. You wonder why you can't sleep beside each other, what would it hurt, why is the world like this, and you kiss her one last time at her door, see the lights go up her house as she makes her way to her bedroom. You run for the holy hell of it back toward your house, roses out, stars up, the maple leaves throwing puppets of shadows from the streetlights. A part of you knows it will never be like this again, not quite, and you smell honeysuckle, hyacinth, soil. You sit at the kitchen table of your house and eat a bowl of Cheerios, it's late, the smell of her on each spoonful, milk, oats, sugar. You put the bowl in the sink, run water, splash it around. Your mom has left you a note telling you you're the last family member in, lock the door, so you do that, turn out the lights, climb the stairs. It is hot upstairs, coolness just outside, and you lie in a single bed, a childhood cowboy lamp beside you, your hand absently on your crotch. You think of her, remember her pulling you closer, using gravity to draw you to the center, and you fall asleep like that, one white sheet over you, your left leg out to get the last of the air on a summer night.

Terrarium

BY SUSAN NEVILLE

IT WAS ALWAYS DAYTIME when she saw him, but there was never light, and there were never other people. He came to her room, and the room was dark with drawn drapes, and after he left, it smelled of sex.

He said this thing would never hurt a soul. He would never tell a single human being. She would never tell a single human being. It was a completely enclosed system. If anyone saw him enter her room, even once, they would deny everything and end it. She loved him, and she knew it had to be that way for now. He was married. He had children. He was a responsible man.

He left dried semen peeling from her skin, flaking off like sunburn, or was it in fact her skin that was peeling off in layers, leaving her unprotected? Or paint from the walls, which were shrinking to fit her? She was convinced the room was shrinking to fit her.

Pretend with me. His sack crawled like the skin of a squid. It was always moving, no matter what his face was doing. She couldn't begin to imagine being him, that particular kind of bondage. He had beautiful eyes and dark hair with flecks of silver. There was the same silver honeycombed in the window glass.

Her room was in a converted factory where once men had manufactured parts for cars. There was still a red Stutz in a room by a former loading dock that was now a restaurant. There was no door wide enough to drive it through. It had been put together in that room as a novelty, like a ship inside a bottle, and it had remained there.

All her clothes were drenched with the smell of him. Nothing would wash it out. Not a thing in the world would wash it out. It was a musty smell, like decaying leaves. If only she were sure he loved her. If only she were sure he wouldn't leave her here alone. Outside the window there were people walking through the sunlight and the dust. How did they get outside? The room was shrinking to fit her. It was a completely enclosed system. When he left the room, she felt the oxygen and moisture seep out around the windows. It drew the walls and ceiling toward her. It was a completely enclosed system. She couldn't breathe. She loved him. She was madly in love with him. Pretend with me, he said.

Outside, there was a city filled with limestone monuments and statues. It was a city like a giant cake, all elegiac, funereal, a place made of stone the color of sugar.

She opened the drapes. A bus went by, with its deep blue windows.

A glass bank tower, glazed with reflected sunset, orange as a Popsicle, shone on his face. An airplane drew its slow descending line near the horizon. Do you see it? he asked. Yes, she said, I see it. You don't need another thing, he said, and she said, No, not another thing. She touched the silver watch on his arm, the warm skin, the dark curling hair, the places where his blood pressed against his skin.

There was a sheen to the monuments, all glassy polished stone, and when she moved her head just right, the light snapped like rows and rows of flashing cameras, aimed straight for her heart.

Talk to me, she said. Straight ahead of her, there was a row of silos. The sunset faded and the silos towered in the blue-white light.

There, he said, and he took her to the base of them. It made her dizzy. She put her hand on the concrete, and it was cool, as though the silos had spent the entire day in refrigeration. A breeze caught a pile of grain dust and it whirled around her face like fog.

The silos were connected to a flour mill. There were trucks lined up outside the silos and the mill. PASS THE BREAD was written on the side of some of them. EAT CAKE was written on some others. She didn't see a single human being, just these trucks and silos and the mill. It was a daylight factory, like the one she lived in, and she could hear the pounding of machines through the long windows, but no sign of people, like one of those neutron bombs had hit, those bombs that burn the flesh and leave the cathedrals.

You know, she said, I read in the paper that viruses replicate by building tiny machines. I swear it's true. They punch a hexagonal hole into a molecule and build something like a nut-and-bolt assembly to turn the DNA into the cell. I read it.

She looked at him. This universe has to be so much stranger, she said, than we can imagine it.

I mean think of it, she said. Little microscopic things inside your cells building simple machines. A few thousand years from now they'll have strip malls and gas stations and ten-cents-off sales, all underneath the skin.

She'd been waiting since she saw him last to tell him this. Otherwise, what was it for? Every bit of information seemed strange and miraculous to her but didn't reach its full potential to amaze her, didn't seem strange enough, or, rather, mysterious or perhaps even real enough, until she passed it on to him and she knew he took it in. This was how she knew she loved him. She was absolutely blind and dumb when he wasn't there to hear her speak.

And maybe we're the viruses inside something else inside something else inside something else, like Russian nesting dolls, and God walks around with us inside and doesn't notice.

Rather than the other way around, he said, and he unbuttoned her blouse to the breastbone and ran a finger down a blue vein to her left nipple. She watched the nipple rise, felt the ping of blood in the tip. It's like they think, she said, these microscopic things, they think. Not thought, he said, but will. The universe runs on sex and will, he said. One feeds the other. I'm older than you. You'll live to see that this is true.

They walked through a laboratory filled with glass tubes and faded Formica tables. There were different colored liquids in the tubes, and the tables were covered with white dust. Beyond the lab, the box of an elevator without a door, these belts and weights that you could see.

She was afraid of closed-in places and heights, and she leaned into the warmth of his body. It was strange being out in the daylight with him. He seemed more vague to her, like something bleached by the sun. She wondered if she looked the same to him. She felt like one of those couples you'd see in beat-up cars, his hand jammed inside her blouse or underneath the waistband of her jeans, and the look on her face too old, a kind of mask, both hard and scared because she could not concentrate or focus on a single thing outside of him.

He said he had worked at this mill one summer when he was a boy. You're still a boy, she said. No I'm not, he said, I'm not a boy.

One of his jobs was to walk on the crust that hardened on the grain and spoiled the suction when it was time to drain the silos. He broke the crust, with a rope around his waist, and then grabbed on to the ladder as the grain began to flow and threatened to pull him under. Grain is tricky, he said, both liquid and solid. Tons of red wheat could stand solid as a mountain and then give way and flow in waves.

In five seconds, he said, you can drown in it. Be so far under that twenty men couldn't pull you out.

She remembers walking in the woods one spring, kicking aside old leaves and looking for crocuses and the red spindly starts of peonies. She had reached down and picked up some rotting leaves, she had crushed the webbing and run her fingers along the spine. She was eighteen and all of a sudden that day the ground had started to feel like a thin crust on top of endless water. Like the ground was fragile, like it would give way at any step and she'd just fall and fall and fall and never stop falling.

Once that occurred to her the feeling had never entirely gone away. She'd just gotten used to it, like learning to walk on a ship. She had sea legs. Once in a while the boat would pitch her forward and she could feel herself starting to drown. She thought she understood what it would be like to drown in the silo. She wanted him forever always. Whatever it is that wants to pitch her forward was always out there, around the edge of her vision, circling.

Hold me, she said, and she leaned into him, his breathing in her ear. Just the thought of being up that high terrified her. Whenever she was up that high she was absolutely certain she would jump. Do you love me? she asked him. He would never say the words, and she knew it was a dangerous thing to ask him, but she asked it anyway. Do you love me? She led his hand up underneath her skirt. Do you love me? Am I important to you? Will you live in a house with me, and read our children stories, and go to church all dressed in a suit and tie on Easter? Could we build a family like a boat for the times when the ground turns to water? Could you do that with me as you could never do it with her?

She was too young for his wife to matter to her, but his children were all too real. She was waiting for them to grow up and then he would be with her all the time, and they would eat in restaurants, holding hands.

He waited a beat or two too long before he answered her. I love you, he said then, but it was wooden, the way he said it. She changed the subject, asked him if he was afraid someone he knew might see them. He told her the mill was, like every place, so automated it was almost empty. Just a man or woman here or there to tend to emergencies and start up the machines. You could go in the largest mill or power plant, he said, and see room after room of abandoned desks. And anyway, though they knew him here, it was a different life. It couldn't touch his present one.

Completely self-contained, she said, and she tried to laugh.

There was motion everywhere she looked, but he was right, no human beings. There were buckets that rose up and down on belts, and man-lifts only one foot wide. You could jump on one, he said, and rise up ten floors like you'd ingested yeast. She tried to put her arm around his waist but felt him move away. When the lift went by from the bottom floor, he stepped onto a step about a foot wide, and he rose into the air. Now she'd done it. She would never again as long as she knew him mention the word *love.* He rose clear to the top of the building. She could see the bottom of his heels six floors above her.

He was nothing more to the person who made that lift than one of the buckets of grain, a container of pulsing blood. Why should he be any more than that to her. She could turn and leave this building but instead she called to him. Don't leave me here, she said. Please please come back down to me. She waited for him to return, like the receipt in a pneumatic tube.

When he came back down, she tried to laugh again, and still it didn't work. She was feverish, she was dizzy, not the least bit well. You scared the hell out of me, she said to him. No matter what you say, you know you're such a goddamn boy.

There were beams in the floor of the mill like a log cabin, bags of barley flour everywhere, soot on the wall from a fire, ink stains on the floor. She followed him then past metal pipes, past giant bags of flour, past boxes marked SWINE STARTER and NIACIN, past gray flour dust and a curving wall that echoed the curve of the railroad track outside of it.

Once he'd brought her silver metal balls you were supposed to roll around the palm of your hand. He'd put them deep inside of her, there were bells inside those balls, and he'd taken his hand and made her come and listened to the muffled sound of the bells. She remembered it now because every inch of the floor was covered with grain that rolled like ball bearings underneath her feet.

She slid several times on the grain and dodged pipes and the lifts that continued circling up and down on thick strong belts.

Finally they walked into a large, window-lined room. The room was filled with enormous golden oak boxes, like armoires, arranged in two straight lines and suspended from the ceiling and up from the floor on black rubber stems.

Look, he said, and she did.

She thought something was wrong with her eyes because every one of those wardrobes was shimmying, twisting around on the rubber stems with a motion like belly dancers. These are the sifters, he said, they separate the wheat and chaff. They shook and shook and a part of the concrete block wall and all the paned windows shook.

Inside the wardrobes the grain fell through metal nets with a thread count as dense and fine as percale sheets. The bran swirled like sparks when he opened the machine and pointed a penlight.

The dark shaking windows, the whole room vibrating. She could feel the power in the engines all the way through her body.

No one else was in there with them. He put his hand on a wooden sifter and held out his other hand to her, and she took it. Why couldn't she stay mad at him? Jesus, she said, oh dear Jesus God, please talk to me. She could already feel the vibrations in the soles of her feet, the shaking windows, through his hand, through his body, to her hand like an electric current. He leaned into the vibrations and pulled her to him, and she lifted her skirt and moved up close to him and pressed her clit against his thigh. She looked over his shoulder, out through the window, to the city. The lights were coming on like the flecks of bran. The wheat, the chaff, the constant sifting and falling, the rising sparks. Underneath the sparks there was all that rolling darkness. The wind through the windows, her skirt, his voice, the wind. His hands, the wind, his voice, the grain from a hundred farms. What was he saying? There's nothing else outside of this, he was whispering, not one single thing outside of this.

Two Cans and a String

BY JACK MURNIGHAN

WHILE SHE FUCKS ME she makes me talk on the phone with various members of my family. Multiple conversations with my mother, my brother, my aging grandmother. And then the exes, the coworkers, the credit card agencies, the pizza deliverers. I ordered the electricity for our new apartment with a shoelace tied around my balls and the back of her teeth dragging up and down my cockhead. On my hands and knees on the parquet making dinner reservations with my pants around my calves and her thumb up my ass. On my back and immobilized cupping the receiver tight in my hand telling Mom the highlights of my week at work trying to keep her from hearing the steaming urine splash off my chest and stomach. When the phone starts to shake in my hand and I feel the exigent tightening behind my balls, I breathe deeply through my nose, holding back through each anxious throb, only to release all at once beneath the cover of a throat-clearing cough. "I'm sorry, Grandma, I must of swallowed funny. Excuse me."

My name is Lucien. I am a line cook. I spend my evenings bent over a commercial grill tending to a massacre of meats. My days I spend with Alice; her evenings—her evenings she spends. I am thirty-eight years old; I don't know how old Alice is. She says twenty-two or twenty-three or twenty-five depending on the situation, but it's clear that she's older, perhaps much older. Quite some time ago I gave her the keys, and she normally doesn't arrive until I've already made the coffee and stirred the eggs in the bowl and am sitting distractedly at the table waiting for the sound of hard heels in the stairwell, the sound of her smoker's wheeze as she tops the final stair, the turning of the lock as she gasps her last breaths to try to conceal that she's unfit, sleepless and entirely overplayed.

She comes to me because I never ask. Never ask if she will come again, never ask where she's been, never ask what she's doing or how she can do the things she does. When she first saw me, she saw what she hoped to see in my hands. Broad, pale and hairless as a child's. She thought I'd be thick and pliant, a sizeable block of workable clay to shape with the insistence of her needs. And this is what I've been for her: a neutral page on which to write her dramas, to play out her fantasies of security. She didn't know, she still doesn't know, that the hair on my fingers and the sides of my hands is perpetually burned off by flame-ups from the grill. She knows that I cook, but doesn't know anything about it. What would I tell her? That you test a steak with a two-fingered push like a doctor percussing a patient's chest? That you turn a chicken breast when the liquid starts to puddle in its center? That when I come home at night and manage to fall asleep, I dream not of golden meadows or armed assailants, but panic my way through forgotten entrees and dropped dishes?

She comes in drunk and often with smudged lipstick, wearing clothes you never see during the light of day. She hurries in and kisses me on the cheek and flops into bed and lets me bring her coffee with her cigarette. Soon thereafter I bring her the omelet but she eats only a bite and then if she's tired she goes right to sleep but if she's drunk enough she pulls me toward the bed with her ashtray mouth and puts my hand under her skirt and rubs my knuckles against her and moans in a way that I can't quite trust. And then she pulls me closer and slides my cock out of my undershorts without really looking at it and rolls over onto her knees. And suddenly I'm inside of her, and I don't have anything on and I don't know if she's protected or if she's been careful but she's moaning so heavily and pitching against me so hard that my fears kind of get lost in the spectacle of her rising ass and something just kind of takes me over and I can't even stay in my mind long enough to figure out if she's really enjoying it. And then I lean my head back and put a hand over my eyes and from my chest to my knees I feel opaline and electric and then my ass tightens to a pinch and I quiver and twitch and just give out inside her like the time-slowed lilt of an airborne leaf. When I open my eyes I can see that she's been panting and clawing and it seems that maybe she too has been delivered. She knows I'm looking and turns her neck and flashes me a smile of playful commiseration that I don't let myself question. Then she wipes herself with her hand and jumps up to go to the bathroom in a dash, leaving me with a peck on the cheek as I get up to do the dishes, awash in the fullness of it all.

God it had been a long night, such a long night already and it was only like two or something. I had been fighting with my ex, had totally fucking had it with him, had to get away or I was finally going to tell him what was going on. I mean, why are they all such creeps, why do I never meet a guy who doesn't turn into a creep the minute I leave his bed? On my way out, he keeps repeating, "Alice, Alice, Alice," and I'm screaming and carrying on and I manage to tear my tights on the edge of his bed frame but I keep going anyway, taking my bag off the kitchen table and telling the fat fuck to go to hell.

So I'm lucky to get a cab and I just tell the driver Midtown, and as we're racing up Flatbush I'm looking at the lights thinking, How the fuck did I let my life get this fucked up? Oh God, what am I doing? What am I doing? What am I fucking doing? And each time I think it, it's like the words start to tremble and get more insistent, and I'm about ready to start crying right there in the cab and I take another swig of brandy and then I think, Oh fuck, I'm not supposed to fucking drink or this medication is never gonna work, and then I'm ready to cry about that too, 'cause I'm itchy and it hurts to pee and it's been two months already and I can't even quit drinking long enough for the medicine to have any effect.

The cabbie starts to take us onto the Manhattan Bridge and I see the downtown skyline off to the side and the Brooklyn Bridge and the East River and Lady Liberty and I'm thinking, What am I doing in all this shit? How did I let it happen this way? Why can't I just close my eyes and make it all be over?

She feels she must test my silence. She tries to draw out my sighs, longs to shake me, to tear me from my moorings, to draw me into her. But then she never notices how my hand lingers when she turns away, doesn't know the savagery of my morning coffee spent wondering if I'll hear the footsteps on the stairs, doesn't know how my stomach drops—from relief or fear?—when I hear the turning of the key in the lock. She would have me lose myself, to consign myself to her without reflection, and sometimes I think she only asks it of me because I would find it the most unnatural thing in the world to do.

I had had lovers before Alice. Quiet and timid girls who I held in my arms without words or understanding. Our sex would unfold at the snail's pace of my own initiative. They would hesitate to touch my cock, and then only touch it furtively, like a hot cup of coffee or someone else's diary. I would love them with my body in a rhapsody of my own unconnectedness. I would see our bodies in a haze, gazing abstractly like I was watching a ritual I didn't fully comprehend. Their pleasure seemed aleatory to me, a function not of my acumen but of their having decided, long in advance, that I was the one. I would listen as their breathing accelerated; I'd hold steady as they lifted their hips from the bed and bit their thumbs forcefully; I'd press my forehead to their shoulders and shadow their movements as they'd buck and spasm and relent. And then I would say, I would always say, as they opened their leadened eyes, "You are beautiful. You are so beautiful."

So I got the cabbie to drop me off at Roddy's and there was this guy sitting at the bar alone, and even though he had B&T written all over him, he was so big and looked so uncomfortable in his ten-dollar tie, it was like he had to be too fucking dumb to start any bullshit. He had one of his oversized mitts wrapped around a whiskey sour with the cherry and the straw still in it and I don't think he realized it's a woman's drink, and then I realized that he probably had no idea what to drink in a bar, and suddenly it all became clear to me that this guy probably works in Hoboken and lives with his bedridden mother and was supposed to meet some coworkers here or something but they blew him off or he got it wrong and he was trying to make the most of a broken evening, his first one out in months, and that I could make this guy very happy and maybe what I needed was someone to make me feel normal, to make me feel clean, like it was me that lived in some ticky-tack house in the suburbs and worked a 9 to 5 and had a kid and a car payment and plans for the future.

When I sat down next to him, he looked up at me with bovine, disbelieving eyes. He was the opposite of what I normally find attractive, but I was thinking, Fuck, all I ever pick are assholes, maybe it's time to try something new. So I turned on my bar stool so he couldn't see the tear in my tights and I asked him for a light and he fumbled in his pockets but it was obvious he didn't have one so I told him to buy me a drink instead and I ordered a whiskey sour and he laughed, saying, "That's what I'm drinking," like I didn't already know, like I didn't totally fucking have his number, the dumb piece of Jersey shit. I've never gotten over how easy it is, how much they're willing to believe. At first I thought it was a kind of magic, that I could be anything I wanted; then I started to see that the only reason they had stars in their eyes was that they were not really looking, that they didn't see anything at all, that they were looking up my skirt and down my shirt and saying yes, yes, but they weren't seeing shit of me. And the sensitive ones would pretend to listen; and the smart ones would finish my sentences; and the rich ones would tell me they'd get me something nice, but I was never anything more than what they wanted me to be, their fantasy of the tramp they'd save or the angel they'd fuck up the ass.

The day I gave Alice the keys I thought back to an evening I'd spent with some people I met through a dishwasher at work. They were passing around a joint and one of the women wanted to play this game. You were supposed to say, if you were shipwrecked on a deserted island and could bring one animal with you, what it would be. My first thought was a dog that would protect and love me and whose love I'd never question, that would follow me and be loyal to my death. But then another idea insinuated itself, truer than the first: I thought of a falcon, that I would fear, but respect. That would return to me, but I wouldn't control it. That would sit blinded on my arm until I'd set it free, to go and kill, and come back only if it so wanted. And each time as I placed the hood back over its head I would wonder why it ever did.

He was so odd, so sad and nervous. I had to keep talking to keep the conversation going. I'd ask him questions and he'd answer in three words then sit silent again and stir his drink. I asked him his name but I didn't really understand what he said—it sounded like "Lucid" or something—and then he didn't even ask for mine back. And part of me is thinking, This guy is a total fucking loser, but then another part of me thinks, Maybe he just doesn't know how to win, and that's when I decided that I'd fuck him in his own car that night and see how long it took him to tell me that he loved me.

Happy, happy—I was going to make him so happy. So I walked him out to his car and got in alongside him and he started to ask where we were going and I just raised a finger to my lips, "Shhh," then ran it down his, then down his chest, and then when I reached into his pleated navy pants he came all over my hand. I felt the laughter rising up in me, and the shame on his face made the cruelty rise up too, but I forced it under and leaned over and kissed him on the mouth and said, "Oh baby, I'm ready to burst now too," and then I ran his come through his hair and laughed and said he looked like James Dean and pushed him back on his seat and told him to close his eyes and I put my hand back between his legs and took him in my hand like it was a broken wing and worked beneath his balls until he started to groan and move with my touch and I told him to keep his eyes closed while I pulled my skirt up above my garters and climbed over him onto my knees with my ankles pressed to the edge of the seat and I held myself open with one hand and guided him in with the other and he started saying, "I can't, I can't, I can't," but I pushed my tongue into his mouth and pulled down hard on top of him and was grinding back and forth until, a minute later, he was ready to lose himself again. And then I stopped on a dime and pulled off him and said, "Uh uh," waving my finger back and forth like a schoolmistress.

And he tried to speak and I said, "Tell me your number," and he said, "Hold on, let me find a pen," and I said, "No, just tell me; I'll remember," and he said, "I work late," and I said, "I know," and he said, "226 2809," and before he could get his pants zipped back up I was out his door and across the parking lot, getting into another cab.

On the first night we fucked; on the second night we were in the car again, and again when I was about to come she lifted herself off me and looked away. But this time she didn't leave, she just turned in the seat so she was on her knees looking out the passenger window and pushed her ass firm against my face. She was wet and sticky and told me not to press so hard and while I was fumbling around trying to figure out what to do with my tongue she just rubbed against me and tucked one hand between her legs. I don't know if anything is scarier than a woman taking her pleasure when you're just sitting there not knowing where to put your hands. So I just ran my tongue up and down her sweaty cheeks trying to stay out of the way until she finally came and looked back at me and gave me a deep heavy kiss. You're the best, she said. And I looked at her and had no fucking clue what I had done.

All my life I've wanted something. The tiara that would make me a princess, the pony I'd ride into my dreams. Later the horse had a rider, and he'd lift me out of the cosmic mess I had made and take me to his castle in the dunes. But then the real men would come with their glittering watches and I'd look the poor fucks in the face and think, Is this what I get? Is this all there is? But Lucien seemed so neutral, so average and grounded that maybe I could get lost in him like in a big field of grain. Just close my eyes and take five steps and never find my way out again.

* * *

It's like looking up from under water, seeing the lights flicker above the surface, reaching up with your hand, and not grasping. I have lived my life this way: wanting to desire, holding back. I am weary of dodging experience. It's like as a wind too brisk to be borne; I close myself and turn away. Perhaps for some passion is a thing both viewable and viewed; for my part, I would rather not dream than dream and be denied. When Alice touches me I flutter. A window opens and, in a blink, closes. She feels me retreat. And like a huntress she pursues. She pursues, not to find me, simply not to be eluded. And ever the acceleration, as if the trigger of my great abandon were simply around the corner, dependent on some key code of positions or perversions. She pulls off of me, turns me over, sticks something in, pours something over, binds or bites or burns me until my well-confected moans convince her she's hit it, that she's touched that part of me she thinks my fear would have me hide. She thinks she can work me like she works every other man, but I see their faces, bent over her, frozen in vulgar masks of pleasure and I feel very far away. Over and over I see it; I see her with all the others, the ones who don't understand her, never cared for her, would take and take and take from her and never bother to find out who they were taking from. Maybe I'm wrong; I've never fucked a man. But then I've also never met one who wasn't selfish. They don't realize that Alice is like a butterfly: if you touch her, you'll rub the dust off her wings and she'll never fly again.

He doesn't even seem to care. I stroll in at any hour strung out of my fucking head and take his coffee and wait for the burning words, the hard hand that never comes. He just looks at me with that pathetic, understanding, impassive face, as if to say, "Don't worry, honey, it's okay, I know you've had a long night," and I can barely fucking stand it. I want to scream out, to smack him in the face, to wipe off that smirk, to humiliate him, to knock him off his angel's peg and make him feel what it's like to feel ashamed. He thinks he's doing me a favor by always being there and "taking things in stride" and doesn't even see that he only sits at home 'cause he's too scared and lost to go out and all his so-called devotion to me is just his need to have someone else call the shots and treat him like a dog and give him the chance to show how noble he is 'cause he keeps coming back for more. Oh, my big hero, how I need you. I need you I need you I need you. And I keep repeating it over and over under my breath as I kneel down and unzip his pants. And he comes, thinking that he loves me.

I wonder whether love is anything other than giving. To lose yourself in commitment, to bend beyond your needs for the other, to be perfect and beautiful and true. Everything else is shit: shit to fuel our ego, our vanity, our greed. With Alice I have learned that events of beauty are hand-rungs in the succession of time; we climb toward the bright window and hope to find stillness.

Bed of Leaves

BY DANI SHAPIRO

LATER, SHE WILL REMEMBER THE LEAVES. The way they scratch and crumble against her back. The way her panties are smudged with dirt and she will have to ball them up and stuff them into her knapsack where her mother won't find them. Years later, as a woman, there will be a moment at the end of each summer when the scent of fresh-mowed grass will fill her lungs through an open car window, and she will close her eyes and her tongue will go soft, her inner thighs moist like the pale insides of a half-baked cake.

Eddie Fish is unbuttoning her shirt. There have been boys before this moment, boys who have stuck their fingers between her blouse and jeans, tugging the fabric loose, pushing their hands up around her bra and cupping her breasts. There have been boys—two, to be exact—who have unzipped her pants in the school basement, pushing their hardness against her cotton panties, eyes squeezed shut. But Eddie Fish is not a boy. Eddie is a man—twenty-eight years old—and Jennie knows these woods are about to become a part of her history. She is writing the story of her life, the story of her body on these damp suburban grounds with the man she has chosen precisely because he is a man. The blond hairs on his wrists glisten as he reaches around her and unhooks her bra. She is impressed by his skill at bra-unhooking, the ease with which he pulls the straps off her arms and hangs it on a nearby branch, a white cotton 32B flag of surrender. She is impressed by his warm dry palms which brush against her nipples, and by his eyes, dark blue in the noon of this clear Indian Summer day, staring straight at her. "Lisa Wallach," he says, murmuring the name of his last girlfriend as he stares at Jennie's breasts.

She looks at him, flushed.

"Sorry," he laughs, "I can't explain it. Your hair, your tits—you look just like her now..."

She doesn't know enough to be horrified. To slap Eddie Fish across his pale stubbled cheek, grab her bra off the branch and streak through the woods, away from him. Instead, she is flattered by the comparison to Lisa Wallach, who is a woman, after all—at least twenty-six—and who is very beautiful in that frosted-blond urban way. Lisa is a lawyer. She has an apartment in the city, and wears leather boots with stacked heels, long velvet skirts almost brushing the floor.

"What am I doing here with you?" he murmurs as he undoes the top button of her tennis shorts, bends down and unlaces each sneaker, pulls off her Fred Perry socks with their small green wreaths. He unzips her shorts and shimmies them down around her ankles, along with her panties. Parts of her have never felt the breeze before. Her ass, her crotch, each nipple seems to braid together into a rope twisting deep into her stomach, twining around itself, a noose which will remain forever inside her.

"Jailbait," he says, kissing her belly-button.

Years from now, Eddie Fish will be a gynecologist in Scarsdale. He will drive a Volvo, own an espresso maker, be the father of two daughters of his own—two daughters he would kill if he ever found them in the woods with a man resembling his younger self. But today, as he lights a joint and places it in Jennie's mouth, he is not focused on his future, the bright golden-boy future which unfurls before him like an heirloom rug. He has no doubts, no fears. His medical school degree is at the framer's, his internship in the city will begin in just a few weeks, and Lisa Wallach is finally a thing of the past. And here is Jennie, the beautiful neighborhood kid with the crush on him, Jennie, twelve years younger than he—sixteen, for chrissake—three years ago he had attended her Bat Mitzvah! His eyes travel over her shoulders, down her breasts, lower to the blond depths of her. A virgin? He doubted it. She had written him letters all through medical school, letters so steamy he and Lisa had read them to each other late at night. He stubs out the joint on a tree trunk, next to a carved heart with no names, no initials inside it.

Gently, he lays her down on a bed of leaves, her head resting against the root of a tree. She crosses her legs, her arms, trying to cover herself. She has no idea how sexy she is. He quickly pulls his polo shirt over his head, undoes his own shorts and steps out of them. Then, in his sneakers and tight white briefs, he lowers himself on top of her, careful to prop himself on his elbows.

Later, after it is all over, a friend will ask him why, after all, he did it.

"She was so beautiful," Eddie will say. "So fucking beautiful."

Eddie's head is between her legs. His mouth is moist, chin dripping, and he looks up at her as he twirls his tongue around and around. With his fingers, he spreads her apart. "Are you using anything?" he asks.

"Yes," she says. She wants him to think she's a woman of the world. A woman whose motto, like a Boy Scout's, is "Be prepared." Her heart pounds as he slides a finger into her. Can he tell that she's lying?

He kisses her on the lips and she tastes herself. She is anticipating something awful, vomitous, some reason why her mother lines up bottles of sweet-smelling potions on the bathroom sill. She is surprised. The taste is not unpleasant: oceanic, vaguely like seaweed. Something dredged from the depths.

She wonders what he tastes like, if she will ever know.

Eddie wriggles out of his underwear and moves up her body so that his thing, this thing that she has been waiting for, is swinging above her mouth like a heavy, hypnotic pendulum. The last one she saw was Steven McCarthy's, back in third grade, when she accidentally-on-purpose opened the bathroom door while he was standing over the toilet.

Tentatively, she opens her mouth, darts out her tongue, runs her lips over the shaft. She is expecting something rough, something that feels like stubble. She is surprised by his smoothness, and she dips her head down and covers him. He moans a high-pitched sound she has never heard before, blending into the chirps and rustles all around them. Suddenly, Eddie pushes himself farther into her mouth with a small grunt and she tastes something faintly metallic at the back of her throat.

"Whew," he says, pulling away from her. "You sweet thing. Where'd you learn that?"

She feels heat rise from her breasts to her cheeks. Without even looking, she knows that a blotchy, red rash has spread across her chest and neck, a map to her inner world. She always turns blotchy when she feels anything complicated. She fights back the urge to gag at the drop of thick slippery fluid trickling down her throat.

"I almost came," he said with a grin. "Naughty girl."

He slides down her body, his stomach pressed against her own, and thrusts into her. Jennie braces herself and grits her teeth, waiting for the pain. Will there be blood between her legs? Will he find out she's a virgin and recoil? Jennie knows this: Eddie Fish does not want her to be a virgin. For the rest of her life, boyfriends and husbands will ask about her first time, and the name Eddie Fish—that unfortunate moniker—will forever be whispered in a progression of beds.

Who was your first?

Eddie Fish.

And how was it, my darling?

It was—it was what it was.

He has pushed all the way inside her and she feels nothing. No pain, no magic. Her insides have widened to accommodate him as if a door has always been open, as if a room inside her has been drafty, just waiting to be entered.

Her breath seems loud to her ears, and her heart pounds erratically as Eddie moves to the rhythm of music only he can hear. She tries to time her heart, her breath, to his. Ba-da-dum, ba-da-dum. A tribal forest beat. The hairs on his thighs tickle her and she fights an urge to break into hysterical giggles. Her stomach is hot beneath him, an interior soup. She twists her head to the left and sees Eddie's hand flat against the dirt, his wrist encircled by a thin strand of leather that she remembers Lisa Wallach brought him from Brazil. The leather strand had magical powers, Lisa told him, and he would have very bad luck if he unknotted it himself. Jennie wonders if Eddie Fish will wear that strand of leather until it disintegrates.

Eddie speeds up. A vein in his throat pops out and he is looking down, down to the place where their bodies are joined. With a gasp and a grunt, he collapses on top of her. Jennie can feel his heart through her chest. Eddie Fish's heart! She will remember this moment, she promises herself: the faded blue summer sky, the worm inching along the edge of a pale yellow leaf, the soft smell of dirt. She will color it with a patina of great beauty. She thinks about Eddie's question—Are you using anything?—and her fingers grow icy. She wonders if it can happen the first time, if the grassy mess oozing between their legs can grow into something more complicated—a punishment, a life sentence. She closes her eyes and prays: just this once, never again, please not now.

"What?" asks Eddie, looking down at her.

"Sorry?"

"Your lips were moving."

"Oh, it's nothing."

"You're not getting weird on me, Jen, are you?"

She doesn't answer. Getting weird. Eddie's words echo and bounce through her skull. She twists her neck once again, her cheek resting on the cool earth, and stares at the empty heart carved into the base of the tree. She imagines her own initials there, and then, like a stack of cards flipping through the wind, a hallucination, she sees the initials of every man who will ever become her lover. There are so many—perhaps dozens! More than she can possibly imagine. She is filled with the knowledge of what she does not know.

Eddie kisses her throat, his lips dry and papery, then jumps up and rummages for his briefs beneath a pile of fallen leaves. He looks down at Jennie and she squints at him, blinded by the sunlight behind his shoulder. From where she lies, he seems like a giant.

"I—I didn't use anything, Eddie," she falters.

He stumbles on one leg, awkward as he pulls on his underpants. "What did you say?" he asks, stopping.

"I'm sorry—I didn't use anything," she says, this time with greater conviction.

"Jesus, Jennie!" He punches the air. "How could you—"

"I didn't know."

"But I thought you were—"

Tears stream down her face. The light, the woods are refracted, kaleidoscopic.

Eddie Fish's face becomes a blur.

"You bitch!" she hears, as if from a great distance. He is walking away from her, heels crunching against the leaves. "If anything happens, it's not my problem, do you hear me?"

Slowly, she gathers her things. She pulls her bra from the branch, stuffs her panties into her knapsack, buttons her blouse and yanks on her shorts. She sits back down against the tree and searches the ground for a sharp twig. When she finds it, she begins scratching her initials into the empty heart, digging deep into the bark. She works carefully, with the precision of an artist. She fills the whole perimeter, so there will be no room for anyone else.

For God's Sake, Forgive Your Mother

BY DARCEY STEINKE

IN THE TAXI, on the way in from the airport, objects moving at her through the windshield had the ability to harm. The green shamrocks painted on the diner window, the Angelina billboard. She could handle artifice, third-rate holidays, giant stylized breasts. It was the everyday objects that hurt, the pay phones, the mailboxes, the 7-Eleven in the strip mall. Fuck them. Fuck the purple bougainvillea twining around the metal fence. She would put each blossom inside her mouth and chew. Fuck flowers. Fuck the moon, the stars. She hated the blue awning on a place called Communication Station. She hated anything that reminded her of that lovely internal configuration created by sex.

In the hotel room, absolutely everything a dull pink, she got out the tiny bottles of bourbon from the mini bar. Closing the curtains partway, she lay out over the bed. Planes, no bigger than floaters in the corners of her eye, moved across the column of sky between the drapes. She thought of the people on the planes reduced to dust motes, the middle-aged lady in the woolen suit. The new mother, her baby's head tucked inside her shirt; the two of them smelling like sugary milk left over after cereal. Without an armature, her desire moved around the woods flinging a nightgown onto bushes, saplings, brambles. Spread over the arching branches of a thicket, the white material looked best. She thought of the last letter she sent him, each word like a day when it rained and she made soup and put on an extra sweater to warm herself.

Then she thought about the last time. How his room was slightly arrogant, with the fireplace, the leather reading chair, the strange print of a dock scene done in neon colors. It was a room from her parallel childhood, one her brother would have inhabited if she'd been a banker's daughter instead of a minister's. She walked over to look at the picture and he had come up behind her exactly as he had in the dream the night before. Turning her around, he kissed her first on the lips and then below the ear. She moved her hand up under his shirt, her palm resting on the slope of his back. Then came the whole economic system of skin against skin. Lips first, the nerves sending subtle charges down her chest out into her limbs. A sort of possession began, desire manifesting first in the touch of his fingertips and then in the proximity of big swatches of warm skin. Her favorite landmark: the moment before all hell broke loose, when he took off his glasses and set them carefully on the nightstand beside the bed.

All this was still pleasant to recount. The figurative confabulations were what pained her, the forms they had created in space. His body hanging over her, cock in her mouth, her finger up inside him. Her tongue ringing around that clenched circle of skin. Somewhere inside of him, there was an ancient Chinese city governed by a boy who was constantly fighting back death. Paper lanterns hung in the courtyard, brightest at twilight. There was a city inside of her too, but more like Baltimore than Peking. Vacant storefronts and a fat lady living over a convenience shop. She was anxious to fuck. And the fucking was very nice, especially the part when they were standing against the wall, she up on her tiptoes, him behind her, and then that moment he leaned over and kissed along the raised vertebrae of her spine.

The hole opened up. For a while she sated it with Caesar salads but then it demanded books of poetry in blank verse. She understood after a time that it would only be satisfied with sex soup. One wet pussy. One hard cock. And a bottle of black nail polish. But that recipe just made the longing worse, elemental to her now as the fallen light at the window, as the feel of her own palm against the bones in her hip.

Had she mentioned that the bed was king size? That its scale in proportion to her body was making her sick? And you should always think twice before slipping out of your skin. You hope it will be this great event, that congress will fill with democrats, that glamour will be unmasked as the fraud she really is. But in the end it's so hard working with people, you want them all to like you and be happy but you get caught up in their frailties, and sometimes you can't help becoming a conspirator in their gloomy conception of original sin.

Flight

BY ROBERT ANTHONY SIEGEL

MY FATHER HAS GOTTEN HIMSELF into some kind of trouble involving money and the law, and for the first time I can remember, I have a role in his life, that of confidant. We spend large chunks of the nighttime hours riding around town while he formulates his plans: compromise, counterattack—all depending on the fluctuations of his mood, which are extreme, from tears to rage and back again. I listen and egg him on toward the more fantastical choices—because at sixteen I'm not aware that they are fantastical, and because they give me the chance to go on more car rides. I am especially pleased when he decides that we are going to skip the country together. "Fuck 'em," he says, his face a pale green in the light from the dashboard. "We'll drive up to Canada, then fly to Israel. No extradition, immediate citizenship under the Law of Return."

"When?" I ask.

"Tomorrow."

But the next day he doesn't show up. I talk to his answering machine, stare into his darkened windows, bang on the door. My valise feels like a ton of rocks in my hand, but I carry it all the way up the Avenue, to Violet's house. Violet is the girl I have been—not dating—no, *circling* is the better word. I am, in general, a circler.

Violet and I sit on the couch in her basement, talking, but I can't really listen because my brain is full of my father's darkened windows—that blackness.

"Running away?" she asks, looking over at the valise in the corner.

"Moving in. Your parents won't mind. Will they?"

"Funny," she says, and I am caught off guard as she leans toward me. I see her face approaching mine, growing larger and larger till it fills my vision, and I smell the sweet scent of her, then I feel her lips against mine, a very light pressure, hardly more than a tingling in the skin. I almost draw back, not because I don't want this but because it's too much, too much and yet not enough.

"How's that?" she whispers. I'm not sure if I actually hear her or am merely feeling her breath on my face, the shape of her words on my skin.

"Wow," I say, a little drunk with the sensation.

She moves back to look at me and her eyes are huge with interest, a childlike curiosity at the effect of her experiment. She looks like a kid who's just built something amazing with blocks that may tumble at any moment. "One more time," she says.

We kiss again, her body against mine, her arms around my back. It is a strangely anchored feeling, like climbing a tree and coming to a fork in the branches, the kind that allows you to wedge yourself in and dangle your legs, suspended in air with no danger of falling. And yet it feels like falling too—falling without the pain of landing. My lips move but no words come out; I can hear the click of our mouths, the rhythmic huff of our breathing. "Umh," she says, "mhrr," and I know exactly what she means: bird, sky, branch, lips. I can feel her hand reaching under my shirt, palm against the skin of my back. Everywhere she touches tingles.

So this is getting laid. I am falling and I am in the tree, watching myself fall. My father is in Buffalo, carrying a tote bag full of money and a passport with a new name on it. He is eating room service with the TV on. He is in his big white Caddy, driving toward the Canadian border, Niagara Falls a silent roar beyond his window. The world is neither good nor bad but huge and a father can get lost in it.

"Stop," she gasps, sitting upright. "Take this off." She begins to work at the buttons of my shirt, fumbling. She looks a little cross-eyed, dazed, like someone coming out of a movie theater into daylight. The buttons come slowly, one after another, and then she is sitting with the shirt balled up in her hands, looking at me with that same expression of curiosity.

"Now you," I say, and begin lifting the T-shirt over her head—to stop the staring, really. I see the white of her stomach, the black lace of a bra, the curve of her throat. And then her face again, smiling through a mess of hair.

"Scared yet?" she asks, brushing the hair from her eyes. It is my first indication that we're playing chicken. She sits with her back straight and shoulders squared, clearly aware that of our mutual toplessness hers is the more powerful.

"No," I lie.

"Well, then." She lifts her hands to the black band of cloth between the lace cups of her bra, undoes the little hook that holds them together. "How about now?" she asks.

"Maybe." I stare for a while trying to make the connection between all the pictures I've seen and these real things, Violet's breasts. They are instantly familiar yet completely new too, and I feel as if I've been waiting for them a long, long time. I lean forward to touch a nipple with my lips. I can feel her hands in my hair. Her body sways and my mouth fills. My father is flying, eating packet after packet of peanuts, the tote bag sandwiched between his legs. He looks out the window and sees clouds reflecting pink and gold. He tells the woman next to him that he is a salesman, a sex therapist, a professional wrestler. The world is huge and anyone can get lost; it's hard to fasten on.

"Oh," says Violet, a sound of surprise. I take my mouth from her breast; the nipple glistens with saliva. I follow the space between her breasts to the top of her stomach, kissing, kissing to the rivulet of hairs down toward her belly button, the waist of her jeans. "Hey, that tickles." She squirms free, gets up from the couch, stands over me, her hair in her eyes. I reach for the button of her pants, unzip her zipper, start pulling them down. Her body sways with my tugging. She watches with a distanced curiosity as her pants clear her hips, her thighs, bunch at her ankles. She is not wearing any underwear. "I'll fall," she says.

"I'll catch you."

I am down on my knees now, my hands on her hips, steadying her. I am face-to-face with the architecture of her pelvis, the tuft of hair that I have dreamt of and wondered about. Of course, of course, I tell myself, this is how it would have to be, this is how women are made. I look up at her face and see that her eyes are squeezed shut, as if it's the scary part of a movie. I kiss the sharp edge of her hipbone, the shallow plane of her pelvis, the shaggy patch of hair. I follow the curve downward between her legs.

"No, don't," she says. "I'm serious, I'll fall. Oh."

The smell is rich and shocking, like the breath of a cave. I feel her sway over me like tall grass, her warm thighs pressed to my ears.

Once abandoned, you will always be a thrown-away thing. You will never be able to possess or hold, will never understand the rituals by which people bind themselves to others. Everything is as fluid as air or water; names are to be changed, money to be hidden. Doors give you an irresistible urge to leave, just for the feeling of leaving. And you watch for this same urge in others: the thinking ahead, the absent laugh, the counting of money. You know people have thoughts they don't tell.

She sits down on the edge of the couch, a sticky look on her face as if she's just woken up from a long sleep. She lifts her feet and I remove the bunched up pants from her ankles. "Your turn," she says. "Stand." I stand up and she unzips my zipper, begins to peel both pants and underwear down my legs. I am careful to pry off my shoes as she works, to step out of the pants when they reach my ankles—I am suddenly worried about looking ridiculous. But there is no helping it: I glance down at my sickly white legs, how they end in brown socks. It's hard to imagine that they're really mine, these limbs, that I stand on them. Is this getting laid, this nakedness? It's like losing your body.

She holds me at the back of my thighs, then takes my penis in her mouth, so quickly that I'm barely aware of it happening. It's not the sensation I expected, not explosive but gentle, like the pull of the water at the beach when it tugs the sand from between your toes. You want to follow, and you want to stay. "Not too much," I hear myself mumble. "I want to take off my socks."

"Leave them on," she says. "They're sexy."

She laughs, lying down on the couch. It is an invitation and I follow, spreading myself on top of her, careful for the sharp points of elbows and knees. "I've never done this before," I say.

"I know. You look like you're in shock."

"I just thought I should tell you." The truth is that I am vaguely worried about hurting her somehow—or hurting myself.

"Don't worry," she says. And I try not to as she slips me inside herself with a single easy motion. But it's a startling moment: suddenly my penis is gone and we are attached. I hesitate, rest my weight on her hips, then begin to move. I have to tell myself to move, actually; there's nothing natural or automatic about it. It is awkward, awkward, like trying to write left-handed, but I find a rhythm of sorts, a careful bumpy rhythm, and things seem to be going okay. It's a precarious, perched feeling, moving over Violet. I'm fucking, I tell myself, as if the word could sum up the mystery of this thing and of how I got here, naked on the couch with Violet. I'm fucking!

I must have said it out loud, because Violet laughs. "You are," she says. "We are." She has a look on her face as if she were standing at the prow of a ship, watching the sea come forward. Her hands are on my back and she rocks in time with my motion, lifting her knees in the air, breathing deeply. "Oh, yes. There. There. There."

Where? I want to ask. We are moving somewhere separately together and I want to know. My father is in Tel Aviv, sitting on a bench overlooking the sea, shocked by the Middle Eastern sun. This strange place is the Homeland, and these are Jews, carrying guns, shouting at each other in a language, both soft and guttural, he can't understand. His tote bag is almost empty now. Citizenship is automatic under the Law of Return, and it is this same law that brings him to the bench every day to watch the light burn on the water. He takes out his passport, just to check his name, his picture. It's easy to mix up who you are and who you're trying to be. One slip and the mistake is made.

"That's good," says Violet. "Yes, there. Keep going."

But I've gone too far already, past the stopping point, and when it is over I lie very still, my eyes closed, listening to her breathing—to the fact of her. I do not move because I can't bring myself to uncouple.

When to Use

BY STACEY RICHTER

THE MOST OBVIOUS time is after menstruation. But you'll want to use it other times as well—after nervous tension has left you not-so-fresh, to wash away contraceptive jellies or creams (check your contraceptive instructions first), after intercourse (of course, this product is only a cleanser, not a means of birth control), to flush away built-up secretions that cause odor or anytime you want to feel clean and refreshed. Remember, this product is to be used for hygiene; it is not recommended as a method of expressing regret for joyless or ill-advised sexual encounters. It is possible, even with repeated use, that some women may not feel clean and fresh. Certain somebodies may look at themselves in the mirror after proper use and notice a halo of taint, an aura of having been "ridden hard and put up wet." If, for example, you've been doing it with a drifter in a parked car behind a bar, with your shoes up against the window, your pantyhose shackling your ankles and your bra pushed up into your armpits (and, furthermore, if you suspect there are a couple of guys standing in the parking lot, smoking cigarettes, drinking beer and watching—and in your drunken state you like this), then this product may be ineffective, despite the light raspberry scent. We recommend you discontinue use entirely if overwhelming sensations of guilt and humiliation ensue when your regular boyfriend finds out. And why would he find out? Because everybody saw you either leaving, sucking face or actually doing it with the weird, over-tan guy with the tattooed forehead, and of course all the products in the world will not restore you to "clean" or "fresh." A word about relief: This product does not support the idea of "do-overs," as when playing pool and missing the ball entirely, in which case certain women feel the right to call out "do-over" and shoot again without penalty of any sort. We consider this cheating. Therefore, it doesn't make it better if, on the night in question, your regular boyfriend was off "taking some time to think about things," which means, as we've learned in earlier sets of instructions, that he's off thinking about how badly he wants to dump you and start "seeing" one of your very stacked friends. Who knows? Maybe he would have stayed if you hadn't drunkenly turned yourself over to the first unwashed mouth-breather who made suggestive comments about the shape of your ass. But it's too late, there shall be no do-overs, and you're destined to remain pathetic, manless and a known slut. You will be largely ignored by your social circle, with the exception of certain guys in shiny shirts who've begun to stare openly at your inadequate breasts. You may start to fantasize while walking or driving around, grief-struck and miserable, about a fresh, clean start where everything is suddenly crisp and blank, like bleached bed sheets, newly washed chalkboards, refinished floors—the ultimate do-over. These instructions have this to say about that wish: Ha! You should be so lucky. Let's face facts, little lady. It's girls like you who force us to include warnings like Do Not Administer Orally. We're not going to let you out of this one that easy.

The Finish Line

BY DENNIS COOPER

Dear Dennis,

I was glad to hear from you, don't worry about it. Whatever fucked-up shit came down between us, it doesn't matter anymore. I don't even remember what the problem was. People change, that's right. I figured you were off doing your own thing and didn't remember me. I've fucked so many people over, I don't expect anybody to give a shit. I've been in AA off and on for a couple of years, and they make you think about what you do, and so I'm better about not going over people's boundaries, like they say. I'm sorry for being a shithead a lot of the time back then. I make people into my dad, and then I have these big expectations that are just stupid. I wish I didn't do that, but I still do. I just fucked up this thing with a guy here in Portland, although I have to say the guy was as much of an asshole as me. I don't have anybody right now, and I get fucked up when I'm alone. I was clean for four months, but now I slipped and everything goes to hell when I'm using. So your letter came at a good time, because I've been feeling like nobody gives a fuck. I'm sleeping in my van right now because I don't have anywhere to live, and I'm getting tired of it. I was doing pretty good for a while there. I got married to this woman, Carla, and we had a daughter. I was with her for about a year and a half, and that was a good time in many ways, but I couldn't play it the way she wanted me to play it, so she kicked me out. That's over. She has a restraining order against me, which I deserve because it got kind of crazy toward the end. I don't know if you want to hear all this shit. You seem to think I'm somebody special, and you always did, no matter how much I fucked you over, which is why I loved you like I did. But it hasn't worked out that I'm so special. That's probably why I was such an asshole to you, because you thought I was so special, and I knew I wasn't, but I wanted to believe it, so I wouldn't let you have what you wanted, because if you got me for real, I just knew it would change. But then it got fucked-up anyway, and later I thought I was a total asshole for not just giving you what you wanted, because it wasn't that much to give, and you were so nice to me, and I should have given it to you, because it's probably the only thing I could have given you to thank you and show you that I cared. But I didn't, so I've always felt like an asshole. I wanted to do it, you know. I was just scared that you'd think big deal, because let's face it, that's what happens. It's not like I've been a saint since I last saw you. I try not to let people have me because it always fucks me up, but then I don't keep jobs very well, and I need money, so I let people have me, just so I can get by, and so that I have something in my life. So I'm not scared of that shit anymore. I don't have big hopes about it. I still had big hopes about it when I was with you. I just thought if I waited until I got out of high school, and had my shit together, it would be better for both of us. Then that time we started to do something, and I freaked out, I thought I blew it. I didn't have my shit together, and now I don't think I'll ever have my shit together, so I feel like an asshole for freaking out. I don't know why you wrote to me, and I'm trying to understand why. The day I got your letter I went to a meeting and told them about it, and asked what they thought. Those people all think I'm a fuckup, because I slip all the time, so I don't really care what they think, but they said maybe I hadn't blown it with you, and that I shouldn't just blow you off, and that I should write you back, and be honest with you about my circumstances and my addiction and so on, and see what happens. So I'm trying to be honest with you, but that's not something I'm good at. I'm trying to think about this, and not just say if you still want me you can have me as long as you give me some money. I told them that's what I wanted to say, and they said that I should say that I love you, and I want to be with you, and not say the money part. Really, I don't care about the money part except that I have nothing right now. So they said I should be honest with you, and that's honest. Sometimes I think the people who go to those meetings aren't being real. It's not real to think you're going to say, I love you for who you are and we should be together. I already blew that, and I'll be honest with you, I think the drugs are always going to be a problem for me. So what I'm thinking is, I could come stay with you for a few days and just see what happens. I was thinking of driving down to LA anyway and trying to get some money out of these guys I know there. I guess I'll just drive down in a couple of weeks and call you, and if you want to see me, cool. If you want to have me, that's cool, and if you feel like giving me some money afterward, that's cool, but I'm not expecting it. You said you don't know what you want with me now, and I don't know what I want either, not just with you but about everything. I know I want to go score, and I can do that, that's easy. I know I want you to have me, if you still want me, and you said you do. I don't remember if that serial murder shit you were into bugged me. Maybe I was scared that you were going to kill me, but I don't think so. I haven't thought about that shit for a long time. But I don't live like that anymore. When I shoot dope, I don't think if I do too much I'm going to overdose. I do as much as I feel like it to get as high as I can. When I let some fucking asshole have me for money, I don't tell him what he can't do, I just go with whatever he wants, because it's bullshit otherwise. I got married and had a kid because I wanted to be with Carla, and she wanted that, and I went for it. If you're still into that weird shit, that's the way it is. If I'm going to let you have me, then you have me. If I don't wake up the next morning, that's the way it is. You were the nicest person to me I ever knew, and I just fucked you over left and right, thinking I had to protect something. There's nothing to protect anymore. I gave it a shot, and it's not happening.

If you want me, you can have me. I used to be so into understanding myself, but now I just want to do things, and not understand them.
I'll talk to you,
Gregg

Dear Dennis,
I'm coming down to Los Angeles next Tuesday. I have something to do that night, and then I'll call you and come over. It's perfect because, check this out, I've got this plan where I can steal a shitload of heroin from these guys down there. They think I'm buying it to sell, but fuck them. I've got it all figured out. So anyway, it'll be cool because I'll just come stay with you, and they won't know where the fuck I am, and I'll have all this dope for us to use. I used to believe in all that Buddhist crap, and then I sort of got out of that, but this whole thing is working out so great, I can almost believe it again. I'm so fucking high. I hope you can read this. When I got your last letter, I had to go celebrate, and fuck those AA guys who say they're my friends. You don't know the bullshit I've had to put up with, about accepting that I'm a fucked-up, helpless person. I started to believe it, so thanks for reminding me that I'm cool. Yeah, I'm not fat, Dennis, don't worry. I'm fucking skinny as hell, but I could still go score with some guy right now, if that answers your question. I've got no problem getting guys to pay for it, as long as they don't give a shit about the tracks. I can still pass for sixteen. I bullshit guys that I'm sixteen all the time, so you don't have to worry about that, and I'm not going to worry about it either, because sometimes I can get really depressed about what I've done to myself, and I'm so sick of feeling like I blew all the shit that you and other guys used to think I was going to do with my life. You used to say I was going to be a great artist, but I haven't done anything in a long time except try to get through every fucking day without killing myself. I tried to kill myself twice last year, if you want to know. The second time I almost did, and I used to be sorry it didn't work, but now I'm excited. Maybe I won't blow this thing with you. I feel like I have a chance. I've fucked up every good situation I've ever been in, and I decided that was because they were

all bigger assholes than me, but you're not an asshole, and you know my problems, so maybe you won't be disappointed, because everybody's always so fucking disappointed with me. If you want to know, I was planning to steal that dope to kill myself, so this is great timing on your part. Thanks for giving me another chance. If I blow this, then that's it. You can go serial killer on me, and I won't even care. It would be better if you went serial killer on me than if you threw me out like everybody else has. Hey, I'm just fucking high. You're going to hear from me soon anyway, so I'll sign off.

Later,

Gregg

Dear Dennis,

Thanks for calling me back the other day. It was a weird conversation, but I'm not going to worry about it. I'm sorry I got pissed off. I just had this idea in my head that you'd send me the money and I'd buy the bus ticket, but I don't blame you for thinking I'd use it to score. You're probably right. Ever since my van got stolen, I've been pretty on edge, so anyway I'm sorry again. So go ahead and buy me a bus ticket, and tell me when to be on it. If you don't mind driving me to those dealer guys' place, that'd be cool, since I'm not going to have wheels. I won't get you involved. You can just wait in the car. Anyway, I'm sorry about the shit on the phone. I was just jonesing, but a guy up here traded me dope for my ass, so it's cool. He said he had a really good time with me, so you don't have to worry about being disappointed with how I look now, if you're worried about that. Don't stop believing in me, Dennis. It was just a bad day. Thank you.

Gregg

Dear Dennis,

I guess you know by now that I didn't make it down there. I tried to call you, but either you don't want to talk to me or you're out of town or something. I fucked up, okay? What do you expect? That's why I want to come down there and see you, because I'm a fucking mess on my own. I'll do whatever you say. If you send me another ticket, I won't sell it. I swear on my life. Please write me back. I love you. Do you know how hard it is for me to say that?

Gregg

Dennis,

Your letter got me really pissed off. I wasn't going to write you back, but I thought about it, and I feel like I don't have a choice. I've really, really fucked things up here, not that you give a shit obviously. So yeah, whatever you fucking want. I'm just worried you don't love me anymore, because you haven't written that in a while, and that's all I've got to live for right now. So if you could just tell me that you do, that would be cool. I'll probably come anyway, but that would help, because I am kind of scared. You're getting pretty heavy on me, and I don't really have a problem with that, but the whole thing for me is that you love me, and if you don't anymore, then I don't know what the fuck to do. If you love me, I'll do fucking anything you want, don't you know that? I fucking swear. I don't know what you want me to say about your rules. I feel like I don't know what answers you expect, and I'm bad when I don't know what people want, because I always make the wrong decision, if it's up to me, but I guess you're saying I have to answer or you won't bring me down there and give me money and all that, so here you go. (1) Fine with you making a reservation so I won't be able to sell the ticket. I won't even get off the bus to take a shit, okay? The thing is, I don't have any ID except for fake ID, so make the reservation or ticket or whatever for James Ravell. It's a long story. (2) I think I answered that. (3) I think it's really unfair of you to ask me that, because you know how hard it is for me. I told you I love you. All I can say is that the only person I've said that about is my daughter. You make me feel like I'm important. I'd be upset if you were dead. If someone fucked you over, I'd fuck them over. I've jacked off thinking about you holding me in your arms and telling me the kinds of things you said in your letters a while back. I don't know what else to say. I'm going to come down there and be with you even though it scares the shit out of me, and part of me is worried you're going to kill me. I mean, I'm not really worried, but you know what I mean. That's a big fucking sacrifice on my part, so I guess that must mean I love you. (4) The heroin deal's not going to happen now probably, because I sort of fucked it all up, so you don't have to worry about that. (5) I ask myself that question every fucking day. I don't think I'm worth shit. You're the one who thinks I'm so great. So I don't know how to answer that question, because it seems like a trick question to me, but then I can be really paranoid. I'm worth all this shit because I'm your friend, and because I'm going to let you do shit to me that I would never let anybody else do, and because you probably couldn't get anybody else to do that shit with you, and because I'm great-looking like you said, okay? (6) I already told you that you can have any kind of sex you want to with me, but, if you don't mind, I don't want to talk about the details anymore. Yeah, whatever you want, Dennis. Go for it. I've been in jail enough times that I think I can deal with whatever you're talking about. Remind me to tell you sometime about the shit I went through in jail, because you'd probably really get off on it. Imagine someone who looks like me in jail, and figure it out. (7) You don't have to worry about me taking off, as long as I have my dope, and you have a TV and maybe a VCR. So does that answer your rules? Now get me the fucking ticket, Dennis, so we can be together. No offense.

Gregg

Dear Dennis,

You're going to be pissed off, but I have to change the plan a little. Just read this and you'll see why this has to happen, and why it'll be great for both of us. I fixed it so I could see those dealer guys after all, but they can't do it on Monday night, so I changed the bus ticket for a different day, and I'll call you from a pay phone near their place when I'm finished with the deal, because you shouldn't have to hassle with it anyway, and it's safer for both of us if I deal with it myself. So I'll call you, and don't be pissed off, okay?

Gregg

Dennis,

Thank you, thank you, thank you. Carlos is going to call you when he finishes doing something he has to do in a couple of hours. Thank you, thank you. You're the only good thing that's ever happened to me. Nobody else would do this for me, I know that. It'll be worth it, I swear.

Gregg

Dennis,

After the mean, evil shit you said to me last night, you deserve what happened. You're the biggest asshole I've ever known. You say you love me, but all you want is my fucking body for your sick sex bullshit. Yeah, so I look wasted and skinny and shit. What do you fucking expect? I was totally going to let you do all that weird shit to me, you know. That's how fucking desperate I am, because I thought you'd love me if I let you do that, because I do love you, you asshole. You've gotten me so confused, I don't know what to think anymore, but I just want to tell you that I had nothing to do with what happened. Yeah, I set it up for them, and they were supposed to give me part of the money, but they fucked me over just like they fucked you over, I swear. I was going to share it with you. I know you don't believe me. Now I'm much more fucked than you. You have money and a place to live, and I have nothing. I had to go down to Santa Monica Boulevard and sell my ass just to get a place to crash. I'm sorry you lost the money and that I didn't stand up for you, but I've got nothing and now I'm stuck here, and this guy won't buy me dope, and I'm sick. So I'm going to ask you if you'd please lend me some money so I can get high and go back to Portland. I think you owe me after all the shit you said. I'm at some guy named Lawrence's place, but I don't think I can stay here past tonight because he's sick of my shit already. I know you don't want to have anything to do with me, and you probably don't even want to do that weird sex shit anymore, and I don't deserve your pity, but I'm asking you this one last favor, and then I'll fucking leave you alone. Fax me, okay? Be cool.

Gregg

Dear Dennis,

Yeah, that sounds cool. Thanks. I'm still totally cool with the sex stuff, I told you that. I'm up for it. I was just pissed off. I didn't mean it, you understand. How about this, though? Just read this and see what you think? I don't really want to go back to Portland. If you could give me enough money to fly to Cincinnati, and stay in a motel there for a couple of weeks, then that would be the best thing for me. Carla and my daughter live there, and I think if I can get there, and get a job, and prove to her that I've got my shit together, she might give me another chance, and I'd be near my daughter. I've been thinking that might really be the thing that would make me get my shit together. I know you hate me now, but I was just thinking if we could go back to that thing before about your rules and all that, and I could stay with you for maybe a week, and do whatever the fuck you want, and I can just be your whore and pretend I don't know you, and that you don't know me or whatever, like you said. Maybe at the same time we're doing all that, I could kick dope, so when I go to Cincinnati, I'll be in good shape. I've kicked a hundred times and it never takes more than a week, and if you want to see me suffer, then you will. Doesn't that sound sort of perfect? You can tie me up, like you were saying, and do whatever the fuck you're going to do, and that way I won't be able to escape and go score at the same time. That's a really perfect plan, isn't it? So what do you say? Fucking great, right? I'm excited. I don't know why I didn't think of this before.

Gregg

Dennis,

Fuck you. No offense. Okay, I've been an asshole, and I've lied to you, but my life is fucked-up right now, and I'm not at my best. What happened to all that shit about me being so great and brilliant, and the most important person you've ever known? Were you lying to me? How can you say that shit you wrote? You're wrong if you think you understand me. I don't have a death wish, and I don't see your fucking logic about your violent sex thing and my death wish being a marriage of fate or whatever. I'm asking you, as your friend, not to go this way, okay? If you want to pretend to do it or whatever, and fuck me up a little, that's cool, and I could maybe get off on that in my own way, because I do hate myself, you're right about that. But you're scaring the shit out of me, okay? You're just tripping out on your fantasy, right? Yeah, it's cool that we'll finally get it together. I'm sure you've got a million things you want to do to me, and I'm very cool with that, and I'll probably love it, okay? I have problems too, and I dig sex, and I've been known to feel right about being treated like shit, and I deserve that, and I've gotten off on it, and it's you, so I'll definitely get off on that, but don't go crazy, because you know I don't have a choice here. What else am I going to do? I've got nothing, and I have to go through with it, and I will, because I don't fucking believe that you mean it. I know when I'm with you, you'll remember why you thought I was great, and I'll remember too. I'll stay with you forever, if you want. I swear to fucking God. That plan about Cincinnati was just an idea. I don't have to do that. I could love you, and be with you, because when I think about it, I really do love you more than anyone ever in my whole life, even my daughter. How about this? Remember you thought I was going to be a great artist? Let's do that. I'll live with you, and do my art. I think that's a great idea. I've been wanting to get back into my art for a long time. So let's do it this way. We'll do the sex thing, and anything goes for as long as you want, that's cool, and then we'll both feel really good, and afterward it will be like it was when we used to know each other, but better because you'll get to do what you always wanted to do, and I'll feel like I finally paid you back for being so great to me, and everything will be cool. It will be like my life never went to shit. Okay? I think that sounds perfect. So I'll be standing on that corner like you said, and you pick me up, and we'll go from there, and I trust you. I feel better now. I hope you do too. Yeah, this is going to be fucking cool, Dennis. I'm excited. See you in a while.

Gregg

Alfie And Joe

BY DEB MARGOLIN

I DON'T WANT to know, honestly I don't. When I'm going away somewhere, I don't want to know where it is; I hate maps, I hate the relativism of Location. The travel agent will say: Let me show you where it is on the map, and I just say: I can't read, I can't write, I'm incapable of this information, I don't want to know where I'm going. Part of what defines a vacation for me is a freedom from the sense of belonging anywhere, of knowing anything, of having any sense of responsibility for where the fuck I am.

So I don't know where Murfreesboro, Tennessee, is, and don't try to call and tell me. I know it's south of where I live; I don't know by how much. I know the original Ku Klux Klan headquarters is a scant thumbnail-moon thirty miles out of it somewhere. I know that the lights of Nashville obscure the darkness of Murfreesboro; that there's a state university somewhere there; that the food in that town, free of charge, couldn't lure a beggar. I know that some native folk stake a claim to Murfreesboro in general, and to a town convenience store in particular, as the literal center of the universe. And for folks in Murfreesboro, it definitely is. I can't tell you another thing about it.

Except that my cousin lived there. My cousin Alfie. I had just gotten out of college, where I read a thousand books and smoked ten thousand cigarettes, had a job and lost it; decided to go visit Cousin Alfie. Alfie was a renegade who made a living suing people and driving a truck for the mob on movie sets and garbage routes. He had a girlfriend, an apartment and a ton of drugs, and he was real gung-ho about the thought of a visit from me. He admired me for being the "black sheep of the family." I never told him how much of a projection I thought that was.

I arrived there in the late summer. I love the late summer, when even the heat feels cool because it's tired of itself; kind of going cool around the edges in preview. Murfreesboro had the stillness of a rattlesnake before the strike; nothing ever happened there except in the obituary section. Alfie picked me up at the airport, and after slamming me on the back a couple of times with genuine affection, he asked me how I was doing, and when I told him how thirsty I felt, he opened a small vial and held out a little white pill. Do this, man! he said. Alfie had a pill or powder for every possible sensation, craving, yearning or biological requirement: if you were hungry you took this, if you were tired, you took that; he was pharmacologically equipped to do away with almost all human experience.

Alfie was so glad to see me that he had absolutely nothing to do with me. I had slated myself for a week in Murfreesboro, but as I write this I can say it was a week of months. I was there forever. Part of me died there, sweetly died. I spent the days wandering the streets. Time was hot and meaningless. I'd leave early in the morning while Alfie and his girlfriend were asleep. His girlfriend hated me the minute she saw me. They had a passionate, violent, friendly relationship, and while I was doing nothing at all, she went to work, came home, smoked, cursed, cut vegetables with a very sharp knife, cooked pork, dyed her hair and read girl magazines. I was told never to touch those.

One night Alfie broke his hand hitting her square in the jaw. I got home late and took an anti-hunger pill, having not found one palatable thing to swallow all day. Back in my room, on this, the penultimate night of my tender visit with Alfie, I heard the fight start up slowly, like a lawn-mower far away, and the sound rose in mass and energy until it turned into swooshes, the sounds of bodies moving, of flying bodies. I think I heard his bones crack, but I could be wrong. I thought I heard her crying, but that wouldn't have been much like her. All I know is, within a short time, she had left with the hair dryer and all the money, and Alfie was sitting in my room sharing his anti-pain medications and showing me the new contours of his fist. It had the shape of a heart in congestive failure.

I took Alfie to the hospital. He told me to get lost, so I left him there. At this time it was 12:20 in the morning, and I had no pills for my sadness, the tainted maudlin kind you feel in a playground empty of children. I walked then, for miles, many miles; I walked for hours and hours, twenty miles maybe, all the way to some little hamlet just outside Nashville. The walk was one of the most exciting I ever had. It was absolutely without promise; it was at the very boundary of meaninglessness. In that state all desire, all sex, all requitedness, all Heaven, is suddenly palpable, audible.

I arrived at the Bickford's Coffee Shop at 5:10 A.M. Bickford's are everywhere. Outside the store was a map, a big map of all the Bickford's Coffee Shops all over the country; green mountains and blue seas punctuated only by the little thatched roofs of Bickford's Coffee Shops. I studied the map with great interest, and I can say to this day it is the first map I ever understood. I understood it deeply, with my body. I realized I hadn't eaten in six days and was literally starving, and I lurched in with a new, profound sense of enfranchisement. I picked a seat in the horseshoe formation of the bar area, picked it the way I've seen kids pick their horses on the carousel. The smell of ammonia and coffee. Bickford's is green, like the face of someone sick; it's lit up without light; it's desperate. I was never so happy to be anywhere in my life. I could sense my proximity to Nashville, my proximity to the rest of my life, my distance from Alfie, my nearness to the woman he just hit, who escaped in a fashion both ancient and heroic. And I was on vacation.

Joseph was in there, dear friends, Joseph. I don't know how I could have missed it: Joseph, Christ almighty, Joseph was in there. I didn't know him, his name, but he was there, sitting directly across from me, staring at me. Staring in general is not erotic to me, but he sucked me with his eyes, pulled my body volume full to the surface.

It's 5:20, don't forget; I'm nothing but thirty miles, I'm nothing but cows and stars, and there's Joseph, the only other patron in the place. Joseph's looks are not important, not important at all. Someone with that degree of sexual power doesn't look like anything. You can't see them, only feel them, experience them; I doubt Alfie would have had any pill that could have gotten me out of this one.

We took our time, we had nothing but that. I asked for coffee, but the waiter didn't seem to know that word, so I mimed holding a cup and bringing it up to my lips, and he suddenly understood. For Joseph the little pageant was obscene; his eyes showed me that. Gravity behaves just this way: powerful, impersonal, supremely unavoidable, the pull of a body on another body, the compulsory fall to the deepest possible level. Gravity lets you roll down a grassy hill; I belonged to this man without speaking to him. A long time went by. I noticed he had a piece of cherry pie in front of him, and that seemed cartoonlike and ridiculous, and I burst out laughing. That passed, and it was silent again. At that moment the waiter put coffee in front of me in a chaste white cup and Joseph got up and was near me in an instant, against me; he put his hand between my legs, whispering in my ear. I didn't even turn to look at him. He picked up my coffee cup, drank a slow draught of it, then pulled my face to him and kissed me, so I could taste the burnt, the unsweetened. He deprived me of his tongue, which was curious; he was flirting with me, he was teasing me, he wanted me to suffer. That kiss was an enactment of all my hunger and when it was over I somehow knew his name without his telling me. He pulled me up off my barstool and dropped some bills onto the counter. It took the bills forever to fall, like leaves from a great height; that was my last image of Bickford's. The rest was all him.

He took me outside and pressed his body against me. I hadn't understood how tall he was. His crotch was against me; it was volcanic. He owned me, and that gave him great gentleness, like God's. Slowly, involuntarily, I reached up, stood on tiptoe and got my arms around his neck; this caused me to cant dangerously, and he caught me before I fell. It had begun to rain. I begged him for his tongue, but he started talking. He put his hands under my shirt. Heat flowed into his hands like milk. He started talking. He said:

My parents are coming today. I want you so badly. You're Jewish, I know that. I want you. I'm a friend of Isaac Bashevis Singer, I know him, I'm a writer, I love you, I wish my parents weren't coming or I'd take you to meet him, you're a writer, I can tell that, don't say anything, he's old now, I'd like you to see him, his eyes would glow, he would steal you. My parents are coming today or I'd take you out of here, take you down to Memphis where we could just live and die as long and as hard as we chose to, baby, you're a writer, I know that, don't say anything.

And he finally gave me his tongue. He put his hand behind my head, pulled my hair from its ponytail, a gesture I'd seen in a thousand movies and never understood before. My hair fell like light from a source, down to the ends of itself, and bounced like water, and he pulled me to him with the force of the tide and gave me his tongue. It was a terrifying, beautiful muscle that moved like a fish. I felt it in my stomach, my esophagus. It was spiny, riddled, like a wall with bullet holes. It burned. It went around me and around me until I came to know it, the second map I ever understood. His tongue was a condition, it was a cartography and it hurt me, it made me want more, I was lost, I just wanted. I said:

Your tongue is spiky.

And it hurt him to hear my voice, he wanted silence and he said:

Does it pierce you?

He took me in his car. Before we got in, I asked, Are you a rapist or a murderer? and we laughed.

I love Isaac Bashevis Singer, with his dybbuks and his spirits and his quaint way of lusting and Chekhovian sense of loss, but Henry Miller was the writer who made me want to write. In one of Hen's exuberant Tropic novels, he sang of wanting to fuck a woman

so she stayed fucked

And that's the image that made me see language, or what they call a tongue, as the means to that kind of fucking, that kind of fuck that never leaves you, that's fixed like a town on a map, that sets the standard, that fixes the nature of one's hunger. He did that to me, Joseph;

he marked me; he promised me things. He fucked me so I stayed fucked. People see that, just looking at me; it makes them want to do it again.

I called him from the airport, my beauty, he gave me his phone number, which shocked me. He didn't want me to speak, he wanted to be the one who helped me from speech like a grand dame from a prop plane. I called him from the airport. When he answered the phone I heard Yiddish being spoken, an old lady's voice speaking Yiddish... I said, Joe? but he didn't say anything and I hung up.

On the plane there was a map of the airline's hubs and stops and other places, with arcs connecting dots to show aviation routes. I wiped my mouth with that when I lost my napkin.

The Wedding of Tom to Tom

BY KEITH BANNER

THE FIRST TIME I saw the two of them doing something was also the first night I worked alone at the place. I was nervous from the start, and the woman on before me was a total alkie. As soon as I got there and clocked in down in the basement, she went, "They're all in bed and they got all their pills."

Then she was gone. I guess she walked off the face of the earth, because she didn't come back the next night, when she was due on. Never called or anything.

Anyway, I was walking up and down the hall of the old house after she left, nervous, like I should be checking on something. It felt like a haunted house, but I felt I belonged, like I was a ghost but didn't know it yet. I could hear the retarded people, all five of them, snoring and tossing and turning. Sleep's never been so loud. Then I heard real intense moans coming out of the back bedroom. They didn't sound like they were from sleeping people at all.

I went to the door at the end. It had this great big poster on it of Michael Jordan shooting a basketball through outer space. The door was halfway open. Suddenly, the moaning became like some weird song. Like singing and going crazy at the same time. I slid the door open the rest of the way, thinking that somebody might have been having a seizure. I'd just seen the training video on that the other day at my orientation. They had this dramatization about a woman dying from drowning on her own vomit while having a seizure. God knows I didn't want that my first night. I'd made a decision from the get-go: I am keeping this job, no matter what. I was gonna stop living like trash.

I opened the door, turned on the lights.

Tom B. was on his knees in front of Tom A. They were both naked and very white. I didn't know either of them at the time, so I just stood there. Tom B. is skinny and short, and Tom A. is big-bellied with short legs and no butt. Both are about middle-aged or older. Tom B. has a burr cut, and Tom A. has curly dark hair.

So there they were, like that. Blow-job position.

I wanted to scream or laugh or cry, all at the same time. This was my first night alone, remember. I figured they shouldn't be doing that, but I didn't know what else to do, so I shut the door back, like a maid in a sitcom catching people in the middle of something.

Of course I forgot to turn off the lights. I was getting ready to open the door and turn them off when I saw that one of the Toms had already got it. Almost as soon as it was dark in there again, they were making that same crazy silly sex music.

I went back to the living room. I lit up a cigarette, wondering if I should call somebody. Kate Anderson-Malloy, the home manager, told me when I saw that video the other day that if I had any questions just to beep her. "Just beep me," she'd almost yelled, smiling like a wacko left in charge, but you had to respect her enthusiasm.

I could still hear them. I smoked real deep and seriously contemplated just walking off. Not beeping anybody, just going. Two retarded men participating in a blow-job. I mean, I'm not some Pollyanna by any means. But yes, it shook me the hell up.

I was about to go back there again, stupidly afraid that maybe Tom B. might get choked or something, I was on my way, when I heard footsteps. I stopped right toward the third bedroom and I saw Tom B., back in his pj's, tiptoeing back to his room. He had this serious face in the emergency exit–light. Half-demonic, half-angelic and dramatic, like he had gone off and now he was returning from his journey filled with beautiful new things to tell. I felt sorry for him, sort of. I heard him close his door real careful. Heard the rest of them continue with their loud, gurgled sleep.

Sleep deprivation—and witnessing a retarded blow-job—made me feel kind of paranoid that whole damn night. I kept smoking cigarette after cigarette. Kate Anderson-Malloy had told me at orientation that sometimes state people come out to check on group homes in the middle of the night to make sure the staff isn't getting paid for sleeping on the job. I kept seeing headlights scatter across the walls all night.

Plus there was my whole ex-boyfriend thing brewing too. I was being stalked, so to speak. He didn't know it, but his ass would soon be in jail. Anyway, to keep myself busy, I started snooping through the filing cabinets over by where the scales are, near the door to the basement, in the little makeshift office there.

I got out Tom A.'s and Tom B.'s files. I read Tom B.'s first. It said right at the start that Tom B. suffered from moderate mental retardation and also possible schizophrenia. He could talk but had trouble with his speech. He had lived his whole life in an institution in Columbus called the Orient, but was sent here when it closed down, as was Tom A. In fact, at that place, according to Tom B.'s file, both Toms had a reputation for being "obsessed with each other's presence" so much that they often had to be split up and put into separate parts of the institution. Usually, though, according to typewritten reports in the file, they found their way back to each other. Tom A. could not talk, and was more retarded than Tom B., so his file was pretty skimpy, except I read one part about when he was four years old, his stepdad burnt him with cigars.

By that next morning, which was a Saturday, I knew the whole damn story by heart. Since no one had to go to the sheltered workshop, Kate Anderson-Malloy had written me a note in the log that said they all could sleep in till eight. I made a big breakfast, to let them know I was an okay chick. I mean, the works. Now that I'm a full-time shift supervisor, lead direct care in fact, I just put out the boxes of cereal and gallons of milk and they go at it. But that first morning, I made waffles and heated up the syrup in the microwave, had some sausage patties that I also nuked. Full glasses of juice and paper napkins, picnic-type dinette table set, like the Waltons were about to come down and eat. It was ready around 7:45 that morning and no one was up, so I got antsy and went down the hall again, like the warden who makes breakfast.

When I woke up Tom A., he looked at me like the way—I'm sorry, this sounds pretty awful—like the way my cat does. Lonesome inside, without the capability to explain, and yet also relieved that he was off the hook from having to tell me anything. In fact he smiled at me, and I said, "Why, aren't you chipper!"

I almost added, as a joke, "Looks like you got some last night."

But I didn't.

He sat up. His belly hung down quite a bit. He had a boyish face though. I noticed on his back all those cigar scars. He walked over to me and put his hand out, like a gentleman in a silent movie.

I shook it. He let out this huge scream that about killed my ears.

"Thanks," I said.

I went and got Sally, this little woman with Down's Syndrome who may have had Alzheimer's too. She was in her canopy bed in her pink bedroom—that's the way her sister painted it for her. She had on a pink flannel nightgown and looked like a melted doll in a playhouse.

I got Damon, a black guy with a big head that had water inside it. He had a pump installed in his skull that kept the water from drowning out his brain. I knew all this stuff from Kate Anderson-Malloy and from the files. I knew Damon used to live with his prostitute mother and she used to sell him out to freaks. He was very quiet and could only say, "Mona Lisa."

Got Larry up. He talked too much. Soon as he was up, he started gabbing.

"Hello. You're new here. Your name is what? May I ask what?"

His eyes were open great big. He was sitting on a rocking chair in his room with posters of big-breasted women hung on the walls with black electrical tape. Tall and bony with a big bald head and very red lips.

"Anita," I said.

"We ain't going out anywhere today," he said, looking out the window. You could totally tell he hated going outside.

"Okay," I said. "I made breakfast for you."

He turned his head toward me and clapped his hands in an exaggerated, almost sarcastic way, but his voice seemed for real. "How nice," he said. "Don't smoke around me. I have asthma."

I said okay.

Tom B. was the last one, as his room was at the end. There was Michael Jordan staring at me. His door opened as soon as I got there, and he was in a pair of dress pants and a wrinkled mint green dress shirt, feet in brown vinyl slippers. He looked uptight and yet really wanting to please. His eyes still had sleep in them. I saw him from last night, naked, going down on Tom A.

"Breakfast is ready," I said.

"Tanks," he said. Speech impediment.

"You're welcome."

His smile was unnerving, shaky around the edges, and it almost made me angry at him.

"Tanks berry much," he said, and then started walking toward the kitchen.

I followed behind him. All of the retarded people were seated at the picnic table now, and the shock on all their faces almost made me burst out crying. It was like Thanksgiving with breakfast food. I know I'm sounding like some sentimental idiot, so I won't go on, but they really loved what I'd done, and it had been a while since I got that kind of reaction from anybody.

"Look at dis Tommy," Tom B. said to Tom A. "Look what she did fow us."

Tom A. smiled bigger. He grabbed his fork in one hand and his knife in the other, like any minute, any minute.

"Mona Lisa," Damon said, his voice very low. "Mona. Lisa."

My relief came in at eleven. She seemed a little drunk too. A lot of drunks work in group homes, like it's their way of paying penance: a vodka binge, then they go in and wipe up a retard's ass and they think they don't have to quit drinking. But this woman, named Raquel, could be drunk but it didn't seem obnoxious, even at eleven in the A.M.

Right when Raquel walked in and went down to the basement to clock in was when Archie called me, my drug-dealing ex-fiancé. This job was sort of my antidote to all I had just gone through with him, kinda like I was paying penance too but just for being a total fucking fool. But Archie kept following me. I mean, I was living with my dad, and I was moving all my stuff out of the town house we were at one time sharing, and every time I went to get more stuff he was there, hangdog in the face. Sometimes when I was going around doing my business and shit, I would see him in his Escort in the rearview mirror with that same hangdog, stalker look. Like he was having his picture taken for the cover of *Pathetic Small Town Dope Dealer* magazine.

"What? How did you get this number, you son of a bitch?" I was whispering, hoping Raquel wouldn't hear. Everyone was out in the living room, watching VH1, doing whatever. Tom A. and Tom B. were sitting on the love seat, of course. Holding hands. Sally was in her pink sweatsuit, on the floor, talking to a piece of a jigsaw puzzle. Larry was really the only one watching the TV, while Damon rocked in his lounger with his eyes closed, kind of like Stevie Wonder does.

"I hired a private detective," Archie said. He laughed.

"Bullshit. Listen, I'm at my new job, and I am trying to make something outta myself."

"Okay, okay."

"So it's over."

"I love you so much."

"Go smoke your crack, Archie. Just fucking go smoke your crack."

I hung up. As if she'd been waiting at the bottom of the stairs for me to finish, Raquel marched up, her hair all ratty-looking, in a pair of nylon sweats and flannel shirt. She smelled like perfume and cigarettes and just the thinnest vapor of Jack Daniel's, almost sweeter-smelling than the perfume.

"Hey," she said, not looking at me.

I had just finished up with the kitchen, so I was ready to go. Pulling an eleven to eleven was more than I thought it would be.

Raquel looked out in the living room. Then she got panicked sort of. She turned around and told me, "You're letting Tom and Tom sit out there like that?"

"Yeah," I said.

"Good God, if Kate found out..."

Raquel yelled, "Tom. Hey Tom. Don't hold Tommy's hand now. You guys split up. It's time for some alone time. Okay?" Raquel's smile was nervous, like she was talking to someone during a hostage crisis.

Tom B. looked up, responding to being called Tom. He smiled. But his eyes were afraid at the same time. He blew out a sigh and let go of Tom A.'s hand and stood up and went over beside Sally on the floor, small and polite like a little Japanese guy.

Raquel turned to me. "If you let them do that, they don't know when to stop. They'll get so into each other, they'll not know when to quit. One time they locked themselves in the bathroom for a day and all they did was—well—you don't want to know. Let's just say they went through a whole bottle of hand lotion." Raquel laughed into her hand. She flopped down at the picnic-type table, lit up a cigarette.

I smiled. Sally was talking to Tom B.'s foot now. I wondered just what the fuck I was getting myself into. Heard Archie's voice in my head, pleading. At one time, he was gonna do construction and I was gonna go back to community college for something in nursing. Ha.

"Guess I'll go," I said.

"Yeah," Raquel said, smoking.

She stood up and, with her cigarette dangling, walked out into the living room.

"Look at all my babies," she said kind of loud, but then she looked up at me and her eyes were real clear. They were the eyes of a drunk lady who used to have kids but for some reason lost them and now she was in a roomful of retarded people that she was claiming as her own, and she was saying it like a joke on herself, on the retards, and on me. But it wasn't mean-spirited. It was pathetic and it was sweet.

I laughed a lot right then. Probably from being so sleep-stunted. Tom A. and Tom B. were trying to sneak off for a quickie, and I saw. So did Raquel, squatting next to big-headed Damon. She grabbed two throw pillows from the couch and tossed them at both the Toms, hard.

"Stop right there." Her voice was joking and not.

They stopped, went to separate corners like obedient prizefighters. I wanted to give them permission right then. Go for it. I wanted to get the hell out of there worse though.

I left that day without saying anything else. Thinking I was not ever going back.

Time sure flies when you're having so much fun. So to speak. I mean, it really does. That was about a year ago, all that I just explained. Of course I went back for my next shift. Actually, if I remember correctly, I got called in to cover the other drunk lady's shift, the one who never came back.

Now Raquel and me go out and get drinks together all the time. I am on my way to becoming a drunk-lady-direct-care-worker myself. Raquel and me practically run the place.

Some things, even with time, don't change, however.

"You want to get together?" It's Archie. I'm standing in my dad's house right now and can hear Dad out in the garage sawing on something.

"Good God," I say, and I laugh because Archie's voice sounds so familiar and yet shocking, like a CD you think is fucked-up and you press play and it's not.

"It's me."

"You were up for six years."

"Time out for good behavior. Plus Butler County ain't got no room, and it was my first offense."

He laughs, smoky-voiced. I can picture him, going bald but with a rugged face, and skin color like dank wood. And his mouth, I always can remember that fondly. Big-lipped and smiling with strong white teeth. He is so into dental hygiene.

Dad comes in sweaty, mouthing, "Who is it?"

I just roll my eyes. "Listen, I gotta go."

I hang up, and Dad looks at me: "Archie?"

"How'd you know?"

“You had that look. He calling from jail?”

Dad is washing his hands in the sink, over all the dirty dishes. He is a tall guy with freshly cut hair. He goes to the barber three times a month. On disability because of his back, so it’s about the only place to go during the day, outside of his old work site and I think they might have told him to stop going there so much. Now he spends his time out in his garage/workshop making things like a vacuum cleaner with a digital display. Inventions he hopes to patent. He takes a lot of pills for pain.

“No. He’s out.”

Dad dries his hands on paper towels.

“Wow,” he says. “You know what, I had a vision.”

Dad thinks he’s psychic. He even has a license to be a practicing one and goes to psychic fairs in Cincinnati and Dayton. Even has business cards: ROLAND SIMMONS, L.S.P. (Licensed Spiritualist Practitioner). With that license, he can legally marry people. He’s marrying Tom A. and Tom B. tonight, in fact. Not legally, but still.

“You did?” I say.

“Yeah. I didn’t want to say nothing.” His eyes go so sincere, like Bill Clinton, when he talks psychic talk. It’s a sad yet joyous thing, his psychic powers. Like a person who can’t read suddenly being able to. The psychic stuff is one of the primary reasons Mom dumped him though.

Dad looks at me with big puffy Darvon eyes. “But I saw you and Archie together in a motel room.”

He laughs but stops.

“Thanks, Dad. There is no way.”

I go into the living room. I’ve straightened it up for the wedding tonight. It’s all planned. Me and Raquel planned it. I have white and sky blue streamers and I made a cake and punch. Dad’s technological shit is still everywhere in piles, cables and old TVs and VCRs and computer monitors and stuff, but I scooted all of it around to make it look like an aisle. At first, we were gonna rent a hall, but that would have drawn attention to it. This is sort of a secret operation, of course. If Kate knew, or if Tom A.’s brother, his legal guardian, knew, we’d all be fired, possibly up for charges or something.

“Think about the headlines, Anita,” Raquel said one night at Applebee’s after work, over cocktails and cigarettes. “Two Group Home Workers Force Clients into Homosexual Marriage.” We got tickled and started making up juicier and juicier ones, ending with: “Shotgun Homosexual Retarded Marriage Performed by Crazed Psychic While Group Home Workers Get Drunk and Laugh Their Asses Off.”

Anyway, Tom A. is being made to move, or at least that’s the threat. Kate Anderson-Malloy caught them one morning, about four months back, doing it in the bathroom, and since then she’s been on a campaign, although she’s totally professional about it. At a staff meeting, where all of us gather at the main office in Middletown, Kate, kind of flabby with really nice hair and an excellent pantsuit, got into a sort of tirade. I mean, she’s a bitch, like most managers afraid of doing any real work are, but also there’s this weird, loud lovingness in her face as she pronounces her proclamations, like against her compassionate instincts she’s always having to tell us these things. And so she looked at all of us in the paneled conference room, and she went:

“Look. We have tried everything with those two. I mean, I’m not against love. I’m not against human sexuality. I’m against obsession. Those two are obsessed. I mean, I talked to Mr. Allen, Tom A.’s guardian, last night on the phone, and he told me they’ve been like that since they were boys, and it’s hard to stop that kind of behavior. I mean, you can’t. So we’re just gonna move Tom A. over to Franklin Street and move Juanita from over there to our place. Juanita’s real cute. You guys are gonna love her. I mean, Tom A. and Tom B. can still see each other, but supervised. I mean, what I’m afraid of is that they are gonna end up hurting each other. Physically. There’s all kinds of issues here. I mean, when I walked in on them the other morning, Tom A., excuse me, but Tom A. was anally penetrating Tom B.”

The way she said “penetrating,” I had to laugh. Raquel looked over at me, and our eyes kind of got conspiratorial.

When Kate looked at me, she had to laugh too. I mean, it was funny. Eric, another guy who works with us, laughed, and then all the people, mostly new hires, well, we all got the giggles until finally Kate had to stop us.

"I know, I know," she said. "This is the people business, and yes, the people business can be pretty funny. But let's just try to make this happen smoothly, okay?"

Then it got quiet, like we were all suddenly little kids and Kate Anderson-Malloy was the teacher.

Dad's standing at the podium he made for the wedding. It's in front of the living room window where the TV used to be. He looks kind of silly, standing there, politician-dumb, like he is thinking how to talk about a big issue in little-people language for the masses.

But I love him. One of his visions about me, and he usually has them after eating late at night, is that I am going to be famous somehow. He sees me getting an award on a show.

"Now," he says, making sure the hair he combs over his bald spot is still in place, "so I'm just gonna treat these two like man and wife?"

"That's what we want," I say.

The phone rings again, and we let the machine get it. It's Archie's voice. He's singing this Boyz II Men song I used to really like, "The End of the Road." It kills me, and I get embarrassed, Dad standing there, smiling.

"What a singer," Dad says.

Archie stops then, and the answering machine has that hang-up dial tone sound for a sec. I get closer to the podium, pretending like I'm one of the Toms so I can see what it looks like. Dad's eyes go serious. He says, "So this is the wedding of Tom A. to Tom B." He's reading it off an index card. Practicing. What a perfectionist.

"Ladies and gentleman, I now pronounce them Tom and Tom."

The plan was secretly hatched in the basement, by the time clock. Raquel was taking a drink from her Super America mug, filled with vodka and red pop. One time she offered me a sip and I took it and, boy, was it vodka and red pop.

Anyway, it was the evening right after the staff meeting where Kate told us Tom A. was gonna have to move. We were both kind of bummed, and Raquel said, "You know, all Tom B. has ever talked about was getting married to him. I think that is so sweet." She took a big drink.

The dryer was going. Big industrial one for all the piss-soaked bedsheets and other assorted piss-soaked items. I knew that already, about them wanting to get married. Not only because Tom A. had a stack of old-time bridal magazines, worn out from looking at them, stacked in his room, but Tom B. and I had gotten into many discussions about marriage too. By this time, we were pretty good friends. Tom A. was more aloof, since he couldn't talk, but Tom B. let you know he was proud of what he and Tom A. had accomplished: twenty-four years of staying together, and when Orient shut down and they were going to be moved out, he knew Tom and him would be in the same group home because, "It went alphabetic. So I knew. It was luck. It was God too. Tink about it, Anita. Tom A. and Tom B."

It made sense, didn't it? His face, as I was trying to do my paperwork, was sincere and stupid and scary and beautiful. You can't say no to that. Well, maybe other people can, but people like me can't.

By the way, Tom B. and me never did talk about me seeing them that first night I worked there, them doing the nasty, but I'm sure he would have just laughed it off like nothing. Raquel said they used to line people up at Orient in the shower room, forty at a time, and tell them to hold their noses, and spray them down with a gigantic fire hose, and then say, "Now soap up," and forty men would soap up real quick, and then get sprayed again and some people, the people who worked there, would laugh as they sprayed them.

So Raquel said that night with the dryer going, "Let's let them get married."

She looked at me like we were both out of our minds. Even though she was a lifer, she was also pretty much timid and obedient, scared of Kate Anderson-Malloy and not just because she had two last names, but because Kate had sense to everything she said. Obviously it made a lot of sense to move them away from each other. Because they were getting worse. They weren't going to workshop some mornings, clinging to each other nude in one bedroom or the other. Other times too, like they were losing their fear, like they were getting brave. Helping them to get married would only make them braver, wouldn't it? And it definitely would not stop them from having to move away from each other.

But Raquel took a big gulp from her vodka and red pop and swallowed and said, "Maybe if they get married it won't be so bad that they can't live together. Like Dolly Parton and her husband."

I smiled. That didn't make any sense, but it seemed right.

Raquel is already at the group home when I pull up. She had already helped pudgy Tom A. into his suit. It's a light blue leisure suit from when he got de-institutionalized and they gave them all new clothes, back in the late seventies. It barely fits, and he looks like some tourist guy having nerve problems on vacation. He and Raquel are sitting on the couch, and Damon and Sally and Larry the big mouth are all in the living room.

I step in. Eric is in the back with Tom B.

"He's showing Tom how to shave good," Raquel says.

Larry asks, "Are we going anywhere? We're not going anywhere are we?" He's got that totally freaked-out look on his face.

"No. Just me and Raquel and Tom A. and Tom B.," I say.

"Thank the Lord. I am just so tired, Anita," he says. He was raised by two aunts in a mansion, kept a secret there with them for years, and that's his personality: old-lady stubbornness and laziness and gentility.

Sally comes over, spit dripping down onto her pink shirt. Her face has a sweet and scary emptiness to it. She is walking around without knowing anything but with her eyes wide open.

"Pop," she whispers. "Pop, candy. Pop. Candy."

She has gone into this repressed memory thing, where she is always thinking she's brushed her teeth real good and now she deserves some pop and candy. That's the way they used to get her to brush them.

"I don't have any, honey," I say.

Raquel, dressed in a long jean skirt and a beautiful orange blouse, her ratty hair pulled back into a bun, gets up and gets some Tic Tacs out of her purse. "Here."

Sally seems happy, and sits on the arm of Damon's lounger. He pushes her off, saying what he says: "Mona Lisa."

Sally flops down and grunts and kind of laughs.

Then Tom B. comes out with Eric, a slump-shouldered high school dropout who wants to be a chef. He has one of those sad mustaches that is barely there. But Tom B. is perfectly clean shaven in a navy blue suit, black shoes. Handsome, I think.

Eric looks scared. "You guys, if anybody finds out."

Larry comes in. "We ain't going anywhere."

"I know, Larry. Calm down," Eric says. He starts to whisper, "I told Tom that he can't say nothing, and he agreed, right, Tom?"

Tom B. nods. "Right. I won't." He shakes his head real hard, and goes over to Tom A. He gives his hand to Tom A. and Tom A. looks dumbfounded for a sec. He is realizing they are actually going somewhere to get married. It doesn't make sense to him, but still, it's exciting.

"Come on," Tom B. says. "Come on, Tommy."

They're two boys going to church. Two kids, it seems like. True love does that to you.

Raquel opens the door. They walk out. I look at Eric, who's still worried.

"God, if anybody finds out," he says.

I just go on out.

Raquel's car is bigger, so we go in hers, both Toms in back, holding hands. It's dark and chilly and the headlights shine on piles of silver gravel. I need a cigarette. I think about Archie's voice on the phone. Pathetic but rich with feeling, and I think about the way he would look coming out of the shower, naked, and anybody naked looks like they did when they were kids, even with hair and flab and all the years added on. Something about being dripping wet and shivering and clean: that's what a kid is. I remember loving Archie when he was wet and naked. Pretending not to see him, but he was showing off, even with his rotten body. Coming over to me while I was trying to read course descriptions.

"Baby," he said.

"You're getting water all over the fucking floor."

He laughed. It was all I could do not to laugh with him. Maybe he was on crack right then, for all I know, because he kept all that hidden from me. In fact, maybe the crack was buried when he saw me. Put away in the chest of drawers in his head, and this was love, without crack and without any lies and without his petty-assed, trashy ways.

Maybe, maybe not.

I see them back there in the rearview. Tom A. and Tom B. Looking straight ahead.

"Tanks, you guys," Tom B. says.

Dad awaits. So do Raquel's two friends, drag queens who go to her AA meetings. They are dressed conservatively, like ladies who go out to lunch but who also might have some mental health issues. Big, big hair, and they sit on my dad's couch, my dad offering them punch or something stronger.

"Punch. That sounds so innocent and sweet," one drag queen says. Right when we came in, Raquel introduced us. This one is Mimi. The other's name is Salsa.

"This whole thing is sweet," Salsa says.

I smile, and Dad goes to get the punch, and on his way he stops by and pats both Toms on the back. They are standing near a little table of gifts. As Dad pats them, though, his face goes white as a sheet. He almost falls down and has to go over to a dinette chair, panting real bad. The Toms and Raquel all look scared, but I focus on my dad, as Mimi and Salsa march over, Mimi saying she used to work in a hospital and knows CPR.

But Dad is not having a heart attack, I don't think. His face is pale but not pained.

"Wow," he whispers to me.

"What?"

"When I touched those two," he says.

"Tom and Tom?"

"Yeah." He laughs. People are leaning into us, and I kind of nicely push them back.

"What?" I say.

"I saw this airplane hangar. You know. Great big corrugated metal, big as hell, and it had this red, well, this pink and red light. And I was at one end of it," Dad says, and he sits up, and I back away and all the others stand, listening. It's suddenly quiet as hell.

"I was in this hangar, at one end, it was empty, and just that pink and red light. Like you know there was a fire somewhere. Then I heard this stampede coming from the other side. I swear to God. That was strong, people. Wow." He laughs some more, and Mimi goes, "You psychic, honey?"

"Yes, I am," Dad says. He looks up proudly, his bottom lip shaking like he might start crying. He's always been emotional.

"He's got a license," I say, to back him up.

"Wow," Mimi says, looking over at Raquel, like thank you for bringing us here. "Well, kiss my hand and tell me what I want for Christmas!" Mimi and Salsa laugh real loud, but Dad just stands up and walks over to the podium.

"Bring them over now. It's time," he tells Raquel, and Raquel brings Tom and Tom over in front of the podium. I run over to the lights and flick switches to make it more intimate, turn on low music.

"This big hangar building," Dad says, from the podium. Tom and Tom are right there in front of him. "Pink light, like exploding roses. The red-light district. Ha ha. No. A stampede. You gotta hear it. A thousand-plus feet. I am on the other side and I look up and all these shaved-headed people are running right at me in the red light. It's like they just got freed, you know? Like the concentration camp just opened its doors and they got out and they're running. They don't know where they're going or nothing. They're coming right at me. And I want that to happen. I want them to run me over."

My dad is smiling with glassy eyes.

"I want them to run me over," he says, looking right at Tom A. and Tom B. "And they do. They stomp all over me. They gotta get somewhere, don't they?"

He's asking the Toms, and Tom B. goes, "Yes."

"They gotta get somewhere," my dad says, and he closes his eyes. Then he opens them real quick.

"That's love," he says.

After taking a sip from her punch, which she had to go get herself, Mimi says, "Amen, brother."

It goes easier after that.

"Do you, Tom, take Tom here to be your husband?"

Tom A. nods his head, silent-movie sincere.

"What about you, Tom?"

"Yes, I do." He kind of knows this is a joke, doesn't he? Tom B.'s pretty smart. He knows that life is filled with little jokes you have to take serious so that something means something.

"Well, okay then."

My dad's face is plush and full of pride. I can see all those people coming at him, then at me. That big airport hangar or whatever, the red light. In my version, they are all smiling the way Tom A. does during a blow-job session. The light is blossoming from all of that, that red light is blood light. Love light. Lava-lamp light. Archie has a lava lamp in his bedroom, or used to. He would turn it on in the dark while we made love. "Real cheesy," he would say. "Just call me your lava-lamp porn stud." The ceiling would get translucent blisters, like jellyfish were splattering into themselves.

When they kiss, Tom and Tom in my dad's living room, it's embarrassing, sure. They kiss long and hard, two retarded guys kissing really wet. Dad just has to look away.

"That is so sweet," Mimi says.

Salsa says, "Look at those two go at it."

Raquel gets up, goes over and whispers to the two Toms, and they stop, both out of breath, standing back.

"I now pronounce them Tom and Tom," Dad says.

Raquel comes over.

"I called Motel 6. They have adjoining rooms. I was gonna take them over and stay in the next room," Raquel says. "But Mimi wants me to go with her. She's in some drag show. You think you could stay with them till I get done?"

Mimi's right next to her, begging me in high style, both long-nailed hands pressed together.

"Sure," I say.

Raquel comes over to me then and hugs me tight, "We are so silly," she whispers. "Ain't we?"

I look at her as we pull apart. She's in her forties but looks about sixty. Her hair is dyed. She's about to go bald. Those eyes though. I see us at some bar next week laughing about all this.

"We are," I say.

Mimi and Salsa and Raquel go. Dad comes over, holding his head. "Migraine," he whispers. "Tell both Toms goodbye for me. I can't. I'm gonna go to bed."

"'Night," I say.

I don't know what else to do but tell them to get into the car. I drive them over to the Motel 6.

Tom B. looks at me in the mirror as I drive.

"We didn't have rings, Anita," he says, like he's just realizing it.

"You know, you're right. We'll have to get you rings tomorrow. We can go over to Kmart and get rings." I try to smile.

They start kissing deep again in the backseat.

As soon as I pull into the Motel 6 lot, I tell them to break it up. I check us in. Our rooms are ready. It's doomed, I know, Tom and Tom. Or maybe Tom B. will escape and go and rescue Tom A. from the other group home. Maybe they'll walk across America and find themselves in paradise.

Tonight is paradise, isn't it? The Motel 6's rooms are beige with orange bedspreads. Yellow carpet. They march into their room, and Tom A., in his leisure suit, sits down and grins. Tom B. closes the door to the adjoining room, smiling.

I sit down on my bed and right then is when I see him, standing in the window. Out on the patio.

He starts tapping on the glass.

I can't help it. If he had a crack pipe I would let him stick it in my mouth, but instead I just let him into the room. He's shivering, he's jailhouse thin. He is in a long cowboy coat and jeans and a cowboy shirt. His eyes look hurt and happy and they seem to glow. My heart feels like all those shaved-headed freaks are marching over it. Love has to happen at the end of every night or you don't know yourself.

"I'm working," Archie tells me, standing in front of the TV.

I nod my head. "You are, huh?"

"Who the hell are they anyway?" Archie asks, and he comes over and sits down on the bed next to me. "Are they those retarded people you work with? Why'd you bring them here?"

"I just did," I say. "For the hell of it."

Archie laughs. It's wheezy and warm. I want to crawl into his laugh like an orphaned baby onto a luxury liner. Go across the ocean to Europe where some kind lady wants me.

"I love you so much," Archie says. "I should have told you and you could have helped me get off the stuff, but I was just ashamed. I'm sorry for what I did. I lied so much. I was sick, babe. It was like the drug took over, you know?"

I want to tell him to shut up. Want to kick his ass out. That's the next instinct, right after being overjoyed at seeing him, happy at being stalked. I remember when I first met him. It was at a bar in Hamilton, skanky redneck place me and a girlfriend used to go to shoot darts and get drunk. He was standing by the dartboard drinking and smoking, still in his work clothes, and I threw a dart and it almost got him. But he wasn't pissed.

"Cupid's arrow," he said.

Then Archie and me hear them. Screaming. Silly crazy sex music. There's bumps and thumps against the thin walls. There's laughter.

"Good God," says Archie.

But he isn't disgusted. He isn't even perturbed. He doesn't understand, but he's here with me, and that's next door.

"Are they having a good time or what?" he asks. He smells of cigarettes and beer and Brut and old pizza and sweat and love.

I guess I love him. I kiss him. That's all I can do.

Perverts.com

BY LAURIE STONE

WHEN YOU GO on the Internet and check out the pervert sites, it refreshes your respect for range. It's a rainbow world out there, and depending on where you stand on the pervert spectrum, it can make you feel small-time or pretty pleased with yourself. Take Aboveaveragedicks.com. It's modestly named. The dicks are substantially above average. The dicks of my acquaintance that are anatomically attached to people do not look like the cocks of stud racing horses or the limbs of 300-year-old trees. The "above average dicks" do. One was photographed from a worm's-eye view and curled up toward its host's ripped abs like an elephant's trunk. I wouldn't be surprised if it could pick up peanuts. Recently, my friend Bruce offered to show me a video of a guy pissing into his own mouth. I was eating dinner at the time and asked if I could take a rain check. Mr. Elephant Dick could certainly accomplish that feat.

The sites endeavor to protect the young. "Leave now if it is illegal for you to see naked women," they entreat grade-schoolers who may not have boned up on the law. Even if they have, they're free to view pictures of naked men employing their orifices in imaginative ways. There is no evangelizing, unless, of course, you're into that. It is a come as you are environment. Although many of the menu choices strike me as ingenious, they are presented as if you, yourself, have already thought them up. Fuckmeharder.com and oneblondefingeringanother.com are unlikely to surprise as options, but I was impressed by the novelty of pregnantandlactatingsluts.com and sodatbitchruinedyourlife.com. Domain names can be a mouthful.

Exxxtremegermanmovies.com doesn't offer Nazi porn, as might be expected, but rather hetero couples blasély performing vanilla sex while speaking German. It's a spin on tongue perversion. Some people just want you to talk German to them. Clitcritic.com is an orgasm-friendly site, with a soupçon of gynecological-exam perversion. Facials.com is for those who enjoy watching semen ejaculated on women's faces and for women who like to use jism for pore-reducing masks. Puckerup.com heralds the joys of anal penetration with objects attached to strings. And the homepage of spanking.com sports a businessman in shirt and tie with a naked woman across his lap, her butt high and her face near the floor. As his hand beats a regular tattoo, her rump turns bright pink.

While some perverts prefer other people's fantasies, an alternative group (among whom I number myself) enjoys inventing their own. For us, there are such sites as newbiepornsters.com, for beginners, mentalspycams.com, for erotica themed around surveillance and paranoia, and poetsandfilth.com, about which I can speak from personal experience. We assemble in chat rooms and arouse each other either during real-time conversations, on which others may eavesdrop, or in emails sent to individuals or posted to the group. The rooms tend to be genre specific. The members of "Futuristic Switch Hitters" write about people who have multiple sets of genitalia and are therefore not, strictly speaking, either male or female, though butch and femme role-playing is still big in this world. "Fabio's Secret" hosts bodice-ripping pornographers. "Prufrock Sent Me" attracts mongers of sleaze with a bent toward pantoons and villanelles. I gravitate toward "Fetishes R Us."

In general, we are a permissive community, and my chat room of choice is open to fetishists of all stripes. Recently, two newcomers entered with the screen names: scratchandsniff and everydayfiend.

They arrived at nearly the same time, though I don't know if they had prior knowledge of each other, and I don't know either's sex. People can declare whatever they like, or refrain from declarations, without fear of detection. Sometimes, members of our group collaborate on a chain story, leaving off at a cliffhanger and passing it to the next writer. Some of the tales are more comical than lubricious, though they can be both. A chubby chaser might begin about removing the underpants of a 400-pound virgin—"They flapped like the sail of my childhood Sunfish." A voyeur might shift the point of view to a neighbor with a peephole. And next might come an installment about wet suits, or one about toe sucking.

Scratchandsniff and everydayfiend didn't collaborate. Rather, each presented installments of two separate erotic diaries. Scratchandsniff wrote as Peg, everydayfiend as Alex. Peg was a nineteen-year-old ex–street punk, who was bartending at a club on Avenue B and writing poetry and music reviews for the online zine *Bristle*. Alex, a former heroin addict in his mid-thirties, lived in Tribeca and composed electronic music. I became captivated by these characters and felt irritable if, for some reason, their authors failed to post an update.

In her first entry, Peg wrote:

Dear Cyberpals,

Rolled out of bed around eleven. The sun was like a disgusting eyeball. Everything hurt. I stumbled into the bathroom and checked myself for damage. Face okay. There was a man-in-the-moon-shaped bruise on the top of my left thigh. Have no idea how it got there. I didn't do any shit last night, though one of the regulars was handing out Ecstasy as if he'd sold all his shares of AOL. I wasn't going to go home with anyone, because I wanted to kick living like a vampire, but around three, Goldie comes in looking hot. She's got this blond pageboy wig on. She looks fucking like she could eat the world and suck on the pit. She knows I like a little pain but not in public. I really want to go home so I can write the next day. That review of the Puff Adder concert is due. But she says, "Come in the bathroom. I wanna show you something." I wipe my hands on a towel and follow her like a dog. Traffic at the bar is thinning. It's almost time to close. We're in the dark hallway near the phone. It stinks from cigarettes and spilled beer, and I get a whiff of piss that's overshot the toilet. What she has to show me is a pair of lace undies she is going to give me after she takes her knife and slices off the ones I'm wearing.

She pushes open the bathroom door. She tells me to bend over, with my hands on the sink, and put my ass in the air. Real romantic. I hear her flip open her switchblade, and now I wish we weren't in a toilet and having to be quick but were back at my place, sipping beer and talking about what we were gonna do before we did it.

Gotta split.

Love,

Peg

Alex wrote,

Dear Friends,

Lila and I are in the kitchen when I ask what I could do that would scare her. There is no irony in my voice. I can't maintain a sense of the absurd and an erection at the same time. She's leaning against the fridge. There's a shopping list attached to it with a magnet. "Semolina bread with raisins and fennel." Lila likes it. I forgot to shop. She doesn't laugh, doesn't even crack a smile. She's wearing the bustier with the laces in the back, the nice fetishy thing she bought for two hundred and fifty dollars earned by proofreading legal briefs, so I would get a woody when I saw her.

Lila has on a trancy look. Her eyes are at half-mast, and she licks her bottom lip. A part of me wishes that, in bed, she would reach underneath it and retrieve not the riding crop I keep there but a seltzer bottle. If she did, I would probably look for another girlfriend. She says, "Tying me up and leaving the apartment." It sounds like she's saying, "Sweetie, I made that chocolate mousse you like," or "You'll win a Guggenheim with that piece you just finished." She asks what would scare me to do, and I think: Nothing. Do I have limits? Well, yes, eating dead people. Not that I wouldn't if I were in the Andes and my plane crashed…

I make up something I would actually do, so we can look forward to someday doing it. "Piercing your navel." I don't want to do this now, even though I still have a sweet spot in my heart for needles. I want to spank her a little and watch her squirm. I want to put my hand inside her while I give her whacks, spacing them out, making her wait for me to give her more. Tonight, we don't do anything for a while, except kiss. Lila knows how to swirl her tongue. She's taking acting classes. When you role-play with an actress, it makes you wonder whether she's acting the role-playing or really into it. If I think about this too much, I can get that "do not resuscitate" look on my face, but Lila knows how to lure me back. She doesn't attract me apart from sex, which is a relief, because that way I'm not liable to fall in love and make the usual mess of things that causes women to hate me.

Over and out,

Alex

These letters were different from the postings I was used to finding in my mailbox. In the mornings, after preparing a double espresso and playing with my cat, I check my email. Typically the porn goes like this: "Late last night, thinking of you, I made myself come. I came hard. Hit my face. I imagined you tied, very tightly, so you could scarcely move. My come was on your nipples. You looked up at me as I rubbed and pinched my come into your nipples until it was gone. I studied your eyes, your sounds, your odors, and your wetness. I used my fingers, hands, teeth, lips, tongue, nipples, hair, cock, and toys on you. I played with your anticipation. After prolonged teasing, my fingers pushed deeply into you, and my tongue made you come—long and hard. I like to orchestrate and control my lover's arousal. I'd like to fuck and dom you. What are your thoughts on this? I think of you as attractive. You need to know my looks, and perhaps you will. You will be pleased."

Variant letters propose that I do the "orchestrating" and use my body and toys for stimulation. Given my screen handle, "privateparts," my correspondents can't be sure of my sex or erotic preferences, though most assume they are writing to someone who has them. One writer addressed me as "mischiefdujour." Sometimes the scenarios I receive are long and detailed, with several sessions of sex, the inclusion of voyeurs, and the possibility of being discovered.

Women write, men write—at least people identifying themselves as men and women. I hear from tops, bottoms, leather freaks, rubber devotees, whip masters, etc. The letters are intended as lines to inhale or substances to roll up and smoke. Throwaway intoxicants. Something to make me come or to make the writer come. New ones arrive as regularly as pigeons on the sill and *The New York Times* at the door.

The letters from Peg and Alex hardly ever culminated in coming, didn't even get that far into sex.

"Dear Cyberfreaks," Peg signed on again,

I was nursing a bagel at Limbo and feeling majorly pleased with myself for not being hungover. Like my mind could see all the way across the Hudson to New Jersey, to the fucking Palisades Parkway, where I think there are picnic tables my dad once pulled over to. I picked up a copy of NY Press *and saw an ad for a writer's workshop. I don't have the bucks, but it got me thinking I should try and save. I've never been able to do that without tricking, and I can't look at another dick and pretend to be happy to see it. Then I think: Why the hell not? A lot of stuff people have to do is gross. Like cleaning bedpans.*

I'm wondering why I am making a case for myself as a hooker or as someone who cleans up other people's shit, when Goldie comes in. She seems surprised to see me and goes to the bar to get a coffee, giving me a little wave. She takes forever adding milk and sugar, then decides she wants a scone and waits at the bar again. I'm thinking of leaving, so I don't have to see her deciding whether or not to sit with me, but I don't want to go. I want to think about the rest of my life. Goldie places a packet of jam next to the scone. Her coffee is in an aquamarine cup. The saucer is salmon, and the plate with the scone is lilac. Festive. She turns and walks in my direction, still not making eye contact. I look at my bagel. It's cold and hard. After what seems forever, Goldie stands in front of me, places her coffee on the Formica table, and pulls out a chair with her free hand.

"Hi," she says, with a lopsided grin that works on me like a hot knife in butter. She's not even pretty when you look closely. There are little lines around her eyes that are way premature. Maybe from the sawdust she kicks up building people's lofts. She asks what I've been up to. I

want to tell her about my writing, but when I do she looks like she'd rather be waiting at the dentist's. She likes to hear about my turning tricks. She likes to imagine me working over guys, having the upper hand, which I never have.

She tells me she is building a set at a theater on Franklin Street. It's a challenge, because the stage slopes down toward the audience and, because the play is about a dream, the walls have weird angles, too. I ask if she's read it. She says no, then breaks off a piece of her scone, puts jam on it, and offers it to me without saying anything, expecting me to tilt back my chin and open my mouth. I do. She places the morsel on my tongue like a communion wafer. I lick the tips of her fingers, which taste salty and sweet, and now I don't care about saving money or the writing workshop. I can't see to New Jersey, can't see to the next block. I want Goldie to invite me back to her place. If she does, I will go knowing that, when I leave, she won't say when we will meet again. I will tell myself it doesn't matter, even though it does.

Later,

Peg

The same day Alex wrote:

Dear Fellow Pervs,

It warms me knowing you are out there. Otherwise, my heart is cold, and this sometimes worries me, but not today. Today I feel hopeful, though everything that sucked yesterday is the same today. The leaves of the maple tree outside my window are glossy and rustling in a whipping breeze. I haven't seen Lila in a few days, and maybe this explains my optimism. It has become difficult even fucking her. I never thought I would say this, but I'm bored with sex. No matter what we do. No matter that these things if I just fantasized them with an unknown partner I would come in two minutes. She is rehearsing a play. I feel guilty not calling. I repainted my bathroom, which had been looking like a bog since the pipe busted. Every time I feel like jacking off, I sit down at my keyboard.

Fancy that,

Alex

Some members grumbled about Alex's defection from our focus. If anything could be said to be taboo, it was admitting you were bored with sex. I was not among the naysayers. I liked Peg and Alex, not merely as sources for titillation. I still read the other letters, feeling a jump in my groin or a flutter in my chest if an image or fantasy hit the right receptor button, but I did not look forward to these postings as much as to those of Peg and Alex. I felt a bit off my feed about the chat room, too, in the same way that Alex had gone off Lila.

In his next posting, Alex wrote:

Dear Pervs,

I was pacing the streets last night. The air caressed my skin, and I started imagining a woman on her stomach, stretched out on a beach towel, her muscled legs extending from a well-toned butt. I begin to rub lotion on those legs, very slowly, inching toward her thighs, as if a massage was what she needed and had been waiting for, though she didn't know me before I touched her. She feels the pressure of my hands, the warmth and firmness of my palms. I smell coconut oil, and it reminds me of summers as a kid, when my mother would rub suntan lotion on my freckled shoulders.

I cannot see the woman's face, but I can tell from her skin that she's young, barely past girlhood, though there is something knowing in her flesh, the way it receives my pressure. I see the back of her neck, exposed under her short, boyish bob. Little ridges stick out in her backbone. She is naked, and there is no one else around. The sun is going down, and the sky is ribboned with orange and peach. Gulls circle and swoop. I hear the waves breaking, but the sea, for the moment, is glassy. Still, she doesn't turn to see who I am. I begin to tease her, allowing my hands to slip between her thighs and lightly flicker over her silky hairs. My hands take possession of her ass, massaging the cheeks, giving her more pressure, which she takes. Little moans escape her. Her skin is reddish brown. She could be Middle Eastern or from North Africa.

I press my hand into the small of her back, where, just below, two dimples etch the cheeks of her ass. I work my way up her back to her shoulders, making her wait for me to return to her ass, which she lifts slightly in anticipation. When she is relaxed and soft to my touch, I open her legs wider, so I can explore her with my eyes and fingers. She lets out a little gasp and closes her legs. I push them apart a little roughly, and she doesn't resist, rather waits for what I will do next.

By this time, I had arrived at Avenue B and 6th Street. I noticed a club where people were crushed against the bar and hanging around outside. It was late, but the energy was up. The jukebox was blasting "Start Me Up," and it seemed that Mick was telling me I needed a new train. I was thirsty and lonely. Not for anyone in particular. I worked my way to the bar, and the girl serving drinks looked exactly like the one on the beach. Her small face was oval, with wisps of short dark hair feathering her forehead and cheeks. Her nose was narrow but long and swerved slightly to the left, giving her a peculiar authority. Pure symmetry would have made her just another pretty chick. Her dark eyes met mine when I ordered a Coke. "Designated driver?" she asked, dryly. I said, "Yeah, but no passengers."

Later,
Alex

The letter drew me further into Alex's life. I didn't know what he looked like, but I imagined him rangy, about six feet tall and slim, with a shag of light-brown hair over a wide brow. I saw him with long fingers that could play the scales of a keyboard and the corridors of a body with equal dexterity. I could imagine him floating through the city, at once guide and ghost. His beach was real, and I could see from his perspective as well as the girl's. When I went out for walks, I found myself looking for him, as well as for Peg.

Somehow, I was sure it was Peg he had met at the bar, sure he would have more to say about her and that she would comment on him, and I speculated now that the creators of Peg and Alex had meant to bring them together all along. Or maybe not. Perhaps the game was unspooling as they read each other online, unfolding in cyberspace the way romance does in life—a gradual peeling back of layers.

The next day, Peg reported in.

Dear Readers,

What attracts me to Goldie is that she doesn't care if she never sees me again. There is freedom in this for me. I just can't enjoy it. I'm not sure if I should work on appreciating it or get rid of Goldie. The next time she shows up, I will leave the room. She has nothing to talk about except sex. She's leather. She doesn't whisper, "baby," or "honey" when we fuck. I'm supposed to ease into the absence. I'm supposed to hold my breath the longest.

This guy came into the bar last night. He had a sad look on his face, even when he smiled. Made me wonder whether I look that way when I'm not falling on the floor laughing. Maybe I'm a gloom magnet. Turned out he was feeling good, just has a kisser that doesn't show it. He smelled like a bakery. It's weird me liking a guy's smell. Most of them remind me of rusting iron or balloons. Turns out he was carrying bread. He's got these deep-set eyes that look like they're strip-searching you—something between a narc and a pimp. He orders a Coke. I think, good, he's not going to get weird on me.

The whole time he's there I don't think about Goldie, except to realize she's not in my head for five minutes. The guy asks what I do. He doesn't mean will I blow him. I lean over so my nose is five inches from his and then straighten up, because I don't want to come on to him. My body just does that automatically. The bar is zinc, and I can see my reflection, wavy, like in water. My eyes have dark circles under them, and I look like roadkill. I say I write for Bristle, *as if anyone's heard of it. I don't know why, but I say, "I scare myself." He laughs. "Yeah, well, it's either that or heroin."*

Gotta sleep,

Peg

Our bulletin board jumped with the kind of debate you see on subway walls and public toilets.

Chickenfingers: "Alex, fuck someone, anyone, just do it. Then you can write about it."

Headgirl: "The guy can have something on his mind besides sex."

Sizematters: "Hey, this here's a porno site. Haven't you noticed?"

Holehearted: "Don't define sex so narrowly."

Ninewide: "Are you getting hot from this stuff?"

Holehearted: "I can't say I get off, no."

Chickenfingers: "I wanna see him spread-eagle her, backside up, and drill her in every hole till everyone's happy."

Holehearted: "I didn't know happiness was our goal."

Headgirl: "I think they're sexy."

Chickenfingers: "Maybe she won't do it with him."

Holehearted: "Maybe that's not what he wants from her."

Sizematters: "What else could he want?"

Headgirl: "Maybe he wants to know her."

Ninewide: "People don't know each other on a porn site!"

Headgirl: "People don't know each other, period."

Scratchandsniff and everydayfiend didn't respond to the messages. That a romance was budding no one could miss, however. And romance was deviant in our midst.

Alex wrote next.

Readers,

I took her home. I had to go to the bar four times before she'd leave with me. The first three nights she told me her name was Alice. We walked across Canal Street, then down West Broadway to my place. I suggested a cab, but she said, "Christ, I could live on that money for a week." I didn't give it to her, didn't want her to think I was buying her, though the thought crossed my mind. So much easier that way. The first night I was carrying bread, the kind Lila likes. Peg acted like it was catnip, so I got some for her. I'm wondering if it's me or the bread they go for.

We get inside my place, and I ask if she wants anything. She says bread and tea. She sits in the kitchen, and I put water up to boil and slice the bread. The fennel smells like licorice, and it feels as if I'm making tea for my grandmother. She puts her head on her thin arms, and her body looks like it doesn't have bones. Don't get me wrong, sex is in me. A junkie pal used to say that sex is the buzz you hear in the jungle when everything is quiet and asleep. Sometimes I can't tell if I want to punch my fist through a wall, tear pieces of meat off a bone, or stick my tongue in a funky hole. I ask Peg if she wants toast. She says okay in a sleepy voice. The toast smells even more intense. I put out some but-

ter, and honey for her tea, and she opens her eyes and smiles, and I wonder why I want to be kind to her. I'm suspicious of it, like there's a trick that's going to spring out at me. After she eats, she curls up on the couch and falls asleep. I don't touch her.

Later,

Alex

I didn't know if I wanted to watch these two tangled in each other's limbs or if I wanted to see what else could happen. Sex was why they had come together—sex in the sense of the buzz. Thinking about Alex and Peg, I felt a bittersweet tug, wanting them to stay and knowing that in time they would have to leave. Or change. I liked their candor, which did not cost them anything. I saw them as bold in comparison to myself, though I think we reveal ourselves, too, in our methods of concealment.

"Dear Pervs," Peg wrote,

I asked Alex if he'd ever sucked a guy's cock, apart from his own. He said he couldn't reach his cock, though he'd tried a number of positions. He wasn't limber enough, and his torso was too long, or, as he put it, "You could also say my cock is too short." As for other guys' cocks, he said that when he was doing dope, he got all liquidy and that almost anything was possible. He said junkies'll go pretty far to stay high and they'd think an idea was swell that, if they were straight, they wouldn't be able to wrap their brains around. So he guessed at some point he'd sucked a cock, sucked a crack pipe, sucked milk out of a tit. Made me feel better. I could see how living a long time had given him this acceptance, though God knows you can be old as dirt, like my old man, who is not a helluva lot older than Alex—maybe like eight years—and who would kill himself if he ever sucked a cock.

I told him about Goldie, even though it's not like I'm involved with her or anything. He said he had someone, too, a woman named Lila. She wasn't a shit, but he was going to break up with her, because he didn't feel anything, and it was making him feel bad to feel nothing. Feeling nothing sounded good to me. Alex picks me up after work, and we go back to his place. I fall asleep, and he leaves me alone. Like I'm his kid sister, or something, but I know it's not that. Even if I really were his sister, there would still be this vibe there. I sit in his bathtub, because the tub in my place is cold and grotty. I don't mind when he pees while I'm there. Afterward, he puts down the toilet seat and watches me, and we talk. I tell him about the times I tricked, and he explains why he started shooting heroin and how kicking was the hardest thing he'd ever done. He doesn't want me to be impressed. We eat breakfast in the morning, and then I leave. He hasn't touched me, not even a kiss. Exciting.

Gotta run.

Love,

Peg

On the bulletin board, ninewide wrote: "Jeez, I could watch Oprah if I wanted this shit."

Sizematters: "Hey, man, everything we talk about could be on Oprah."

Headgirl: "They'll hate each other if they fuck. She's better off with him as a friend."

Holehearted: "Bring back Lila! She's the kinda girl you could give a butt plug to for Christmas."

Sizematters: "You'd give your mother a butt plug for Christmas."

Holehearted: "I have a big heart."

Chickenfingers: "Bring back Goldie. Let her beat the crap outta Alex, that pussy."

As if prompted, Peg's next installment began:

Hey, Maniacs,

I haven't seen Goldie in I don't know when, like maybe two weeks. I told Alex I had a story in Bristle, *and he went to the website to read it. Like Goldie'd ever do that. Like she can read! My story is about having sex in Central Park with an alien who looks like one of the chicks on* Baywatch, *with tawny skin and green eyes, and she has two little velvet-*

covered horns on her head. Alex touched the back of my neck, ruffling my hair, saying the story made him laugh and that my writing was musical. I felt good, and it scared me.

We go out to the deli. Alex is at the counter, ordering bagels, and I'm at the front, getting apples and chips, when Goldie comes in. She's wearing tight jeans, worn out at the butt, and I feel that jolt go through me. She comes up and stands close enough for me to smell Marlboros on her breath, and I say she looks good, because I'm one of those dolls where you pull its string and out comes a recorded message. But all of a sudden, I don't want anything. It's because Alex is there, though I don't know exactly what this means. I'm not trading one mean fucker for another, because Alex isn't mean. Yet. He sees me talking and he doesn't come over, and I think that's cool.

Goldie is used to seeing me whipped, so she doesn't know what to do with the new information. She catches me glancing at Alex. "You with that guy?" I tell her we're friends, and she laughs so hard she looks pretty. She takes a step back, and then she squeezes my left tit like she needs it to develop the muscles in her hand. I let out a little gasp, but I don't want to give her too much. She says she'll come by the bar tonight, and I shrug. She buys a pack of cigs and a cup of coffee and leaves. I don't say anything to Alex, and he doesn't ask me anything. I say I have to split, and he says okay, but he looks sad.

Later,
Peg

The next letter was from Alex.

Hello from downtown. I'm writing a new piece of music, and I'm forgetting the other parts of my life, except wanting to get off, and I don't know whether it's from the excitement of composing or the anxiety of maybe failing. Before, I'd shoot skag, but now it's only sex. I feel like one of those chimps that got launched in early space shots. He must have known he was in the hands of people who did not, shall we say, have his best interests at heart. He's catapulted up in a rocket and his brain fills with fear, and what can he do but jam his paw into his space pants and hang on to his pud for dear life, fiddling away and doing a little dance.

I'm cheerful today, and I attribute this to Peg. Fellow drooling idiots, don't worry, I have designs on her silky, unblemished flesh. I contrive scenes in which I take her in every imaginable way, scenes of delight for me. I like that she is a child. It's possible she only likes girls. It's possible she doesn't like sex. But she comes to me every night. I gave her a key. Maybe what I like is that she asks for nothing. I don't see need in her eyes, the thing that usually makes me want to smash someone. Maybe we are easy, because I don't like women and she doesn't like men.

Gotta work,

Alex

Then suddenly the letters stopped. Neither scratchandsniff nor everydayfiend posted messages of any sort. Some members of the chat room complained. They wanted a conclusion to the story. Others said good riddance. Each morning after making my coffee and feeding my cat, I would turn on my computer, but now, instead of a quickening pulse, I felt deflated, and I either opened my email with a sense of duty or just deleted it.

I am masked by temperament, not as a strategy, but after a while, to others, it amounts to the same thing. I might be straining your patience now, relating my experiences, yet offering no clues about my life. But what I tell you is the most salient thing I have to share—my responsiveness—which can be conveyed independent of my sex, or what I like to do in bed, or how I make my living, or whom I spend time with. None of these things weighs in, especially with my reactions to Alex and Peg.

I wished for their return, not to see a resolution to their tale but just the opposite. I wanted them never to conclude it. They made me feel a little less numb, a little more alert. They were my companions, even though I only eavesdropped on their lives. Unlike the characters in a book to whom one might become attached but whose fates were typeset by the time you read the first page, Peg and Alex were in a constant state of becoming. Or so it seemed to me.

I had never written to either scratchandsniff or everydayfiend, but now seemed the time. "Dear scratchandsniff and everydayfiend," I wrote,

I am saddened by your absence and wish you would return, for I have greatly enjoyed your revelations. You give flesh and personality to horniness. How many times have I masturbated in the arms of a blank? No name. No face, sometimes. Often, no words. The script is engraved on the brain, the code scribbled on the laughing part of the double helix. I am a droid. (Not really.) Have you grown tired of displaying yourselves? I see Peg at the bar, with her miniskirt and fishnet hose, leaning over to get a glass and flashing her rear, as if it were in a spotlight. The mini's made of leather, and I smell it. Ah! Peg wears red lipstick, though she chews it off and has to reapply it often, in a little round mirror—a gift from Goldie. I see Alex in his loft. He's sitting at his keyboard, when his gaze drifts to the leather-covered bench across the room and beside it the set of barbells. He feels less like a ghoul when his body looks fit. He's been lifting lately and sometimes walks around barechested in front of Peg. She asks him to show her his scars, and she runs her fingers over the insides of his arms. The first time she touches him.

I could go on, but you know them better than I could ever hope to! Please return.

Faithfully yours,

privateparts

When there was no immediate response, I became melancholy, as I do at the exit of a beloved person. I sought consolation in the flesh. The need would sneak up or would dog me all day, until I could find a few minutes to be alone. What is it about the thoughts that are summoned, the pulsing of the body, the going out for those moments of bliss until the shudders subside and you return to the place you left, no better no worse, though feeling peculiarly detached from the desire that only minutes before seemed so urgent, and you wonder when the desire will return?

About a month after the letters stopped and just as my hope was nailed in its coffin, everydayfiend returned. There was no explanation for the break, and I took it for a game of suspense. "Readers, I took her. Peg, that is. Took her in every part," the note began.

Last night around three, I hear the key in the door. I'm not asleep. I know when the traps are being loaded and how to nab the cheese without getting my snout snapped off. It's gotten so all I think about is the soft skin of her inner thighs and the tiny hairs that glisten there. I can taste her pussy, though I have never so much as sniffed it. Her youth, coupled with her brash attitude, make her seem innocent. She trusts me. I want her to split herself open for me. The tape just loops in my brain. I'll risk anything to make the pictures there dance in real life. She's trying to be quiet. She stifles a yawn, and the sight of her in silhouette, with her little shoulders slightly bent from fatigue, fills me with tenderness, and it's confusing, because a part of me wants to fold her in my arms and protect her from harm, and another part wants to consume her, until there's nothing left but her miniskirt and the stockings that make her look like a downtown cliché. She places her backpack and jacket on my workout bench and tiptoes to the bathroom, where I hear her run water into the tub. I'm on the bed. I ask myself why I can't continue as her friend. Why I can't allow her to come to me, if that is ever her choice.

I swing my body off the bed and knock lightly on the bathroom door, as I push it open. She's in the tub, her knees drawn to her chest, with bubbles floating around. I smell gardenias. I'm wearing a shirt and boxer shorts. Ones she bought me, with little red hearts pierced by an arrow. Fresh towels hang on the hooks. She's draped a large purple one over the edge of the tub. I see a dab of toothpaste in the sink and the wet bristles of her brush sticking out of its cup. There is a brick of glycerin soap in the dish beside it and another by the tub. We were walking past a shop with expensive stuff like this, and she looked at it longingly. She doesn't turn around, just waves over her shoulder. I want to hold on to things before they change. I feel like wax.

I have not thought what I would do if she wanted to be with me, wanted me there for her, and I push down the idea, because the possibility that she will refuse me drains my cock. On the other hand, my cock will say anything to get what it wants. I think of Peg when she is away, as I write the score for the play, see her plump lower lip when composing themes. What is sex without an open question?

"Were you awake?" she asks, languidly. She trusts me. To do what? Not to do what?

I kneel on the mat beside the tub, feeling shy, as if she is the one with designs and I'm not sure how to respond. "You look sad," she says, pulling damp fingers through my hair. She runs an index finger along the lines in my forehead, as if to erase them. I take her hand and kiss it. I think my chest will explode when she lifts her chin and laughs, and I see her nipples peek out from the bubbles. The feeling surprises me. It's fear.

"You want me," she says, matter-of-factly.

"I do."

"I don't like men," she says, but not with distaste, rather to remind herself.

"You don't have to think of me as a man."

She laughs again. "What do you want to do?" she asks, as if willing to eat some ice cream, though not every flavor.

"I want to wash you everywhere, dry you, and carry you to the bed. I want to explore every inch of your skin, and hurt you a little if you like. You have to tell me what you want. I want you to feel the same way about my body. I will not do anything unless you ask for it."

"I like the way you smell," she says, enjoying the power of not wanting. I feel she has the upper hand, my little top, and to test her, I pick up a washcloth and soap it for a long time. I make her wait, so her mind can catch up with her breathing. I begin washing her slowly, and she says nothing as I work my way down her back and part her legs and slip my fingers into her slick parts. She says nothing, but she meets my eyes and says, "Take off your clothes." I do, easing myself beside her, and when we kiss I plunge my tongue deeply into her mouth, though I can't tell whether she wants me to or has no choice.

Later,
Alex

I did not believe a word of this and therefore wasn't surprised when, the next day, Alex admitted he'd imagined the seduction and that Peg actually "got out of the tub and went to sleep."

The next letter was from Peg.

Dear Freaks,

I don't see Goldie for weeks, and I think, good, she's gone. My life feels regular, which is weird. I write, go to my job, sleep at Alex's. I'm not having bad dreams. Alex is working on a new score. He's eating and working out. We're good for each other, I guess. How much longer? No guy has ever left me alone. They want something they think is there. I'm like a magic trick they are sure they can figure out, and when they can't they feel cheated.

Maybe that's how I see Alex, like a promise I'm afraid is a lie. Or maybe that's how everyone sees everyone else, until they understand that the promise is what they want and the lie is what has been there all along. I'm in this space, after shit happens and before more shit happens, and I'm trying to remember it for the time when I don't have it anymore.

Then boom, Goldie's back. She walks into the club like she was there the day before. In one minute, I bite. She is the promise and lie wrapped in one. She looks me up and down, taking her time. Other people know how many plants grow in Brooklyn, or what the population of China will be in 2005, or how much money it would take to cure AIDS. Me, I know how to feel all the parts of a second.

"So is that guy fucking you?" Goldie says, leaning toward me, as if she doesn't want people to hear, although she is speaking loud enough for everyone in the bar to be clued in.

I say, "Goldie, how come you can't talk about anything but sex?"

Her eyes uncloud, and she shoots me a goofy grin. She seems like a girlpal now, and I think she isn't as mean as she is simple. She scoops up a handful of bar mix and cascades the pretzels, rice crackers, and peanuts into her mouth. She doesn't chew. She's a fucking machine you fill with fuel. "I've been thinking," she says. I grip the edge of the bar in mock suspense. "Maybe we should do a threesome with whatshisname."

"Alex."

"I could show him how much you like me to eat your pussy, and how I make you so wet before I even touch you that you drip on my hand when I put my fingers inside you, and how I rub my spit and your cunt

juice around your little asshole and make you wait for me to go inside, and how I never know whether you are going to laugh or burst into tears after you come."

This is the longest string of words I have ever heard Goldie unspool. I say, "So what's he supposed to do?" I'm getting hot listening to her, and I'm sort of imagining the scene as she talks, seeing Alex watching, and I wonder how one minute I can be thinking about him as a friend and see myself curled up on his couch, and the next minute I can slink him over the edge of the pot Goldie is stirring up.

She takes a drink from her beer and wipes her mouth with the back of her hand. "He holds his dick and entertains himself. He asks me to whip him and fuck him in the ass with my strap-on. After that I say he can fuck you, while I watch and you suck me off." Her mouth curls in contentment, and if I didn't know she was incapable of irony, this would be it.

Since she mentioned this, I can't get the pictures out of my head. Knowing Alex, he'd probably go for it. If he did, I would feel let down.

Confused,

Peg

The message boards revived like dogs after a nap.

Holehearted: "I want the threesome!"

Chickenfingers: "I want to see Goldie do Alex with the strap-on."

Headgirl: "He'd probably like it."

Sizematters: "They're much hornier now than they used to be."

Ninewide: "They haven't been fucking anybody for weeks."

Headgirl: "How long can they go without it? Anybody want to get up a pool?"

I would have said, "They can go on without it forever."

I have a small confession: I recently suffered the loss of love. In the first part of our romance, we used each other like spoons, to dig ourselves out of our lives. There was no second part. My lover left, uninterested, perhaps, in seeing what would happen next. There is nothing like part one. It makes you feel most alive, though it may be the least real part of life. When you are left, what you need is a suspension bridge, solid enough to absorb the shocks of wind and tremors. A bridge to a time when life will again barge in, demanding names, dates, and serial numbers, demanding you strip off disguises, spread yourself open for inspection, turn your attention outward, to the other's fragility, until you well with so much tenderness it seems an oasis in a desert. Until then there are imagined smells and drumbeats sounding across a wilderness.

What can happen between Alex and Peg? Can he bear their relationship if it doesn't move to sex? Will he still want her after they have sex in every imaginable way? In time he will leave her or she will leave him. Or maybe not. Perhaps one day years off we will see them at a party, a fabulous event with tables of food. He will go to the desserts and pile up a plate of meringues, tarts, cookies, and chocolates. He will move slowly, and young people will watch him return to her with the spoils. He will place the plate before her. He will select a miniature blueberry tart and lift it to her lips. She will tilt her head back and open her mouth, as if on command and as if it still excites her.

Perhaps in time they will disappear from this website. Perhaps in time I will be more occupied with my life than theirs.

But not yet.

Without Leaving Gone

BY MARTIN ROPER

I AM INSIDE HOLFY, bruising myself against her creased arse, thinking about Ursula. Imagining it is her. When I'm with Ursula, she struggles but secretly she enjoys it. That weekend we spent at her father's home, the shy way she bent away from me, her hands gripping the mantelpiece, lifting her skirt, warm pert arse against me, her father's laughter out in the garden (even his laughter sounded English), shuddering at her cheeks brushing the curled hairs on my stomach. Only later realizing the thrill for her was doing it in her father's bathroom; I squirmed at the odd relationship she had with the man. The evening we spent in Searsons'. Ursula noticing me noticing some skirt walk past. The moment is irretrievable. Neither of us pretend it has not happened. I am not the kind of man to be tactless and I bite my tongue for the mistake. A marriage has many endings. We said nothing. The first slip. Cracks in our lives we fall into, cracks become walls around us. I curse and curse and Holfy comes and all the time it is Ursula's back I am looking at in anger, it's her moaning I hear, her cunt surrounding me.

I have been lying for years—telling myself I want this kind of woman or that kind of woman. I want a woman I can fuck forever but have been too afraid to admit it. Ursula is a paragraph out of some feminist pamphlet. Holfy has changed my life. She fucks. She likes my seed leaking out of her. Soft bubbling of her cuntfarts afterward. I was afraid of my wife's silent standard. The standards in her eyes she could never hide. That night in Searsons' I went and got another drink and looked at her in the Smithwick's beer mirror. She was biting the end of a hangnail. I thought then (and this was before we were married), I should walk out now. The coward leaves a thousand times and never leaves.

The Resolution Phase

BY ELLEN MILLER

I FEARED FOR the worst. But it seemed Dick wanted me more than ever, now that I was dead. Back when I still burned the Shavian flame that's always burning itself out, my sex drive was spirited and lively, even—especially—in the throes of moribund relationships. Sayonara sex. Last gasp sex. Don't-let-the-door-hit-you-on-the-way-out sex. In earlier affairs, impending departure was always vivifying. I cleaved this way, hungry, detaching and adhering simultaneously to my beloved's body. With Peter, Willie and Rod, sex was the first thing to start and the last thing to go. That was before, back when I was a breathing, locomoting, warm- and red-blooded female American organism. Being dead, I assumed things would taper off. I mean, how sexy can a girl feel after dying, when the maggots begin to lay eggs, when the pockets of liquid collect inside, when the lips start to drift? And how worked up can a girl get over the little death when she's already had the big one?

Still, Dick couldn't keep his hot hands off me. The fact that I had joined the great majority apparently didn't matter. He'd come home, find me lying supine in bed, and interpret my horizontal pose as an invitation to fuck. "You want me, eh?" he'd say, unzipping his fly. I was flattered, at first, by his continued sexual interest. How romantic! In life, I'd been so fearful that a single misstep, even a missed bikini-line waxing, would turn him off and away. How I'd underestimated his desire! Even death wasn't sufficient to make him stop wanting me. In hushed, heartfelt tones, he kept declaring undying lust and then proceeding accordingly, his passion and loins overcoming our unfortunate obstacle.

It kind of went like this: He'd separate my thighs to try to get in, but then they'd snap shut, bouncing a bit on the sheets before settling into a tight clench. When he'd finally get my legs apart, he'd hold them in a V and rub and thump his body up and down like a pile driver, but it wouldn't be long before he lost his grip and my legs would push inward, squeezing, then crushing, his balls. Undeterred, he'd hoist one of my legs on each of his shoulders like a swashbuckler donning a cape. My feet would turn out into second position, my ankles would slide precariously down the slope of his shoulders, but before my legs crashed to the bed like timber, he'd grab each ankle and hold on tight.

Afterward, he'd give me a chaste kiss. "You look so peaceful. Your lips are so nice and cool and dry. Your skin, too. A little pale maybe. Are you anemic? Doctor Cummings sells a great chelated iron supplement. It'll give you energy, put color in your cheeks. And you know, your hair looks good when you don't wash it. It's growing so fast. Don't cut it. But maybe we should trim your toenails. They're getting a little long."

This technique worked until my body lost its stiffness. Everywhere my muscles slackened, lost their tone. Unable to grab and resist, my vaginal walls provided insufficient friction, then none. Dick couldn't come. "I see you've stopped doing your Kegels," he harrumphed. "This is pointless. How about a tit-fuck?" I didn't respond. "Cool."

But eventually, my lack of enthusiasm started to turn him off.

"What's up? You won't touch me. You won't talk to me. You just lie there, not moving, not saying anything."

I had no response.

"I see you have nothing to say to that either. Don't you know that your passive-aggressive silence is sabotaging any chance we have of reviving this?"

Again, no comment.

To him, it was all a symptom of a larger, underlying problem. He'd been in analysis for six years. He knew about these things. Analysis had given him back his life and it could give me back mine, if I wasn't so passive, so lifeless, so stubbornly still. Dick was an American optimist. Although death is the universal complaint of the species, Dick believed that all problems could be "worked through." Every complaint had a corresponding therapeutic intervention. When the overt symptoms were properly controlled the core issues could be exhumed. My inertia, my lack of "proactive, help-seeking motivation," my empty stare into space with open but unseeing eyes, my "depressive, delusional" conviction that my existence could not be resurrected from its present state of decay—all these, Dick said, were things that skilled professionals could heal.

Finally he demanded, "Come with me to see Dr. Buttram or I move out and leave you here to rot by yourself." Couples counseling was a shared investment, he said, so I'd have to pay half of Dr. Buttram's fee. I don't know how Dick expected me to generate the money. He knew I wasn't working, but I didn't protest. Pleased, his posture softened, and he cuddled up next to me in bed. "Sweetheart, please, don't freeze up on me." He breathed hotly into my ear, then moved his foot toward mine. Before recent events—that is, before I paid the debt that cancels all others—I had liked for our feet to touch. He had delicate, sensitive feet, with smooth soles and toes aligned in perfect size order. Now, just before his toes curled around mine, he gasped. "You've got some wicked cold feet." I didn't move. He pulled the quilt over both of us. "Let's get your tootsies roasty-toasty. You've got to relax." He rubbed my neck, my shoulders. "You should go see Hyman, my massage therapist." His fingers moved down the bones that were becoming prominent in my neck, chest, arms. "You'll feel so alive afterward. You've lost touch with your body. You act so stiff." He rolled on top of me so that the warm tip of his nose touched the cold tip of mine. "I'm stiff, too." He chuckled. "In all the right places.

I haven't lost touch with your body. Or mine." I remained silent. "Don't worry, baby, I'm a well-oiled machine. I'll do all the work. It'll relax you. Warm you up. Thaw you out. If you want me to stop, just say so.... I'll take that as a yes."

Before our visit with Dr. Buttram, Dick discovered a new sexual domain—a horny, deviant purgatory ruled by demonic experimentation. I couldn't ask what accounted for the shift. Instead of wooing me with reassurances that nothing could part us sexually—that he wanted me despite my immobility—he seemed to want me because of it. I wasn't moving, but he didn't seem to notice that I was dead. Of course, at the outset I figured he had to have noticed, but was enjoying his chance to mine the romantic potential of my paralysis. But then I became less and less sure, as Dick used the occasion to tap his deepest, strangest proclivities. *The Sex for Dummies'* make-the-best-of-what-you've-got message inspired him. "Let's view this not as a problem, but as a challenge. An opportunity," he said, hard-on in hand, "for enormous growth. Enormous. Heh-heh. Call it an adventure.

"All along it's been so obvious that I couldn't even see it. In your silence, you've been crying out loud for something new. Lady that you are, you'd never ask directly, or complain or demand anything. I understand now. Please, princess, chained in your lonely tower by the moat, if it excites you to feign indifference, to be cold and still and silent, to pretend that you don't want me to ravish and ravage you, that you don't love it when I take you against your will—go for it! Two can play. I'm comfortable in my masculinity. Really. I am. I'm confident enough not to need my desirability validated all the time. You want a good game of cat-and-mouse? Of hard-to-get? We're both adults. We can be creative."

I said nothing.

"You want cold?" He jangled a pair of steel handcuffs. "You want still?" He tossed four black bungee cords onto the bed. "You want silent?" He moved toward me, like a Looney Tunes kidnapper, with his gag-rag and duct tape. With a knee against each of my ears, Dick cranked apart my jaw with his penis until we fit like a ball-and-socket joint. "That's it. Close it up tight. To the hilt. No bitching. No moaning. No choking or gagging reflexes allowed. Even if it kills you."

As if.

Doctor Buttram nattered about the age-old sex-drive differential in the opposite sexes, recommended *Mars and Venus in the Bedroom,* pontificated—with emphasis provided by a wagging, erect index finger—on the universal female laments of never being heard, of being seen only as a sexual object, of compulsory participation in deadening, male-identified heterosexual patterns.

"Things are coming to a head," Dick fumed. "I'm about to blow my stack. I had to literally drag her out of bed this morning. She was lying there like always. Like a dead weight."

"Resistance to treatment, in the beginning, is to be expected, to be honored but not indulged. Tell me"—he turned to me—"Do you find talking about sex difficult?"

I slumped in my chair.

"Is it hard for you to talk to Dick about sexual feelings?"

Dick spat. "She doesn't have sexual feelings."

Doctor Buttram's expression turned grave. "How does it make you feel to hear Dick speak that way?" He steepled his thumbs and index fingers, and looked above their apex at my face. "How do you feel right now, talking to me, a stranger, albeit one trusted by your beloved, about sex?"

I made no reply.

He suggested hearing from Dick while I took the time I needed "to warm up to the process." I didn't object to the idea. Doctor Buttram flipped to a new page of his legal pad, switched pens. "Dick, why don't you tell me what your perceptions are of what happens when you initiate sex."

"I've told you a million times. She's like a corpse."

"You might have told me in individual sessions, but your life-partner needs to hear you give voice to your concerns out loud, in her presence. At precisely what phase of the arousal process—the desire, excitement, orgasm, or resolution phase—do you see your sexual exchanges breaking down?"

Dick laughed. "Let's go for the short list and say where it doesn't break down. She never starts me up. When I initiate, she's reluctant and stiff, like she can't be bothered. She doesn't seem to miss it. I can't sleep I'm so horny. She sleeps all night. All day, too. Doesn't even notice I'm shaking the bed with my pud-pulling. I've never seen someone sleep so much.

"The silence is killing me. It's got to be killing her, too," Dick blubbered unattractively. "All this passive-aggressive shit. Covert strategies."

"Dick, why don't you try to avoid abstraction and intellectualization. Let me be the doctor. That's my job. Yours is to describe what you feel."

They carried on, absorbing themselves in each other's polysyllabic lingo. Who would use the biggest, longest words? Eventually Dr. Buttram broke off. "We have to stop. We're not going to resolve this overnight. There's a great deal to talk about, and it's all quite rich. Before we jump to any conclusions, we need to eliminate all possible physiological etiologies of hypoactive desire. I want to send you to some specialists. Run some tests. You'll need a pelvic, to check for atrophic vaginitis. I can refer you to someone for that, too." He smiled a knowing smile, as if he'd had a pelvic. "Or do you have your own gynecologist?"

I didn't reply.

Doctor Buttram nodded gently, his sympathy as plastic as a speculum. "I understand. Internal exams aren't fun, I know, but it's crucial. In case we're dealing with dyspareunia or other sexual pain disorders. We might even be seeing a vaginal numbing syndrome."

"I hope she can rouse herself to take a shower before anyone looks too close," Dick said.

"I sense that you're feeling some hostility, Dick. You'll have to try to contain that until our next session."

"You know, Doctor, I don't feel like a man anymore. I used to feel good about my sexuality. I was virile. I could make a dead woman come."

"Our time is up. We'll start next time by exploring those feelings. Here's your bill for this month."

Then he asked if I wanted to offer any last words before departing. But it was too late. I had done all that already.

"A diminished sex drive can be a problem unto itself: hypoactive sexual desire disorder: HSDD," droned Dr. Buttram. Dick smiled. He loved the bureaucratic officialdom of initials, abbreviations, acronyms. He loved the booming voices of experts, like narrators of nature documentaries, like Dr. Buttram, who continued, "Hypersomnia points to a clinical picture including, but not limited to, a major depressive disorder. Besides the presenting loss of libido and excessive sleep, social withdrawal, loss of interest in conversation or previously pleasurable activities, food apathy, hunched body posture, and absent zest for life all suggest major depression. I'm not ruling out HSDD, but what I see right before my eyes is a patient who presents six out of seven diagnostic criteria for major depression."

"Does that mean we aren't going to talk about sex?"

"Worry not, Dick. Sex is a central component of the human experience, carrying the symbolic cargo of the gestalt of the human dilemma." Dick loved jargon. Dick loved German. "Another question worth exploring is whether the desire reduction is global, encompassing all sexual expressions, or limited to one particular activity. Some HSDD patients I treat have no desire for intercourse, but enjoy masturbation, mutual or solo, enhanced by pornography or marital aids, or driven simply by our wonderful, prehensile hands, our fingers like ten little lovers who know exactly what we enjoy."

"I doubt that she masturbates, but she won't say. Don't bother asking her."

"Masturbation is difficult for any of us to talk about, even when we're feeling our best. Before we push such matters, Dick, we also have to consider this." Doctor Buttram's voice dropped, turned avuncular, unctuous, soft: an I'm-going-to-level-with-you-man-to-man voice. "Sometimes one partner's low desire actually reflects an excessive need for sexual activity—a compulsion! an addiction!—in the other partner. Usually, the clinical picture isn't that extreme. Or simple. More often, both partners have levels of desire within the normal range, but at different ends of a healthy continuum. In that case, we need to work on compromise. And communication."

Holdin Heat

BY TOURÉ

HOLDIN HEAT V. 1. To be armed with a gun. Watch yoself, man. That nigga's holdin heat. 2. To date a very desirable woman. The reason why he lost that fox is cuz he don't know bout holdin heat.

It's Saturday. Good writing, sun shining, Miles playing, and I'm just chilling. Not even answering the phone cuz I'm deep in my own groove and ain't nobody gonna knock me out. But then the phone just purrrs so sweetly. What could be the harm? Could be my heart... After seven months of deep talking and slow dancing and deep kissing and slow loving, we in love, sweeter and warmer than I could've imagined. Any time, every time, I pick up the phone I hope it's her. I say hello.

"Hello, Touré?" an unfamiliar man's voice comes back. "This is C., you know, D.'s boyfriend." My heart nosedives to my toes, then comes bounding back up. Knew this shit would happen. Knew, after the first date, she had a man. Knew the pertinents of her situation (four years, live together, on the rocks). But, circa that first date, I didn't care.

Back then my niggas and I spurred each other on to chase girls with boyfriends, fiancés, husbands, whatever. Seducifying an occupied woman, we postulated, was the ultimate proof of your power, proof that you were in the big leagues, proof that, unlike her man, you knew how to hold heat. When I met her I saw a black Audrey Hepburn, a world-class dancer, a honey-sweet thang. Stealing her from another man was a little tasty icing.

She went on tour. I mailed letters off to Paris and Stuttgart and Cairo and got letters back from Cannes and Berlin and Tel Aviv. At the beginning she wrote...how you would look walking out of the water, all wet, wearing something loose that would cling to your... Months later...You are a part of my life and I have to take care of you. She got me open. She got me to feeling as though the doors of my chest were literally unbolted and her white, hot love, thick like gooey molasses, was being poured directly in. I was feeling her. I began to wait for her to choose between him and me. And on my plate he was that tasty icing quickly decomposing into something rancid and crusty as, again and again, I woke up alone, knowing my sweet was not alone, was in another's arms, in his arms, one of which is now holdin the phone.

"I have to jet in a minute," he says sounding shaky, almost geeky, "but I just wanted to introduce myself."

My heart bungee-jumps up and down my frame. In the commotion I catch bits of our conversation. He sounds nervous, I think. He gropes for words, stumbles a bit, finds a few, lumbers on. He shrinks. I had expected tough, confrontational, a puffed-out chest. I had prepared an if-ever script, sprinkled with What you want man?s and Why don't you ask yo woman, if she is yo woman?s. But here is no roaring Harley-Davidson, no itching Smith & Wesson. He is a cracked plate, some tamped snow, a light, melancholy rain. In his humanness I lose my script.

"Cool," I say.

"I just felt that...uh...you had been...in the shadows too long... you know. Uh, so, um...Now the door's open."

I say, "Alright." I think, This is so fucking absurd! What can we say to each other? Nothing you could say would hurt me and there are a million truths I could tell you that would shatter your cuckolded heart. But those million truths would end up right back in her face and in mine. So, we're just going to talk without saying anything. "Is there anything you want to ask me?" he says, a bit of a cringe in his voice.

What do I say? Yeah, why don't you step aside and let D. and me get to our life together? No good. Why the fuck are you bothering me, yo? I can't, he's too nice. Okay, Touré, something simple and negative. How about, Naw, nigga? It's natural, simple, and far too complicated. *Nigga* would hint at brotherhood, shared space, the potential of respect. But also, since we ain't friends, he might take *nigga* for *nigger*. Then, war.

"Nope."

"Well...um...the door's open so...uh...uh...if you want to call me or I want to call you."

"I'm here."

We say goodbye. I begin to laugh. Don't quite know why. Some at him, some at me, some at our static chess game—two twenty-something black men talking to each other like white boys. I laugh uncontrollably, still not certain why, soon not certain who it is laughing. My stomach starts aching and I crawl into myself. Maybe he's not the thorn in our rose. Maybe I'm the thorn in theirs. He's gotten me open and, through the laughter, coming louder and harder now, I wonder if it's time to look at my sweetheart, my heat, my dream girl, his woman, and, maybe, somehow, maybe, let go.

Scene

BY COURTNEY ELDRIDGE

DO YOU WANT to talk about "play"? he says, and she says, Yes. Then let's begin with the House. I wouldn't know where to begin, she says. For starters, relax. Then, tell me the first thing that comes to mind. When she says nothing, he says, Anything at all. And when she still says nothing, he says, If you don't want to—No, I do want to. So tell me the first thing that comes to mind when you think of the House? She hesitates again, then says, The phones. The phones? Ten in the morning, any given morning, and I hear them ringing before I step foot through the front door. What else about the phones? There's no call-waiting on the flake line. Good, continue. Please don't praise me; it's embarrassing. But he ignores her and says, There's no call-waiting on the flake line. What else? They're big talkers, flakes, at least those who talk. What about those who don't talk? They hang up. Hundreds hang up. Probably leaves them feeling giddy all day, just thinking about hanging up. Then he interrupts her, What is a flake, anyway? and she says, Slang for a first-time caller or an unreliable client. In order to conserve time and energy, you learn the distinction between a hopeless flake and someone who's going to pan out. How do you tell the difference? Experience.

And practice, she sighs, you've got to practice; memorize and personalize the script. But you couldn't handle a flake, much less juggle three or four calls and handle the books, all at once, if you weren't working—you aren't even allowed near the phones until you have a good twenty or thirty hours of sessions under your belt, depending. Some have a better phone manner, which certainly helps if you're thinking long-term. Why not hire someone to answer the phones for you? Sure, she laughs, what do you suggest? Take out an ad for a receptionist? I'm sure someone could—No. We don't bring outsiders into the House, ever. Not only for the obvious security reasons, but because you have to know the other women and their play styles, first-hand, in order to book them, and because you couldn't possibly field the range of questions asked or answer with any authority unless you've been there and know the language. It's a matter of fluency. Then how do you begin on the phones? First, you study the book, log your hours in session, and listen for a month or two, before you get to take your first call. It requires a lot of coaching. I can imagine. How? she asks, and he says, I meant the necessity of coaching. I doubt you can imagine. Some of the absolute worst days I've spent at the House were answering phones. It's incredibly draining. Then tell me about the script. Pretty standard: "We cater to a wide variety of fantasy, fetish, role play, all aspects of BD and SM, with seven fully equipped play rooms at our disposal; we're located in an elegant, private residence, with professional dominants, submissives and switches on staff—and, of course, there is no direct sexual contact involved in any of our sessions." And you actually repeat this script for every flake? Each and every, fifty times a day, she sighs. Then how do you recognize a potential client as distinct from any other flake? Telltale signs: articulation, action verbs, correct usage, knowledge of slang, lingo, euphemistic terms, personal referrals—He interrupts her again, What euphemistic terms? I've told you before—Tell me again, and she says, A.P., for example. A.P.? She sighs, and he says, Humor me, and she says, Anal play—but we joke about that particular term all the time. What would you think if I said that I had "pussy play" with some guy, she says, laughing. But I thought you said there was no sex in any of your sessions? I did; I was speaking of euphemisms.

But any flake who requests anal play in the course of conversation doesn't know protocol; sounds flaky. How many callers solicit anal sex? No—excuse me, how many request "anal play"? I'd say a third to a half of flake calls, more on a bad day. I mean, can you imagine having to answer twenty, thirty calls per day from strangers asking if you'd fuck them up the ass, however euphemistically? I thought you said the term was "anal play"? I said the euphemism is "anal play," but I certainly didn't say that all flakes know the correct terms. Yes, well. Other euphemisms? Douche is classic. They want to watch you douche? and she says, No, douche, as in: "Mistress, I douched for you this morning." She drawls, "Oh, you douched? For me?" That's so faggy, though of course we welcome all sexual persuasions. Couples and doubles, especially. What's the difference between a couple and a double? A couple is you and your acquaintance, male or female; a double: two professionals and you, alone. Or various combinations of sexes and sexual persuasions. Triples and group walk-ons are a total blast too—a much-needed break from the monotony. Of course, he says, and she continues, Seriously, I wish more women would call, we cream ourselves whenever a woman calls, practically fight for the scene. Were those all of the telltale signs of flakes? Not by a long shot. Those are a few basic indicators, but there are always those who have done their research—even though you can only fake so much—and then there are notorious flakes, the ones who call once or twice a week, every week, for a month or two, then drop out for five or six months. Notorious flakes book appointments, but never show. But if you know they're flakes, why do you book their appointments? That's the problem with flakes, unpredictability. Some flakes book and confirm their appointment—Wait, what do you mean by confirm? Flakes must book and then confirm their appointment twice before we give them directions. We refer to the second round as "finals," as in, "Hey, your flake is on finals!" Why two rounds? To ensure discretion. We expect the vast majority of prospective clients will lose their nerve at the last minute. Also, anyone who calls and seems mostly concerned with obtaining our physical address sounds extremely flaky. And, often enough, flakes make finals but still don't show. So it's like being stood up by a blind date? Pretty much, but with twice the relief, or disappointment. Why would you ever feel disappointed? Oh, maybe their session sounded interesting, or challenging, or both. But just the same, even if you have an extremely enjoyable conversation with a flake, you really seem to hit it off, you can't get your hopes up—that's something you only learn from experience as well, even though you're warned. Because most times, flakes get off on calling, the discussion is a rush in itself. That's why we call them phone fucks. I'm still not clear on this. Often enough, we use the term literally, when you hear them jacking off. With heavy breathers, you can just hang up. But figuratively, loosely speaking, phone fucks are flakes with no intention of showing, who really get off on talking about their fantasy and hearing themselves being heard, and so some will call and call, hoping a different woman answers. That's why flakes are unique to Houses, greater chance of speaking to a different woman. Go on. Another example? Please. Okay, take anyone who calls and asks if it is possible for two women to kick his ass, to really, really kick his ass. If he mentions a baseball bat, or if he mentions the duo repeatedly kicking him in the balls, if he mentions cleats or hiking boots, if he repeats any particular detail five or six times, for example: "Their fierce spikes trampling my groin..." apparently hoping you might clarify and embellish the scenario with your own adjectives, then chances are he's a phone fucker. They actually request trampling? Trampling is not uncommon. What do you do in those cases? Put him on hold, take a deep breath, return, and reply, "Yes, I'm sure we can arrange that type of session. What time were you thinking?" So how do you know when to humor them, and when to hang up? That's the trick. Sometimes it's really hard to control your first impulse, like this guy who calls about once a week, and there's always a baby crying in the background, and I finally said, "Excuse me, is that a baby?" and then he came right out and told me all about his divorce and the custody battle. He still calls us on his days off work, when he's watching his son. The point is, never ask. Is the tipoff usually that obvious? Yes, and no. There are lots of clues—phrases, accents, a recurring noise. This one guy always sounds like he's calling from a kennel, with this horrible yipping in the background. Would you like to hear more? Please. There was this one flake, the "brother-in-law." This guy calls and says, "My brother-in-law gave me your number, and my brother-in-law says you're the best he's ever seen," and I say, "Thank you." Setting aside all concern for any sister/wife related to this guy, I say, "Can you tell me what you're looking for?" and he stammers, as they often do, claiming, "I never talk about this with anyone." Whatever—I don't argue with him or ask about his brother-in-law. I just give him a moment, tell him to take his time, as I always do, and finally, the man says, "What I'm looking for exactly is a drop-dead gorgeous woman who gives good head in the morning, and takes it doggy-style," and I say, "Well, aren't we all?" You didn't actually say that, did you? No, of course not—that's my point. Are you ever surprised by a request? Ummm, nothing comes to mind. Nothing? Once in a while, but not too much anymore. I'd like to be surprised, but when I am, it's usually for the worse. Specifically? Well, generally, you hear the stranger requests while fielding calls for submissives. Like this Ob/Gyn who kept calling, and who wanted to do things he couldn't do to his patients—something involving ovaries. Are you kidding? Why would I kid about such a thing? There was this one other caller who wanted to gag a submissive with a soiled pair of his little girl's underwear. How did you handle that? I avoided further discussion by explaining the reasons why we don't allow our subs to be gagged, then I hung up. As it turned out, they dealt with him elsewhere, eighty-sixed him, and called to let us know, as a professional courtesy. Eighty-sixed? He's never allowed to return. Occasionally, clients who've been eighty-sixed try to sneak back into the House by calling on the flake line, and changing their name, or their date of birth, or they lower their voices a register, she laughs, Some will cop a fake accent—another reason why we don't put new girls on the phones right away: they haven't heard all the stories, yet. Also, any prospective top who tells you that he's been doing this for twenty-five years or more, I never believe them, especially flake sadists, not until proven guilty. Regardless, I certainly wouldn't book them with an inexperienced sub, I'd probably book them with a switch, tell her that he's looking for a straight submissive, and not to blow their cover. Why the deception, if they're paying to see a submissive? If they've never been to the House, we don't know anything about them, and we have to look out for each other. Book them with a green sub, and you're asking for trouble. Honestly, most new tops will pick up a whip, without any training, not even five minutes of training—they'll pick up the most vicious whip available, all impressed by the eye candy, but they don't think about the fact that you have two kidneys, a spine, muscles. When you correct them, however many times they wrap—Slow down, wrap? Technical term for when the ends of the whip literally wrap around your waist, hips—really jarring, and you can bruise someone pretty easily that way. Of course if it's intentional, that's another story... So what happens when you inform them of their poor technique? Well, usually when you finally tell them that they'll have to learn to use the implement if they want to see you again, however gently you might suggest that they take lessons from a dom, or switch with you, chances are you won't ever see them again. Not that you'd want to, either, but the point is that most don't care to be corrected—they'd rather risk injuring you than learn proper technique. And once warned, they usually either deny any wrongdoing, or they'll suddenly feel guilty about endangering your body and get all sheepish, or some bullshit. Or, there are those who will say, "You aren't a true submissive..." You hear that enough times from some flake, walking in off the street. That's when most subs start to burn out, or they switch, or they go strictly dom—usually the latter, if they're going to work long-term. Switches burn out almost as quickly as subs; you're up, you're down, day after day. Not to say that you don't get some phenomenal players, there are definitely those who've been doing this longer than I've been alive. Total pros. You still work as a submissive, then? No, but even if I did, I would never admit the fact to any submissive client. Tell them as much, and they're likely to think, You aren't a true dom... Then he pauses, and says, I don't think I could handle the masturbatory element of the job. She laughs, Masturbatory element? You know what I mean. Yes, but we prefer "self-release." Isn't that much nicer? And he laughs, and she says, I knew you'd appreciate that one. But as far as the masturbatory element, you're probably right about your limitations. Isn't that standard, though? Not in my scenes. The first year or so, you don't think of it as much, you aren't as confident in your ability to pull off a scene without allowing them to jack off. But you find out who the real players are. That's one more reason why it's important to screen properly on the phone, find out their actual intentions. If their focus is sex, they'd do better looking elsewhere, because their getting off is definitely not our priority. That doesn't strike me as completely honest—it's sex work. Yes, it's highly sexual, sexually charged and motivated, but that's the line. And that's why they won't hire other sex workers, strippers, prostitutes, different boundaries. He says, A fine line, just the same. Only if you've never played before. Haven't you ever called? No, you know I haven't. Why not—you're so curious—have you thought about calling? Not exactly, but I am curious, yes. Well, whatever your reasons, get your information right. Because it really pisses me off when I hear rumors, when people lie. Lie? Lie, joke, exaggerate, or claim that we solicit these conversations. We offer nothing, we never get up and offer to beat someone, that's bullshit. The same goes for the "whips and chains" line of inquiry, which is so lame I find myself laughing. Don't you realize it just covers up what really goes on? Then why do the jokes bother you so much? If you had to check the answering machine every morning and deal with the freaks and belligerent drunks who call. I mean, if you heard some of the messages we receive, you'd understand. How do you expect me to understand, if you won't tell me? Like, "You filthy whore, I know where you are, and I'm gonna fuck you with a hunting knife, and you're gonna thank me when it's over"—stuff like that. He laughs and she says, Does that sound funny to you? I'm sorry. Was that you who called? Of course not. Then don't apologize. Then he pauses, and says, Personally, I don't like pain. Now who's starting? Talk about misinformation, masochism is not a prerequisite—over half my scenes involve no physical pain whatsoever. A dom once told me a story about this submissive, after my practice session. The story goes that she took a heavy pain scene as her first professional session, and she never used her safe word; she thought the whole point was to see how much physical pain she could humanly endure, and she was left pretty beat up. Exactly why were you told this story? As a comparison—he was comparing me to her.

But the point is, I was completely ignorant when I began. You've never actually told me how you began. You never asked. I'm Old School, and before he interrupts, she says, Old School means you train to dom by working as a sub first. Paying your dues. The vast majority of women drop out within six weeks of starting. That's how you start at a House? Yep, you interview, and if they think you're for real, and you can handle it, then you sub to a man in a practice session, which is similar to an actual session in that you're naked with some man you don't know, likely never laid eyes on before. They find out how you'd handle the real thing; your limitations, responsiveness, and not just the physical side; they might try any number of mind games, mindfuck you, just to see if you'll break, what might set you off. If I could do it all over again, I'd train with a well-established independent, even though there are definite advantages to working at a House. It's like a sorority, an incredibly depraved sorority, the things we do together. Are we through with the phones, then? No, what I was going to say is that even independents—I assume you know what an independent is? Yes, thank you. Even independents answer their own phones, at least during their phone hours. Why? Smart business—you'd be surprised how much information you can learn simply by listening to their questions: how they ask, what they ask, tone of voice, how nervous they are. Your own questions, for example, are self-evident. How so? What do you think I've told you about myself? You're passive-aggressive, so you'd likely try to top from below, and chances are you wouldn't be particularly responsive in your first scene, probably intellectualize the experience, assume you understand based on what you've read—Then he interrupts her, I don't think there's any need to—And then she interrupts him, I am speaking, and he says, Excuse me, you were saying? And she pauses a moment and says, To finish answering your question, my guess is that you'd probably be somewhat vague in negotiation, sidestep and say something like, "I will leave myself in your most capable hands," or "Do whatever you most enjoy," and he laughs, and she says, That always drives me up the fucking wall. Why? What's wrong with that? Isn't that a sign of their desire to please? No. It's a sure sign of their desire to be pleased. And a submissive would never say such a thing;

the very redundancy of the declaration casts plenty of doubt, besides which, I hardly need some novice telling me how to do my job, thank you very much. Then he laughs, and she says, If you said such a thing, I'd recommend you give the matter far more thought, beforehand, and decide if it's something you're genuinely interested in, beyond the novelty. Because the fact is that I'm paid to be perceptive, not clairvoyant. Just the same, I would guess you were into bondage, sensory dep, and a few other things, but again, I think it's your responsibility to figure that much out, yourself. Sensory dep? We prefer sensory deprivation, as opposed to "Do you enjoy blindfolds, sir?" Or, "Do you enjoy ball gags?" That tends to scare off the timid, you understand. I'm familiar with the term, I just hadn't heard the abbreviation. How would you? You cannot assume based on a handful of conversations—On the contrary. By the way you've handled yourself in this conversation—you dip one toe at a time, then back off, it's your entire mode of inquiry. Fine. Let's pretend that I do call. Why pretend? Are you calling, or not? I'm willing to try. All right—but you aren't the kind of flake who's going to hang up on me, are you? No, I'm a potential-client flake. Then let's have it, already. Give me some hints how to begin. There! From the start, I know you're not a potential-client flake, besides which we never give hints. That's not our job, at least not at this initial stage. Why don't you tell me where you found our number? I saw your advertisement. I would note that, as well. Pardon? Advertisement, short-i, emphasis on second syllable, as opposed to advertisement, long-i. You're well educated—not that that makes you special or provides any assurances. Where did you see our ad? Your voice changed. I know, I'm in role. Soothe, lull, arouse, provoke; you know. Where did you see our ad? In a magazine. Which publication? I forget; and she says, I would never coerce an answer to a question, but, seeing as you sound promising, perhaps *Black and Blue,* or maybe *Bitches With Whips?* and he says, Yes, I saw it in *B.W.W.* Strike two: You've reassured me that you are not in the know, because we have no qualms saying *Bitches With Whips.* It flows. Just the same, what do you enjoy in session? What's the difference between a session and a scene? Intensity. In my case, you assume it would be a session? You want an educated guess? Never mind. You've really never done this before, have you? No. That's fine, we welcome novices, provided they're open-minded about the experience. Are you open-minded? I should think so. Naturally. Where would I have seen an advertisement, someone like me? Well, how serious are you? Very. Do you have any personal experience? None. You would have seen us on the Net. Why the Net rather than a trade publication? Partly due to changing demographics—when I started, less than three years ago, you would have used *D.D.I., Dominant Directory International.* It's *D.D.I.,* but not *B.W.W.?* Correct. *D.D.I.* costs twenty bucks, so it used to be anyone who'd shell out twenty bucks seemed far more serious than those who only coughed up a buck-fifty for a weekly sex-trade rag. Regardless, you still have to speak to them on the phone, beforehand, and feel them out. Never underestimate the power of a woman's voice. Good phone skills make all the difference between a flake who shows, and one who calls elsewhere. One last question? One. What is good phone manner, in your opinion? You involve them in the conversation, encourage them to open up and speak freely; you provide information, and pique their interest without offering too many specifics, whether that means you sound domineering, or disinterested, or naive, or confiding, or any combination, depending on personal style. Really, whatever makes the caller feel most comfortable and trusting, granted that they interest you. Manipulation, basically. You were saying? Yes, I saw your website, and I was interested. You're interested in general information, or in booking an appointment? Both. Wonderful. But before we continue, you wouldn't call on a cellular phone, would you? No, I have a cordless. You'd have to call from a hard line. Why? House policy, we only accept calls placed from hard lines; cellular calls are routinely monitored by scanners, and that's not very discreet, is it? So first, why don't you tell me what interested you about our site? Why don't you tell me what interests you? Now you sound like a genuine-article phone fuck—remember, I didn't call you and we aren't here to discuss my fantasies. I'm only interested in finding out if you actually want to understand, if you're genuinely willing, as you say you are. If you aren't up for it, that's fine, but don't tell me you want to understand, and don't think for a second that you understand anything about my line of work. Do you want to play or just talk about it, because I still think that you want something for nothing. That is certainly not my objective, and don't overestimate your powers of intuition; I already told you that I was willing. Yes, you told me you were willing, but you still haven't told me what interests you. I don't know, I've never played before. I'm not so sure of that. So let's try again. What intrigues you? B&D, D/S. So you have done some homework, after all. Nevertheless, are you asking me, or telling me? I'm telling you. You're telling me what, exactly? You're telling me that you might enjoy B&D, that sort of thing? Yes. Fine, but could you possibly be any more vague? I doubt it. If you don't want to play—No, I do. Then I need you to answer as specifically as possible. Let's just start with the first thing that comes to mind…

Fifty-five Fucks

BY SAM LIPSYTE

ONE IS HER, Heidi, maybe, or Helene, Heidi with the hair, the face, the nips that ended in little pink knots. Two is Betsy in the shrubs at pottery camp. Three is Lucretia, three is always Lucretia. Four is Kenneth by the lake. Five is Kenneth and his brother Keith by the lake, their cocks like great, quivering cocks by the lake. Six is Moira with the tragic scar from tennis. Seven is me coming in Heidi, or Helene, in the front seat of my Dodge Dart, and me, or maybe not me, thinking nips, or thinking nips, knots, nips. Seven is me or rather not me coming in Heidi, or Helene, but also me throwing my hand over the vinyl seat to clutch the hand of Donna who is topping Brian, who is maybe bodkinned there by Brian, who is coming in Donna in the backseat of my Dodge Dart. Eight is me and Donna, later, near the trestles next to Main. Nine is Ann Anteater, but only my finger, like a great, quivering finger by the lake. Ten is Heidi, or Helene, again. Eleven is very much the same. Twelve is the swine-herdess, dressed as a nurse. She was the love of one of my lives. She lays down, or maybe she lies down, with men of other lives now. They suckle, I suppose, that mole on her hip, and I hope they taste me. Thirteen is there is no taste of me. Fourteen is with the girl with the poster of Fanon. Fifteen is somebody and Fanon. Sixteen is what is the strangest place you've ever had sex with? Seventeen is reamed by the Space Needle, or sticking it deep in the loop of Orion's Belt. Eighteen is buggered by chance. Nineteen is the girl who said no. Is it twenty yet? Yes, it is twenty, yet. Twenty is begging those two women leaving the party to let me in their car. Twenty-one is me on my knees, begging them to bugger me in their bed. Twenty-two is me thinking twenty-three. Twenty-three is me waking to me bathed in their blood. Head to toe. Neck to knee, really. Twenty-four is wanting them, the bleeders, to bleed on me over and over again. Twenty-five, twenty-five is to stand before God and confess my fifty-five sins. Lying, after all, is a sin, whereas laying, who knows? Did I say fifty-five? I just wanted the others to like me.

STORY OF MY COCK

Listen to this: I had a wee-wee, then I had a dick. Now I have a cock. What's so crazy about it? I thought I had small balls until she told me they were big. I thought I had a small wee-wee until she told me it was an average-sized dick. Cock, I corrected her. If you prune the pubes the way the men on the videotapes do you get more cock, or more shaft of cock. You get more of a sense of shaftness. You can kneel over someone the way they do in the videotapes, you can bend yourself over them and what you have in your hand is referred to in certain circles as a superabundance. I use my dead mother's sewing scissors.

STORY OF MY PUSSY

What was that about, the way we used to put our things away to make a pussy for ourselves? You fold it down and under, press it into disappearance. You get half of a hairy Star of David down there. It feels like God singing through you when you make a pussy for yourself down there. I don't want to hear a theory for it. The Nazis are coming. That's Dad's car in the garage. You better make a pussy for yourself quick.

PHONE SEX

You can get it all the way up in there, but I'd be careful.

PHONE SEX PART II

Here's a good way to go about having what you can never have denied you: Restrict your carnality to the fiber optic kind. What I mean is make sure you do your fucks long distance. Get a headset, do the lotion with both hands. I'm talking as a man here. I'm talking headsets and lotion and I'm talking as a man. I'm also talking as a man talking on a headset to a woman in another country, or in another kind of country than this one. What she has in lieu of lotion is something small and silver (she says), something mechanical and of a genius beyond my means. That's okay. Most things are of a genius beyond my means. Could I have invented the can opener, for example, that genius device for opening canned-meat cans, if it wasn't already invented? Not on my life. Still, I do alright. Like the Incas. Look at the Incas. A whole civilization without knowledge of the wheel. How many roads did those Incas build without figuring out the wheel? No can openers that I know of, either. No knowledge of canned meat, that I know of, in terms of knowledge imparted to me. Still, they did okay, the Incas, for a while. They did great until that prick Pizarro dragged his horses to the beach. Which is my point about phone sex, exactly. Point being, have you ever played King's Fifth? What you need is lotion, a headset, a small and silver thing, a smattering of Spanish and ancient Andean dialects, some canned chicken, and a burning desire to deny yourself what you can never have.

AUTOINFECTION

Get this: I was celibate for a few years, and after most of it I got a thing on my thing. Do you know what that means? Jesus, can you even get your head around what that might even possibly mean? I'll tell you, so you can pretend you're not one of the dumb ones who can't get his head around what it might possibly mean. It means I gave it to myself. It means I gave myself the syph, the clap, the clyd, the King's Fifth, whatever the hell you want to call that thing on my thing.

Beat that.

A SEXY NARRATIVE FOR THE EROTIC MARKET

I wanted to make her come. I wanted her to love me for trying to make her come. I wanted her to think of me as Jesus come back from my daddy's throne room just to make her come. I wanted her to come in a way that all the times she might ever come afterward with anybody else or all alone would just be some twitchy thing to do instead of reading that book again or making that call she didn't want to make. I wanted her life to be somehow ruined by the exaltation of this one moment of coming, ruined in the sense that life in its wake would be a kind of falling away.

Guess I had some problems.

Guess I still do.

So what, glass houses, pal, know what I mean?

Natoma Street

BY TERMINATOR (J. T. LEROY)

IT'S LIKE I'M PUSHED from behind, pulled down the slope of Natoma Street like it's a ramp down into another world. All the buildings are low and tight, huddled around me. Heavy-gated sweatshops, sunken-down tenements, windows filled with dusty laughing Santas and graying fake snow, ancient slaughterhouses with rusted metal beams jutting suddenly out above me. I watch my shadow slip underneath them, sharpen under the piss-colored street lamp and slide unsliced over the green and white pebbles of smashed glass almost worn smooth from streams of urine. And behind me somewhere is the rainlike sound of a car window being smashed, and in front of me the *crunch-crunch* under my boots, pulling me forward. I tilt my head to listen to the blood in my own ear and all I hear, and all I feel, is a cold ache. The sheet metal door glistens in front of me like an axe blade, and the sound of my pounding fist on the door echoes through me and down Natoma Street. Each split second of contact with the frozen metal is like a jolt trying to wake or stop me, but all that's racing in my blood is too old and too known and too mechanical to be turned back. I stand and wait and watch delicate white puffs of air float out from me. And it's amazing anything can come out of me.

Soon nothing will. I bang on the door as hard as I can, bruising my knuckles, and wait a few seconds.

"C'mon."

My teeth are clamped. I kick the door with my boot. They're gonna find me collapsed here, as drained and empty as if a vampire had fed on me. I kick the door again and again, and it shudders. I feel the panic and desperation in my stomach spread as my blood roars away, feeding on itself.

"You're supposed to..." I kick and hit the metal door. "Fuckin' be here!"

From behind me a window slams open.

"People sleeping, people sleeping!"

I turn and look up to see a bald Chinese guy, his face so chubby and squished he looks like a smiling Buddha. Christmas lights flash like a strobe around him.

"You go way, go way!"

I stare as he points the way out with a stubby thick finger. From behind me, I hear heavy latches and bolts moving. I twist in the direction the finger points, and it's like an opening in the world, with cars, lights and people passing the mouth of Natoma, and they have no idea I'm here.

"God damn, you're eager." The door pulls open like a bank vault and blue light reflects onto the sidewalk. "It's just 11:30 now; I don't start early," he says in a deep radio-announcer tone.

My ears pound, and I look back up to the Buddha man, but he's gone, just the empty flashing space of his gaping window.

"Let's go," he orders, and I turn to face him, but he's gone too. I step into the door that's framed in steel, and it slams behind me. "Bolt it," I hear from ahead of me. I stare at a puzzle of red and black painted locks and bolts. "The bottom," he says. It's a padlock that will need a key to unlock. I feel a clink in my stomach as I watch my hand seal me in.

I walk down an unpainted narrow Sheetrock hall with bare blue bulbs poking out like lights in an arcade. The ground is concrete and cracked.

"C'mon!" he says impatiently. "Off to the right."

The hall opens to a huge warehouse with two giant Harleys parked in the middle and a maze of other halls, lofts, ladders, and doors surrounding it. I follow the blue lights into a smaller room that smells of rubbing alcohol and something else I recognize but can't recall.

"Over here."

He's sitting in a director's chair in the middle of the room, holding two Fosters. He holds an open one out to me. I watch my shadow like a black fog moving toward him. My shadow head hits his feet, black in engineer boots, and I trace up faded Levi's to a leather vest half revealing shining silver hoops through his nipples. His arms are like air-drawn traces of a woman's figure stretched long. I avoid his face. I reach out for the beer.

"Uh, thanks." I stand a few feet in front of him.

"How old are you?" He crosses his legs.

"Eighteen," I say automatically, and sip some foam. He laughs.

"Try again." His boot wags.

"Fifteen," I mumble.

"Fifteen?" he repeats.

I follow the floor to a brick wall to my right. There are things hanging, attached, from the wall. A warm wave rushes over me. I swallow loudly.

"Fifteen, I like that."

I nod my head. "But I have ID in case."

"In case of what?"

I look up at him. His cheekbones are cut too sharply, like eroded ridges pushing out. His lips are small, tight, and curled up like old newspaper. His hair is black and slicked straight back. His eyes are reddish-brown like dried blood.

"This is between you and me, got it?"

"Mmm." I feel awkward and stupid. "I got your money!" I say too loudly, and start to reach back to my pocket with my beer hand but spill some. He laughs, shakes his head. "Sorry... shit!" It takes me a few seconds too long to figure out how to maneuver my money out with only one free hand.

"Blondes," he sneers. "Fuckin' geniuses!" He takes a big gulp of beer. I hand him 100 dollars. "So, how's it feel being on the other side?" He smiles, crooked little teeth.

"Huh?" My throat clicks, he holds the money up and shakes it, eyebrows raised. "I had to borrow it." I look away.

"Stop rocking."

I didn't know I was. I feel like my eyes are telescopes I'm peering through, somewhere far away. "Uh, sorry."

"You will be." He smiles sarcastically.

"Huh? Oh." I nod. "Yeah." I feel my face getting hotter and hotter.

He nods, grins and says, as if I don't speak English, "You are paying me, how does that make you feel?" He starts fanning the money.

"I dunno." I sigh. His foot taps. "Umm...weird."

"How?" He leans in.

"Uh..." I rub my face, it feels red. "Embarrassed, I guess." I can't explain it, paying for it does humiliate me and I want that, I need that part, it calms me in some way. You can't trust people you don't pay.

"Hey, hey!!" He snaps his fingers. I look up. "Stop rocking!" He puts his arm out and waves his hand like he's trying to move something aside to see me.

He sighs loudly. "Just, just sit down." He leans back. I look around me. "Right there."

"Yeah...sorry." My left eyelid starts twitching. I sit on the cold concrete, and chew on the inside of my cheek.

"I've heard about you," he says with a little laugh, and stuffs the money away.

"Uh huh." I nod. My blood swirls around faster and faster.

"No limits for you, right?" His beer clanks on the wooden chair arm. My eyes shift from side to side. "No safe word, right?"

"Mmm."

"You can take it all, huh?" My head twitches in a nod. "Coz you," he points at me and laughs, "don't give a fucking shit, right?"

"Well..." My voice sounds too high. "I'd like, umm, I'd like it if, uh...I'd like..."

"Sssay it..." he says, sing-song.

"Ummm...I'd like it if you would..." My head jerks.

"Would what?" He leans forward again.

"Um... give a shit, I mean, ya know..." I swallow hard. "Sorta like, um, care." My bottom lip starts to quiver.

"Yeah." He sighs. "You know I care. Shall we get going?" He gets up. "I don't got all night."

I take a few huge gulps of the beer, and push up, like I'm pulling myself out of a pool, and follow him to the exposed brick wall.

"Take your clothes off. You can put 'em on that chair."

A chill jerks my head, and I close my eyes. "Yes sir," I whisper, and start to undress quickly.

"That's right, you call me *sir,*" he responds. I hear him moving things, setting things up. "Any other special words?"

"I dunno." I lean down to unlace my boots. He comes over to me and I feel his hands sliding along my naked back, down my open jeans and underwear.

"You do take a lot, huh?" he says. "Dad? Stepfather, right?" He's running his hands across the little gullies and streams lining my back and ass.

"Can't get this fuckin' knot!" I yell, and punch my boot top.

"Hey!" He grabs my face between his hands and leans over me from behind. I keep punching. "Hey, hey, hey, not yet, stay calm. It's okay." His voice is soothing. I hear a moan escape me.

"It's okay, it's okay, it's okay." Like a lullaby.

"Please," I half whisper, and reach one of my hands up to his hand holding on to my face.

"Tell me," he says into my ear. His breath smells like warm beer and saliva.

I bring my other hand up around his other hand, cupping my face. I feel his hard cock leaning into me from behind, and I release into containment. "Tell me," he whispers. We breathe together, him leaning over me, in-out, in-out.

"Fix me," I murmur. "Fix me."

"What's it say?" He points to the words cut on my stomach, ass, thighs.

"Bad boy." I pant. "Evil." I spit. "Fix me, you have to!" I feel like I've been hooked to a train that's speeding away from me.

"You are a bad boy, aren't you," he says above me, squeezing my head like a zit. I feel it loosening. "Sinner, aren't you." I close my eyes, and my stomach cramps, and a chill runs through me. He wraps his arms, crisscrossed, around me. I moan. "Tell me, now," he says quietly.

"Punish me," I pant.

"How hard?" His chin digs into my shoulder.

"Till I learn... please? I need you to. Please?" My body is shaking.

"Safe word?" he whispers.

"No, no, not till you're done, okay?" I pant. "Just not my face, okay?"

"It's a very pretty face." He pats my cheek, and I try to lean my head into his touch.

"Yeah, yeah, tell me that," I gasp, and his cock rubs into my ass through his jeans. "Tell me I'm beautiful. Please." I can't stop.

"You are, and that's why I need to help you," he whispers, like a kiss.

"Save me," I groan, and he squeezes his arms tightly around me, and I hope he'll never let go.

"I will, you beautiful, conceited, bad, evil bitch."

"Sir," I whisper, and I feel the tears swelling in my gut. "Sir, hold me after. Please, I'll pay extra, please, after hold me."

He says nothing.

"I'll pay extra." I sound pathetic but I can't shut up. "Please."

"Oh, he'll cry!" My mother squeezes and twists my wrist.

"Never done seen a thief, young or old, so bold-face remorseless," the white-haired security guard says, wagging his finger at me. The steak and six-pack of beer from my knapsack sit on the table in front of me. "See all the trouble you put your poor mother to?!"

The young, frizzy-blond checker that busted me shakes her head at me.

"Steals it for his no-good gang friends."

"Oh, we don't let gang members in this store, ma'am." The manager quickly shines his shoes on the back of his pants legs.

I feel my mom smiling at him. She fans herself with her hand.

"Well, that's a good thing, sir." Crosses her legs. "We have special services for them at our church, the Virgin of Perpetual Love and Mercy, but all in vain I reckon." She sniffles, and I can't help but laugh. Her hand reaches out fast and slaps my cheek. I keep my grin despite myself; I know I'll pay later.

"Yes ma'am, the police won't do a thing to help you, 'cause of his age. He is amazin'." The manager leans down over my face. He smells of tuna and pickles. "Have you no shame, boy?"

My mother clears her throat. "He's been a bad boy since his father passed, few years back. Remember that big blaze? Was a firefighter, over Tallahassee." Murmurs of sympathy. "Thank you, Lord rest his soul. Boy hasn't had the father he badly needs to give guidance and discipline."

I spurt out a laugh at the thought of her being married to a firefighter. Her hand smashes across my face again.

The manager clears his throat. "Well, I think this is the best way to handle this, ma'am."

"Mary." My mother nods.

"Mary, Howard." He reaches out, and shakes my mother's hand a little too long.

"Howard, sorry we're meeting in such a way, but I'm sure it will help save my boy more than police or I can." I roll my eyes and groan. My mother's nails dig into my wrist. "You're an evil boy. You thank Mr. Marsh."

"Thanks," I say flatly, and grind my teeth.

The checker girl flashes her braces and flips her hair. "We should whoop all the shoplifters like him."

"Way it used to be, and hardly anybody thieved," the guard grumbles. I look up and see two bag boys, a little older than me, peering in wide-eyed through a broken, small window. "Well, no time like the present."

My mom stands, and pulls me over to the table. My heart pounds louder. "Please," I whisper.

"Oh, now we see the remorse," Howard gloats. He opens his belt. "Soon you'll see the tears."

My mother jerks me forward. "Take down your pants." I look up at her, and her eyes flash a private message of rage. She didn't tell me to get caught.

"Excuse me," Howard says to my mother as he pulls the belt from the loops.

I stare at the checkout girl biting her lip. "Oh, I'll leave." She starts to get up.

"Oh no, darling!" My mother waves her back. "He stole in front of you, so he'll pay in front of you."

I look over to the boys in the window and point. My mother shakes her head and smiles slightly at me. I feel everyone's stares, and it's like a heat and ice spasm racing through me. My body shivers, and, like Batman sliding down his tunnel, I am suddenly prepared to endure the impossible. I am suddenly able to lean over the table and pull my pants below my underwear. But I pull as much as possible of my jeans in front of me, and I pray and pray. At some point I feel Howard's belt beating me, as he will almost every other day as my new loving father till we move out of his trailer three and a half months later, stealing all his cash, his gold cuff links and his school ring.

I pray during my punishment. I pray so hard I drown out the horrible whipping sound. I pray that God or Satan or whoever won't let them see how sinful and repulsive and bad I truly am. I pray something won't let them see what my mother knows and has tried to punish me for, but which only worsens. And the tears that eventually come burn through me and only heighten it all. For hidden in my bunched-up jeans is my erection, like a gleaming badge of guilt, waiting to be discovered and ripped from me.

The belt is slamming into me all over, my back, ass and thighs. The tears are streaming, and confessions of every sin and every evil thought or action I ever did or almost did pour out from my mouth. I cry harder and harder as the truth washes over me. Even as he takes the belt to between my legs and the pain is unbearable, I am still excited. Excited as hell, though my thing has long been cured of its ability to have erections. I beg for it, harder and harder, so perhaps I can outrun it, but, like my shadow, it is next to me. It follows me. It is permanently attached. As I hang from the gray bars, swaying, wet and throbbing, I recognize the scent from earlier as blood. His switchblade at my crotch slices like I begged him, to try and help save me. One hand caressing, one hand cutting.

I remember when I saw Peter Pan when I was little. Afterward, the other kids wanted to reenact the battles of the Lost Boys, pirates and Indians. All I could think about was the part where Peter Pan sits still while Wendy takes a sharp needle and, with concern and maybe love, sews his shadow onto his feet. And I wonder if his pain excited him as much as it excited me.

I hang here, all the old voices still bleeding in my ears. I watch my shadow, solid like a police outline of a dead body, and I pray. Maybe one more slice, just one more, will sever it forever.

Flare

BY MARCIA ALDRICH

HE HADN'T TOLD her. He had put his mouth on hers, and he hadn't told her. He had put his tongue inside her mouth, keeping it there, and he hadn't told her. At first a small bump in the middle of her upper lip. At first a mild crescendo, nothing more, in the middle of her upper lip. At first a slightly fuller lip, a crescendo, not unattractive, nothing more. Then, the bump grew, it grew into a large sore, a loud crescendo in the middle of her upper lip. More than full looking. The bump was growing hard and tight with what he hadn't told her, it was growing into a large sore. She was cleaning the large sore tight with what he hadn't told her; her tongue was diligently working the crescendo, darting completely to the sore in the middle of her upper lip. She was tonguing it, learning the touch of what he hadn't told her. The sore was growing, ready to pop. She had a sore the size of a cherry tomato growing on her upper lip. She was growing a cherry tomato on her upper lip, ready to burst. She was trying to talk but the cherry tomato was getting in the way. She was slurring, she was slow sliding into language. She was still trying to talk when the sore began popping. Not just one clean swift pop. The sore that was finally ready to pop began popping. It was popping extravagantly as if there was no end to its popping. It could go on popping all day. At first a liquid something like nail polish remover but not nail polish remover began to ooze. It began oozing out of the sore. Air made it burn like his mouth on hers. She wanted to put her mouth in snow. There was burning and there was wanting to put her mouth in snow but there was no snow.

She thought, That's the last of it. The sore would disappear now. She was home and the sore was multiplying. It was filling up again and spreading even though it had popped. Why didn't it snow, a huge blizzard, snow covering the whole world. She wanted to open the door and put her mouth in snow. It was October. The sore was spreading to all the corners of her mouth, opening like fiery tulips in the fleshy flaps of her mouth. They were erupting on the roof of her mouth, a field like the one they had rolled in—Indian paintbrush on fire. They were not disappearing. She stood at the mirror looking at her sores. She did not show her sores to others. Rashes on arms or legs are not pleasant nor desirable. But they are different from sores on the lip. Rashes on arms do not arouse suspicion or shame. Sores on intimate places spread, invite suspicion, even shame. Sores spreading on other places make something private public. There are places that speak for us and there are sores on these places. Her body was turning on her, turning on itself.

She went to the doctor and said, Look at my mouth, it is turning on itself. The doctor said a word that surprised her, a word she never associated with herself. There was nothing to be done. Once the sore begins, there is nothing to be done. There never is, the doctor said, there never is anything to be done. She opened her mouth, but no sound was coming out. Unexpectedly a sore will appear for the rest of your life.

Inside her mouth she could no longer see where the sores had flowered. They had burst and disappeared. The sore on her upper lip had disappeared, but there was a scar, a crescendo of tissue, where what he hadn't told her lived.

Third Party

BY JAY McINERNEY

DIFFICULT TO DESCRIBE precisely, the taste of that eighth or ninth cigarette of the day, a mix of ozone, blond tobacco and early evening angst on the tongue. But he recognized it every time. It was the taste of lost love. Alex started smoking again whenever he lost a woman. When he fell in love again he would quit. And when love died, he'd light up again. Partly it was a physical reaction to stress; partly metaphorical—the substitution of one addiction for another. And no small part of this reflex was mythological—indulging a romantic image of himself as a lone figure standing on a bridge in a foreign city, cigarette cupped in his hand, his leather jacket open to the elements.

He imagined the passersby speculating about his private sorrow as he stood on the Pont des Arts, mysterious, wet and unapproachable. His sense of loss seemed more real when he imagined himself through the eyes of strangers. The pedestrians with their evening baguettes and their Michelin guides and their umbrellas hunched against the March precipitation, an alloy of drizzle and mist.

When it all ended with Lydia he'd decided to go to Paris, not only because it was a good place to smoke, but because it seemed like the appropriate backdrop. His grief was more poignant and picturesque in that city. Bad enough that Lydia had left him; what made it worse was that it was his own fault; he suffered both the ache of the victim and the guilt of the villain.

His appetite had not suffered, however; his stomach was complaining like a terrier demanding its evening walk, blissfully unaware that the household was in mourning. Ennobling as it might seem to suffer in Paris, only a fool would starve himself there.

Standing in the middle of the river he tried to decide which way to go. Having dined last night in a bistro that looked grim and authentic enough for his purposes but which proved to be full of voluble Americans and Germans attired as if for the gym or the tropics, he decided to head for the Hotel Coste, where, at the very least, the Americans would be fashionably jaded and dressed in shades of gray and black.

The bar was full and, of course, there were no tables when he arrived. The hostess, a pretty Asian sylph with a West London accent, sized him up skeptically. Hers was not the traditional Parisian hauteur, the sneer of the maître d'hôtel at a three-star restaurant; she was rather the temple guardian of that international tribe that included rock stars, fashion models, designers, actors and directors—as well as those who photographed them, wrote about them and fucked them. As the art director of a boutique ad agency, Alex lived on the fringes of this world. In New York he knew many of the doormen and maître d's, but here the best he could hope for was that he looked the part. The hostess seemed to be puzzling over his claims to membership; her expression slightly hopeful, as if she was on the verge of giving him the benefit of the doubt. Suddenly her narrow squint gave way to a smile of recognition. "I'm sorry, I didn't recognize you," she said. "How are you?" Alex had only been here twice, on a visit a few years before; it seemed unlikely she would have remembered. On the other hand, he was a generous tipper and, he reasoned, not a bad-looking guy.

She led him to a small but highly visible table set for four. He'd told her he was expecting someone in the hopes of increasing his chances of seating. "I'll send a waiter right over," she said. "Let me know if there's anything else I can do for you." So benevolent was her smile that he tried to think of some small request to gratify her.

Still feeling expansive when the waiter arrived, he ordered a bottle of champagne. He scanned the room. While he recognized several of the patrons—a burly American novelist, the skinny lead singer of a Brit Pop band—he didn't see anyone he actually knew in the old-fashioned sense. Feeling self-conscious in his solitude, he studied the menu and wondered why he'd never brought Lydia to Paris. He regretted it now, for her sake as well as his own; the pleasures of travel were less real to him when they couldn't be verified by a witness.

He'd taken her for granted—that was part of the problem. Why did that always happen?

When he looked up a young couple was standing at the edge of the room, searching the crowd. The woman was striking—a tall beauty of indeterminate race. They seemed disoriented, as if they had been summoned to a brilliant party that had migrated elsewhere. The woman met his gaze—and smiled. Alex smiled back. She tugged on her companion's sleeve and nodded toward Alex's table. Suddenly they were approaching.

"Do you mind if we join you for a moment," the woman asked. "We can't find our friends." She didn't wait for the answer, taking the seat next to Alex, exposing, in the process, a length of taupe-colored, unstockinged thigh.

"Frederic," the man said, extending his hand. He seemed more self-conscious than his companion. "And this is Tasha."

"Please, sit," Alex said. Some instinct prevented him from giving his own name.

"What are you doing in Paris?" Tasha asked.

"Just, you know, getting away."

The waiter arrived with the champagne.

Alex requested two more glasses.

"I think we have some friends in common," Tasha said. "Ethan and Frederique."

Alex nodded noncommittally.

"I love New York," Frederic said.

"It's not what it used to be," Tasha countered.

"I know what you mean." Alex wanted to see where this was going.

"Still," Frederic said, "it's better than Paris."

"Well," Alex said. "Yes and no."

"Barcelona," Frederic said, "is the only hip city in Europe."

"And Berlin," said Tasha.

"Not anymore."

"Do you know Paris well?" Tasha asked.

"Not really."

"We should show you."

"It's shit," Frederic said.

"There are some new places," she said, "that aren't too boring."

"Where are you from?" Alex asked the girl, trying to parse her exotic looks.

"I live in Paris," she said.

"When she's not in New York."

They drank the bottle of champagne and ordered another. Alex was happy for the company. Moreover, he couldn't help liking himself as whoever they imagined him to be. The idea that they had mistaken him for someone else was tremendously liberating. And he was fascinated by Tasha, who was definitely flirting with him. Several times she grabbed his knee for emphasis and at several points she scratched her left breast. An absentminded gesture, or a deliberately provocative one? Alex tried to determine if her attachment to Frederic was romantic. The signs pointed in both directions. The Frenchman watched her closely and yet he didn't seem to resent her flirting. At one point she said, "Frederic and I used to go out." The more Alex looked at her the more enthralled he became. She was a perfect cocktail of racial features, familiar enough to answer an acculturated ideal and exotic enough to startle.

"You Americans are so puritanical," she said. "All this fuss about your President getting a blow job."

"It has nothing to do with sex," Alex answered, conscious of a flush rising on his cheeks. "It's a right-wing coup."

He'd wanted to sound cool and jaded. Yet somehow it came out defensive.

"Everything has to do with sex," she said, staring into his eyes.

Thus provoked, the Veuve Clicquot tingling like a brilliant isotope in his veins, he ran his hand up the inside of her thigh, stopping only at the border of her tight short skirt. Holding his gaze, she opened her mouth with her tongue and moistened her lips.

"This is shit," said Frederic.

Although Alex was certain the other man couldn't see his hand, the subject of Frederic's exclamation was worrisomely indeterminate.

"You think everything is shit."

"That's because it is."

"You're an expert on shit."

"There's no more art. Only shit."

"Now that that's settled," said Tasha.

A debate about dinner: Frederic wanted to go to Buddha bar, Tasha wanted to stay. They compromised, ordering caviar and another bottle of champagne. When the check arrived Alex remembered at the last moment not to throw down his credit card. He decided, as a first step toward elucidating the mystery of his new identity, that he was the kind of guy who paid cash. While Alex counted out the bills Frederic gazed studiously into the distance with the air of a man who is practiced in the art of ignoring checks. Alex had a brief, irritated intuition that he was being used. Maybe this was a routine with them, pretending to recognize a stranger with a good table. Before he could develop this notion Tasha had taken his arm and was leading him out into the night. The pressure of her arm, the scent of her skin, were invigorating. He decided to see where this would take him. It wasn't as if he had anything else to do.

Frederic's car, which was parked a few blocks away, did not look operational. The front grill was bashed in; one of the headlights pointed up at a forty-five-degree angle. "Don't worry," Tasha said. "Frederic's an excellent driver. He only crashes when he feels like it."

"How are you feeling tonight?" Alex asked.

"I feel like dancing," Frederic said. He began to sing Bowie's "Let's Dance," drumming his hands on the steering wheel as Alex climbed into the back.

Le Bain Douche was half-empty. The only person they recognized was Bernard Henri Levy. Either they were too early or a couple of years too late. The conversation had lapsed into French and Alex wasn't following everything. Tasha was all over him, stroking his arm and, intermittently, her own perfect left breast, and he was a little nervous about Frederic's reaction. At one point there was a sharp exchange that he didn't catch. Frederic stood up and walked off.

"Look," Alex said. "I don't want to cause any trouble."

"No trouble," she said.

"Is he your boyfriend?"

"We used to go out. Now we're just friends."

She pulled him forward and kissed him, slowly exploring the inside of his mouth with her tongue. Suddenly she leaned away and glanced up at a woman in a white leather jacket who was dancing beside an adjoining table. "I think big tits are beautiful," she said before kissing him with renewed ardor.

"I think your tits are beautiful," he said.

"They are, actually," she said. "But not big."

When Frederic returned his mood seemed to have lifted. He laid several bills on the table. "Let's go," he said.

Alex hadn't been clubbing in several years. After he and Lydia had moved in together the clubs had lost their appeal. Now he felt the return of the old thrill, the anticipation of the hunt—the sense that the night held secrets that would be unveiled before it was over.

Tasha was talking about someone in New York that Alex was supposed to know. "The last time I saw him he just kept banging his head against the wall, and I said to him, Michael, you've really got to stop doing these drugs. It's been fifteen years now."

First stop was a ballroom in Montmartre. A band was onstage playing an almost credible version of "Smells Like Teen Spirit." While they waited at the bar, Frederic played vigorous air guitar and shouted the refrain. "Here we are now, entertain us." After sucking down their cosmopolitans they drifted out to the dance floor. The din was just loud enough to obviate conversation.

The band launched into "Goddamn the Queers." Tasha divided her attentions between the two of them, grinding her pelvis into Alex during a particularly bad rendition of "Champagne Supernova." Closing his eyes and enveloping her with his arms, he lost track of his spatial coordinates. Were those her breasts, or the cheeks of her ass in his hands? She flicked her tongue in his ear; he pictured a cobra rising from a wicker basket.

When he opened his eyes he saw Frederic and another man conferring and watching him from the edge of the dance floor. Alex went off to find the men's room and another beer. When he returned, Tasha and Frederic were slow dancing to a French ballad and making out. He decided to leave and cut his losses. Whatever the game was, he suddenly felt too tired to play it. At that moment Tasha looked across the room and waved to him from the dance floor. She slalomed toward him through the dancers, Frederic following behind her. "Let's go," she shouted.

Out on the sidewalk, Frederic turned obsequious. "Man, you must think Paris is total shit."

"I'm having a good time," Alex said. "Don't worry about it."

"I do worry about it, man. It's a question of honor."

"I'm fine."

"At least we could find some drugs," said Tasha.

"I don't need drugs," Alex said.

"Don't want to get stoned," Frederic sang. "But I don't want to not get stoned."

They began to argue about the next destination. Tasha was making the case for a place apparently called Faster Pussycat, Kill Kill. Frederic insisted it wasn't open. He was pushing L'Enfer. The debate continued in the car. Eventually they crossed the river and later still lurched to a stop at a club beneath the Montparnasse tower.

The two doormen greeted his companions warmly. They descended the staircase into a space that seemed to glow with a purple light, the source of which Alex could not discern. A throbbing drum and bass riff washed over the dancers. Grabbing hold of the tip of his belt, Tasha led him toward a raised area above the dance floor that seemed to be a VIP area. Conversation became almost impossible—which was kind of a relief. Alex met several people, or rather, nodded at several people who in turn nodded at him. A Japanese woman shouted into his ear in what was probably several languages and later returned with a catalogue of terrible paintings. He nodded as he thumbed through the catalogue. Apparently it was a gift. Far more welcome—a man handed him an unlabeled bottle full of clear liquid. He poured some into his glass. It tasted like moonshine.

Tasha towed him out to the dance floor. She wrapped her arms around him and sucked his tongue into her mouth. Just when his tongue felt like it was going to be ripped from his mouth she bit down on it, hard. Within moments he tasted blood. Perhaps this was what she wanted, for she continued to kiss him as she thrust her pelvis into his. She sucked hard on his tongue. He imagined himself sucked whole into her mouth. He liked the idea. And without for a moment losing his focus on Tasha, he suddenly thought of Lydia and the girl before Lydia, and the girl after Lydia, the one he had betrayed her with. How was it, he wondered, that desire for one woman always reawakened his desire for all the other women in his life?

"Let's get out of here," he shouted, mad with lust. She nodded and pulled away, going into a little solipsistic dance a few feet away. Alex watched, trying to pick and follow her rhythm until he gave up and captured her in his arms. He forced his tongue between her teeth, surprised by the pain of his recent wound. Fortunately she didn't bite him this time; in fact she pulled away. Suddenly she was weaving her way back to the VIP area, where Frederic seemed to be having an argument with the bartender. When he saw Tasha he seized a bottle on the bar and threw it at the floor near her feet, where it shattered.

Frederic shouted something unintelligible before bolting up the stairs. Tasha started to follow. "Don't go," Alex shouted, holding her arm.

"I'm sorry," she shouted, removing his hand from her arm. She kissed him gently on the lips.

"Say goodbye," Alex said.

"Goodbye."

"Say my name."

She looked at him quizzically, and then, as if she suddenly got the joke, she smiled and laughed mirthlessly, pointing at him as if to say, you almost got me. He watched her disappear up the steps, her long legs seeming to become even longer as they receded.

Alex had another glass of the clear liquor but the scene now struck him as tawdry and flat. It was a little past three. As he was leaving the Japanese woman pressed several nightclub invitations into his hand.

Out on the sidewalk he tried to get his bearings. He started to walk toward St. Germain. His mood lifted with the thought that it was only ten o'clock in New York. He would call Lydia. Suddenly he believed he knew what to say to her. As he picked up his pace he noticed a beam of light moving slowly along the wall beside and above him; he turned to Frederic's bashed-in Renault cruising the street behind him.

"Get in," said Tasha.

He shrugged. Whatever happened, it was better than walking.

"Frederic wants to check out this after-hours place."

"Maybe you could just drop me off at my hotel."

"Don't be a drag."

The look she gave him reawoke in him the mad lust of the dance floor; he was tired of being jerked around and yet his desire overwhelmed his pride. After all this he felt he deserved his reward and he realized he was willing to do almost anything to get it. He climbed in the backseat. Frederic gunned the engine and popped the clutch. Tasha looked back at Alex, shaping her lips into a kiss, then turned to Frederic. Her tongue emerged from her lips and slowly disappeared in Frederic's ear. When Frederic stopped for a light she moved around to kiss him full on the mouth. Alex realized that he was involved—that he was part of the transaction between them. And suddenly he thought of Lydia, how he had told her his betrayal had nothing to do with her, which was what you said. How could he explain to her that even when he bucked atop other women, it was still her who filled his heart.

Tasha suddenly climbed over to the backseat and started kissing him. Thrusting her busy tongue into his mouth, she ran her hand down to his crotch. She took his earlobe between her teeth as she unzipped his fly.

Alex moaned as she reached into his shorts. He looked at Frederic, who looked right back at him and seemed to be driving faster as he adjusted the rearview mirror. Tasha slid down his chest, feathering the hair of his belly with her tongue. A vague intuition of danger faded away in the wash of vivid sensation. She was squeezing his cock in her hand and then it was in her mouth and he felt powerless to intervene. He didn't care what happened, so long as she didn't stop. At first he could barely feel the touch of her lips, the pleasure residing more in the anticipation of what was to follow. At last she raked him gently with her teeth. Alex moaned and squirmed lower in the seat as the car picked up speed.

The pressure of her lips became more authoritative.

"Who am I?" he whispered. And a minute later: "Tell me who you think I am." Her response, though unintelligible, forced a moan of pleasure from his own lips. Glancing at the rearview mirror, he saw that Frederic was watching, looking down into the backseat, even as the car picked up speed. When Frederic shifted abruptly into fourth, Alex inadvertently bit down on his own tongue as his head snapped forward, his teeth scissoring the fresh wound there.

On a sudden impulse he pulled out of Tasha's mouth just as Frederic jammed on the brakes and sent them into a spin.

He had no idea how much time passed before he struggled out of the car. The crash had seemed almost leisurely, the car turning like a falling leaf until the illusion of weightlessness was shattered by the collision with the guard rail. He tried to remember it all as he sat, folded like a contortionist in the backseat, taking inventory of his extremities. A peaceful, Sunday silence prevailed. No one seemed to be moving. His cheek was sore and bleeding on the inside where he'd slammed it against the passenger seat headrest. Just when he was beginning to suspect his hearing was gone he heard Tasha moaning beside him. The serenity of survival was replaced by anger when he saw Frederic's head moving on the dashboard and remembered what might have happened. Hobbling around to the other side of the car, he yanked the door open and hauled Frederic roughly out to the pavement, where he lay blinking, a gash on his forehead.

The Frenchman blinked and winced, inserting a finger in his mouth to check his teeth. In a fury, he kicked Frederic in the ribs. "Who the hell do you think I am?" Frederic smiled and looked up at him. "You're just a guy," he said. "You're nobody."

Sailors

BY GENEVIEVE FIELD

IT'S THE FOURTH OF JULY so everything is burnt and everyone has a dry mouth they'll make a job of keeping wet. It's 104 in the shade so there is no shade. My high-heeled sandals beguile me, collapsed in the corner of my bedroom like broken ankles. I strap them on and we are no longer broken. We catch a cab and take it to the Lower East Side and climb twelve flights to the roof. We weave a little at the top, shallow-fucking the sweaty tar with each step toward my friends, Cintra and Melvin, in matching sailor suits. The cute bastards are kissing, Cintra's platinum pigtails tied in star-spangled ribbons, swinging. Melvin's black-dyed spikes won't let the sailor cap sit. Sweet. And that's not sarcasm talking. What kind of gargoyle-heart would begrudge a dominatrix and once-junkie their cute? Not mine, though I'm told it's been carved a funny shape. I'm from the suburbs, yes, okay. My friends admire my efforts to run the other way: rope tattoo healing pretty around my wrist, prophylactic tank in black, Kleenex-thin skirt (waxed waxy under that). "Look." Cintra points. It's my date, on top of the water tower, having a smoke. He hasn't met Cintra and Melvin, but they know him because they are good listeners. "Didn't I say he looked like a lion, minus the mane and muscle?" "Yes, you did, honey." He delights me as much as the shoes did before I put them on. The shoes climb to him, slipping a little on the metal rungs. Someone's built a deck up there, it's scattered with butts. He adds one, lights another. His eyes are a dry gold fire hazard, when they crinkle they might spark. But like the mouth around his cigarette, their smile is narrow. I wipe his brow like a humid window and run the sweat through his hair. It would be gentle to hold his hand, so I kneel and place it between my legs instead. "It's me and the shoes," I say. "Together we are possessed." "You mean repressed," he teases. "This is repressed?" "Yeah." It's our fifth date, counting one apology over drinks. "Let's fuck right here then." "You're sad," he says, "I have to find the bathroom." On his T-shirt, a picture of a gun. "Go then, I think there's a place up the street like fifty blocks." He shakes his cub-head and takes the ladder in a step and a jump. Down on the rooftop his shoulders square and the crowd unzips. He pauses to admire a halter-topped girl passing out firecrackers and other dangerous favors; he slides through the trap-door floor. I kick off the shoes, lie back and watch the smog blush redder than this. Cintra and Melvin climb up and lie down on either side of me. She presses a cold beer to my cheek and the three of us hold hands, flinching together when the bottlerockets start to explode. I don't have to tell them what else has walked away.

26 Hours, 25 Minutes

BY DANIEL HAYES

HOW DO YOU ASK a woman out? Bob asks me. Just like that, I say, pointing at Bob and encouraging him, lying just a little about the simplicity of it all. You just ask, I tell him, like you're asking her for the time. What about the small talk? No small talk, I say. If you have the small talk, that's fine, but if you don't, that's okay, too. So you skip the small talk? No, I tell Bob, you don't skip it. You give it a try, but if it's not going well, go ahead and just ask her out. To what? Bob asks. To what what? Ask her out to what? To whatever you want, Bob. A vacation? Okay, no, I say. Not a vacation. To ask a total stranger to go on a vacation is like shooting yourself in the foot. Or giving her the gun and asking her to shoot. Instead, I say, it's sort of step-by-step: the coffee, the lunch, the dinner, the trip to the seventh arrondissement in Paris. So why the stalking? he asks. This bothers me a little—the way the word *stalking* has lost its prohibition in our conversations, as though Shoshana, my ex-girlfriend, was doing the talking. As if she had wormed her way into the safe, male bastion Bob and I create during these late-night discussions. I don't want to talk about Shoshana, so I ask Bob whether he ever gets the feeling that maybe he should go outside more, junk the television, rub shoulders with the masses, get some exercise, do some girl-watching if nothing else. Some stalking? Bob says, adjusting his thick glasses. No, I say, that's not what I mean.

When Shoshana gave me her phone number, after I'd actually met her in a drugstore—a pharmacy, she always insisted—I can remember staring down at the little piece of paper and feeling warmly satisfied that the numbers, in that particular configuration, met up exactly with what I already knew her phone number to be. Like magic, like coincidence. It only made sense that Shoshana's phone number, address, place of birth, place of employment, ex-boyfriend's name—not to mention her brother's dips into religious activity of a questionable nature—were consistent with what I'd already found out by following her and doing a little investigative work on the Internet. And somehow I'd thought of that as a good sign—the consistency. What was I thinking? Now, a year and a half later, I know everything there is to know about Shoshana, but I've got nothing to show for it—just this one picture of her taken in a photo booth in Galveston, Texas, of all places. And, who knows, maybe I was splitting hairs, not admitting to it all, trying to separate myself from the image of some crazed, drooling loser in a cum-stained trench coat. Maybe the whole time I'd been trying, in the narrow corridors of my mind, to give it a slightly romantic flavor, as though stalking, or whatever—following, let's call it—was just the first, initial step in the path of any romance. Like picking up a dropped pen or shaking hands or exchanging names and phone numbers or making conversation about the tabloids with a total stranger, who happens to be wearing a killer bikini, in a coastal town's supermarket checkout line. Yes, that could've been my mistake.

Truly, the first thing I ever noticed about Shoshana—besides whatever scattered information I'd gotten from furtive glances in public places—was how the bridge of her nose rode an almost uninterrupted path from her forehead to the nose's tip. Not quite a straight shot, but it was the not-quite that made up its beauty in the miniature museum of my mind. It was impossible for me—and there's no telling, but maybe it would be for you, too—to look at Shoshana without feeling as though the strength of her face emanated from the upper slope of that nose. The nose itself wasn't large, but the straightness of the bridge gave it, for me at least, an irresistible weight. Coupled with an unconscious habit of slightly elevating her chin, so that she showed off her elliptical nostrils without a trace of shame, Shoshana's nose drove me crazy. And I have no shame in telling you—though I wouldn't tell Bob, since he might incorporate the image into his daily wank—about how a month into knowing Shoshana I asked for, and was granted, the privilege of putting that nose in my mouth. No teeth, I swear. Just holding it there, giving it a place where it could secretly shine like some fistful of flashlight in a dark cavern. But then maybe I'm just speaking of my own private obsessions. After all, when I showed the Galveston picture to Bob, a few weeks into my relationship with Shoshana, he said nothing about her nose. But he did sort of shudder at the sight of her: a sudden sucking-in of air, a hand shooting to his mouth. A moment later he pointed out Shoshana's resemblance to Elisa O'Donnell, the actress. *Resemblance* is too weak a word, Bob said. The eyes, the hair, the smile. You've seen her, he said, as though speaking of some ubiquitous presence in the neighborhood. And then Bob mentioned an HBO movie, which I told him I hadn't seen. I claimed ignorance; I didn't want to add to the fervor, I guess. Yes, okay, I'd seen her in a couple of lousy movies, I finally admitted, but so what? Was Bob saying what I thought he was saying? I tried to erase the resemblance from my mind, and yet for days afterward—in bed, lights out, during frenzied sex with Shoshana—I found myself thinking of Elisa O'Donnell, over and over, in inappropriate ways.

So why did you tell Shoshana that you'd stalked her? Bob asks me. I didn't, I say. Not then. You did eventually, Bob says. It was a mistake, obviously. I heard the same voices you hear. I got vulnerable. It must've scared her, Bob says, to learn more about you than you thought you were revealing. This just comes flying out of his mouth, and I have to take a moment to consider. Have you ever stalked before? Bob asks, and I wonder why he's asking. Is he trying to depress me? Would Ricki Lake, in this situation, ask that question? Is he trying to make himself feel better, since clearly he's not the type of man who takes chances? Anyway, how am I to respond to this question? As a kid, I say—and I know what I'm doing, skipping right over the real answer and slipping into its place a convenient truth of the past—I once followed a girl named Dorothy all the way home and just stood there, out on the sidewalk, and got invited in without even asking. In her backyard, it turned out, she had a white-haired pet llama. And it wasn't even in a cage. Everywhere you took a step, there was llama shit. And her father had white hair, too—I remember that—and he was a minister in a local church, even though he didn't seem like a minister. She didn't seem like a minister's daughter, either. Bob listens patiently to the entire story and asks, What was the llama's name? Grace, I say, with no hesitation.

So that was my mistake. After living with Shoshana for a year, I happened to tell her that in a strange sense I knew her even before I'd actually met her. Not very precise, I know. It begged the question, which she went about asking after first giving me a frown that spoke painfully of confusion. Innocent confusion? So I went on to say that before I met her I'd been following her. I meant following in a couple of different ways, but I was hoping that she'd see it as the idea of a person giving thought, or paying attention, to another person even though that first person doesn't really know the second person, not personally. Like following someone's career. I may've even said that, trying to make her feel like someone other than a lonely victim of a lonely man. A movie star. I can't remember, but I probably said, You know, Sho, like someone following someone's career, like with a movie star. And she said, You mean stalking. Stalking? I didn't think that was exactly the word. But after she waited, and I gave her a complete explanation—it took five minutes or so, a quick speech that didn't really go very well, or it didn't seem to make much difference—she looked at me and said, So it was stalking. And what could I say? She made it sound like I was one of those guys who owns a restaurant and sets up a hidden camera in the ladies' room. And so, in short, that was my mistake—surprising Shoshana, popping it on her, telling of this little secret about how I knew her before I actually knew her—because it changed the nature of our relationship. I won't say it ended our relationship, though within weeks it was over. If you were to ask Shoshana why the relationship ended, she'd say something about how she lost trust in me or began to think that maybe I wasn't the person she thought I was, which scared her. How couldn't it? But take away the secret, take away the stalking, and there wasn't really much to the idea of me as an untrustworthy person. Not that I am trustworthy, mind you. Just that Shoshana didn't know enough to have any reason to think otherwise.

It's funny what you find out about women, even after you meet them. Whenever possible, Shoshana ate with her hands. Honestly, I used to marvel at it. I remember one time spending an afternoon conjuring up my specialty from cooking school: *poulet aux champignons.* And there I was, that evening, switching the fork from my left to my right hand, having ripped off a piece of savory chicken with the aid of a knife, and there she was, across the table, with the breast right up there in her face. She was using hands and fingers and, most of all, her teeth to tear the meat away from the bone, without so much as a drop of sauce smudging her face. I tried this once, just to see. Very messy on the hands and face, not to mention the food slipping through your fingers. I had to get up twice for another napkin, and it was the second time when Shoshana sighed. You're just afraid, she said. Afraid? Afraid of what? I asked her. I don't know, she said. You tell me.

One day, after the breakup, under the illusion that Shoshana might actually want to talk to me—not exactly to take back her rejection, but maybe just some of her outrage—I dial her number. Free and easy. How does this happen, after not having talked to her for all of those weeks? Well, we all suffer momentary lapses; forgive me for saying this, but I'm no different than you in that department. She might've even been expecting my call, I told myself. And so, suffering this lapse of reason, I dial Shoshana's number, and, in dialing—in remembering having punched those numbers before I'd even met her, just to hear her say hello—I begin to realize, if somewhat vaguely, my mistake: This sequence of numbers is tantamount to a secret entrance code to a place where I'm not entitled to go. Don't go there, you shouldn't go there. As it turns out, she isn't there anyway, and I hear her voice all over again and then I leave a message. The message says the following, and I'll try to keep it factual: Shoshana, hi. It's me. Don't know if it's okay to call or not. I hope you don't think I'm trying to bug you. Just calling on a lark. I was hoping, you know, just to say hello and see how you were. Are. And I guess to ask you whether it was okay—for you, I mean—to try one more time in explaining. That's me explaining. About following you, way back when. And I hope you don't think that that's what I'm doing. Following you. Now. I mean, just by calling you. I'm not that crazy. Boy, the lessons I've learned. So anyway, as usual, it's always nice to hear your voice. On your outgoing message, I mean. And then, pausing for a moment and thinking of the awful, out-of-control spontaneity of leaving a message on an answering machine—that is, my message, this message, this awful explosion of verbal mumbo-jumbo—I stop talking, hesitate, close my eyes, and then reach to hang up the phone. I put it back in its cradle like it was a long-dead baby. *Resignation* isn't a strong enough word. It's like lowering myself into a casket, which in turn gets lowered deep into the ground.

What's the hope? Bob says. The hope, I say, trying the word on for size. What hope? You mean by calling her on the phone? I ask, trying to see what Bob has in mind. But he's already shaking his head. Forget the phone call, he says. Say you never made the phone call, so then what's the hope? What do you want her to do? Bob asks. Or what did you want her to do, he says, in making the mistake of telling her in the first place? Hey, listen, I say to Bob, I just wanted to own up to our own origins. Share the stalking. Get it out there, up front. Not stalking, Bob says. Following. And then he brings a finger to his closed lips as though to emphasize the sudden importance of words in the private, dark universe of his studio apartment. I just wanted to tell her about it, I say. Let her get an inside look into the mind of someone like me. I guess I figured she'd get a kick out of it, I say. Imagine that! she'd think to herself—and I slapped my own cheeks, in pantomime—a man who follows me around and takes an interest, both from afar and up close, and I never even knew! Bob looks at me without expression and says, No, women prefer fate. Like he's standing there in a khaki jacket, a field guide in his hand, and speaking of some aboriginal tribe. Fate? I question Bob's knowledge on this point; he's guessing, I worry, or repeating something he's heard on television about the often amusing gulf that lies between men and women. Or, who knows, it could be true. Maybe you're right, Bob. Maybe she wanted to just meet me in the drugstore, pure and simple. Pharmacy, Bob says. And he brings the same finger to the same lips, like he's kissing the whisper of a dandelion.

Okay, I know what you're wondering. So the first time I ever seriously followed someone—setting aside Dorothy, the llama girl—was back in my early twenties. She was a woman who'll go unnamed who danced for a city-based ballet company, which was very impressive, since back then I was living in a city where ballet meant something. Now, living in a cultural necropolis, my balletomane days are over and gone. Anyway, I went one night and saw her perform—the piece, I remember, required her to do fish dive after fish dive, in the arms of anonymous men—and then, for the next week or two, I kept thinking about her. I thought about her a lot. I thought about what it would be like to be a part of her life. I made up a cozy picture in my mind of her apartment, its interior—a lonely place in spite of her gold-framed family photos and her nostalgic collection of stuffed animals. And, of course, I got closer: I found out things about her by reading newspapers and dance magazines and, while masquerading as a writer for a small weekly located out in the suburbs, I even made calls to the ballet company. Once, I actually made the mistake of talking to her on the phone. After that fiasco—stuttering, mumbling, excusing myself, reaching for a glass of water and sending it plunging toward the kitchen floor—I kept a lower profile. I followed her just once, one day as she came out of a morning rehearsal in a black, sweat-drenched cotton outfit that left me dizzy. I kept count, and I ended up following her for the next twenty-six hours and twenty-five minutes. Just for the experience. Without sleep, or at least none for me. And for that period I was her guardian. She wore the tutu, but I was the angel.

So one night I'm sitting in Bob's dungeon of an apartment—where else?—and he asks me to name my favorite memory of Shoshana. The question itself, hanging there in anticipation of my answer, had a little flame of wistfulness at its core. In another world, I might've thought Bob was leading me somewhere—if I managed to somehow provide an answer from the heart. But Bob's mind doesn't work that way; he just wants to know, and he doesn't know why, or he doesn't care to know why. And so I tell Bob about this one time, during our only shower together—after Shoshana and I had first slept together—how she leaned her wet head against the tiled wall, looked up, and gave me a kind of beastly snarl, sans sound. And this is your favorite moment, Bob says, very slowly, as though to give the television audience a wink of incredulity. The snarl wasn't meant to be taken seriously, I explain to him. It was meant to be playful. And so I said to Shoshana, What was that? What was what? That sneer, I said. That snarl. And then, before she could answer, I said to her, I feel like I've been granted entry. Did I actually use the word *granted*? Bob shrugs his shoulders. I can't remember for sure, I say, but I can remember that she seemed somewhat taken aback; she obviously thought I was commenting on the lovemaking we'd just finished, back in her bed, banging away in a rudderless frenzy. Getting inside of her, entering her—that kind of entry. No, no, I said to her. I like that, too, but I meant a different kind of entry. That snarl, I said, it means something about you, it means that I know something about you that I didn't know. And Shoshana did it again, showing off the shoddy orthodontic work of her adolescence. It does, it does, I said, almost exuberant in seeing the snarl again. She looked exuberant, too, maybe in the act or in seeing how much it meant to me. She asked me what it meant—this snarl of hers, this split-second baring of misaligned teeth—and I wasn't sure, but it said something about her. So what did it say? Bob asks, drawing his eyebrows up and over his thick glasses. And I tell Bob I have no idea whatsoever. But it was in that moment—not quite the snarl itself but the feeling of discovering something about her and feeling, because of it, exuberant—that I got sent right over the edge. Tumbling head over heels. Even in only now remembering it. And maybe you, too, know how it feels.

Reservation

BY SIMON FIRTH

THE ROOM WAS a wreck. She saw that now, and felt suddenly, overwhelmingly tired.

Leaning against the door, its cool paint a welcome balm against a pain she felt spreading diagonally across her naked back, she tried to work out if anything was broken. The room was on her credit card, she remembered, so she'd be the one charged for breakage. With relief she saw nothing smashed, just everything out of place. Only her flight bag seemed to have been untouched—still zipped, set square to the wall on a luggage support, the only straight lines in a room of disturbed curves and folds.

Her clothes were scattered everywhere. The curtains were only half closed and beyond the small balcony she could see the dawn beginning to dim the artificial lights of the airport, the first planes taxiing on the runways, a single jumbo taking off into the familiar early morning mix of cloud and fog. Looking for the rest of her uniform, she remembered that her skirt was ripped. Was that her bra behind the TV? She wondered where she had put her contacts.

Knowing she had to move, she rocked forward, testing the idea of motion, but instantly her limbs pleaded back: no, not yet. Her every muscle ached; it was as much as she could manage to keep where she was. It was as if she had had a month of massages; she felt wrung through. Was there a part of her, she wondered, that had not been held and kissed, lifted and bitten, that had not thrust against some part of his?

Besides, she liked the cold of the door on her back and buttocks. It contrasted with, prolonged for a few precious moments, the warmth she still felt in the last places he'd touched her, lovingly, his hands cupped, almost a ritual with them now. If she didn't move, if she stayed there at the room's door where they had last embraced, she could still sense resonating within her the tremor of his final soft caress.

Across the room the low-set mirror of the dressing table reflected back to her a pair of legs. She studied them. They were pale, not as thin as they used to be, but still good enough for her job. The distance obscured the veins, she knew, the front view better than the back, but there was something new in the reflection, just below her knees: two patches of skin rubbed to a raw red. She leaned down and gently examined one. It was puffed and sore to the touch. Where had they been, she wondered, looking back up at the room, when she did that? Were her stockings on at the time? Did she ruin them? She remembered and smiled.

Still not ready to move, she tried to recall if she had a spare pair in the suitcase. In there, too, was her wash bag. She marveled that she hadn't even opened it. To not even think about her face, the creams she always used at night—to make no pretense that she was getting ready to go to sleep, shutting herself in the bathroom, making him wait. This time she must have needed him badly. A sudden small wave of the tiny hairs on her breasts and belly pricked up at the thought. But the rash of goose pimples that followed, spreading to her arms, persuaded her she was actually getting cold and that she should move.

Pulling away from the door her back stuck slightly to its surface. She pulled a little harder and felt a sharp sting as her flesh broke free. Turning, she saw impressed across the paintwork a faint broken line of dried blood. A little startled, she reached behind her to find a long weal running from one shoulder blade down into the small of her back. She looked at her nails, wondered what she, in turn, had done to him.

Standing free now of the door's support, her legs felt suddenly weak, her head slightly dizzy. She registered the digital clock on its side by the bed, not really absorbing the time but knowing she was late. She stepped over and unzipped her bag, fished out her bathroom things and made for the shower, but midway across the room she tripped on something in her path and collapsed sideways onto the bed. Lying there she realized just how tired she was, how little sleep she'd had, how much she wanted to just roll the blankets over herself and shut her eyes against the breaking day.

The bathroom, too, was a mess. A towel was dumped in a corner, the soap in the sink had been unwrapped. He'd left the toilet seat up. On the floor she noticed a few of his graying hairs. Picking one up, she thought of his body, of its covering so different from hers, of the line of small tight curls that ran up to his stomach, of how it was always a surprise how firm he was under his skin, year after year.

She tried to imagine where he was now, if he had washed completely before he left or if he would try to keep her smell on some part of him. She asked herself again whether he was truly as faithful as he always claimed, waiting for her, seeing no one else but his loveless wife.

An itch in her crotch reminded her how much of him she still had inside. She looked around—no bidet. Fine, she thought, I'll keep him for a while. Setting down the seat of the toilet she peed, amazed at how she could forget for hours her usual bodily routines.

As she wiped herself, the nub of her thumb brushed lightly against her clitoris. It, too, was rubbed sore, but the touch reminded her of the excitement and anticipation she always felt walking off the plane in San Francisco, knowing he was in his truck, driving over the bridge and across the city to meet her. She thought about what they did for each other, what they had found they could do together, and she wondered if it really wouldn't be the same if they had decided to make it something more permanent, if they had broken off the tangle of their separate lives and made a go of it somewhere in the world.

She caught herself staring at the opposite wall. Chastising herself for doing what she had promised herself she would never do, she got up and stepped into the shower. For a brief moment, as the hot water hit the wound upon her back, the pain was intense. But it was a welcome shock and it melted quickly as her stiff muscles surrendered to the battering, her mind now a little more awake, beginning to take her forward into the coming day.

With the heat of the spray her knees had turned a new, more livid red. Perhaps they'd swell so much she'd be unable to work the returning flight. There had been close calls before—the worst when he actually broke one of her ribs—but she had always made it through. She knew no one better at disguising pain. Asbestos hands, they called her in the galley.

Bending over to soap her feet, she wondered what her colleagues would think of her if they knew. Going off with a passenger: at least she hadn't done it right after the flight, like some. On that flight, years ago now, she'd seen him look at her, returned his glance, felt foolish, told herself off for even thinking of breaking the rules that in those days the other girls broke nightly.

She thought it would be just that one time as she took him back that night to the hotel by the airport. But in that room she had found what she had despaired of ever finding: an education in the possibilities of pleasure, a trusted body against which to dash her own. Relief. She had found that despite feeling it had been wrong to do, perhaps even because she felt that way, she wanted nothing more achingly than to experience the thrill of it again.

Since then there had been times when they didn't speak for tens of months, when she thought she was finally over him. They had set up separate lives but as she grew older, as she had grown further from the person she was when she was with him, she had come to need these meetings more and more. From that first night it was only in this room—their room—that she could ever release herself from herself. In some way, and it shocked her that she didn't know him well enough to know how, it was the same for him.

She looked down at her legs to see if they needed shaving, but she'd done them specially for him and they were fine. And he had noticed, too, he always did—he went over her every pore, kissed each square inch of her every time.

She forced herself to concentrate on leaving. She needed to dress and tried to empty her head of thoughts as she went around the room collecting the pieces of her uniform, putting them on in turn, trying at the same time to straighten what she could. The doors to the balcony, where they had stood not bothering to hide themselves from the planes that landed through the night, wouldn't open now. The room would just have to go unaired.

Reaching under the bed for her jacket, she felt a sudden stabbing pain rip down her arm, through her shoulder, spine and hips, into her legs. It ended with a cramp that clenched her thigh and made her gasp in shock. She knew that if she tried to back out now she'd only make it worse and that she was stuck there, until her muscles relaxed and she could ease herself back out.

Frustrated at herself, at being late, at being stuck alone and too embarrassed to call for help from under the wreck of a bed that stank of sex, at the indignity to which her desire had driven her, she felt a wave of self-disgust. How had she come to crave a relationship that left her always covering her tracks, alone, in pain? Why couldn't she be satisfied with what she had in London? Why, when she got to SFO, did she always make the call? If it was such a good thing, if it was what she lived for, why did they meet so rarely and why did they need to keep their meetings secret? She couldn't let it end as it always did. Instead of walking out of the door and onto a plane that would take her half a world away from him she wanted to stay there, have him return to her, help her up, pull her onto the bed, hold her, press inside her again and stay there for days, his moans loud in her ear, his nails dug deep into her flesh, his arms enfolding her.

Utterly exhausted now, she picked herself up, put on her jacket and bent down to grab her bag. From deep within she felt slip some of what he'd left inside her. She wondered if she should quickly use the loo. Then she decided: no, this time she wouldn't.

Instead she grabbed the bag, unlocked the door and stepped onto the threshold. She could not, and now she would not, leave alone. As she walked down the plane's long aisle, she would feel him with her, dampening her, perhaps a drop running down the inside of her leg. As people beckoned to her she would walk toward them, placing one foot in front of the other, so that her thighs would rub together; and as she walked so each drop would slip away from its still moist mooring and fall onto the white cotton of her briefs, drying and fusing with her red-brown hairs, until a bend, a reach, the fetching of a blanket or the stowing of a coat would tear a single hair from its swollen follicle, and the sharp pain of each momentary prick would force her other, proper self to admit that she was intimate with him, that he could give her pleasure, that they should be allowed at last to find some other heaven than the awful prison of this airport hotel.

Complex
Electra

BY ILISE BENUN

THIS IS WHAT I remember. My father was an imposing man, tall, with ink-black hair in short, hard waves that lay back from his temples. He was bearded and wooly, his heft covered with a coat of coarse and curly dark hair, like a grizzly bear, like a caveman. Thin-lipped and heavy-jawed, he had a wide neck, with a prodigious Adam's apple, set atop a pair of broad shoulders.

At thirteen, I was thick in the waist, wide in the hips and not what you'd call smooth-of-skin. But my father saw none of that. To him, I was Beauty, and he always had a compliment for me, whether it was about my outfit, my hairstyle or my calves, muscular from years of ballet.

One Friday, my father was working late at the factory of our family business and I'd offered to help with the paperwork. When I arrived, the cutters and sewers were lined up at the time clock, chatting with my father as they punched out. He shook the hand of each one of them, thanked them for their good work that week, and patted them on the back as they left. I stood close and, as he talked, I smoothed under my palm the dark hairs that blanketed the back of his hand.

When everyone was gone, my father turned to me and opened his arms for our hug. I reached around his waist, pressed my face against his chest, took a deep breath and squeezed as hard as I could.

"You're pretty strong for a girl," he said, following our script.

"The tighter to squeeze you with, my dear."

His long arms hung over my shoulders and his hands came down to rest on my schoolgirl skirt. "Oh, man, this little bottom of yours," he said, with a firm squeeze. "I just can't help myself." And for a blessed moment he held me with such authority it was as if I were suspended above the ground. Then, with a pat, he let me go.

"Okay, Beauty, enough horsing around. Let's get to work. I have a new job for you today, so sit right down here." Like a gentleman, he held the chair and like a lady, I curtsied.

"Here we have today's orders." He rapped on a stack of papers with the eraser end of a pencil. He was standing behind me, leaning over so that his arms encircled me and I could feel the heat from his body. "In each of these columns, I want you to write the store name, the dollar total and the shipping date. Got it?"

I lifted my chin and breathed in his warm exhale, blended with the cinnamon gum he chewed all day. His Adam's apple stared down at me, then promptly disappeared. He was talking, saying something and pointing with the pencil back to the pile, but I couldn't hear a word. I could only smile up at him and nod.

"Okay, get to work." He walked over to his desk and sat down. I shifted in my seat, coughed, sniffled and sneezed, erased loudly, shuffled papers, even came close to dropping them on the floor. He didn't budge. Then I pushed the chair back and walked toward the door.

"Taking a break already?"

"I'll be back, " I said, and picked up my book bag.

In the ladies' room, I dug hurriedly among my books and old sandwich remnants until I found the small vinyl makeup kit I'd bought several months before at Bullocks. I leaned close to the mirror and inspected my nose, my chin, my upper lip. With a tiny dollop of foundation, I covered a bright red pimple on the tip of my nose, then dusted it with powder from a compact that clicked open and closed.

Mascara baton in hand, I isolated, elongated and thickened each eyelash. Next came the blush, which I applied in long, clean lines up along my cheekbones and toward my temples, as I had practiced in my own bathroom with the door locked.

Moving quickly now, I pursed my lips and applied Rouge Sublime. I pulled my hairbrush down my back, through tangles that wouldn't give. As a final flourish, I undid two buttons on my white shirt and leaned toward the mirror to see what a view from above would reveal: a peek of black lace and a tiny pink rose.

Dad sat at the conference table, his back to me, and I stood at the threshold of his office, leaning against the doorjamb, my elbow extended as high as it would reach, my cheek pressing into my upper arm. Imagining myself as Lauren Bacall, or Lucille Ball, tall and sleek and thin in a floor-length red dress, I shifted my weight back and forth, my hips swaying, almost circling.

Then I approached silently and stood behind my father for a moment, stealthlike. With a deep breath, I reached forward and placed my trembling palm on his shoulder. I squeezed once and held my hand there.

"Thank you, honey. My shoulders are a bit stiff." I squeezed again.

"Do you want a massage, Daddy?" My voice was high and tight, not what I'd intended.

"No, Beauty," he said. "We've got a lot of work to do."

I stepped closer, put my other hand on his shoulder and began to knead gently. I pressed my thumb over the neckline of his shirt, inching my finger slowly along his clavicle. A low moaning sound arose from him, and I pressed harder. Then with both hands, I spread my fingers up his neck, and softly raked his scalp with my nails.

"Honey, really," he said, waving his hand above his shoulder. "We don't have time to play."

I leaned in toward his throat at that moment, my lips parted, and my chest grazed his back.

That's when he stood up. Suddenly he was towering over me, his eyes wide and full and I watched as they moved slowly, seeing my strategically unbuttoned shirt, the tiny flower, my red mouth. All I could do was stand there waiting, for punishment or absolution or ecstasy.

At first, nothing happened. He didn't smile with pity. He didn't take me in his arms. He didn't sit me down on his lap for a little talk. He just stood there, motionless, looking. His watch ticked loudly and a car passed by outside.

Then his face changed, it softened a little and he sighed deeply. He drew me toward his chest, and said quietly, "No, honey." He cradled my entire head in the hollow of his hand, repeating over and over, "No, honey, no." I began to weep. All that unspeakable desire I'd been nursing for so long, melted and drained out in long, deep sobs. All the while, he held me to him.

When my sobs tempered to a sniffle, he released my head, took me by the outer arms and pulled me away from him. "I love you," he said, bending down and looking directly into my swollen, mascara-bleared eyes. "You know that, right?" I nodded and kept nodding as I buried my head back in his chest. Again, he pulled me away, this time with a little more force. He kissed me once on each wet eyelid and whispered, "Okay. Now, go clean yourself up, and we'll get back to work."

Robbery

BY KAREN BENDER

ELLA ROSE SAT BESIDE her husband, Lou, as they drove through the streets of the San Fernando Valley. It was dusk, and the streets were grand, golden with the vanishing sun. The car was quiet, for Lou did not turn on the radio, and the two of them did not speak. They had just dropped their retarded daughter, Lena, and Lena's husband, Bob, off at Panorama Village, a residence for people who could not live on their own. Now Ella and Lou were going home.

Ella was in her early sixties, as was Lou, and they had lived in their home on La Buena Street for about forty years. But now she and Lou approached their home cautiously, like robbers. With Lena gone, it seemed an unfamiliar, almost illicit place. Ella could not remember how it felt to have the house belong only to them. Lena had been born thirty-one years ago, and for all that time she had been a constant presence.

The car stopped in front of the house. Lou had left the sprinklers on, and enormous glass flowers seemed to be sprouting out of the lawn. The spray sent thousands of clear droplets sparkling into the air, and the front yard, in its mist, seemed like an unearthly place. Ella and Lou got out of the car and, for a moment, watched the spray.

Then Lou switched off the sprinklers, and the grass glittered in the blue-pink dusk.

Her husband's eyes seemed raw, young to her. "After you," he said to Ella, with a gentlemanly bow.

It had taken Ella a long time to decide that Bob and Lena should live at Panorama Village. Ella had chosen it carefully, and slowly, examining room sizes and dessert offerings and the kindness and number of aides. It was the place that satisfied most of her stringent requirements. That afternoon, Ella helped Lena and Bob arrange snapshots of themselves and the family up on a bulletin board. "Bob's picture goes at the top!" Lena announced, gazing at her prize, her husband of five months. Her admiration made him blush; he watched as she gave his photo its own special spot. Ella understood, in some honest part of herself, that this was where Lena and Bob would live for the rest of their lives.

And it was where she had left her daughter. She did not know what she and Lou would be like now in their home. She went inside and stood in the kitchen. She had made sure to thoroughly clean up before they left, so as to come home to a house in order. Lou grabbed a black cherry soda from the refrigerator and downed it quickly, with great thirst.

They looked at each other like restless children. A variety of feelings hovered, like clouds, in the air. She wanted, just now, to avoid them. They would come upon her, powerfully, soon enough.

Lou stood on the gleaming tile, his hands thrust into his pockets. He was utterly irreplaceable to her. She had not known, when she was first married, what it would be like to love this person, a husband, for so many years. Every marriage was a secret, containing its own bargains, frustrations, and theirs also had its own dealings, its own limits and joys. But right now she felt completely vulnerable to him.

He smiled, a little evil smile, for he sensed she was thinking kind thoughts about him. He shuffled his feet a little and swayed his hips in a silly, hopeful way.

"And, God, could that man dance," he said.

He looked so absurd she could not help laughing. She ducked in to give his stomach a little slap. He grabbed her wrist and held it.

“Let’s look around,” he said.

She and Lou had to reclaim the house. They both understood this. Holding her hand, he stepped into the hallway first. He had always been braver than she was.

Lou did not bother to turn on the lights. It seemed enough to get used to the rooms like this. They walked into the living room. Suddenly, she felt him behind her, his hands on her blouse.

“Don’t move,” he said, softly. He held her waist firmly with one hand, and with the other unbuttoned her blouse and slid it gently off her arms. The air was cool on her bare skin. She looked at him, surprised, a little thrill going up her spine, but could not see his face.

“Let’s go,” he said. She followed him, now in her skirt and bra. His hand was warm, paternal, encircling hers.

Her eyes adjusted to the darkness of the house. In each room, he stopped and removed a piece of her clothing. He did it stealthily, throwing each item onto the floor. He did not touch her besides removing her clothing. Her bra fell onto the floor, then her shoes, then her skirt. He left articles all over the house—strewn beside her cabinet filled with porcelain figurines, tossed onto the wing-backed divan, little piles on the powder-blue carpet.

By the time they had walked a circle around the house, she was naked, and he was still clothed. She could see him gazing at her, and she loved to hold his attention like this; she turned around slowly for him, letting him see all of her.

He came up to her and tenderly stroked her hair, her cool shoulders.

“What about you?” she whispered.

How utterly she knew his body, in all its lives. As a young man, its hard arrogance, the illusion of infinite strength. Then the lovely softness that evolved as he grew older, more successful; in his fifties, the ways he grayed. She did not think either of them looked that different than they did when they were younger. It was only when she saw old photos of them, forty years ago, that she was shocked by the naivete in their expressions, the slickness of their hair. She had always imagined she would look back at the two of them at twenty, envy their smug beauty, but now the untouched quality of their former faces seemed less lovely to her. The young versions of themselves were so greedy. They wanted everything to be easy and right. They could not have known how their shared sorrows would sweeten their lust for each other.

Love was the ultimate form of robbery. She needed to take his body from the rest of the world and make it hers. She went to Lou and removed his clothes quickly, hungrily, and she felt his naked arms, soft but strong, curve around her.

They knelt, carefully, on the carpet of the living room, this most illicit place, and she felt the exquisite pressure of his lips butterfly against her neck, her shoulders, her breasts. "Shh," he said, bringing her down to the floor, beside him. He touched her skin slowly, tenderly, for they took longer now, as though, with age, both of them had become more female. They understood each other's bodies, the responses that delighted and annoyed them utterly, yet now their bodies seemed to be revealing new secrets. He touched her ear in a light way that felt marvelous; she kissed his neck and unearthed a new kind of sigh. Their skin was soft and babyish in the light; her long, steely hair fell out of its clip and tumbled onto him. No one would find them in their living room, trespassers, as they loved each other's hair and skin and lips. In the darkness, in the luscious quiet, they kissed and fell into each other. That night, they made the house theirs.

Aubade

BY CAROLYN BANKS

THE OBITUARY PAGE stared up at her from the foot of the bed. She looked at the faces of the people pictured there: husbands, wives. One day her own photograph would be there, or his. One day she would live alone, or he would.

And what then?

She would feed on remembering those skin-on-skin mornings, the cache of warmth beneath the quilts and blankets of that otherwise cold, high-ceilinged room. The way her eyes would fall on things: his easel, her books.

"Listen to this," he would say, Sundays mostly, in bed with all the fat sections of newspaper. Some bit of news, ironic, unruly, or both.

What else would she think of? Cigarette ashes falling like snow. Light from the north.

And how they wore tops to bed, usually, and were slow to take them off. He would lift his and she hers, and they would yearn against each other. She would feel his ribs and marvel, thinking always of the first time they'd been together and how each time after was the same: delicious and fierce and sweet.

His arms and legs would wind around her. He was climbing her, he said, climbing her higher than he thought a man could go.

And she was tiny beneath his fingers, tiny like the Carolina wren just outside the bedroom door.

Oh, that spring.

He pulled a thick white sweater over his head and went outside without putting on his pants.

They were in the city and she stood in the doorway watching as the darkness lifted. She sneaked back into bed without his knowing she had seen him out there, eyeing the sky near dawn.

And she laughed to think of their neighbors.

When he slid back beside her the room was gray with morning and his knees and his belly and his testicles were cold until she kissed them.

You were awake, he said in mock reproof, reaching for the radio. And then Neil Young's voice, its remarkable innocence, was there in the room too.

No one wins...

No one wins...

"What a fucking lie," he whispered in her ear.

He would paint that morning, day breaking like a blossom, sky bleaching pink. "Baby-ass pink," he would say. And he would tell her how hard it was to find the color, and how long, how long, he had tried.

Anniversary—Eleven Years

BY VICTOR LAVALLE

HIS FACE WAS BAD AWFUL but I loved him because he loved my eggs. I promise. He would say it sometimes, same as last night, when we got down for sleep.

—I love your eggs. You are not barren.

This morning, very early as always, he woke, showered and tried to put a pick through his hair, but the naps had all set in. Real hard. I told him not to get them out, that they were beautiful like the tangled nets when fish are caught—they're full of life. I meant it, I don't lie to my man any more than the minimum—which is thirty percent. You really think he wants to know I've had bigger? Truth is, he fits fine enough so that's what I call him, Fine. He takes it complimentary since he thinks I'm talking about his face; you get to have your little jokes when you're married.

Our home is small, but the bedroom's big. We bought it for that; with both of us working as we do he'd said—We'll be sleeping or out so let's forget a den and all that.

We have enough space in here for two beds, cots too. When relatives visit it becomes like a monastery—we all say our prayers and are otherwise chaste. But as we were alone this morning he hopped about—even in front of the window—and as he stood in the sunlight the blemishes up and across his back came out sure and proud. It looked like he'd been ticked by wasps all over but there was none of that. This silly man had such skin from driving a bus all times and in the heat he would sweat but not move and it ruined his flesh so I can barely rub his shoulders. What a mess.

So he was flipping about like we were young and I pulled the covers over my head, called out—You are a fat fool! To which he answered by perching at the side of the bed where I turn my head when sleeping and slapped a salute against his rump loud enough to sound like lightbulbs being smashed in the next room. When I pulled down my covers he was laughing hard enough for two. Then he said—It's Sunday, better dress for church.

He walked off, his cheeks a bit red from his foolishness, to the closet where he'd prepared a suit and my dress on hangers the night before. But I sat up and let the sheets fall, told him to return to bed presently, that we would be lax this morning and bear the scrutiny of our neighbors and friends next week. I peered to the wall where he'd hung our marriage certificate, all framed as he'd prepared it six years ago, as a gift. Today, if I may say so, I didn't want to share him, even with God.

Fourteen Days and a Possible Cure

BY KARLA KUBAN

HER BOYFRIEND OF EIGHT YEARS took her twice around the world and lavished her with everything. But he withheld what was most accessible: sex, babies. He didn't want babies. Then one day, he packed up and moved to Canada, and for some time they exchanged letters and telephone calls until they agreed that they were *finito*.

For a month after the end, she ate apples and popcorn and toast. She had no appetite for anything else, not because she was so brokenhearted over him, but because she had betrayed herself, fooled her own heart. Her colleagues at the university told her she looked gaunt and depressed. She was nearly forty. "I want a child," she told them. Some sighed and others offered remedies. That new professor in the German department, good genes there. Artificial insemination, maybe? What about a good, safe, one-night stand?

In her fortieth year, a year after she and the boyfriend had split up, here is what occurred: She was artificially inseminated for six months but didn't get pregnant. Her doctor put her on fertility drugs. Her body made big, ripe egg follicles and finally she succeeded. In the fourth month of her pregnancy, she had an amniocentesis. The baby, as seen by the sonogram, bounced inside her womb. The doctor measured its little femur bone. Then he ran a damp, cold cotton swab around inside her navel, disinfected a coin-size area of her stomach, pushed Lidocaine into the disinfected skin and told her to watch the screen. The needle's tip could be seen white, peeking into her womb. He told her to hold her breath and to keep very still. She stopped breathing and the needle broke through. There was a little cramp, but nothing horrible in light of the tumbling baby, beautifully spiderlike, nimble-bodied, bucking. The sonogram was being recorded for her to watch at home.

In seven days, the amnio results came back and indicated that her baby, a boy, had Down's Syndrome. She put a hand to her mouth to keep from crying out. The baby's disabilities and deformities could not be predicted, her doctor said, and she thought: How can I raise this child? Will he live? For how long? She spent the night awake, and in the morning phoned her doctor: "Please. Make the arrangements."

For months after she terminated the pregnancy, she played the videocassette over and over of her baby floating in her womb, flexing and somersaulting, the amnio needle plunging in and withdrawing the fluid. She watched the four-minute video with deadened eyes. She slept on the fold-out couch because she couldn't face the bed (she had spent so much time there, nauseated and tired during her pregnancy). She lost sixteen pounds. She went out only to teach, to hold office hours, to get groceries and stamps. At night she read and read, wishing the words would put her to sleep.

Then one morning, she went to her sliding-glass door and looked out over her backyard. It was small, had a cedar fence around it and a lilac bush in the corner where raccoons had been leaving their droppings in the snow. The nasturtiums and impatiens in red clay planters were bare and brittle, brownish, dead against the snow. She had not taken the cushions off the metal furniture. She hauled them into the basement, each cushion frozen in chair form, stacked them there and went back outside to sweep away the snow on the patio, to pull the dead flowers from the planters and fill the bird feeder with seed.

She went to the music store and bought two CDs, one Renée Fleming, the other an old Donna Summer her ex-boyfriend's dog had taken and buried. At Dunn Bros., a green-haired boy made her a double Café Mocha. She opened the weekly newspaper, *City Pages,* and read the movie reviews. Then the personals. She read "Women in Search of Men" to see if any women advertised for a baby-maker. None did. Then "Men in Search of Women." No men were searching for women to make babies with. There was one that looked as if he might be willing, as if he had the wherewithal: M.D., recently transplanted from Anchorage, 6'1", blue eyes, patiently starved (was this a pun?) ISO SWFDDFHWP (she had to check the key on the back page to decipher the acronyms), who wants/loves walks around Lake of the Isles, Jimi Hendrix blasting, a tent for two in Costa Rica, 911 Turbos, Gorecki, a raw love machine.

She telephoned the voice mail of the *City Pages,* punched in his ad number, left a message and that night he called her back. In their thirty-minute conversation, she learned many things about him: Bob was an only child, he ran six miles a day, had been married and divorced twice, no children. He was an anesthesiologist, not on-call the following night.

They met at the Palomino restaurant. There he was, sitting wide-kneed at the bar. His hair was short and blond; he wore tiny, round, wire glasses; jeans tight as duct tape; black cowboy boots and a white T-shirt. The way he said *Bobby* made her think of the Beach Boys' song "Barbara Ann." Bob Bob Bob. Bob Bobberan. He was halfway through a martini.

She thought of making a joke about his putting people to sleep all day, but she couldn't think of anything too funny. She was looking at him, at his boots and hair and mouth, thinking of making a baby with him. She saw babies, babies, babies in their imagined sex. In his ad he hadn't specified wanting a long-term relationship, a commitment. Weren't non-specifiers out for a good time? They weren't out for babies, were they? Maybe he'd be open to it? No strings attached. No parenting required. He kissed her goodnight at her car door, her back against it, his body pressing urgently into her.

Three nights later, they went to a reading at the Hungry Mind bookstore, and as Michael Ondaatje read, Bob's eyes were brimming with tears. "Did you like that poem?" he whispered into her ear.

Sex, she thought, feeling the forward edge of prospect.

They had dinner and drank a bottle of wine, and he asked her what she wanted to do next.

"Your place," she said.

They went to his car, a neon yellow Porsche, and sped off. He ran a red light. She asked him to pull over and he apologized for scaring her.

"I want to tell you about my baby," she blurted out.

"Oh?" he said.

Then she told him. She told him she wanted to try again, and he said they would have to talk about it, but he was flattered, and then he frowned and asked if she was using him.

"I'm not lying to you, am I?" she said. "If I were using you, I'd lie. I suppose asking for your sperm is asking for something free, for a part of you, but I'm telling you now what I want, so it's your decision."

"Are you ovulating?"

"I might be."

"There are tests for that. You can buy them anywhere."

"I know."

"When was your period?"

"Twelve days ago."

"Then you're ovulating, or about to. Are your periods regular?"

"Yes, and you know the score. I told you. What do you think about it?"

"I'm thinking." He said almost nothing the rest of the way to his place, and she thought, If he doesn't go for it, I'll find another one, and I don't have to be so honest. That's all. I'll keep looking. It's not a perfect situation, but it's rational. It is what it is.

They took the elevator to the twenty-first floor. In the kitchen he leaned her back on the table. He didn't take off her panties, he just pulled the crotch aside. Artificial insemination—a lousy way to get pregnant. A pinch like a straw through the cervix. You don't even feel the semen; it goes directly in so the swimmers don't have to work so hard. Bobberan, she thought.

What did he have to say about her egg and his sperm? Not a thing. He wasn't worried or didn't care. Why ask? Their relationship wasn't founded on stable expectations or committed love. If they pondered over the hows and whys, it might ruin everything.

"I'm tired," she said. "Can we go to bed?" She wasn't hostile or happy. She was hopeful. He led the way to the room and pulled down the covers. In bed, he touched her gently at her temples and down her neck.

The morning-after-Bob was a disappointment for her. He was a doctor; he knew the dope on disease, on sperm and eggs. They hadn't even discussed STDs. Stupid. She was a grown woman. Stupid. She was a masochist, she thought, and wanted to run out of there. Was he really a doctor? Maybe he was sterile. Had he had a vasectomy? She should have checked for the tiny vasectomy scar. Maybe Bob (he had asked her to shout his name, Bobby, Bobby, as he fucked her, and she had whispered it, then shouted Bobberan—God, the things we do when we have sex) was a psycho-killer, and maybe the next time she went to him, he would strangle her. How could she know?

But he called her, they went to a movie that she hated, then back to his place. They undressed in his bedroom, he with a lofty air of superiority, staring at her thinness so she felt mocked and desperate. What did he have in mind? He knew what she had in mind with him. He asked about her siblings, said she was lucky not to have been an only child. Only children are lonely, he said. Then they got into bed.

"What if I'm pregnant?" she asked quietly, so quietly that he asked her to repeat it. When he felt her leg and around her buttocks, he squeezed hard and she told him it hurt.

"Do you think you might be?" he asked, squeezing her breast.

"That hurts. Don't. I told you," she said abruptly. It was as if he'd never heard her say that she wanted a baby. And why would he be so willing to have unprotected sex? She asked this question over and over, but she didn't ask him.

"Good night then," he said, and rolled over. She stood up, turned on the light and dressed. He didn't move. She went to the kitchen and called a cab, waiting in the doorway for the headlights.

He called her the next morning and apologized. He was exhausted, he said, frustrated at work, had been unfair to her. They talked about going to Santa Fe. It would be romantic, they agreed. He said traveling was a good way to get to know each other. She had to admit she was surprised by his suggestion of romance, and she was pleased and willing.

Was he really a doctor? She called the state medical examiner's office. Born in 1945. Graduated from the University of Nebraska. No pending actions against him. "What does that mean?" she asked the clerk, " 'no pending actions'?"

"No pending actions," the woman said.

"Does it mean someone, for example, may have filed a malpractice suit but it hasn't gone to court yet?"

"I don't have that information."

"Lawsuits can take ten years."

"I'm sorry, I don't have that knowledge."

Was her hair right? Did she dress more provocatively when she ovulated? She was not particularly successful in her career, not especially patient in her teaching, wasn't happy in love or socially confident. She was lonely and isolated, and she thought, Buck up.

It snowed two feet and she didn't feel like meeting Bob. She called and told him so, and he said that he'd already bought tickets to the symphony. He would go alone though, he told her, not a problem.

She didn't have the safe option of calling a mutual friend, one who might have set them up, one who could explain Bob's almost obsessive fascination with Bill Gates and the digital watch on his left wrist that illuminated phone numbers (how many eligible women's?), one who could clarify his high school nickname, Roamer (but really, what needed to be clarified about a name like that?), or say why he kept dead roses in a brown bag by his bed, their heads small and shriveled like cherries? When she asked he said, "I don't know," and she felt pathetic for asking. Not knowing didn't bother her so much as the vacant, calm manner of his response.

On the airplane to Santa Fe, they did it in the bathroom. She was convinced by then that because of the reckless manner in which they were doing it, never mind whether she had ovulated or was about to, whether she had or had not lied about her menstrual schedule, he must have had a vasectomy and that was why he was so gung-ho. His eyes in the bathroom seemed vacant one minute, and earnest the next.

The thought of a vasectomy made her cringe. In their seats, she eyed him with contempt. What were the odds of a vasectomy reversal? Fifty percent, no better. She cried now and was embarrassed and turned away from him. She missed her baby. She cried because this man wanted to fuck, but not for a baby. How could she have been so optimistic? But in truth, she'd known all along.

"What's wrong?" he asked.

"I don't know what you want from me."

"Why do I have to want anything?"

"Do you?"

"Sure," he said. "I like you. Let's not get heavy, let's not have one of those discussions I keep sensing you want to have."

"You do?"

"If you want me to define this relationship for you, I can't. We've only just met. We're in the process of getting to know each other. Isn't that okay for now?"

It made sense. Sure it did. She put her head on his shoulder and he kissed her hard on the mouth. He pushed his tongue through and she pulled away.

"Better?" he asked. "We're going to have a very nice time."

"I hate this," she said, and he turned to look out the window. Finally, he looked at her.

"Do you want to tell old Bobby what's wrong?"

"No thanks."

"Is it something I said?"

"It's something you didn't say," she said, "but I'm not myself and it's not your fault." She dismissed the whole thing with a wave of her hand. He put his hand on her thigh. Her smile was as tight as a bootlace, and she practically mouthed the words so that he had to lean in to her. "Do you do this very often? Take trips like this, with women?"

"This jealousy," he said, "is getting to me."

"This is the first time I asked."

"I can sense it with you all the time."

"So I'm a mess. Shoot me."

He picked up his Bill Gates book and buried his nose in it. She watched him read. He looked over at her and cleared his throat. He cracked his neck by moving it right and left. He smiled at her. She smiled back. He told her her eyes were so bright, such a blue, in the light there. With his face in the light, the light of the sunny blue, above-clouds sky, she noticed a small, barely visible line at the bottom of his teeth, slightly up from the ivory edge. Inside were lines of his authentic teeth that laminate had overlain. She noticed his hair, streaked the many colors of blond, the colors summer sun puts into tawny or auburn hair. But his roots were dark. So he's vain. Big deal. Or adventurous. So what?

At the Albuquerque airport, they rented a Jeep. At the hotel, they checked in and threw their luggage in the room. It was late, nearly ten, and they hadn't eaten. They had dinner downstairs and crashed into bed, sleeping without touching.

In the morning, they ate bagels and drank grapefruit juice and went out to shop in the plaza. She bought a pair of silver crucible earrings with malachite orbs. At a street kiosk, they ate two burritos. They went back to the hotel and took a shower together, and she lathered his cock with soap. He put it in her, soapy, and it stung. She pulled away. They rinsed and dried off and waltzed to the bed, and he entered her from behind, her mouth over the cool pillowcase.

"Bob? You said you were tested for AIDS. But there's a six-month window. You know?" She suddenly felt as if anything she spoke about was unimportant, out of context and silly. He slumped back on the sheets and groaned.

"Have you ever had sex with a man?"

"What?" he said angrily. "Don't I seem slightly hetero to you?"

"That has nothing to do with whether or not you've had sex with a man. Have you ever used needle drugs?"

"I don't think this conversation has anything to do with me. What's the matter? I mean, this is ridiculous."

"Why don't you answer me?"

"I'm exhausted. I could strangle you."

He rolled over and put the pillow on top of his head. She imagined herself a mother dangling a puppet, her child the only audience, clapping at the marionette. Then the image wheeled away and she saw the back of his head and the deception and awkwardness between them. She wanted to talk, wanted to fix it, but she would wait. She lay there for another hour, thinking how he might react to her tomorrow, how he would feel and be, whether he would touch her or not. Maybe she'd be surprised.

In the morning she woke up to little fish kisses up and down her spine. He tried to roll her under him. When she would not dive, he tried to push her head down on him. At first she resisted, but she wanted to go below to take a good look at the place where a surgeon might have opened him up and sealed him. The light was dim. She couldn't reach the nightstand light, and when she tried he asked what she was doing. She took his cock in her mouth and bit it slightly. He moaned in pleasure. She bit harder. He slapped the top of her head. She pulled back and went into the bathroom. "What's wrong?" he called.

She closed the door and drew herself a cool bath and felt something just short of guilt, wished she were here alone, could walk and walk, not sense the changes in his mood and her own neediness. She decided to towel off and go out there and apologize, to ask questions, tell him more about herself, dance with him, spit on the floor—anything but this cool bath and her own volatile fears. She was eager to get out but the blood of eagerness drained, and she slid deeper into the suds.

They drove ninety miles to Angel Fire to look at land. Bob had considered buying a ten-acre parcel and building a log home on it. The land up there was just about to take off, investment-wise. While he rattled on, she could only think of her baby and the way it had fluttered in her womb. One more month and she would have felt the baby as more than butterfly wings.

Bob didn't like the realtor. He didn't like East Coast men, he'd whispered to her while the realtor answered his phone. She liked the realtor just fine. He told them how he'd cleared his own land, how he and his wife owned a nine-acre piece with a view of the ski mountain, about his recent heart attack, his grandchildren. He tried to talk Bob into a steep ten-acre plot in back of the trailer that was his office. They walked up and down the property and when the realtor asked, "How do you like it?" Bob said, "It's a dog. Why don't you show me something decent, okay?" The realtor, twisting his hands, told them, "All right, let's take a ride."

He took them to a flat piece with a creek running through. They got out and walked up the creek to the edge of the property. Bob stood by the trickle of water (it was winter and the water wouldn't run hard until late spring, the realtor said), asking about trout and paved roads. It was there in the afternoon light that she saw it. He had put a finger up to scratch his cheek and pulled the skin forward, and the sun caught the thin white scar. When the skin came back after his fingers left his cheek, the skin-fold covered the scar. As they walked back to the car, she thought of the ways in which she was vain, and that charm was vanity, giving to get something back. She knew how to be charming, but she'd lost her will. She was real with him. Real in a puttylike way and unable to concentrate.

"What's wrong with you?" he asked quietly.

"This is the third time you've asked today," she said.

"But what is it?"

"Well," she said, rolling down her window. Cold afternoon air filled the Jeep and the windows crooned from the wind. Bob turned on the heat. "Well," she said again, "did you have your teeth fixed?"

"What does that matter?"

"I saw the lines of your real teeth under the laminate, or whatever it is."

"Is that a crime? My teeth are bad."

"If I had a baby with you—"

"A baby? What are you—"

"—what color hair do you suppose it would have?"

"You know, we were getting along so well. This is crazy. A baby?"

"I guess it would have brown hair; I don't think it would be blond."

"I don't think I need to apologize for that. Do I?"

"The scar on your ear. I'm hungry. Could we stop at the next fast food? I could go for a cup of coffee. Did you have a facelift? And did you have the big V?"

"The what?"

"You act pretty stupid for a smart guy. Did you?"

He veered the car to the right, to the west, where a gravel space for a scenic overlook narrowed into a dirt road that seemed to roll all the way to the horizon. The land was wavy with violet sage, the Jemez angling south, the peaks coated in glistening white.

"Have you flipped your lid?"

"Drive on, please," she said. If she had a knife, she would hold it to his throat. She'd make him drive. She didn't want to be stuck with him here, looking out at such beauty. It would make her cry again.

He pulled onto the highway and drove with one hand, reaching over with the other to touch her hair, her cheek, the oval hollow part of her neck. At least they had sex, she thought, something that people had had since the beginning of time, naked people, people who scavenged for food and whose teeth rotted and who died from abscessed teeth. In the beginning of time when people had nothing, and the making of a fire was something, and charring meat, when the wet red body of a baby slid out of its mother's tunnel and its blanket was tree boughs or moss, there was always sex alone or with someone else, and love, or the attempt to love.

"Did you have a vasectomy?" she asked, small, cold tears running down her chin.

"Enough!" he said, hitting the steering wheel with the heel of his hand. "I think we should fly back tonight. Really."

"You think, or we should? Did you?"

"You take everything I've ever done to try to make myself more seem like less. You try to humiliate me."

"A vasectomy makes you more, and you think my asking the question is humiliating you?"

“Whatever I want to do with myself, that is my business. Please shut up. Let’s catch an early plane and go back.”

“Everyone fakes it from time to time. You’re phonier than most. Maybe that’s why you’re such a good fuck.”

“I beg your pardon?”

“Don’t act so shocked.”

They checked out and drove silently back to Albuquerque, where they caught the plane two days before their scheduled departure and flew back to the Twin Cities. He was not speaking to her, not at all, and his neck had broken out in a faint rash. The sky littered her front yard with a translucent coating of snow.

“Why don’t you come in?” she said, leaning into his car window.

“Thank you, no.”

“Please. Oh please, Bob. I have something to—”

“What is it—a gun? A bullet?” He half laughed. “Because I’m scared of you. You’re one scary woman.”

She opened her mouth a little but did not speak for a few seconds. He was already backing out. When she yelled, Stop, he kept going, and she ran into the street and threw down her fisted hands.

She stormed into the bathroom and took a pregnancy test. Negative, as she’d suspected. In her living room, she slid the baby video into the VCR, watched it once, then rewound and watched again, attentively, the one part: the baby’s left thumb upturned, leg extending, at which point she remembered, in the doctor’s office, she had felt the boy’s foot graze her like a butterfly wing. She held her breath now as she had held it then, as the rounded needle tip, rounded so as not to hurt the baby should he bump against it, popped into his ellipse. She turned on the television and tapped through the channels, hunting for something to record over baby.

Music for Torching

BY A. M. HOMES

[THEIR OWN HOME damaged by a fire, Elaine and her husband, Paul, are staying with their suburban neighbors, Pat and George. It is a weekday morning; the kids are at school, the husbands left for work hours ago.]

Elaine is awake. She is embarrassed to have slept late. She lies in the bed thinking that what she has to do now is get up, get dressed, and go home. She has to fix the house, fix herself, and focus on what comes next. She has to plan for the future. Her plan is to go downstairs, have a quick cup of coffee, and then go home.

Pat is in the kitchen. She is on the phone and also ironing. "Good morning," she whispers to Elaine.

"Morning," Elaine says.

The coffeepot is on. Elaine pours herself a cup and leans against the counter. Pat is still in her robe. Her hair is a mess. On the table is a bowl of pineapple slices, left over from the night before—no muffins, no warm morning pastries, no fresh-baked bread. Elaine checks the clock—ten A.M. How odd. Pat in her robe, Pat serving leftovers. If Pat can't keep it together, who can?

Pat is smiling at Elaine, practically grinning. Why?

"What?" Elaine asks.

"You're so lovely," Pat says, and Elaine isn't sure if Pat is talking to her or the person on the phone.

Elaine sits down with her coffee and begins reading the paper. In the background Pat is ordering lamb. "Page forty-three. Could I have three racks and then one leg?"

Elaine had never heard of anyone having meat mailed to them.

"Over the phone. Door to door. Hardware, underwear, shoes, food, everything," Pat says as she's hanging up. "It saves me so much time." Pat sprays starch on the last of the shirts and digs in, wrestling the wrinkles.

"I slept late," Elaine says sheepishly.

"Every day isn't perfect," Pat says. "Some days start strangely."

Is that why she's still in her robe? As Elaine reaches across the table for the sugar, the coffee sloshes, it splashes onto Elaine's clean white shirt. "Shit," she says, jumping up, running to the sink, blotting it with a kitchen sponge.

"Take it off," Pat says.

"I'm not dressed," Elaine says, pulling the stained fabric away from her skin—she's braless.

Pat takes something out from under the sink, squirts it directly onto the shirt, and rubs thoroughly with her bare hand. The spot disappears. "Will you let me iron it?" Pat asks.

Elaine hesitantly unbuttons the shirt and slips it off.

Pat moves to the ironing board to press the blouse dry. Steam rises from under the iron. Goose bumps come up on Elaine's skin. She crosses her arms over her chest.

Pat holds the shirt open for Elaine, like a bullfighter's cape. *Toro.*

"Thanks," Elaine says, sliding her arm in.

There's something delicious about the shirt, crisp, bright white against her skin. The cotton is hot on the spot where the coffee spilled, the place where Pat worked it. Hot against cold, Elaine closes her eyes and lets the warmth soak in. "Thanks," she says again.

Pat is moving in a slow circle around Elaine, lifting Elaine's hair out from inside the neck of the blouse.

Something brushes against Elaine's neck. What? What was that? A prickly triangle. Elaine turns toward it, turning toward the trouble, wanting to see what's what. It's Pat. Pat kissing her. Pat kisses her again. Pat kisses her on the lips. "Ummmm, ummm," Pat murmurs.

A whirl, a dizzying spin.

The purple press of Pat's lips is insistent and sure. Pat is kissing her, and Elaine isn't sure why. She pulls back and looks at Pat. Pat's eyes are closed, her face a dissolve coming at Elaine again. Elaine turns slightly to the side, avoiding her. The kiss lands on Elaine's cheek. Pat's eyes blink open—baffled. Something. Guilt. Confusion. Elaine can't think, can't see, can't breathe, but she doesn't want to give Pat the wrong idea, she doesn't want to say no, she doesn't want Pat to be hurt. Elaine kisses Pat.

The kiss, unbearably fragile, a spike of sensation, shoulders the frame. Everything Elaine thinks about who she is, what she is, is irrelevant. There are no words, only sensation, smooth sensation. Tender, like the tickling lick of a kitten. Elaine feels powerless, suddenly stoned. Pat is kissing her. She is kissing Pat. They are standing in the middle of the kitchen, giving and getting every kiss they've ever gotten or given; kissing from memory. Kissing: fast, hard, deep, frantic, long and slow. They are tasting the lips, the mouth, the tongue. Elaine puts her hands to Pat's face, the softness of Pat's skin; the absence of the rough scruff and scratch of a stale shave is so unfamiliar as to seem impossible. Pat rubs her face against Elaine's—sweeping the cheek, the high, light bones, muzzling the ear, the narrow line of the eyebrow, finishing with a butterfly flick of the lashes.

Elaine's mind struggles to make sense, to find familiar coordinates—it spins uselessly.

Pat reaches for Elaine's hand. "Come," she says.

"Where are you taking me?" Elaine asks in an airless voice.

"Bedroom."

"No," Elaine says, fast, firm. Bed, that's breaking a rule—a rule she didn't know she had. It is like being a teenager again. There are things you will and won't do. Bed is too much. Pat and George's bed, their twins' twin beds—no. Bed is out of the question. So far it is a kiss, just a kiss, nothing truly unforgivable. "No," she says again.

"Am I frightening you?" Pat asks, coming in close, whispering the question right into Elaine's mouth. Kissing. "Am I?" Pat's hand is on Elaine's shirt, on the buttons.

Elaine, not wanting to offend, breathes, "No," even though she is terrified.

Pat undoes the buttons. It feels amazingly good. Pat is unbuttoning the blouse, brushing her lips against Elaine's neck, her clavicle, going lower.

Elaine fixates on the blouse, holding it against her body, worrying it will get wrinkled.

"Don't worry," Pat says, pulling the blouse away. "I'll iron it. I promise, I'll iron it again when we're done."

The shirt falls to the floor.

Elaine bends to pick it up. She stops to drape it over the back of a chair.

It's fine, Elaine tells herself, if it's only a kiss. Fine as long as the clothing is on, fine if only her shirt is off, fine if... She's making rules and instantly breaking them.

Pat is at her breast. A noise escapes Elaine, an embarrassingly deep sigh—like air rushing out of something. Elaine can't believe that she's letting this happen; she's not stopping it, she's not screaming, she's enjoying it. Pat is kissing Elaine's belly, tonguing the cesarean scar that no one ever touches. Elaine reaches for Pat—there's an incredible strangeness when they touch simultaneously. Elaine can't tell who is who, what is what—Marcel Marceau, a mirror game, each miming the other. Phenomenal confusion. Elaine touches Pat's breast, pressing. Her knees buckle, she collapses to the floor. Pat goes with her.

They are in the kitchen, down on the linoleum floor. It is fine, Elaine tells herself, fine as long as Pat is dressed, fine as long as Elaine keeps what's left of her clothes on.

"Is this all right?" Pat asks.

"Nice," Elaine manages to say.

Luscious. Delicious. Pat is smooth and buttery, not like Paul, not a mass of fur, a jumble of abrasion from beard to prick. Pat is soft, enveloping.

Elaine is thinking that it'll stop in a minute, it won't really happen, it won't go too far. It's just two women exploring. She remembers reading about consciousness-raising groups, women sitting in circles on living-room floors, looking at their cervixes like little boys in circle jerks, women taking possession of their bodies. Only this is far more personal—Pat is taking possession of Elaine.

Pat is pulling Elaine's pants off. Elaine is lifting her hip, her khakis are tossed off under the kitchen table. Pat is still in her robe. Elaine reaches for the belt, half thinking she will use it to pull herself up, she will lift herself up and out of this. The robe opens, exposing Pat.

Pat spreads herself out over Elaine, skin to skin, breast to breast. Pat against her, not ripe, repulsive. She almost screams—it's like a living thing—tongue and teeth.

And Pat is on top, grinding against Elaine, humping her in a strangely prickless pose. Fucking that's all friction.

She reaches her hand under Elaine's ass to get a better grip. Crumbs. There are crumbs stuck to Elaine's ass. Horrified, Pat twists around and begins licking them off, sucking the crumbs from Elaine, from the floor, and swallowing them like a human vacuum cleaner. "I sweep," she says, wiping dust off her mouth. "I sweep every day. I'm sweeping all the time."

"It's all right," Elaine says. "It's fine."

Fine if it's only on the outside, fine if it's just a hand. Fine if it's fingers and not a tongue, and then fine if it is a tongue. Fine if it's just that, and then it's fine. It's all fine.

They are two full-grown women, mothers, going at each other on the kitchen floor. A thick, musky scent rises, a sexual stew.

Pat reaches up. Pulling a pot holder shaped like a bright red lobster off the counter, tucking it under Elaine's head—from above Elaine looks as if she has claw-shaped devils' horns sticking out of her head. "That's better," Pat says.

"Thank you," Elaine says. "I was starting to get a headache."

"Mmmm," Pat says, spinning her tongue in circles.

"Mmmm," Elaine echoes involuntarily.

Pat's fingers curl between Elaine's legs, slipping in.

"Aooww," Elaine says, combining "Ah" and "Ow," pain and pleasure. It takes a minute to figure out what hurts. "Your ring," Elaine pants.

The high diamond mount of Pat's engagement ring is scraping her. Pat pulls off the ring, it skitters across the floor, and she slips her hand back into Elaine, finding the spot. She slips in and out more quickly, more vigorously.

Elaine comes in cacophonous convulsions, great guttural exaltations. She's filled with a flooding sensation, as though a seal has broken; her womb, in seizures, squeezes as though expelling Elaine herself.

And just as she thinks it's over, as she starts to relax, Pat's mouth slides south, and Elaine is flash-frozen at the summit of sensation, her body stun-gunned by the flick of Pat's tongue. She lies splayed out on the linoleum, comparing Pat to Paul: Paul goes down on her because he saw it in a porno movie, because he thinks it's the cool thing to do. Paul goes down on her like he's really eating her, like she's a Big Mac and he's got to get his mouth around the whole burger in one big bite.

Elaine is concentrating, trying to figure out exactly what Pat is doing. Every lick, every flick causes an electric surge, a tiny sharp shock, to flash through her body.

She is seeing flashes of light, fleeting images. It's as though she's losing consciousness, losing her mind, dying. She can't bear any more—it's too much. She pushes Pat away.

"Stop," she says, closing her legs. "It's enough."

Pat lies next to her. Pat kisses her. Elaine tastes herself on Pat's lips, a tart tang, surprisingly slick, a lip-gloss lubricant. Their mouths move over each other, hungry.

They begin again.

She owes Pat something.

Elaine's hand moves down, over the rolling hill of Pat's belly, the slow arch of her pelvis. The absence of balls, of the ropy, rock-hard root, is strange, simultaneously familiar and un-. Elaine rubs Pat, working fast and furtively in the swampy heat, doing what needs to be done, not lingering. Pat fills with blood, becoming thick, fibrous, seeming to swell, to tighten on Elaine's hand. Out of character and undignified, Pat writhes athletically, enthusiastically, on the floor. She comes with a long, low moan.

They are finished.

Elaine looks around the kitchen—at the cabinets, the counters, noticing that the coffeemaker is still on and that they kicked the kitchen table, knocking some of the sections of the newspaper to the floor. Her thigh is stuck to the linoleum; she peels it up; it makes a thick sucking sound. She is naked on the kitchen floor with a pot holder tucked under her head as if she's had some strange household accident. Her underwear is across the room, by the refrigerator; her khakis are under the kitchen table; her blouse, draped over the chair. She is doused in the queer perfume of sex, drowsy—as though awakened from a dream before it ended.

"You're a treat," Pat says. "A delicacy. I never get to kiss. George doesn't like it."

Elaine is crawling around on all fours, rounding up her clothing, wondering, What do you do now? How do you bring yourself to standing? How do you get up, get dressed and move along?

"How about a bath, a long, hot bath?" Pat asks.

Elaine pulls on her underwear and looks at the kitchen clock. "I can't," she says. "Look at the time; it's eleven-thirty. Aren't you worried about having gotten off schedule?"

Pat shrugs. She finds her ring on the floor and puts it in her mouth, sucking it to clean it.

Elaine is dressing as fast as she possibly can. She can't believe what she's done: Okay, so Pat kissed her—George doesn't like to kiss, and Pat needed a kiss, but what about the rest—did it really happen? Has Pat done this before? Does Pat think it was all Elaine's fault? And why is Elaine thinking fault? Why is she blaming herself? Pure panic.

"Are you all right?" Pat asks.

"It's fine," Elaine says, hurrying.

Elaine needs to be in her car going home, she needs to be someplace familiar and safe, she needs a few minutes alone. She is suffering the strange anxiety of having risen so far up and out of herself as to seem entirely untethered. She's scared herself—as though this has never been done before, as though she and Pat invented it right there on the kitchen floor. She wonders if she's suffered some odd injury—did she hurt herself? Did Pat scrape her? Will she get an infection? Will she have to tell someone—explain it? She fumbles frantically with the buttons on her blouse.

"You seem upset," Pat says, slipping back into her robe.

"I just feel...like I'm running late. I slept late, and then, well, this happened. And now I'm really late. I should go." Elaine practically runs for the door.

"Something special you want for dinner?" Pat calls after her. "What's your favorite food? Wednesday is grab bag. Everyone puts in their wishes, and each person ends up getting at least one thing they want."

Nothing, Elaine wants nothing.

"You can't leave without naming something," Pat says.

"Beets," Elaine says, racing.

"Oh, that's good, that's great. I never would have thought of that," Pat says.

Elaine throws the car into gear and pulls away—she hates beets. Why did she say beets? She drives around the block, pulls up in front of the house, and blows the horn. Pat opens the door, thrilled that Elaine has returned. She leans forward, as though expecting Elaine to make some declaration along the lines of "I love you," or at least "Thanks, that was fun." Elaine rolls down the window and shouts her confession across the lawn. "I hate beets. I don't know why I said that."

Pat's face takes a fall.

"Asparagus," Elaine says. "Asparagus is fine."

"Oh," Pat calls back, recovering. "Oh, good. Asparagus is a good thing."

A Story Problem

BY DARCY COSPER

LET X = X. There are things to solve. There are many variables. There are elements to be accounted for. There are trajectories to identify. There are forces to be reckoned with.

Your answers will count. You must show your work. Pay attention.

You are at a party. Let us say, for the sake of argument, that it is a large party, it is a large city, it is deep summer. Let us say that there are many people and that they are restless in certain ways and dressed with intent and the room is big and less than bright but more than dim.

The party is very large and crowded and the music is loud and heat is close and pressing and the women twist their hair up off their necks and pluck at their shirts and people flap their hands and everyone says to everyone else, It's so hot it's so hot.

There is only one person in this room you have fucked more than once. Let him be represented by the letter *A*. You were with him for years. It was not so long ago. He leans against the wall, you see him in pieces through a mass of people. He is talking to a woman, B, who is a close friend of yours. She is the former lover of C, a close friend of A's. Three of the four of you once shared a bed, a night, made certain exchanges, ignored consequences.

C is on the other side of the room, talking with D, frail and sleepy-eyed, a childhood friend of B's who C tangled with for a month before some resistance brought things to a halt. Standing with them is E, sultry, sulky, once wooed and tumbled by A, the only time you know of that he stepped out on you. She is large and absurdly beautiful and angry tonight and you travel along her gaze to a corner of the room. She is looking at F, who has fucked B, D and, long ago, G, who is talking to him while she waves to you. J brushes past and his hand lingers at your waist and he is with the girl he was cheating on when years ago you let him seduce you and now she is his wife and K, whose marriage is falling apart, comes to drop a kiss on your brow and asks you to dinner the following week, and he is with the woman he would not harm though he wanted to when you tried to seduce him and didn't sleep for weeks imagining the length of his body and the shape of his face, and you are all smiling and dazed and everyone says to everyone else It's so hot isn't it so terribly hot let's have another drink.

Later you will talk to F, lean, dark-eyed, and he will let one finger come to rest on the delicate sharp point of your hip and E will come in her lovely rage to slip between the two of you and she will not cast a glance back to acknowledge the space you occupy nor will you move. Later F will take E home and return to the party and G will tell you that E is another in the string of women F has been with between the sheets, and for a moment you will imagine fucking H, the man who broke E's heart—you will imagine this not out of malice but out of a desire for continuity.

Later still, G will leave with a boy who pressed you against the bathroom sink, and you will wonder how many more people each of you would have to fuck for the sake of perfect symmetry. You will wonder what is to be added to this equation tonight.

Let us say that you are at a party and it is a dense late summer night and the weather will never break, never, and your shoulders are bare and slick, that there is a hand resting on one of them, and the hand belongs to a man and there is a wedding ring on this hand. He is standing beside a woman who is not his wife, a tall woman who gave you a slow, appraising smile that made your breath catch when she arrived. Now it is later, it is late, and this tall woman hands you a glass of wine and slips her arm around you and leans to kiss you, and when your wet mouths part the man who is married lets his hand slip from your shoulder and stares and asks Are you for real? And she tells him No, we're just a projection of your desires and you think that she may be right.

Let us say that everyone has had a certain amount to drink, and that you are watching L, a round-eyed cupid-lipped girl introduced to you by B, a girl who has pursued your friendship with a force that unsettles you. Tonight she is an object propelled and drawn by the heat of others. You watch her careen from one group to another, easing herself into the crevices that separate their bodies. Later tonight, so much later, she will kiss A, and he will walk away from her into the dark and call you from the street. And when he calls, one of the people in this room right now will be in your bed, and together from the tangle of sheets you will listen to the answering machine absorb his confession and his anger and his love. You will wish to be alone, you will regret nothing but the rawness between your legs, the rawness of your mouth, the ferocious roughness of the hands that gripped you tonight. You will stand naked in the dark at the door to your apartment and wave goodbye.

Let the letters not yet assigned stand for variables, individuals, situations you don't know, can't see.

Now solve for these things:

The weights of wine and ice and bourbon.

Melting points and breaking points.

The salt content of sweat, of semen. The surface area of naked skin.

The equal and opposite reactions.

The distance from all centers, the gravitational pull of bodies, the relation of objects.

The velocity of desire.

The probability of grace.

The sum of longing.

The space between us.

Alex

BY ELIZABETH WURTZEL

HE STANDS AT THE ENTRANCE to his apartment as I walk up the stairs. His face is between the door and the post, as if it is stuck in a picture frame. He says hi and pulls the door open to greet me. The knob is missing. He is wearing gray sweatpants and a cut-up Jack Daniel's T-shirt with a red bandanna tied on his head. I remember his publicist telling me he is bald underneath.

I follow him across the room. His apartment is just one room. A long one. The bed is at the other end, underneath the window, which faces south but is too coated in white dirt to let much sunlight in. All over the walls are *Playboy* centerfolds and pictures of motorcycles and of various heavy-metal acts—even a poster of his band. To the side of the bed are a TV and VCR, and the tape in the player says SEX KITTEN. On the other side of the bed are a stereo and some records and tapes, mostly groups I haven't heard of. He falls on the bed as soon as he approaches it, which is understandable since there is no other furniture in the whole place. I'm so tired, he says. I guess that is an explanation. He clings to his pillow and squeezes the covers between his legs like a little baby. I keep wondering if he ever takes the do-rag off.

I sit on the edge of the bed. I am wearing a long, straight, blue cotton skirt, a sleeveless black shirt and black suede boots. I rarely look so conservative. All I can think to do is sit there and say, Great place. I notice a Polaroid of a little white cat on the mantel over the bed. It doesn't look like something Alex might own.

I ask, How is your cat? And he says, Bad question. He's still in the hospital.

I ask, How is your bike? Another bad question, he tells me. It's still in the shop. It needs $700 worth of repairs.

Oh, I say.

Listen, I volunteer, I can see you're tired, so I can just leave. We can do this some other time.

No, he says. His voice is muffled. Please stay. His hand clasps on to the empty side of the bed beside him. He pats it the way I pat my futon when I want the cat to come curl up with me.

Lie down, he commands.

A few days before, we are on the phone making plans. I suggest we have a drink sometime, and he says maybe Monday or Tuesday, and then we are talking about our cats. He tells me that Alby is in the Animal Medical Center because while he was on the road in Asia, the cat ate some telephone wire and got dehydrated. Alby was alone in the apartment, although people came by to feed him, but the cat ate the phone cord in protest. It would cost Alex $600 to get Alby out of the hospital, and he didn't have the money to do it. So he misses the cat.

He's just like me, Alex says of Alby. He gets self-destructive when he's angry.

Yes, I say, it sounds that way.

I feel sorry for Alex. It seems like he really loves the little animal, and I think a person like him should not be deprived of the one thing he might really care about. I feel bad for Alby because he is being deprived of the person who loves him. And then I think, if the cat got into such bad condition living with Alex, maybe he is better off at the hospital.

Don't you find it strange that almost all we've been talking about for the last half hour are our cats? I ask.

No. Alex doesn't think so at all. He says, Compared to most people I know, my cat is really cool.

I lie down on the bed next to him, thinking that there is nothing wrong with having a conversation while prone. There's no other furniture in the apartment, after all. No chairs to sit on civilly. And he is tired. As I get near him, he stinks of whiskey, definitely hard stuff. He told me he's been up for three nights straight partying. His publicist told me that he'd given up on drinking, that all he does now is work out. His arms and chest are muscled and rippled like a person who lifts weights but his face is lined and puffy like a person who doesn't do anything good to his body.

I am facing him. I try to make conversation. I hear you got thrown out of prep school.

Yeah. Lawrenceville. I got pretty well educated before I got expelled.

I ask what he did wrong but he doesn't answer. Did you ever finish school? I ask.

Yeah. In Florida.

Is that where your family lives?

Yeah.

Still?

Yeah.

He rolls me to my side so that I'm not facing him, and pulls me close so that we are layered in fetal position, curled up like two plastic spoons that got bent out of shape by the heat. Maybe he wants to cuddle up when we talk. I'm sorry, he says, pulling me tighter, but this is all I can do right now, I'm so tired.

I am surprised by how nice it feels to be in someone's arms. I examine his bicep, and look at the tattoo from Hawaii. A girl in a bikini and hula skirt says, WISH YOU WERE HERE. There is another one, the Hell's Angels logo: RIDE HARD, DIE FREE. He has tattoos across his knuckles, up his arms, on his chest and back. All I have is a tiny tattoo on my shoulder blade. It says FTW, which stands for *Fuck the World.*

The first time I met Alex was at the recording studio. He was being interviewed by a reporter from some metal magazine in the lounge while the producer was mixing tracks and adding some twelve-string guitar lines in the other room. She was asking Alex about his tattoos when I first walked in.

Some people think of it as an art form, but I just like them all over my body, he tells her.

I ask him if it hurt. I bled a little, he says.

I tell him about my tattoo, which a boy I had an affair with at college gave me, using a sewing needle and thread and some indelible black ink that has faded to a greenish-bluish gray by now. It said FTW on the boy's hip, which was pretty much the only thing I liked about him, the only reason I was so eager to pull his pants off night after night so I could look at that mark and feel like he was a skate punk instead of a Harvard student like me. The night he did it I drank a whole bottle of white zinfandel and half a bottle of Wild Turkey so that I wouldn't have to feel the needle prick at my skin.

I say, It didn't hurt at all.

He asks to see it. He is sitting on a couch next to the woman who is interviewing him. I know she really isn't interested in seeing my tattoo. His publicist stands across the room, offering us some fruit: oranges and bananas in a basket. I can tell she is curious about the tattoo. I open a few buttons of the green cropped sweater and pull it over my shoulder. I am glad that I have a nice black bra on. I pull the strap over my arm too.

Alex looks at it.

I tell him I want it fixed since the guy did sort of a sloppy job.

He says, If you give me your phone number, I can call you and tell you the name of a good tattoo artist.

He pulls me close and kisses my ear. He must know he stinks of alcohol because he reaches over my head and grabs something, I can't see what it is, but he sticks it in his mouth and starts chewing. At first I think it is some pill to keep him from falling back to sleep. It is green Trident. He turns me onto my back and starts kissing me on the mouth. I taste the mint and I taste the whiskey it hides. He kisses me all over my face and digs a hole in my ear with his tongue, which makes my throat hurt. He leaves a trail of sticky stuff wherever his mouth goes.

I don't know how to say this is unpleasant.

Does your family still live in Florida? I ask.

Yeah. It's a shithole down there.

I don't ask why. I just wonder why they left Canada in the first place.

'Cause they're dumb.

It occurs to me that he probably didn't like school very much. This is a hard concept for me to grasp because teachers were always my friends, I always enjoyed reading—I just liked learning a lot. Alex has tattoos all over his body and he plays in a heavy metal band and he doesn't have a phone because he never bothers to pay his bills, but I only begin to understand the difference between me and him because of his attitude toward school, toward family, toward home. All those things make me unhappy too, but for different reasons.

I thought for a while that he was a rich prep school refugee who just does heavy metal as some sort of act of rebellion. But lying here, I understand that he is what he is and that's it. He is not slumming. He is white trash. He hates life. Compared to most people I know, my cat is really cool. He has no choice but the one he has already made. It is the prep school career that was an aberration. Everything that has happened since he got thrown out makes perfect sense.

He is now on top of me. Kissing my face some more and nibbling on my hair, which is getting stuck together with green gum. I think, We can just kiss. There's nothing wrong with this.

Then his hands move underneath my skirt. I have no underwear on. He massages the most inner part of my inner thighs and I say, Alex we shouldn't be doing this.

I know, he says. That's why we're going to.

Alex, I say. Today my editor just asked me if I've been fucking around with Don Henley and Steve Tyler from Aerosmith, because he heard some rumors about that from someone at *The New York Times*. Funny thing is, they aren't true. I've never even met either of them.

Oh, he says.

But this is true, I continue. And this is bad for my professional decorum.

Decorum's the wrong word, he says.

My professional standards then—you know what I mean, I say.

Standards is a better word, he says.

Alex, I ask, giving up on the last conversation. Alex, how come you never hit on me before? I didn't even think you found me attractive.

The time wasn't right, he explains. You can't analyze these things.

His hands move under my shirt and under my bra. He rubs my chest and his thumbs make circles around my nipples. I say, I'm probably the only woman in New York who wears a bra and doesn't wear underwear.

That's okay. I like bras.

I decide to stick my hand under his shirt, to seem like I'm participating. He pushes my hands down his stomach and pulls my fingers below the drawstring and into his pants and the flesh I touch there is so hard and so long and so large, it surprises me a little. I usually think that tough guys are trying to compensate for what they lack between their legs. But no.

I hold it tight at first, because it's all I can do, and then I run my fingers along the ridges, curious, interested. I worry that I'm not doing anything to make him feel good. Then I realize, he's not doing anything to make me feel good either. But I feel obligated to act like I'm enjoying myself.

I moan. I wonder when this will stop. Usually, with most guys, maybe on the first date, you neck until someone says that maybe we should stop. Just because you've kissed somebody doesn't mean you're going to fuck them, and certainly not the first time you're together.

But I understand that with Alex I don't stand a chance. I crossed an invisible line as soon as I walked through the door. If I stay, I have to do it. My other option is to leave. And I don't want to leave.

I am seeing the band in concert for the first time after hearing an advance tape of their new album, which I like a lot. Alex is wearing a white, rather sheer blouse and tattered jeans. The shirt hangs loosely around his hips. He has dark spectacles on. He doesn't sing; he growls. He reminds me of Jim Morrison.

A friend of his is in the audience. Alex introduces him and pulls him on the stage. Big Joe here is going to be a big star, he promises. Come on, Joe, show us your rock star collagen smile.

I think it is clever of Alex to modify "smile" with "collagen." He must be pretty bright, I think.

Next, he reaches out to the audience and does a high five with a tall blond guy with dreadlocks and a red bandanna who looks a little like Alex. He is actually better-looking than Alex, his features sharp, his skin smooth and clear. Alex minus the damage.

This is my little brother, he says as he pulls the lanky blond boy toward the stage. My fucking little brother. I guess he's not so little, he's got at least four inches on me. Height-wise, that is. I don't know about his pecker. Is there anyone here who's done a comparison?

Backstage after the show, Alex is sitting and drinking beer with some skinny frail-looking blond woman-child at his side. At various intervals, she gets up and crosses the room to retrieve him more bottles of Bud. She is pretty, even natural-looking, surprising because most groupies aren't.

I bend over to talk to him. Can I catch you later? he asks. I kind of want to chill out after the concert.

I feel like an invasion. I realize that I am one. I am a journalist. I am not a groupie. I suddenly wish I could give up my job, except then I realize that I would never have met Alex if it hadn't been for my job. Besides, Kent is waiting outside. I should go.

Alex says, Look, I'll call you next week.

Will you really? I want to know.

I promise.

His hands are now under my skirt again. He touches me, fingers me over and over again, and I realize I am so wet. There is no way to explain how this happened. His idea of foreplay is taking his clothes off. And actually, neither one of us has any of our clothing off. He has hardly done anything to merit any sort of reaction from me besides a voice in my head that is saying, Don't do this. But my body is acting on its own and I am wondering what is it inside me, where is this mysterious place, this crazy hidden female thing that wants him so badly that I am wet without his doing anything. My body is begging for it.

At least it won't hurt.

My skirt is straight and tight. He pushes it inside-out up around my hips. He presses my thighs to the bed and I remember what all those years of ballet were for. He pulls the drawstring open and the sweats slip down on his hips and I almost gasp at the sight of him. There is so much there. I think men worry about size a lot more than women do, especially since its variations have very little to do with the amount of actual physical pleasure I've experienced. But the more there is, the more confidence the man has, so it ends up being a turn-on anyway.

Alex, you don't want me to get pregnant, do you? I ask. I realize this is a very prosaic concern.

You won't get pregnant, he says, and I'm sure he is right.

So he fucks me. No matter how deep inside me he is, there seems to be inches more of him that still haven't penetrated. This doesn't feel particularly good, but it doesn't feel bad either. There is a spot, a small and sensitive spot that he bangs against as he moves back and forth and these incredible noises just come out of my mouth every time he hits it. It's not because it feels good. It's just because it feels at all. I don't know where I am on the pleasure-pain continuum.

He is sitting up on my hips the whole time. He never lies on top of me. I realize that one of the great joys of sex is the feeling of being pressed so close to the flesh that what separates me from him kind of disappears. The one reason I have always thought homosexuality is not natural is that women and men fit together, like a complicated jigsaw puzzle, when they have sex. Where you jut out, I recede, and so on. But right now I am being deprived of the part of sex I love the most because my shirt, my skirt, even my boots are still on and I cannot feel Alex tight against me.

It's hard to move in this skirt, I say.

You don't have to move, he answers.

He keeps pumping away, and after about a half hour, it begins to hurt. My membrane has been stretched as far as it will go, and it's about to split like Saran Wrap on a jagged edge. I wish he would come already so that we could stop. But he doesn't.

Eventually, he pulls out of me without any warning and I am relieved. This is when the pain really starts because the accompanying pleasure stops and I am left with a womb too small and too tight for all it has been filled with and emptied of. Alex falls on his back on the bed. His head strikes the pillow like a match and he curls up to go to sleep.

Once I was over at the record company to hear some reel-to-reels off the new album. Alex was there too, making phone calls. There were lots of other writers there as well, mostly from fanzines, but the entertainment editor of *Seventeen* showed up, so I had someone to talk to.

I wandered outside of the conference room to the desk where Alex was answering his messages and I stood over him. He was talking about meeting some people at a bar. He was saying he'd probably end up doing things he didn't think he should do and saying things he didn't want to say because that's what happens whenever they all get together. Then he hung up the phone.

I'm sorry, I began. I don't want to bother you. I always feel so weird when I deal with musicians because there's this kind of us-and-them thing going on—you know, we're the press and you guys have to watch what you say when we're around.

Don't be silly, he said. We're all people.

Well, I was just wondering, you once told me that you knew where I could get my tattoo fixed and—

Give me your number and I'll give you a call.

You always say that, I said.

I was moving at that point, for the third time in six months, and I couldn't really be reached. I never gave Alex my new phone number. He told me where I could leave him a message when I settled in.

But I never left one.

Later that day, his publicist brought out a birthday cake for him. It was early in February, so I knew he was an Aquarius. I was sitting on the floor at that point, and as he walked out of the room I asked, How old are you? He didn't answer, so I pulled his leg until he bent down and whispered, 31, in my ear.

I lie down next to him but I have no interest in sleeping. I hope you don't mind if I sleep, he says.

Oh no. Of course not. You're tired.

I pull my skirt back down over my thighs as I sit up on the edge of the bed and feel my hair, how it sticks together, and touch my ear, which is not just gooey but also in pain from being pushed into so hard. My whole body has been pushed into pretty hard. I feel at my lobe that an earring is missing, but I get up to leave because I don't want to look for it right now.

Can you pass me the soda at the side of the bed? Alex asks.

I hand him the liter-size bottle of Orangina, which he gulps down.

Maybe I'll go running, I say as if I'm looking for a better suggestion.

You're a very energetic girl, he says.

Yes, I suppose.

I stand up and look at him lying there. I think I'm going to marry my bed, he says. He starts telling me that he'll be at a concert I am going to at the Bottom Line later on, but I know he won't. I look at my watch. It's 4:20. I arrived there at 3:30. Fifty minutes. Not bad.

He shows me to the door, even though it means getting out of bed, not because he is being chivalrous but because the knob is broken and he knows I'll never figure my way out alone.

It was fun, I say, because that's what you say. Let's, um, do it again sometime.

Yeah, he says.

Did you have fun? I turn around and ask before I walk through the door. I want to know this because he didn't come, at least not as far as I could tell.

Yeah.

I want to ask him why we did this since it seemed so unmonumental. I want to ask why he didn't say the things men always do in bed, whether they mean them or not, like, Ah baby you're so pretty.

Or whatever. I want to ask what the point of this was but instead, the only words I say are, Do you do this often?

What? Screw? Yes.

No—invite strange women to your apartment to fuck?

He doesn't answer.

When you asked me to come up here, did you know this was going to happen?

Yes.

I must be very naïve because I had no idea.

I kind of doubt that.

I do too, I think. But I realize that I really did assume we'd hang out, maybe go for a walk, maybe watch MTV, maybe get something to eat. I thought he was just one of me disguised as one of them. I thought heavy metal was just a show and offstage everyone is married and has kids and that the Jack Daniel's in the bottle is really just iced tea because that's what David Lee Roth once admitted. I thought that we were all people really.

He opens his door to let me out. I tell him I really want to go for a ride on his motorcycle. You got $700? he asks.

No, I tell him. No, I don't.

I'd like to go for a ride on my motorcycle too. Maybe we will when it gets repaired.

I offer to try to get his cat out of the hospital, but he says he's got people working on it already.

I'll see you tonight, he says as I turn to leave.

The review had already been written before any of this stuff happened, so I didn't feel conflicted about what I'd done. Of course, had I actually written the damn thing afterward, I wouldn't have felt bad either because sex can be so separate from everything else, including feelings, including critical faculties, including my own judgment, which is usually pretty good.

But the review came out on a Monday. I was up all night that night, finishing another assignment, and 5:30 Tuesday morning the phone rang. It was Alex. I didn't know who Alex was when he first said his name, and then I put it together. I was about ready to go to sleep.

Come over, he said. Come over right now. I'm going down to Washington in an hour, so you have to come here right now.

I probably would have but I was tired. Not too tired to go there and hang out for an hour or so, but too tired for his breaking and entering routine. Too tired to fuck.

I kept saying, I can't. He kept saying, You can. He said, I won't take no. I said, You're going to have to. I said—confusing sex and love as usual—If I say no, will you still like me? He said, It's not a matter of no because you're going to come over here right now.

I finally said yes to get him off the phone. But when I didn't turn up at his door twenty minutes later, he called me three more times so we could go through the same discussion again.

I saw your article, he said during one of the calls. It was great.

Thank you, I answered. I'm glad you like it.

Come over now. My ride will be here in an hour and I need to see you now. Besides, I'm running out of quarters.

Alex, you're crazy, I said.

I know I'm crazy, but you're crazy too.

Why are you calling me now? Why not call me at a normal hour?

Why are you awake now?

I've been up all night. What about you?

Same thing, he said. What he was trying to show me is that we are the same: we both don't sleep at night. And there is a camaraderie that I feel with all nocturnal creatures, which is maybe why I love my cat, maybe why I feel bad that Alex doesn't have his cat. But now he is mistaking me for one of him disguised as one of them. He doesn't realize that I've been up all night working while he's been up all night partying, mainlining, nodding off and drooling.

And I know something isn't right. When he calls me for the last time, I let the machine get it. I don't go.

Months have gone by. Maybe it's been longer. Alex still doesn't have a phone. Sometimes I think of leaving a message for him with the record company, but I never do.

Sometimes I think of writing him a note, but I don't know what to say. His band will be playing again soon and I know I can go to the gig if I want. It's a free country. I can see him there, surrounded by girls, girls who don't write for a living, girls who probably don't do anything for a living. I can feel like shit if I like.

But instead I walk by the building where he lives, day after day, night after night. I wonder why he's never there. I wonder if he's ever coming back. I wonder if I will ever see him again. I wonder how things would have been if I had gone there that morning, and sometimes I wonder if he wasn't sending me some kind of cry for help, if maybe he wanted me to come over because he too was suffering from the intense loneliness that I feel day after day, night after night as I wait for something to happen to change to make my crazy life seem settled and then throw it to pieces again and make my settled life seem crazy. I wait for another Alex. Or maybe I just wait for Alex.

I look for him all over my neighborhood. Every time I see a man on a motorcycle, I think it might be him, and then I see that the hair isn't long and black, the stomach isn't smooth and strong. A friend of mine said she saw him doing his laundry one day, so now I think every man with a bag of clothes might be Alex.

I break up with my boyfriend. I look for a new apartment. I move around a lot. My phone number changes so many times and one day I realize I am in one place, my stuff is in storage in a warehouse on Avenue D, my cat is in my old apartment until I find a new one, there is an answering machine taking messages for me in still another place, and it feels like my life is disappearing. And I can't find Alex anywhere. It is no comfort for me that if he wanted to, he couldn't find me either.

I feel everybody disappearing.

I sit around the house doing nothing a lot. I lie in bed and listen to records, kidding myself that I am actually doing my job and then realizing that, in fact, I am doing my job. I hear Tom Petty singing: "But not me baby / I've got you to save me / Yer so bad / The best thing I ever had / In a world gone mad / Yer so bad." And I know what he means. Maybe sometimes everything is so crazy that what's worst for you is what's best because if nothing really matters anyway then the one thing that might make you remember that you're alive at all is something that's black when you're blue, something that's wild when you're so tamed you can't even see to the other side of the cage much less consider escaping.

And then I hear Don Henley: "I was either standing in your shadow / or blocking your light / Though I kept on trying I could not make it right / For you girl / There's just not enough love in the world." I feel certain he's singing to me, that's the sort of person I am. I watch my boyfriends, and there have been so many, so many more than I ever thought it would take to make me feel okay, and I see that after a while they all get that same baffled look on their faces, that shoulder-shrugging look that says I have no more ideas about how to make you happy so maybe I should just give up. In the beginning, every one of them thinks he will be The One, the savior, the person who will be different from the last failure who would dig ditches to China, who would stop traffic, who would fly across the country, who would wake up for phone calls at 4:38 A.M. just to hear me say, I feel such pain I don't know why please help me.

It never works for me with anybody because of the gaps—gaps between my legs and in my mouth and in my heart—that are maybe deeper and wider than the Mississippi, that love needs to fill up but there just isn't enough of it. Never has been. Never will be.

Late at night I feel desperate and think of calling old boyfriends who were never good enough when they were around but who I could maybe talk to right now to make it okay, but instead I roam the streets until the morning light peeks through, thinking about all the work I could get done in the time I spend feeling bad about all the things I don't do, and I know that one of these days I'm just going to throw my body across Alex's doormat and I'm not going to move until he comes back from the Far East or Avenue A or wherever he is because it would take something as empty as him to fill up a void like me.

BY T. K. TAWNI

I. NO MORE RENAISSANCE PICNICS

My friend Bennie told me about a scene in a porn film in which a handful of executives in business suits sit drinking from tall glasses on lounge chairs beside a swimming pool. A young woman in a bikini is called over, and one of the men says, "Show us your asshole."

At my party they won't even have to ask.

II. MY PARTY

It will be a time of judicious revelry, a time of cakes and ices, with other novelties thrown in for those friends who need to learn a particular lesson. My boss, Marlena, hypochondriac and Francophile, will have to listen to a loop of slow jams while trussed and wearing a ball gag. Nan, one of my dearest friends, will have her lipstick removed...directly from her lips. For years she has presented herself to men mouth-first, hungry and agreeable. That same mouth, denuded of hubris the next morning or afternoon, will moisten the telephone receiver for over an hour, pouring into my sweaty ear everything he said, what he might have meant, what he did, inquiring what I think might happen next. Also on the short list is Jerome, who I have nothing against personally except that he treated Nan badly during the two weeks they were lovers. I kept telling her how easy he'd be to punish, his vanity a fragile mushroom. Truth was, I'd wanted him for myself, but he hadn't noticed. Fortunately, neither had Nan. You, Jerome, will have to be ugly all night: your carefully torqued hair, flattened; your sexy vintage shirt slashed from your Apollonian torso and replaced with a Blimpie uniform.

III. IMPRESSIONISM

Once, just as we were about to go at it, a guy asked me, the way a waiter inquires how you'd like your meat cooked, "What do you want me to do to you?"

"Anything an airplane can do to a cloud," I told him.

My new lover, The Painter, in the moist calm of an afterfuck, asks gently, "What are your fantasies?" Which drops a certain pall on my afterglow. I cannot bring myself to tell about that scene from the long movie about the life of Christ, in which Mary Magdalene, wearing only jewelry and tattoos, gets fucked on a pallet in an open room while a line of guys with hard-ons stand waiting a turn; the party where everyone gets Mary. Instead I say something about a phone booth and something else about a ladder.

IV. PANTIES

In the midst of party planning, Bennie launches into a discourse on panties, remarking on how charmingly ill-fitting they are. "You know," he says, "they're so compromising, women have to pluck at the elastic all the time. Guys love that."

"They make them better now," I assure him. "They hug right where they're supposed to."

"Oh no," he says. "Even on the little girls?"

Then he wants to know what The Painter is going to get at the party. I'm not sure. Maybe I'll tell him my most relentless fantasy, which begins with my ex-boyfriend Ford appearing at the screen door one evening, lit by the porch light. He has on a yellow T-shirt and red shorts. The kitchen is dark, and as I move through it I can see him, but he can't see me. All I have to do is see him, and my erogenous zones, in the short time it takes to cross the kitchen, form a kind of Bermuda Triangle. I'll already be lost, that is, by the time I reach the door.

Should Ford ever truly reappear, there'll be no pretending I don't want it. I'll want it. Whatever makes sex hallucinogenic and time-altering, like a drug, was always in the mix. We seemed as likely to fuck ourselves to death as save each other's lives. The problem is, I remember everything: the living room that winter in the old farmhouse, how the propane heater cooked the air, the green couch we dragged across the floor, not watching *Scott of the Antarctic.* The elevator in the public library. Fingerbangs and thumbfucks. The sweet round note of a choirboy he sometimes sang when he came.

The problem is, you can't live on any of that, but living without it seems like waiting.

V. THE OPEN BOAT

After Ford departed for Alaska there was the mechanic, a hale swimmer, against whose stomach and through the layers of my underwear and shorts I ground my pelvic bone and came three times, his mouth all over my tits. Once I was riding him and his knees were up and he did some butterfly motion with his legs that popped me off, but at the time, for some reason, I was thinking of the Kennedys.

Next I took up with a cardiologist whom everyone endorsed because he had a good job and did not look like a doctor; he looked like a man with a motorcycle and a rap sheet. But he fucked like a doctor, if that's not impolitic to say. He always wanted my legs straight, tightly together, sometimes locked at the heels. I always wanted my legs apart, my ass tilted up so every stroke he'd hit the sweet spot. When, after some weeks of this disjunctive choreography, I intimated a need for follow-up care so that I too could have an orgasm, he was surprised. For a woman, he asserted, coming was rather like dessert—sometimes it was part of the meal, and sometimes not. Who cared if he had a good job?

Now, as we approach the date of my party, there is The Painter, a dark and brooding man who rarely leaves his house. I go over there and drink the syrupy coffee he makes and smoke his hand-rolled cigarettes and can't keep my hands still because I want them on his face. I want to put my mouth on his face. Everything I like I want to put in or against my mouth, including the flat part of my dog Pippa's head. Bennie says I'm wearing the fur off, kissing her too much. He says The Painter is depressed, and that the kind of light I've got under my bushel should not be wasted on a sad renderer of old fruit and fierce self-portraits inspired by Rembrandt.

"But what if I love him?" I say.

"You don't," Bennie replies. "I'd be able to tell." Ten years of observing my sexual behavior have given him an edge. I appreciate his candor, and the aspersion he casts lightly on my ability to know my own heart.

My heart is an inveterate liar, though it means well. And everyone invited to my party is sick of hearing me wax on about these flash infatuations, inflated, as they tend to be, within an inch of exploding. When everyone gets theirs, I guess I'll get mine too. It will be time to tell the truth: I have always wanted sex. I have pretended, to myself mostly, that I might love whoever-he-is in order to fool my body. A pox on me then, because those men are ambushed by the glazed look in my eye, the gyrations of my hips, the lube job, the open mouth; by the letters I send in the early days, addicted as I am to words and their power to persuade: "Dear X, I can't do anything but think of you. And it makes me wet. I prop my feet on the kitchen table on either side of the typewriter and make myself come. It isn't enough. I go to the couch and assume a four-point stance and press what Walt Whitman called the chuff of the hand hard against my clit, employ my middle finger for the in-and-out, cup my ass around the sensation and come, whimpering like a baby coyote. Get over here and put your mouth on me," etcetera.

"Stop writing those letters," Bennie tells me. "Or don't send them."

"I have to send them," I explain. "It gives them incentive to move me."

"How moved do you need to be?"

VI. CUBISM

It's a limpid afternoon in August, the day of my party, when The Painter tells me that he can't. He says it like that, exactly: "I can't." Given how we've spent the last hour, a pair of dummies crash-testing sex, his meaning is obscure.

"Oh, can't," I repeat, glaring at him. The prospect of an argument puts me in a good mood. The timbre of my voice changes. I practically sing out, "Can't what? Come to my party? Live without me?"

"We can't do this anymore," he says, waving a hand over our corporeal forms and the rumpled bed whereon they finally fell. "I need to find someone with a similar temperament. Someone like me."

"Ah," I say. Bear in mind, he's going through his blue period. "You mean a woman who rarely leaves her house?"

"No." He flashes his dark eyes, amused but unwilling to cede. "Someone who approaches these things, relationships, cautiously. Slowly. You go at things hard. Maybe it empties them out."

"But I like that about myself, that I go at things headlong." Heretofore, it's been part of my charm.

"I can't keep up with you." Here he shrugs, gives a half smile, which makes a sexy dimple near its quirk. He's lazy about shaving, and today he's rough. His sweat smells like lavender and fresh tobacco. Maybe I do love him, partly because he's getting ready to deny me. Nothing compels a cliff diver like a long drop.

I know the frantic, exhaustive, panting shapes of love. Maybe I choose those, because I do want to empty things out, to pass through them and extricate myself. But love that is studied, careful, slow-growing as a rhododendron is not something I've ever had the patience for. Nor do I now. Where is someone who wants what I want, who, similarly driven by the laws of thermodynamics, can move forward, toward the other person, me, with an equal and opposite momentum?

"I appreciate your candor," I tell him. "It makes me want to shave my pussy." I bought the clippers to trim the dog, but what the hell. It is my party.

"Really?" he says, and I get a glimpse of the lover he might be, if he would reach for me, if he would stop hiding behind the posture of a Platonist, waiting for some idealized woman to materialize proximate to his hard-on. He could keep up with me, if he wanted to. It is this suspicion of mine, that he has chosen to isolate himself behind the curtain of an idea and simply does not want me enough to push it aside, to choose real flesh, that drives me crazy.

"You make me peevish!" I yell, and with the fingers of one hand I tap his chest, his hairy chest, a feature I do not ordinarily find appealing on a man, but it's on him and I like him, so I like it, and isn't that the point, really, that the real is, finally, what most compels us? We live with a composite of what we want, and as we move in and out of bed and in and out of relationships we refine it. When we come upon something else, and it exerts an unfamiliar pull, we don't know how to act, or what to do. We shave our pussies and rant, perhaps. But I can rant all I want and it will make me no less willful, less greedy about sex, less hell-bent on intimacy. I want it now, The Painter wants it later, or he may not want it at all, ever, with anyone. "You won't let anyone in there," I say, and press his chest.

"You are not a good guest," he points out, laying his hand over mine. "You'd wreck the place."

And I probably would.

The Velvet

BY WILL CHRISTOPHER BAER

NEW ORLEANS DISAPPEARS behind her. But she remembers to take the lithium and tomorrow she will have moments of clarity.

Sally doesn't know what to do about the car. It's falling apart. It leaks and the dashboard lights are dead. It scares her to drive after dark because she can't see the speedometer. She thinks the car was given to her. She examines the ring of keys. One for the ignition, the other for the trunk. The engine is in the trunk and for some reason this disturbs her. A twist of leather on the silver ring, but no house keys. It's possible she stole this car.

Public radio and the hiss of insects.

The voice of someone she used to fuck, relentlessly deconstructing Sylvia Plath. She gassed herself while the children ate bread soaked in milk. And her skin was bright as a Nazi lampshade.

Miles and then miles. It's not so easy to disappear.

She sleeps with the doors unlocked, but she feels safe. The car will never make it to California. Sally assumes there is a lover involved, a shattered boy with a red mouth. A young girl eating a plum in the rain.

The sky is fleshy, the color of lips. Sally wakes to the hiss of traffic.

The seats are slick and cold with dew. She leaves the keys in the ignition and starts walking. A field of dead wheat. She wishes the sun would come out. The wheat surrounds her. It blurs her vision, becomes powder in her hands. She turns to look back and the path she has left appears random, violent. She begins to run, her eyes burning. If she falls she will surely die in the wheat. Then an access road, trailing away like black ribbon.

Her tongue is strange and misshapen. Her memories are encrypted, binary.

Dementia, she suffers from dementia. Her hands feel brittle. The skeleton of a bird's wing.

Headlights rise and swallow her.

Sally has an irrational fear of the word *panties,* of heat ripples on the highway. She looks up and the river drops into an unseen chasm. She tells herself this is only the curve of the earth, the trajectory of its orbit. The sun is cleverly hooded, like the eye of a corpse. She is hungry and her period is off by days.

Under a white light, the skin around her eyes appears yellow. She avoids mirrors. Aliens and dead souls have yellow skin, she is sure of that. And she doesn't really care to see the pale web of scars around her left eye. Deformity is so easily memorized. Sally stares at the road until she can't feel her legs. She veers abruptly into a field of cotton and crouches to pee in the dust. As she nears the city the sadness in her resumes, like a pulse. She smells urine and she touches herself.

She hitchhikes back to the edge of the French Quarter. It's late summer and bitterly hot. Sally is thirsty and walks into the first lighted doorway. There is sawdust on the floor. In a shadowy corner are a pinball machine and an apparently broken jukebox. Two drunks sluggishly hammer and kick at the machine. They stand there panting, staring dumbly at her in the doorway. The sun is behind her and Sally is confident they can see through her thin dress. The drunks nudge each other and continue to abuse the jukebox. Sally steps to the bar and asks for iced tea. The bartender is a large woman with very bright blue eyes. She is slumped on a stool behind the bar, staring at an untouched jelly doughnut on a plate before her. Her eyes flicker like two blue insects and soon she produces a tall glass with a twist of lemon at the lip.

I added you a drop of gin, she says.

Thanks. You have beautiful eyes.

The bartender is embarrassed, briskly wiping the bar with a rag. Her eyes don't avoid the scars on Sally's face, but they don't linger there. Sally puts two crushed dollars on the bar, the very last of her money. There is a brief silence as the drunks take a break from pounding on the jukebox. They rest and smoke cigarettes. One of them has a mustache; the other does not. Otherwise they are identical. The clean-shaven one whispers to the machine, You're a cunt. Your mother's a cunt.

He spits on the jukebox, then resumes his attack.

The second drunk shakes his head. Escalate, he says. You got to escalate, Bob. Give that cunt a little nuclear war.

This is nothing, says Bob. This is like fucking Panama.

What's your name, little one?

Sally flinches. The bartender is peering at her, smiling.

Rachel, she says. My name is Rachel.

And you live around here.

Sort of.

Are you okay?

I think so.

You don't look it.

How do I look?

The bartender hesitates. Your arms are bleeding, she says. For one thing.

Sally examines her arms, which are indeed scratched and bleeding.

I'm just tired, she says.

The bartender shrugs. You call me Dolores. And holler if you want anything.

Sally sips the tea cautiously and the gin is like metal to her tongue. She turns to watch the drunks, who still pound and curse at the jukebox.

I guess your jukebox is broken, says Sally.

It's unplugged, says Dolores. I don't have the heart to tell them.

One of the drunks notices Sally looking at them and nudges his partner. They grin at her, their mouths fat and wet. Sally swallows more of the tea, then touches her lips with a napkin. She turns away.

Are you sure you don't want something for those cuts? says Dolores.

Sally stares at her. You don't even know me.

No, says Dolores.

How can you possibly care?

I guess I don't.

Dolores is flustered. She's reluctant to offend the cripple. Sally has seen this before, in the rare eyes of sympathetic cops and social workers.

Do you want half a jelly doughnut? says Dolores.

Would you mind, says Sally. Would you put your arms around me?

Dolores hesitates.

Sally spreads her arms wide and closes her eyes. The heavy red hands pull her close and for a moment she can hear another heartbeat. Dolores could crush her like an egg, but Sally feels weirdly safe.

Oh my, says the drunk with the mustache.

Bob Junior, says Dolores. Shut your face.

You kidding? says Bob Jr. I dream about this shit.

Sally swivels on her stool, remotely conscious that her dress has risen up to mid-thigh.

You're delicious, says Bob Jr. You're sweet as pie.

He steps closer. Sally trembles and wonders if this is rage.

Thank you, Bob.

I'm Bob Junior. He points at the other drunk. That one's Bob.

Is he your father? says Sally.

They're twins, says Dolores. One of them wasn't enough, apparently.

Bob is three minutes older, says Bob Jr.

Sally concentrates and her shoulders simply stop shaking, as if she has flipped a switch. Dolores comes around the bar and goes to plug in the jukebox. Bob shakes his head and laughs.

You like a model, or what? says Bob Jr.

Sally frowns. No, she says.

Bob ambles over to stand alongside his brother. Sally smiles at them and reaches to tie her hair back in a ponytail. Her scars are more visible this way. Bob Jr. recoils visibly, while Bob develops a sudden coughing fit. Dolores feeds a quarter into the jukebox and Willie Nelson begins to croon, his voice full of rust. The brothers barely notice.

I dance at The Velvet, says Sally.

You're a stripper, says Bob Jr. With that face.

Bob grunts. No shit. Your face is a fucking freak show.

The jukebox abruptly fails. Willie Nelson ominously slips into a drunken warble, then dies.

Sally puts her drink down, her lips wet. She doesn't know what to say. She is rather amused to think that anyone might be interested in a stripper's face. Dolores is not amused, however. She offers to fetch her husband's shotgun. Bob and Bob Jr. might learn some manners, she says, if they spent the weekend picking buckshot out of their thighs.

It's okay, says Sally.

The brothers shuffle away, their faces pink and confused. Sally wishes she had a few dollars, if only to buy them a beer or two. It must be thirsty work, beating a machine to death like that.

Sally walks in circles until she comes to the black apartment. Everyone calls it that, because the wall behind the television is painted black. She's not sure who is living there now.

Tripper is there. He doesn't look up when she comes in. He's eating a bowl of cereal and watching a cartoon on television. His face is apelike and he literally hoots at the TV. There is something wrong with his mouth, as if it's numb from the dentist. The milk drools from his lips, a damp cornflake stuck to his chin like a smudge. Sally sits down on the couch. She takes her shoes off and pulls her bare feet under her.

Anyone home? she says.

The Penguin, he says.

Sally looks at him. Tripper is not much older than she is. A thin mustache crouches beneath his pink nose. He wears stained white pants with no shirt. His eyes are close together and his hair is wispy, prematurely gray. Most of his teeth are gone. His mother drank when he was in utero. When he has money he spends it on crystal meth. Tripper grunts and swipes at his mouth with his clubbed left hand. The hand is fingerless and reminds her of a child's foot. His other hand is muscular, callused.

Who? she says.

The Penguin, he says. That's me, huh.

Your name is Tripper.

People call me the Penguin. Lately.

You shouldn't let people make fun of you.

Tripper shrugs. His face brightens. Huh. Yuh got any cheese.

Cheese? says Sally.

You know. The white, says Tripper. The crystal.

Crystal, she says. I never heard anyone call it cheese.

Huh. Now yuh have.

Sally offers him a thin smile and wonders what time it is.

Anyway, says Tripper. Do yuh?

What? says Sally.

Got a little cheese for the Penguin?

Are you a circus act? she says.

Tripper gazes at her, his eyes round and blank. She might as well have asked him to explain time travel. The door slams and Horse walks in, the heels of his boots loud. He grins broadly.

As I breathe, he says. An angel has fallen.

Hello, she says. I'm back.

Are your wings broken?

She looks away, at the window. Not quite, she says.

Horse is part Cherokee. His hair is black and straight, his skin like chocolate. He used to be a Marine. He wears a long white shirt, unbuttoned and swirling about him like a cape. Black jeans tucked into knee-high motorcycle boots. Horse smokes tobacco from a carved pipe. He sits cross-legged on the floor, blocking the television. The flicker of cartoon light like a halo.

Tripper whines.

Hush, boy. I have something for you.

Horse reaches into his coat, pulls out two cans of spray paint. Tripper giggles and makes a whooping noise. He lunges, grabbing at the cans. Horse gives him one and Tripper pulls a filthy red bandanna from his pocket. He happily sprays paint into the rag and presses it to his nose, breathing deeply. Sally moves to the far end of the couch. She watches Horse carefully. She always feels like a rabbit around him. Afraid to look at him, afraid not to.

Nice, she says.

Horse lights his pipe and smoke drifts blue against the black. He nods at Tripper.

It's his birthday.

Really, she says.

He's eighteen. He's a man today.

Tripper has red paint smeared on his mouth and face. A string of snot catches the light.

A man, she says.

Horse blows a smoke ring.

Sally, he says. What do you want from me?

She feels the blood rise in her cheeks and hates herself for blushing.

Nothing, she says. Really.

I know you don't like me, he says.

Sally shrugs, helpless. I do. I like you.

What the fuck do you want?

I need help. I need to get out of town.

Money, he says. He smiles and smoke twists away from his teeth.

The tickle of goose bumps.

Money, she says. Beside her Tripper writhes, panting.

What would you do with my money? says Horse.

I could get a car, she says.

And where would you go in your new car?

Anywhere. Memphis, maybe.

Horse smiles at her. No one will love you, he says. No one will ever love that face.

His eyes paralyze her. She breathes evenly and concentrates on the sadness in her chest. She glances at Tripper, who is staring at his strange left hand as if he's never seen it before.

Horse shrugs. You might as well go home to your idiot husband.

He's not my husband, she says.

Neither here nor there. Horse yawns as if bored.

I'll do anything, she says.

Don't you have a job? he says.

Sally is silent. On the television, game-show contestants hop about in apparent ecstasy.

I believe you were dancing at The Velvet, he says.

I was. I quit three weeks ago.

Why?

The men depressed me, she says. They were like ferrets.

Horse points his pinkie finger at Tripper.

It's the Penguin's birthday, he says.

So what?

And he's never had a woman.

Sally closes her eyes, thinks of the money. The sadness is warm and deep. She lets herself sink. She slides next to Tripper and sniffs him, doglike. He smiles at her. He's a child, she thinks.

Hello, Sally.

Hello, Tripper.

I'm the Penguin.

With one hand Sally unzips Tripper's pants. His penis flops out, soft and massive. It's as fat as her arm. She blinks at it, confused.

Impressive, isn't it? Horse laughs.

It's too big, she says. I'll choke to death.

Oh, please. Have faith.

She looks at Tripper. His face is placid and staring. Sally pokes and prods the thing until it's relatively hard. She takes a breath and bends over him. Tripper begins to struggle and moan, as if she's attacking him. Then he relaxes and begins to chant the names of actors who have ever portrayed Batman.

Adam West, Adam West. Michael Keaton. Val Kilmer. George Clooney, oh no.

She tells herself she's sucking her own fist. It doesn't take long and Sally pulls away, her mouth wet and sore. A gout of come narrowly misses her face.

George Clooney, George Clooney.

Sally looks at the coffee table and thinks of slug tracks. A terrible smell rises from Tripper's crotch. The smell is familiar and she stares at Horse in disbelief.

He shit himself, says Horse. Interesting.

Sally tastes gin in her throat and runs to the kitchen.

Laughter and running water. Sally washes her face and spits repeatedly into the sink. She opens a drawer. Bits of foil and rubber bands and books of matches. A small knife with a black handle. She picks it up between two fingers. The blade is thin and bends easily and she tests the edge with her thumb. A line of blood runs to her wrist and she lets go of the blade. She slips the knife into the waistband of her underpants and sucks the blood from her thumb.

Tripper is gone. A damp spot where he was sitting. Perhaps a shadow. Sally sits on the floor, near the window. The length of a body between herself and Horse. She sucks her thumb. Sunlight swims in dust and smoke and she realizes she doesn't know if it's rising or setting.

Alone at last, angel.

Where is he? she says.

Horse smiles and she feels herself shiver.

The Penguin? I told him to have a bath, he says.

The sound of running water. Distant and soothing.

I wish you wouldn't call him that.

He doesn't mind, says Horse. It makes him feel like a superhero.

What about the money?

Horse closes his eyes and sinks away from her. He lies flat on the floor. Sally looks at the flickering television, where predatory teenagers glare back at her with superior, indifferent faces. It might be an ad for blue jeans, or a push for safe sex.

I want fifty dollars, she says. At least. That's enough for a bus ticket and a grilled cheese.

You aren't going anywhere, angel.

Sally stares at the heels of his boots. There is another game show on television and she decides it must be morning. After a few minutes Horse breathes slowly, as if he is asleep. Sally sits very still. She watches television for two hours, three. The game show becomes a soap opera. She tells herself to demand at least a hundred. Her legs begin to hurt. Horse has not moved. He's not going to give her any money. He's only amusing himself. She stands up and there is a cracking noise, like knuckles. Horse still sleeps and she edges past him, like a whisper. A finger strokes her ankle and Horse smiles up at her. His teeth are terribly white.

I will give you the money, he says. I promise.

Horse's bedroom is dark and sensuous. It always shocks her, somehow. The ceiling is a mosaic of silk scarves. There are blue paper window-shades glowing in the afternoon sun and the air has a dreamy, underwater quality. In one corner are a table and chair of scarred cherrywood, both piled high with books. Beneath the blue window is an antique chest of drawers that looks very fragile. The surface is littered with masculine accessories: a silver cigarette lighter and matching cuff-links, a collection of pocketknives, a wooden hairbrush, three pairs of expensive sunglasses. Sally turns to face the bed, a simple futon with white cotton sheets and five or six puffy pillows on an iron frame. On the wall above it are two framed photographs, blown up to uncomfortable proportions. One is a naked, red-haired woman wrapped in gauze bandages. The other is a dying horse, its body white with foam. Sally takes her dress off, drops her underpants to the floor. She looks at herself. A girl's body, but the breasts are too large and her nipples strange, translucent. Her thin pubic hair is growing back. Faded white razorblade scars on her arms and legs. She hates this body.

Horse watches her, his eyes lidded. His tongue flashes between his lips and the silence is like the prick of a needle. Sally holds her breath, waiting for him to say something.

Then he whispers, Very nice. I've got to have a piss.

Sally stands there, conscious of herself. She forces herself to recline on the bed, her hands hiding her crotch. Horse leaves the bathroom door open and pees endlessly and loud. The toilet flushes and now Sally rolls over to wait on her belly. When she looks up Horse is standing naked in the doorway. His muscles are fluid, his skin smooth and hairless. He laughs, softly. He has a nice laugh.

He sits next to her, kisses her hair. She looks down and his penis is sleek and pretty.

Are you afraid? he says.

Yes. I'm afraid.

But why? he says. We have done this before.

I remember.

Horse laughs again. His finger moves slow and faint as breath down her spine.

I want some protection, she says.

My body is a temple, he says. I assure you.

Protection, she says.

Relax, he says.

He produces a condom in gold foil. She opens it with her teeth and the lubricant tastes of copper and bad breath, of shoe polish and dead skin and wet hair.

I love the taste of spermicide, she says.

You have beautiful feet, says Horse.

The rubber is also golden. She thinks of locusts and salamanders. Horse slips his fingers inside her. His tongue is everywhere, touching her and disappearing and tickling her asshole like a feather, like the tail of a cat. Now he lifts her onto his lap. Veins stand out along his penis, fat with blood. The rubber is still clenched in her left hand. There is a wound on his shoulder, like a bite. She stares at it without recognition. Horse grunts as she slips the condom onto him. Her hair falls over her eyes and she hides behind it. Horse lifts her by the armpits. Sally is weightless. He can't seem to get inside her. He lowers her again and prods at her ass and pelvis with his ridiculous gold penis. Sally stares at the bite mark and remembers: the police use the teeth to identify victims.

Please stop, she says. This isn't working.

She feels his muscles tense. But he stops trying to push his penis into her. She feels it soften against her thigh and is temporarily sorry for him.

Maybe a handjob, she says.

Don't insult me, girl.

Sally pulls her underpants on and feels sticky. She picks up a shirt and realizes it's not hers. The sleeves hang down to her knees. It doesn't matter.

I'm going to pee, she says. Horse doesn't open his eyes.

She shuts the door behind her. In the bathroom she washes her hands and stares at herself in the mirror. Then she turns to the toilet and sees the body. Tripper is sprawled with his legs like scissors, his arms around the toilet. His head is somehow wedged beneath the tank.

Horse, she says. Then she says it again, she screams it and he is standing there, still naked.

I know, he says.

Tripper has one shoe on. He still wears the fouled white pants.

What happened?

He had a fit, maybe. An air bubble in his brain.

There is a window above the toilet, small and dirty. A word is scrawled in the sun-bright dust.

You might have warned me, she says.

Horse scratches his belly. Then tugs absently at his scrotum. His penis is shriveled and damp.

The way I see it, he says, the Penguin was taking his shoes off and his bubble burst. Hit the floor and started thrashing around like a chicken. Then he grabbed hold of the toilet and got his head stuck.

The bathtub is full, the water murky.

He just freaked out and died, says Horse.

The water, she says. It was running.

I turned it off, he says.

When you came to pee?

There is a cigarette butt on the sink. Horse puts it in his mouth and looks around for a match.

I heard the toilet flush, she says.

Horse smiles.

He was dead, she says. He was dead.

I stepped over him, says Horse. I emptied my bladder and flushed the toilet.

Sally stares at him. She feels vaguely sick.

Horse sighs. He wouldn't be any less dead if I pissed in the sink.

What is that word? she says. On the window.

The word is *dodo,* he says. Another, more exotic, bird that can't fly.

Horse turns and walks back to the bedroom. Sally looks at the body once more, then climbs into the bathtub. The water is clammy, room temperature. She sinks until her ears are below the surface and everything is flat and gray.

Horse is sleeping. She watches his chest rise and fall. Water runs from her hair. The shirt is soaked, the long sleeves cold and heavy. Her blue and white dress is a wretched clump on the floor. She tells herself to get dressed and go. He's not going to give her the money. She takes off the shirt and suddenly is shivering. Her T-shirt smells like sickness and her stomach heaves. She crouches there, staring at her little black shoes. The knife from the kitchen glitters brightly, tucked into her left shoe like a gift, but she doesn't remember leaving it there. It might have been Horse, playing a game with her. He would think that was wildly funny. She looks at him. His breathing is steady as a metronome.

Sally kneels on the bed beside him. She holds the knife gently, like it was a bird's blue egg.

His skin is the color of wood.

Between the ribs, he says.

She doesn't move.

Slip the blade between my ribs, he says. Poke a hole in my heart.

Sally backs away and he smiles, his eyes still closed. I would die in seconds, he says.

She dresses in the other room. It takes several false starts to get her shoes tied. Her hands are shaking and she sits down to smoke one of Tripper's cigarettes.

The television is still on.

Sally changes the channels until she finds one that is silent and blue. She wonders how long the body will be there. Another day, or two. The chest and stomach and thighs will turn purple, almost black. The blood will settle. She can see Horse waking up in the middle of the night, stumbling to the bathroom in the dark. He will surely step on Tripper's outstretched hand and curse at him. She pushes the television over with a violent shrug and it crashes against the linoleum. There is a dull popping sound as the screen goes black.

On the table before her are two cans of spray paint. Sally picks them up, listens to the distant lead rattle. The can that Tripper was using seems unclean somehow. She pulls the lid from the other can, rips a square of cloth from her dress. She folds it twice, like a bandage. She shakes the can back and forth then sprays into her fist until the can is cold. The paint is yellow. Sally presses the cloth to her face and breathes deeply.

In the bathroom again. She looks closely at Tripper. He hasn't moved and she's glad. She feels dizzy and turns to the mirror. The skin around her eyes is yellow. The color of lemons, aliens. Sally turns on the cold water and soaks her wrists. In her left hand she still holds the knife. She turns off the faucet. The fingers of her right hand brush the curve of her breast, her ribs. She has goose bumps. She feels her heart beating and lifts the shirt, watching herself in the mirror. She positions the knife and tries to push it through. The blade bends and she feels a thread of pain. A long thin cut opens down the left side of her body. A ribbon of blood, pretty and painless.

Drained of color the light creeps up on her. Slow, reptilian. She washes her hands and face. Her mouth is that of a hanged man.

The sun is high and bright. She feels blind. Three wild dogs, their ribs showing. They follow her, circling. For a moment she is one of them. Perhaps they smell blood and they are waiting for her to weaken.

She nearly steps on the swollen, legless body of a rat.

Minutes become teeth. She counts them. Her clothes are torn. The smear of yellow across her face. She wonders about the color of those Nazi lampshades. Would they be yellow or pink.

She buys coffee in a small grocery. She decides a cop is watching her. His eyes behind black glasses. She goes into the rest room, locks the door. She takes out the plastic jar of lithium. Two pills remain. The prescription is expired.

Raw pink punctures. She can't tell dirt from shadow. His genitals were so pale and unthreatening. She won't sleep. Not until dark. She finds herself walking toward the river. She's afraid of the river. The sadness swells when she gets close to it. But the water pulls at her.

Despair. The smell of animal waste. The city is below sea level. The dead are left aboveground and this gives the air a terrible heaviness.

Now at the river's edge. Sally sits on a bench. Two boys throw stones at a foreign object in the water, a shadowy lump that drifts lazily in the current.

What is it? says Sally.

Dead alligator, says one boy. I think.

Bullshit, says the other. It's a sleeping bag.

Which would be more exciting? she says.

The boys wander away and she hears a car. Then footsteps in gravel and a man is walking toward her. He wears an ill-fitting blue suit, with white shoes and hat. He grins, lipless and sunburned.

Pretty day, isn't it?

I guess so, she says.

Do you know a club called The Velvet? he says.

She stares at him. He is nervous, shifting his feet.

I never heard of it, she says.

Sure, he says. I was hoping you might give me directions.

I told you. I never heard of it.

Twenty dollars, he says. I'll give you twenty dollars to get in the car with me.

Sally turns to look at the car. A silver Toyota sedan with four doors. Electric windows and heated leather seats and two air-bags. A roof-rack for luggage and bicycles and skis that he doesn't use.

That's a nice car, she says.

Thanks, the man says. Thank you.

Where shall we go?

Her skin never asks to be touched. It shrinks. His eyes are invasive, surgical. For six days the sun never drops below the horizon. A blunt object, the fist. The size of a heart.

Tragedy in Burgundy

BY JAMES HANNAHAM

Dear Darnell:

I am writing to you because my friend LaKeisha's lying has to stop. It's been more than a year since she started carousing around clubs like some shameless Jezebel, duping straight mens into thinking she was a woman. I can't handle the dishonesty. I mighta left the Baptist church and never looked back the day after some deacon who made a pass at me at a barbecue on Saturday gave a sermon against homosexuality on Sunday, but I can't help thinking in the back of my mind that me an LaKeisha is gonna be bunkmates in flames if we continue to perpetrate this lie. God will punish the wicked. I seen it too many times to doubt that.

This is what's really working me. Last week she went on a date with some brother—one tall, fine brother. We're talking Nubian Prince of Egypt fine, jaw drop to the knees fine, capital F-Y-N-E fine, like "I never knew Adonis had a cuter younger brother" fine. This man is so hot that he could fry bacon in his hand. He could fry my bacon in his hand, that's for sure. Brother used to be a linebacker in school, now he a lawyer. And she ain't told him the truth yet. This is a man who could crush her behind with his eyelid. What if some queen sees her in the street with this brother and runs up going, "Ronald! Ronald!" 'cause not everyone be calling her by her drag name all the time like I do. How dead would her ass be then?

Darnell, I am so scared something is gonna happen to her. She is my best friend in the world, like family, I've known her since kindergarten. She's my twin sister, practically. If something happen to her, I'd be all alone in the world, 'cause I don't got no family around here. And Sheba (that's LaKeisha's cat) just had eight kittens three weeks ago. Who's gonna give a home to these poor innocent creatures if—oh shit, I'm starting to cry again.

It's one week later. I'm sorry it's taking me so long to write this. But do you see what it's come to, Darnell? I cannot live like this. Every weekend it's another club with pastel neon lining the outside edges of the building and fake palm trees and women with big ol' hair-weaves, so much makeup they look like Jason and nine layers of pantyhose on—there's so much fakeness on top of these 'ho's that if you took it all off they'd look like a upside-down mop. And LaKeisha's no different, playing her little game of straight chicken. Have you heard of gay chicken, Darnell? You should do a show on it, it's a good topic. Straight men will pick up a gay man and go through a whole date with them until they "get sick." Ain't that some shit? Buncha closet cases if you axe me. I heard about this study they done, where they found out that if you attach a electrode to the dick of a homophobe and make him watch gay porno, that they dicks gets harder than straight men who ain't homophobic watching the same pornos. It's like, tell me some shit I don't know. But what I do wanna know is, how they get them homophobes to tape a electrode to they dick? I was a homophobe, I wouldn't let nobody with no gay porno and no electrodes within a mile of my ass.

Unlike them closet cases, though, LaKeisha don't wanna hurt nobody, she just having a good time. My girl loves to kiki. She the kikingest bitch around. And I don't wanna be no party pooper or nothing, but I feel like she putting her life in danger (and mines) the way she be carrying on with every Tom, Denzel and Hakim that come up to her with a pup tent in they pants.

Anyways, I still haven't gotten to the A1 tip-top reason that Kiki

Keisha's lying has got to stop, that just happened a couple of days ago. So this guy that LaKeisha went on that date with, you know, Super Fly, he's really into her. I mean really into her. But she don't know that, 'cause he ain't called her or nothing. But here's how I know. The other day, I'm at Fremont and Tamika's House of Beauty getting my finger waves redone, right. And I'm just chatting with Tamika, you know, it ain't too many other people around, talkin' 'bout this and that, whatever. Just chillin' and whatnot. Tamika is very drag-queen friendly, the only one in Boston like that. I love her. And the front part of the House of Beauty is where Tamika husband, Fremont, got his li'l barbershop. So who walks in but Super Fly, and Fremont starts giving the brother a fade. So on my way out, I'm like, "Hi," and Super Fly look at me like he seen a overseer's ghost. He get up out the chair so fast that Fremont gives him a bald spot. A ton of kinky hair go spilling all over the floor. So I'm really charmed, I think the brother maybe like me a little too. But then he goes, "You LaKeisha's friend, right?" And I go, "Yeah," even though my li'l ego's feeling 'bout as big as Emmanuel Lewis' ho-ho.

Then he like, "You gotta give me her phone number 'cause I left it in my pants and took them to the cleaners the next day and they washed it. I been thinking about her constantly. I been back to Ruby's every night looking for her." He start talking about how she's the most beautiful woman, pitcher of femininity, gorgeous, womanly, etc., etc. I'm feeling a little cunty, plus he don't know nearway how wrong he is, so I'm like, "I'd give you her phone number but I ain't got it on me, sorry." Like I ain't had the shit memorized for ninety million motherfucking years. So he give me his business card. And at first I was gonna give it to her. But then I was like, I can't let this continue. I'm gonna call the brother and tell him the real deal. So the next day I try like all day to dial Prince Charming's number. I'd been dialing six numbers and then hanging back up so many times that my index finger be getting a big blister in the middle. So finally at nine last night I call him, hoping I'm gonna get his answering machine, 'cause I have this li'l prepared speech about how LaKeisha has put one over on him and he shouldn't be mad because she was just having fun, whatever. So the phone rings three times, and I'm like, "I'm in the clear." Then I hear Super Fly's voice come on the line and the shit sound like a fucking black velvet couch come to life. Good God almighty, my knees starts shaking, my blood gets hotter than the Happyland Social Club—she's about to have a conniption, honey. So I'm like, "Hi, it's LaKeisha's friend," and he get all excited again—I can tell he's like, drooling all over the phone—and he start talking about her. The phone keep slipping out my hand because of all the sweat in my palms. I can't bring myself to shatter his little world, you know. And I don't wanna be the Grinch that stole LaKeisha's Christmas. So finally I'm like, "There's something I gotta esplain to you 'bout LaKeisha, but I can't do it over the phone. Let's have dinner, I'll tell you all about it." Part of me is thinking he's clocked us as drag queens from the git-go, and he doing some kinda serious denial trip. But some of them straight guys—you could show them Yaphet Kotto in a dress with no makeup and they'd think it was a real woman. Or attach a electrode to they dick without them knowing.

He a little shy at first, so I go, "Okay, you have dinner wit me, I'll tell you this thing, then I'll give you her number so's you could make your own decision, aight?" So he's like, "Tomorrow night at Tiny's." That's a rib joint.

So the next day I'm hanging with LaKeisha and we start talking about guys and whatnot, and she gets to the subject of Super Fly. Like how he ain't called her in a week, and how upset this shit makes her and how much she liked him, and she ain't never gonna find nobody to love her and take care of her. She's a mess in a dress, a tragedy in burgundy. So I do the tough love routine, very calmly, like I was her mama. I go, "LaKeisha, he thinks you a woman, like with a pussy. Hello? He gonna be really disappointed to find that shit out, honey. Imagine you went home with a guy and found out he had equipment down there you wasn't especting and had no interest in, like, he had a catcher's mitt instead of a dick." I was trying to make her laugh behind that comment, but instead the bitch lost it. I mean, really lost it. Got my new velour halter top all soaking wet with tears, honey. Going on about how she felt like he was definitely the one, love at first sight and that he'd assept her as she was even when he found out she had a ho-ho instead of a ring ding. I really doubted that, but at the same time, here's my best girlfriend in my arms, bawling her eyes out over this man she had been on one—let's count that again, one—date with. She's not normally like that. Wait, yes she is.

So that's the dilemma I got on my hands. Right now I'm almost due to meet Super Fly for dinner, but I can't go through with it. I picked up this letter again as a excuse to procrastinate. I'll admit it. It's like I want the brother, but if I go and make a play for him and she find out, she'd feel like stabbing me enough times to make me into some paper dollies. I'd be walking down the street and people be pointing at me like, "There go Save the Children." But maybe I should go and give him her phone number. Maybe the bitch is right, that his mind is open enough, or he already figured her out or some shit. But maybe I should try to protect her from getting hurt so bad. I don't know what to do. That's where you come in, Darnell. I thought if we appeared on your upcoming show, "Your Lying Has Got to Stop!" we could all work this thing out with your guidance and the panel of experts. Maybe LaKeisha would find her dream lover and we could all still be friends and kiki together. But right now everything's such a big mess and I'm concerned that my best friend might do something stupid and get hurt—oh shit, I'm starting to cry again.

Please help us, Darnell. We watch your show every morning. We love you, love you, love you. Seriously.

Sincerely,
Tony Adamson
(a.k.a. Almonetta Rosé)

Dear Darnell:

Thank you so much for giving me and LaKeisha the opportunity to appear on *The Darnell Show*. You have to admit that there was not a dull moment on the show. And please believe me, Darnell, if it was within my budget or LaKeisha's to pay for all the damage, I would be enclosing a check with the $20,000 your lawyer asked for in his very nice letter. Hell, I'd give you a extra $20,000 'cause you so handsome.

But it really ain't our fault, you know? First of all, we had to be up at six in order to get to the studio. Our friend Mazda Miata was doing a gig at this club the night before so we was out until like four. So naturally, when we got to your studio, we was totally out of it, 'cause two hours sleep is just not worth it, so we didn't bother. You shouldn't be doing no show at eight in the morning, 'cause that way your guests gotta get up real early to get there by like, seven, am I wrong? I'm surprised that any of them guests could put a sentence together, now that I know how early you be taping that shit.

Plus you know you shouldn'ta had LaKeisha in the same room backstage with all them mens who's just a buncha dogs. You know she was just her usual self behind that. I was like, we came here to stop this 'ho from doing this kinda thing and it's exactly what she's doing. That's like saying, "I'ma take you to France to make you stop drinking wine," or "I'ma take you to Thailand so you'll stop having all that sex." I'm not trying to say it was a dumb idea or nothing, but Darnell, what the hell were you thinking? She was carrying on like never before, dancing around the room even when it wasn't no music. And I know I didn't see that tight plastic jumpsuit and say it was okay to wear on the show. I just sat there and read my book and I was like, "Never again."

But out the corner of my eye, I was looking at Super Fly sittin' in back of this whole group of brothers, just as nice as nice could be. Mmm-mmm. And still as fine as fine could be too. I felt so sorry for this poor man, about to have his whole world shattered in public, put to shame on national TV by the fact that he was dry humping a tranny in some club. He'd just gotten himself a skin fade with a oil sheen that looked *très* fierce, even though he still had that big bald spot. He had himself a beautiful gray suit on, and these little gold-frame glasses. You could tell he was brought up real well, 'cause them others, with them big sneakers and crinkly jogging pants and baggy shirts and gold teeth and shit—they was tackier than clowns at a funeral. Super Fly had himself a laptop computer, he was making up some laws or whatever lawyers do, just clicking away. Then he put it away and decided he wanted to talk to me. He was like, "Hi," in that deep sexy voice. I got a sweet rush like I'd just gulped a mug full of Bailey's. I was like, "H...Hi!" So he sit down next to me an go, "I like your dress."

But as soon as he said that, he turnt his head and start looking at LaKeisha, trying to tell me how pretty he think she is. He can't even see her for all the dogs sniffing around her li'l fire hydrant, and he trying to get me all worked up about that girl.

Well, Almonetta wasn't having it. I got so mad I almost told him everything right then and there. It was all I could do when he axed me at one point what was the topic we was gonna be discussing. My skin felt all flushed when I lied and told him, "It's a show about, um, girls who party too much." After that I couldn't really say much. I put my nose back in my book.

Darnell, I don't like your li'l policy of not telling people who gonna be on the show what they gonna be talking about on the show until they get onstage, 'cause you never know how they gonna react. You put them in a embarrassing situation like that, who knows, one them gun-toting thugs could be a stone psycho motherfucker and take the whole audience out while you taping. I'm sure it would improve your ratings, honey, but please—think of the grief.

And you shouldn'ta axed me to esplain what was going on. I thought you was gonna step to those brothers like, "Yo, LaKeisha's a man, y'all." Why couldn't you do that? Instead, I had to take me a deep deep breath and break it to 'em gentle, like, "LaKeisha has been keeping a secret from y'all. It's inportant for y'all to know that the person you just been doing all that nasty fly-girl dancing with is not no biological female." I thought I's being all rational and whatnot, but I think if they'da heard it from a guy like you, Darnell, they wouldn'ta taken it upon theyself to start tearing shit up, ripping chairs out the floor, knocking them potted plants over and breaking them framed pitchers on the walls. And no one was more shocked than me when them bodyguards started joining in. Where'd you find those brutal motherfuckers anyway? Did you thaw them out a million-year-old block of ice?

And I think we all know that the final straw was brought on by Miss LaKeisha herself. All I was trying to do was speak the truth. She had no right to get all up in my face and start pointing. She did it on purpose too. She knows I hate it when people be sticking they fingers in my face. And how many times did I warn her? Four times, that's right, Darnell. Once when she pulled my wig out of place. Another time when she said I was doing this because I was jealous. The third when she called me ugly. All that shit I let roll off my back. But when she ripped the straps off my dress—my eight-hundred-dollar dress—and my falsies popped out in front of the nation, it was like every embarrassing thing I've ever suffered from that bitch had all happened at once. I just lost control, Darnell, I couldn't help it. Suddenly her face was the ugliest thing I'd ever seen in my life and I had to beat the crap outta her.

Anyways, Darnell, the reason I'm writing you back at all is so's we could compare our losses. You have lost $20,000 worth of camera equipment, carpeting, Steuben vases, tacky paintings and the services of a perky li'l assistant who out for a few days 'cause of a broken arm and a concussion. If you ain't had all that insured, you a fool.

Almonetta Rosé, on the other hand, has lost her dignity, her pride, a pair of shoulder pads that was essential to her persona, any potential dates that mighta been watching, a dress worth more than three times her life savings, and the once-priceless friendship and love of her former best girlfriend, LaKeisha Lorraine, also known as Ronald Knight.

My very handsome lawyer friend, who just happened to be present during the event that brought on your li'l lawsuit in the first place, told me over dinner last night that should you choose to prosecute, you should bear in mind that the only assets of the defendant is a dirty pile of women's panties. And you don't gotta sue me for that, Darnell. All you gotta do is axe.

Sincerely,
Tony Adamson
(a.k.a. Almonetta Rosé)

A Caring Rescue

BY ANDRE DUBUS III

OFFICER LESTER BURDON left his engine running and walked over to my window and I swung my leg off the seat and sat up. There were sweat stains under his arms, and his gold star hung away from his shirt. "I'm sorry about the coffee, Kathy, I got a call on a domestic. Did you wait long?"

"Just an hour or two."

"I am sorry, I —"

"I'm kidding. Forget it, I drove around." I hoped I didn't sound as happy as I felt seeing him now. "Still want coffee?"

"Yes." He had both hands on the door, looking right at me with a dark look—a wanting, I thought, definitely a wanting. I glanced down at my hands on the steering wheel.

"You mind riding in a patrol car?"

"Only if you're not busting me."

He smiled and I parked the Bonneville behind the truck stop between two eighteen-wheelers. I walked to Lester's cruiser and when I slid in and pulled the door shut he asked about my eviction, his face hard and soft at the same time. I told him about waking up in the house this morning, about the carpenters and the piece of roof in my yard. Lester started to shake his head and get that long-eyed look for me I didn't want, so I told him again how my lawyer promised to have me back home by the weekend and now I had someone I could celebrate with. I felt a little too naked putting it that way, and Lester didn't say anything back, just put his cruiser into gear and pulled out of the truck lot, heading west. I looked at the black radio set into the console, the green and orange scanner lights. There was a shotgun clipped under the dashboard, and I glanced over at Lester behind the wheel. He was shaking his head.

"Does your lawyer know you're sleeping in your car?"

"She thinks I'm with friends. That's what she wants to think anyway."

"What do you mean?"

"I mean there's a limit to how much she wants to help, that's all; she has her limits."

He drove onto the Cabrillo Highway and went quiet a minute.

"There's no one you can stay with, Kathy?"

I shrugged, my face heating up. "You don't meet a lot of people cleaning houses, I guess."

I felt his eyes on me. I squinted out at the bright ocean. I was tired and I wanted my sunglasses. We passed a few cars and I watched the drivers hold their heads still, glancing down at their speedometers and keeping their eyes on the road, only looking up once we'd pulled away.

"You ever get used to that?" I said.

"What?"

I nodded out the window at the slowing traffic. "People you don't know being scared of you."

"You really think they're scared?"

"Scared enough to mind their P's and Q's."

Lester turned off Cabrillo into the lot of a hot dog and ice cream shack on the beach. There were picnic tables on both sides of it and in back, and five or six teenage boys and girls sat at one near the order window. Their arms, legs and faces were tanned or sunburned. When they saw Lester get out of the car they looked away like he was the fourteenth cop they'd seen in the past ten minutes, and I liked being on the other end of that look. I could smell cooked hot dogs, the cigarette smoke of the teenagers, somebody's tanning lotion. The girl working behind the window told Lester they didn't have coffee so he said two Cokes would be fine, but then he looked over at me to check and I smiled at him.

In the shadow behind the shack Les carried our drinks while I walked through the cigarette butts in the sand. We sat at a weathered picnic table, and way ahead of us the Pacific Ocean seemed to be pulling out into low tide, its waves coming in long and small before they finally broke. Out on the water was a blue-gray cloud bank, the kind that usually came in as a fog, and the sky around it was a haze. Lester sat next to me on the bench facing the beach and for a while we just looked out at the water. I drank from my Coke and turned to him enough to take in his profile, his deep-set brown eyes, the small nose and badly trimmed mustache. Again, there was this gentleness to him, this quiet.

"How did you ever end up in that uniform, Lester?"

"Les." He glanced at me and smiled.

"Les." I was smiling too, but like a flirt, I thought. Like I wasn't really interested in the answer to my question.

"I was planning on being a teacher, actually."

"That's what you look like. I mean, that's what you seem like to me." I wanted to light a cigarette, but didn't want the taste in my mouth, not right now. "So then how come you're a boy in blue?"

He shook his head and looked down at the old tabletop, at a plank where someone had carved two breasts with X-shaped nipples. "My wife was pregnant. The academy was cheaper than graduate school, the guaranteed job afterward. That kind of thing."

"You like it?"

"Mostly."

"Mostly?"

He smiled at me, but his eyes had gone soft and he suddenly seemed too tender so I looked straight ahead again, at the cloud bank that had moved closer in just the past few minutes, the haze around it too. The beach sand wasn't as bright as before, and I caught the smell of seaweed. "Fog's coming in," I said. I could feel him still looking at me. I drank from my Coke until the ice slid to my teeth.

"Kathy?"

"Yeah?"

"I'd like to ask you something personal, if I could."

"All right, get it over with." I was kidding him again but I couldn't look at him so I kept my eyes on the green water, on the haze it seemed to make.

"Why is your husband not with you any longer?"

I watched a low wave ride all the way into the beach, and just before it broke, I felt I was rooting for it, hoping it wouldn't. "I wanted kids and he didn't. I don't know, I think if he really wanted me, he would have wanted them too, you know?"

Lester put his hand over mine on the table. It was warm and heavy. "He's a fool."

I looked down at his hand. "Have you been watching me, Officer Burdon?"

"Yes."

"Good."

"It is?"

"That you didn't lie."

He took a breath. "I haven't stopped thinking of you since the eviction, Kathy." I looked at him now. His voice was quiet, but there was something like boldness in his eyes. Our knees were touching. He lowered his eyes, but then, as if he'd made himself do it, he looked back at me, his brown eyes not bold anymore. He reminded me of me. He squeezed my hand and I suddenly felt so close to him that kissing him didn't even feel like a forward movement. His mustache was prickly and soft against my upper lip and I let my mouth open and I tasted his sweet Coke. I held his back and he held mine and the kiss went on for a long time, it seemed, until we finally took a breath and pulled apart and the fog was floating in close to the beach and it was getting hard to see the water. I looked at him, at his small straight nose, his lower lip beneath his mustache, his shaved chin. When I got to his eyes that were taking me in so completely, my mouth felt funny so I focused on his gold star badge, his name etched on the tag beneath it, and I wanted to run my fingertips over the letters. The temperature had dropped and I had goose pimples on my arms and legs.

"Let's find you a place to stay." Les stood up and grabbed our empty cups, and as he helped me over the sand to his car, I didn't say anything. We rode quietly through Corona into San Bruno, where he turned north just before the El Camino Real Highway. Under the gray sky we passed one-story houses with small grass lawns. Behind them was the highway, and I could see the cars and long trucks going south for towns like Hillsborough, I guessed, San Carlos, Menlo Park, Los Altos, and Sunnyvale, towns I'd driven through alone for months now, telling myself I wasn't looking for my husband's gray Honda. Les was quiet behind the wheel and even though we were in his police cruiser, it was so familiar to be sitting on the passenger's side of a car with a man driving again that I felt sort of up and down all at once. Then we were away from houses and in a neighborhood of gas stations, fast-food restaurants and a shopping center right next to the highway. "So where're we going, Les?"

He looked at me, then rested his hand on my knee and turned left, driving past the shopping center to a stretch of motel and travel inns on a grassy hill along the El Camino Real Highway.

"You want a pool?" Without waiting for me to answer he turned into the small parking lot of the Eureka Motor Lodge, a two-story white brick building with a fake-looking terra-cotta roof. Outside the office door were two Coke machines and an ice machine. A carved wooden sign hung over its window: EUREKA: I HAVE FOUND IT!

"This neighborhood's better than the other one, Kathy. I can't let you sleep in your car."

"I'll have to pay you back."

"Shh." He put his finger close to my lips. I pretended to bite it and he smiled, then went into the office, all uniform, gun and wedding ring. For a second I asked myself just what I was doing anyway, but then I concentrated on how good a bath would feel, a firm bed with clean sheets.

The room was in the back, away from the highway, facing the pool. Les helped me in, then excused himself to go to the bathroom. I sat at the foot of a queen-size bed covered with a periwinkle spread. The floor was carpeted and clean. Against the curtained window were two cushioned chairs on each side of a small glass-topped table. In front of me was a color TV on a stand next to a walnut dresser and mirror. I couldn't see my reflection from where I sat, so I started to stand when the toilet flushed; the water ran, and Les walked back into the room drying his hands on a towel he dropped on the dresser.

"Looks like you've done this before," I said.

"Why do you say that?" He stood where he was, a hurt look on his face, his hands resting on his gun belt.

"Sorry, it was just a joke."

He opened his mouth like he was going to say more, then he squatted at the mini-fridge on the other side of the dresser and pulled out two cans of Michelob, handing me one. It was cold in my hands and I looked down at it in my lap, like I was seeing an old Polaroid of somebody I used to know and for a second didn't know why I didn't anymore. Les opened his and drank from it right there, standing over me. But I couldn't even look up at him. I let the can drop to the floor and I flopped back on the bed and covered my face. What was I doing? I wondered if my thighs looked fat from where he stood. I heard him rest his beer can on the dresser, then squat to pick up the other, the leather of his gun belt creaking. The mattress sank with his weight and I lowered my hands and he was looking into my face, leaning on one arm so his shoulder moved up to his ear. He looked almost feminine that way, and for some reason it made me want to kiss him again. He was moving his middle finger over my wrist and forearm, and though his eyes didn't have that boldness, they didn't look sad either.

"You have no idea who I am, Lester."

"I think you're the most beautiful woman I've ever seen."

I put my hand on his warm hairy arm and he leaned down and kissed me. His tongue was cool from the beer and I could taste it and that did something to me. I scooted away from him and sat back against the headboard.

"What, Kathy?"

I wanted a cigarette, but didn't know where I'd left them. I crossed my arms in front of me. Les sat at the foot of the bed looking at me like I was about to say something deep. "I haven't had a drink in almost three years, Lester."

"I'm sorry, I didn't know."

"I know you didn't, but you don't know much about me, do you?"

His lips were parted beneath his mustache and he looked away, stood, then walked over and took his can of beer into the bathroom and I could hear him pouring it down the sink. I wanted to tell him he didn't have to do that, but I didn't trust my voice not to sound bitchy.

"You didn't have to dump that beer, Les. It's not like that."

His eyes caught mine. "What's it like then, Kathy? I'd like to know."

"You would?"

"Yes. I would."

I put my hand on the spread. "Come here." He hesitated a half second, as if he didn't know what I had in mind, and truthfully, I don't think I had anything in mind. But when he sat on the bed beside me, then leaned over and kissed my forehead, my cheek, my lips, his hand pressed to my rib cage, the other stroking my hair back, it was like I was an empty well and didn't know it until just now when he uncovered me and it started to rain and I pulled him on me and opened my mouth and I held the sides of his head and kissed him so hard our teeth knocked together; I kissed his cheeks, his eyes, his nose; I licked his mustache and kissed him openmouthed again. I began to unbutton his shirt and he pulled my T-shirt over my head, then everything slowed down as he touched my breasts. A change came over him, and me too. He looked into my eyes, checking on something one last time, then he sat up and very slowly untied his shoes. He put them aside, unsnapped his pistol from its holster and laid it on the bedside table. When he pulled his shirttails from his pants, I swung my legs to the other side of the bed, unsnapped my shorts, and pulled them and my underpants off. My fingers were shaking, and I was thirsty, but a throbbing heat had moved between my legs and I lay back on the bed just as Les stepped out of his boxer shorts, his rear small and dark. He turned to face me and I made myself look up at his crooked mustache, at his messed-up hair, his narrow shoulders. I was sixteen all over again, Ma gone shopping, Dad at work, plenty of time before we get caught. I gripped his shoulders, drew my heels up along the backs of his legs and pulled him forward.

Folk Song, 1999

BY MARY GAITSKILL

ON THE SAME PAGE of the city paper one day:

A confessed murderer awaiting trial for the torture and murder of a woman and her young daughter is a guest on a talk show via satellite. His appearance is facilitated by the mother's parents, who wanted him to tell them exactly what the murder of their daughter and grandchild was like.

"It was horrible to talk to him," said the talk show hostess. "He will go down in history as the lowest of the low." There was a photograph of the killer, smiling as if he'd won a prize.

A woman in San Francisco announced her intention to have intercourse with 1,000 men in a row, breaking the record of a woman in New Mexico who had performed the same feat with a mere 750. "I want to show what women can do," she said. "I am not doing this as a feminist, but as a human being."

Two giant turtles belonging to an endangered species were stolen from the Bronx Zoo. "This may've been an inside job," said the zoo president. "This *person knew what he was doing, and he was very smart. We just hope he keeps them together—they're very attached." The turtles are valued at $300.00 each.*

It was in the middle of the paper, a page that you were meant to scan before turning, loading your brain with subliminal messages as you did. How loathsome to turn a sadistic murder into entertainment—and yet how hard not to read about it. What dark comedy to realize that you are scanning for descriptions of torture even as you disapprove. Which of course only makes it more entertaining. "But naturally I was hoping they'd report something grisly," you say to your friends, who chuckle at your acknowledgment of hypocrisy.

And they did report something grisly: that the grandparents of the murdered girl wanted to know what only the murderer could tell them. You picture the grandmother's gentle wrinkled chest, a thick strip of flesh pulled away to reveal an unexpected passage to hell in her heart.

Then you have the marathon woman right underneath, smiling like an evangelist, her organs open for a thousand. An especially grotty sort of pie-eating contest, placed right beneath the killer, an open body juxtaposed against the pure force of destruction. Why would a woman do that? What do her inane words really mean? Will she select the thousand, is there at least a screening process? Or is it just anyone who shows up? If he had not been arrested, could the killer himself have mounted her along with everybody else? If she had discovered who he was, would that have been okay with her? Would she have just swallowed him without a burp?

You picture her at the start of her ordeal, parting a curtain to appear before the crowd, muscular, oiled, coifed, dressed in a lamé bathing suit with holes cut in the titties and crotch. She would turn and bend to show the suit had been cut there too. She would "ring-walk" before the bed, not like a stripper, more like a pro wrestler, striking stylized sex poses, flexing the muscles of her belly and thighs, gesticulating with mock anger, making terrible penis-busting faces.

Might the killer enjoy this spectacle if he could watch it on TV? He may be a destroyer of women, but his victims were regular, human-style women: a concerned mother trying to connect with her daughter on a road trip in nature—the trip that delivered them into the hands of the killer.

You picture her reading *Reviving Ophelia* the night before they left, frowning slightly as she thinks of the teenage boy years ago who fucked her bottom and then took her to dinner at Pizza Hut, thinks also of her daughter's co-ed sleepover last week. Getting out of bed to use the bathroom with only the hall light on, peeing in gentle darkness, remembering: grown-up pee used to smell so bad to her, and now the smell is just another welcome personal issue of her hard-working body, tough and fleshy in middle-age, safe under her old flowered gown. The daughter is awake too, and reading *Wuthering Heights*. She is thirteen, and she is irritated that the author has such sympathy for Heathcliff, who abuses his wife and child. What does it mean that he is capable of such passionate love? Is this realistic, or were people just dumber and more romantic back then? She doesn't think that the mean people she knows are the most passionate; they just want to laugh at everything. But then she remembers that she laughed when a boy in class played a joke on an ugly girl and made her cry. Sighing, she puts the book down and lies on her back, her arm thrown luxuriantly over her head. On the ceiling, there are the beautiful shadows of slim branches and leaves. She does not really want to take this trip with her mother. Her mother tries so hard to help her and to protect her, and she finds this embarrassing. It makes her want to protect her mother, and that feeling is uncomfortable too. She rolls on her side and picks up the book again.

Thought and feeling, flesh and electricity, ordinary yet complex personalities, the like of which the killer had found impossible to maintain inside himself from the moment of his birth—and yet which he could erase with the strange, compulsive pleasure of an autistic child banging his head on the wall. You picture him as a little boy alone in an empty room, head subtly inclined as if he is listening intently for a special sound. In the top drawer of his dresser, there are rows of embalmed mice stacked neatly atop one another. At age twelve, he has killed many animals besides mice, but he embalms only the mice because uniformity satisfies him. He likes embalming because it is clean, methodical and permanent. He likes his mind to be uniform and inflexible as a grid. Below the grid is like the life of animals: sensate and unbearably deep.

There are people who believe that serial killers are a "fundamental force of nature," a belief that would be very appealing to the killer. Yes, he would say to himself, that is me. I am fundamental!

But the marathon woman on TV would be fundamental too. She would not show her personality, and even if she did, nobody would see it; they would be too distracted by the thought of a mechanical cunt, endlessly absorbing discharge. However, with her lamé bathing suit and her camp ring-walk, appealing to everyone's sense of fun, she would be the fundamental female as comedy: the killer could sit comfortably in the audience and laugh, enjoying this appearance of his feminine colleague. Maybe he would feel such comfort that he would stand and come forward, unbuckling his pants with the flushed air of a modest person finally coming up to give testimony. Safe in her sweating, loose and very wet embrace, surrounded by the dense energy of many men, his penis could tell her the secret story of murder right in front of everyone. Her worn vagina would hold the killer like it had held the husband and the lover and the sharpie and the father and the nitwit and every other man, his terrible story a tiny, burning star in the rightful firmament of her female vastness.

Hell, yes, she would "show what women can do!"

In the context of this terrible humanity you think: the poor turtles! They do not deserve to be on the same page with these people! You think of them making their stoic way across a pebbled beach, their craning necks wrinkled and diligent, their bodies a secret even they cannot lick or scratch. The murdered woman, in moments of great tenderness for her husband, would put her hands on his thighs and kiss him on his balls and say to him "secret Paul." She didn't mean that his balls were a secret. She meant that she was kissing the part of him that no one knew except her, and that the vulnerability of his balls made her feel this part acutely. That is the kind of secret the turtles are, even to themselves.

But now all natural secrets have been exposed, and it is likely the turtles have been sold to laboratory scientists who want to remove their shells so that they can wire electrodes to the turtles' skin in order to monitor their increasing terror at the loss of their shells. Scientists do these experiments because they want to help. They want to alleviate physical suffering; they want to eradicate depression. To achieve their goal, they will take everything apart and put it back together a different way. They want heaven and they will go to hell to get there.

But still, there is grace. Before the mother met the murderer, her vagina had been gently parted and kissed many times. Her daughter had exposed her own vagina before her flowered cardboard mirror (bought at Target and push-pinned to the wall), regarding her organs with pleased wonder, thinking, "This is what I have."

And maybe the turtles were not kidnapped but rescued: There are actually preserves for turtles, special parks where people can take turtles they have found or grown tired of, or rescued from the polluted, fetid fish tanks of uncaring neighbors. Or maybe they were simply set free near the water, wading forward together as the zoo spokesman had hoped, eyes bright in scaly heads, each with the unerring sense of the other's heartbeat, a signal they never knew to question.

And maybe she didn't start the marathon in a gold lamé suit. Maybe she appeared in a simple white gown with a slip and a bra and stockings and beautiful panties that the first man (hand-selected for his sensitivity) had to help her to take off to the sound of "The First Time Ever I Saw Your Face." Maybe they even took time to make out, acknowledging romantic love and the ancient truth of marriage. It would be the stiff and brassy acknowledgment of showbiz, but deep in the brass case would be a sad and tender feeling—sad because they could only stay a moment in this adolescent sweetness, they could not develop it into the full flower of adult intimacy and parenthood. But this flower comes in the form of a human; it must soon succumb to disease, atrophy, ruined skin, broken teeth, the unbearable frailty of mortality.

The marathon woman is not interested in mortality or human love. Right now, the marathon woman has infinity on her mind. Roberta Flack's crooning fades. The first man mournfully withdraws. Then: the majestic pounding of kettle drums and brisk, surging brass! It's *2001: A Space Odyssey*! The lights go up! The silhouettes of naked men are revealed on the screen behind her bed, above which spins a giant mirror ball! Men step from behind the screen and array themselves about the bed, splendid in their nakedness, even the ugly ones, like gladiators poised to plunge in! This one now, number two, is very short and muscular, covered with hair. His face is handsome, his body exudes physical swagger shadowed by physical grief. The woman cannot know that, at eighteen, he was a gunnery mate on a PT boat in Vietnam, or that *Time* once ran a photograph of him posed with his machine gun, the brim of his helmet low across his eyes, a cigarette sticking up at a jaunty angle from between his clenched, smiling lips. She can't know it but she can feel it: the stunned cockiness of an ignorant boy cradling Death in one arm, cockiness now held fast in the deep heart of a middle-aged man. Just before he enters her, she pictures his heart bristling with tough little hairs. Then she feels his dick and forgets his heart. He pulls her on top of him and she feels another man ready to climb up her butt while number four bossily plants himself in her mouth, one hand holding his penis, the other on his fleshy hip. The referee, a balding fellow in a smart striped shirt, weaves deftly in and out of the melee, ensuring that real penetration is taking place each time. The music segues into hammering dance music, the kind favored by porn movies, only better. The music is like a mob breaking down a flimsy door and spilling endlessly over the threshold. It celebrates dissolution but it has a rigid form and it hits the same button again and again. It makes you think of Haitian religious dances where the dancers empty their personalities to receive the raw flux of spirit—except this music does not allow for spirit. This is the music of personality and obsession, and it is like a high-speed purgatory where the body is disintegrated and reanimated over and over until the soul is a dislocated blur. It is fun! People dance to music like this every night in great glittering venues all over the world, and now the woman and the men fuck to it. They are really doing it and it is chaos! The referee furrows his brow as he darts about, occasionally giving the "rollover" signal with his forearms, or a "TKO" hand-sign barring a man who's trying to sneak in a second time. And because it is chaos, there are moments when the woman's mind slips through the bullying order of the music and the assault of the men. There are many trapdoors in personality and obsession, and she blunders down some of them—even though she doesn't realize that she has done so. Like the killer, she is now only able to occupy her surface because extraordinary physical demands are being made on her surface. By turning herself into a fucking machine, she has created a kind of temporary grid. But underneath, in the place of dream and feeling, she is going places that she, on the surface, would not understand.

What no one would guess about this woman who is having intercourse with a thousand men: She is afraid of men. Her father was an ineffectual man who was enraged by his own weakness, and so his daughter grew up surrounded by his silent, humiliated rage. Her mother smothered her own strength in order to make her father look strong; that didn't work, so the girl grew up with her mother's rage too. She had no way to put male and female together inside herself without rage.

This is the core of her fear. Her fear is so great that she cannot afford to recognize it. It is so great that it has taken on a thrilling sexual charge. Because the woman is courageous by nature, she has always gone directly toward what she most fears. When she began to have sex with boys, it was as if she was picking up a doll marked GIRL and a doll marked BOY and banging them together, hoping to unite herself. As she grew older, the woman inside her became more insatiable and the man became more angry. He became angry enough to kill.

Because this woman is decent, she will not kill. But in deep sleep, she dreams of terrible men. In the worst of these dreams, a killer with magic power came to her childhood home. He bewitched her mother so that she let him in. He turned her father into a dog chained to a post. He carved his name on the girl's face. He butchered her mother like a cow.

This dream was so terrible that the girl forgot it before she woke. It is still inside the woman. He is part of her, the male who would kill. The female he wants to kill is part of her too. Deep inside, she is still trying to bring them together. And for one moment, down a special trapdoor, she has found a way. If the murderer who guested on the talk show had been fucking the marathon woman at this moment, he might've had a feeling of subconscious unease: for she has entered the deep place of sex and it is not a place the killer wants to be. This is a place without form or time. There can be no grid here. Even the shape of his heart will no longer hold; it will be forced to open. Sorrow, terror, hate, love, pity, joy: all human feeling will come in and he will be unable to bear it. He will dissolve. His killing nature will be stripped to abstract movement, a bursting surge overtaking the weaker prey, the principle of pouncing and eating. In this place, all pouncing and eating is contained, because this place contains everything. This place is her ovaries and her eggs, bejeweled with moisture, the coarse, tough flowers sprouting in her abdomen, the royal, fleshy padding of her cunt. Some people say that nature is like a machine. But this is not a machine. This is something else: a million dark wombs giving birth to millions of creatures, wet and rank, eyes sealed blind with darkness, humans and animals, all forms derived from every formless entity swarming in boundless black nothingness.

When male turtles fuck, they thrust deep inside their mates, they stretch out their necks, they throw back their heads and they scream. They don't have to drop through trapdoors or travel down layers. They are already there. Animals want to live because they are supposed to. But they know death better than a human killer. Life and death are in them all the time.

The marathon woman is more than halfway through, and she is

tired. You are tired too, just from thinking about it. The theme from *Chariots of Fire* is on the sound system, but you are hearing a very old song from the Industrial Age called "John Henry." It is about a steel driver of great strength who outperformed the machine invented to replace him. He won, but in doing so, he died. The song ends, "He lay down his hammer and he died." This song is not about sex or about women. The marathon woman is not going to die, nor is she going to win. She has no hammer to lay down. But she is like John Henry anyway because she is making herself into a machine. But she is not a machine. She is something else.

Over
Chinese

BY RACHEL SHERMAN

MY FATHER SAYS that, after twenty years, maybe it's enough. Maybe it is his own fault, those few nights at home, in front of the TV, charging away the hours. And then those other nights, the nights away, when indiscreet smells from his starched shirts would reek from the hamper...

Suddenly, everything felt so raw, as if it had happened yesterday, but twice as bad just to spite me. My father's mistakes flashed from the tube onto his glasses, from the glass table to the infinite snow of our prized and perfect snow globe that was too crazy when shaken and too much of a mess to break.

He takes me out for Chinese.

"Enough is enough," he says, and eats hot and sour soup. He licks his big fish lips. If he were a girl, the boys would tease and call him D.S.L. Dick Sucking Lips. I am a girl and I own his lips. The boys tease less than they used to.

My father kissed me once and it was not a nice kiss. It was on the lips and too wet. It was for my mother.

"Tell me," my father says, over our fourth Bloody Mary, "tell me."

Sometimes I forget who my father is. He wasn't around as much when I was younger and now that I've begun to notice him, his slicked gray hair, his sweet, back-deep eyes, I look for things familiar, for things licked up and pasted in the center of me, connected by more than white saliva, but dreamy as a kiss.

I tell my father about the boy who lives next door, who is so close through my walls I can hardly sleep. This boy, he likes me for the things I can't control: the way my hips jut out like my mother's from the side, my thick and sad pillowed lips.

I tell my father how the boy said we could dress up. I could pretend to be Jackie O and he could be John. I tell my father how I told the boy that he too may die a tragic death—too tragic for me to watch—but that I was good at pretending.

"Stay faithful," my father says, having just ruined his marriage.

Meanwhile, I order egg rolls, feel my father's leg beneath the table and die. I worry that things are off-center, that my watch is minutes fast. I watch the light from the window, the glare from his glasses, his fingers, my hands.

Perv

BY JERRY STAHL

I DIDN'T OFFICIALLY see her go. I made myself look away, pretending to watch for pedestrians. But I heard her, the first quick *wisssh,* then the sputtering gush. I saw the pee run and puddle the damp cement. A frothy stream ran under my work boots but I didn't move. It wasn't piss. It was her piss.

I couldn't believe it. After my whole life, Michele's pussy was right there... and I stared somewhere else. When the puddling stopped, she tugged my pant leg. She raised her face and gave me a funny smile. "You want to?" Her voice was sweet and girlish again.

"Want to what?"

"You know..." Shy and defiant at the same time. "Wipe me. Girls have to wipe when they pee, you know. My daddy always wiped me."

"Your daddy?"

Maybe I could tell her about Mom's cuddle-fish.

My mouth went so dry I could have spit wood chips. The sun peeped out of the clouds and everything looked super clear. More real than real. The wet crease between her legs was the color of champagne. My parents served it every New Year. I never liked the taste, but now sneaking a peek—because it was too much, because I would die or go blind—now I guessed I'd love it.

"I don't have any tissue," I sputtered, but Michele only shrugged. "So?"

That's how it happened: in the middle of the Miracle Mile parking lot, I not only got to feel like I loved a girl, I got to feel when you touch one—down there—and love her at the same time. I trailed my finger so lightly on her slit, I hardly touched her at all. I'd have strangled puppies to do more, but there were all those people, those cars. All that light and traffic. The air felt like cold tinfoil.

I thought, idiotically, What would Bob Dylan do? Then I freaked. I imagined a station wagon owner footsteps away, ready to catch me. But catch me what? All I was doing—and I couldn't believe I was doing it—was brushing my hand along Michele's cleft, feeling the hot wet of her. The warm droplets in her champagne slit mingled with the chilly rain still on my fingers.

"Lick it," she said. Just like that. Matter of fact. "Lick it."

And, still standing over her, sort of leaning in, I slowly brought my hand up to my mouth. Yes! All the traffic noise seemed to fade away. The volume of the world had been turned down, leaving nothing but the roar of blood rushing from my balls to my ears. I let her see what I was doing. My tongue sponged along my knuckles, over the backs of my hands. I tasted the briny flavor of what I guessed was pee. I made a show of it, darting my tongue between my fingers, wiggling it, like a goldfish plucked out of its bowl. Then she spoke up again.

"I didn't mean that, Bobby. I meant this."

I stopped my knuckle lapping, looked down again, to where her finger was describing little circles. Her wrist blocked all but the purple-pink clit. "You know," she said huskily, "the little man in the boat."

"You mean...right here?"

My face got hot. I imagined police. Choppers swooping out of the sky, fixing us in a telephoto lens, filming everything and presenting the evidence to a horrified jury. I could see the witnesses: Dolores Fish and Dr. Mushnik, Ned Friendly, Weiner, Tennie Toad and Farwell and Headmaster Bunton. All of them dying to testify, itching to send me to Perv Jail.

My head wouldn't stop. I saw my mother, pill-drunk and burbling baby country-and-western, hiking up her salmon nighty and tell the judge, "He wuvs to cuddle..." They'd drag her from the courtroom facedown in a box of turtles, yelping for electroshock. Somewhere in sweaty heaven, watching all of it, Mr. Schmidlap would crack a Rheingold with his flipper while Dad banged his head off the nearest wall.

"BOBBY!" Michele's harsh whisper brought me blinking back. "Bobby, GO AHEAD. Bobby, I WANT you to..."

She touched herself and I shivered.

"But there's... I mean... There's all these people."

"I know," she said, but huskily, edging her back against the tire well of the VW bus. She parted her naked thighs slightly further. "I know."

The way she studied me, it's like she was measuring something, seeing how far I'd go. Or else—and this really made my stomach sink—how much I loved her. I was so hard I thought my dick would crack off. But all those people! Those cars! The weather...

You didn't think of sex and weather in the same breath. You didn't have to. Not normally. Not ever. Except for here, in the Miracle Mile parking lot, where Lela the Hare Krishna, who used to be Michele Burnelka, was on the run from Shiva—whoever Shiva was—and on her haunches for me. Whoever I was. That's what I wrestled with. Not, Can I do this? But, What the fuck was it I thought I was doing? And who the fuck was doing it?

Even the raindrops seemed to mock me.

"Michele," I stammered. I was ready, but then... A Negro lady gawked at me from a Dodge Dart and it seized me up. I had to pull the words like olives from out of my throat. "Michele, I can't... I can't do it."

I heard myself and I died. It killed me to find out this was me. I had everything I ever wanted. AND LOOK WHAT CAME OUT OF MY MOUTH!

It wasn't like I was being a "good boy." It was like, I don't know, like I was scared. Or not even scared, just... guilty. That was it. My psyche sputtered like defective neon. One thought wrenched my brain: Mom's seen a husband stroll under a streetcar. She's seen a daughter disappear to Canada, her son fucked-up and flown home, kicked out of a pricey prep school. If that weren't enough, picture her expression when I was arrested for public pee tasting, or whatever the legal term happened to be. How could I face her if I got popped for a sex crime? For the ten zillionth time, I wished I was an orphan, like my long-gone father, just so I could relax.

Just to make things perfect, my voice squeeched into Jiminy Cricket. "Michele, I really like you... I mean, I've always, like, loved you, it's just that..."

"Forget it," she said, her face hardening. She pulled up her pants and launched herself off the station wagon in a single movement, as though she'd been bouncing off cars and asphalt her entire life. "Forget it, Bobby. It's nothing."

"Really?"

This was so hugely untrue, so clearly not nothing, I hated myself for needing to hear it.

I held my hand out to help, but Michele ignored it and dusted herself off.

"You don't," she said with a brittle laugh, "you don't think I was serious, do you? You don't think I'm some kind of exhibitionist."

"Gee, I don't know," I said. I just knew I wanted to rip my tongue out at the sound of "gee." This was worse than Jiminy Cricket. My voice box had been hijacked by Wally Cleaver. Because I never said "gee." Never before and never since. I was not a "gee" type person. But I couldn't tell Michele that. What was the point?

To Michele, from here on in, I'd be the geek who said "gee" and didn't have the balls to lick her pussy in broad daylight. With one move—or lack of one—I'd killed something horribly important. Whatever else happened, I knew I'd spend the rest of whatever time I had left walking upright trying to redeem myself.

When Michele slouched off toward the highway, I resolved to be a badass. A rebel. A daredevil. Keith Richards with Jew-hair. Whatever it took to de-lame myself, that's what I'd do.

With no plan to speak of, I announced, "We need sleeping bags." To which Michele replied, "Sleeping bags cost money."

Remembering that she had all the money, and knowing I'd look like an even bigger lightweight if I asked for it back—suppose she said, "No!" Suppose she said, "Fuck you!" Then what?—I heard myself mumbling, Marlon Brando–style, "Don't worry about it. One thing I know how to do is steal."

And without another word, I headed back to the mall. Before I left, I thought I caught a flicker of respect in her eyes. It gave me hope. (And a partial erection.)

I was back in ten minutes with a pair of lightweight goose-downs, army green and waterproof.

When I handed hers over, I could tell she was impressed. With any luck, I wouldn't have to knock off a gas station to make her forget my cowardice. I could probably kill a man with my bare hands and it wouldn't matter now. *Too-chicken-to-lick*. It might as well have been tattooed on my forehead. What do you do when you're branded and you know you're a man?

Michele's eyes grew huge under her Beatles cap. At some point, she'd dumped the rose-petal grannies, and I didn't miss them. She squeezed the sleeping bag, then smiled. "You... you stole these?"

"No big thing." I shrugged, and pretty much stood still while she hugged me. I didn't want to look too eager. Didn't want her to know what I felt. Most of all, I didn't want her to accidentally touch my ass. The credit card was in my back pocket. The last thing I needed was her finding out I charged the bags to my mother.

Intimacy

BY HENRY WREN

IF I SENSE that they're going to fuck back there (after twenty-six years in the business I can usually tell at the beginning of the evening, sometimes long before either of them have any intuitions of intimacy) I'll drive them to Iwo Jima out in Virginia. Not only is Iwo Jima beautiful at night, all lit up, but it's a good long drive away, it allows ample time for him to move to her side of the seat, to kiss her on the cheek, for her to kiss him back, for him to kiss her neck, for her to crane it, to intimate a moan, for him to touch her breasts, to mess her hours of hair, to begin to undo the preparation like winding a clock hand backward, for her to fumble with his cummerbund, for him to begin work at what is always an inconvenient dress, to look for quick ways in, of which there are never any, for her to help him help her out of the dress—the dark window between the driver and passenger compartments of the car is usually raised for all of this, but not always—for her to lick her palm before taking his cock, for him to move his hand down from her breasts, down to her belly, down to her pussy, which is usually wet, and sometimes leaves a water-soluble mark I have to take care of in the morning, for him to insert a finger or two in her pussy, two or three knuckles deep, for her to moan, for him to think about baseball, or his mother, or anything to distract the seven seconds of come knocking on the door of his existence, for her to lean over and wrap her lips around him, to take off her class ring and use her hand under her mouth, like she was trying to swallow a microphone, for him to pull back her hair to watch her suck him off, for her to sit up, to remove her panties from over her high heels, which she usually won't take off, I don't know why, for her either to spread her legs, bend her knees and pull him unto and into her, which is the most common way of accommodating to the backseat, or mount him, to use her hand to insert his cock into her from behind, to balance and torque herself with her hands against the defrost parallels of the back window, to push her chest into his face, for him to say, sometimes with a whisper into her ear, sometimes with a holler, "I'm fucking you, I'm fucking you, I'm fucking you, I'm fucking you," because he's still in high school, still more aroused by the fact of his having sex than by the sex itself, for him to fuck her, to fuck her all the way to Iwo Jima, to roll down the window, which he thinks is something like a joke, and watch the city pass as they fuck, the city that I choose to give to them: the gay bars and rusting neon of Dupont Circle, the losing lottery tickets of Mount Pleasant, the fluted columns of the Tidal Basin, the baguettes and bag ladies of Georgetown, the numb yellow street lights of the Whitehurst Freeway, the scenery that I choose for them as they fuck in my backseat.

This has been my job for twenty-six years. I drive a limousine. During most of the week I drive rich people who are used to limousines. I drive them from here to there, am never late and never talk unless I'm spoken to. Just before the summer, in mid and late May, early June, I drive high school kids to proms. These kids have never been in a limo before, and have saved up for months to pay for this one magical night. Some will actually call it that: the one magical night. Because of this, they very often have sex in my backseat.

I may have to drive around Iwo Jima several times, waiting to be sure they're completely done, and more than done, that they're at peace, rested, happy. That's my job, if I had to state it in such a way: to make people happy. I'll circle around while they finish up. I'll see our boys' faces, their right sides, from the back. I'll watch the names at the base circle by and blur. I'll try to count the soldiers in the statue, but it's almost impossible because of the way they're climbing all over each other. Every time you look at it you think you see another arm, or another boot. All of these must connect to another soldier, you think. (There are seven of them.) It doesn't bother me to drive as long as they need back there. I've driven around the memorial for hours waiting. Sometimes they'll finish only to start again. How do I know? After twenty-six years, you learn to know. I've memorized every fold in every shirt on the boys in the memorial. I know how the helmets fit on the heads. I know how the backpacks rest, and whose hand is where on the flag that they're so eager to stab into the island. Whose hand is on top.

When they're done in the back, I always get them out of the car to see the memorial. They like it when I do this. It makes the night feel more magical, more unique, like everyone else is in a limo but only they get a tour from their driver. Usually she'll be wearing his jacket, smoking a cigarette, a complete mess as compared to how she looked at the beginning of the evening. He'll look better than he did when we picked her up, more relaxed, I guess, and will sometimes hand me a couple of bucks, although I don't know why. "This is my job," I tell him. Which is not to say that I give it back. "Iwo Jima," I say, pointing to the memorial in front of us. "One of the Volcanic Islands in the North Pacific, south of Japan. Site of the greatest battle in Marine history." They're holding hands, always, this is how it always is, they're holding hands, and his attention is elsewhere, maybe at other girls walking around, maybe off in space, maybe replaying the events of a few moments ago, but she's listening, so I talk to her.

"I've never been to Japan," she says, "but I'd like to go."

"Well, it's amazing. It's an amazing place. My brother wrote me letters from there, every day."

"Every day!"

"Every day," I'll say, and sometimes I'll feel proud of that. "We returned the island to the Japs in '68, so I don't know about since, but it used to be just beautiful. That's what he told me."

He'll kiss her. He'll put his hand on her butt, and she'll smile, as if for me. Am I happy for them? Of course I am. Who do I hate?

"It's a really pretty monument," she'll say.

And then we'll get to talking more. He isn't paying attention. He doesn't care. The further away his mind goes—and he may even go for a walk on his own at this point—the closer we get. I've said everything I have to say for the evening, I don't want to say any more than I already have, so I let her talk. I let her tell me about how she's never been to Japan, but has been to Portugal, which is really pretty. She was there for a semester, because school was becoming too much. Home was. I let her tell me about how she doesn't usually smoke, she hardly ever smokes, she doesn't even know why she's smoking now. I let her tell me how she has a little brother with Down's syndrome, and he can really be embarrassing sometimes, I've never said this to anyone, I'm ashamed to say it out loud, but I've been drinking, you know, God, I hope it's okay that we had a couple of drinks in your car, but, well, it's just that I love him, but. You know. But. And then I let her tell me about her first boyfriend's car, and how the alignment was so bad, you're not going to believe this, but he actually had to hold the wheel upside down to go straight. I let her tell me about where she lost her virginity, it was so long ago, I can't believe how young I once was, I don't know why I'm telling you this, you probably think I'm some kind of weirdo. She flicks the ash, and I let her tell me about her father's girlfriend, and a food called *panini,* they're just little sandwiches, and how given the choice she'll always use a pencil. I let her tell me about her brother's school, which is a special school in Virginia, and the music she likes to listen to, and how her room is decorated, and her friend Tracy's night in Atlantic City when she won four hundred dollars but had to give it back when they asked for some ID. I let her tell me about what college she wants to go to, and her mom's sleeping pills. And after everything she tells me is my implicit response. "It's okay." I don't say it, I don't say anything, but it's there, hovering like the dust between the spotlights and the statue. I let her tell me again that she doesn't usually smoke. "It's okay." I really want to learn to drive a motorcycle. Do you know how to drive a motorcycle? "It's okay." All the while, she doesn't even realize that we've been walking, that I've been leading her around the memorial, around our young boys blown up huge like heroes against the night. The breeze makes her shiver, and I let her tell me about how she's allergic to peanuts, how if one touches her lips, even touches them, she could die, and I lead her to my older brother's name. HENRY J. TILLMAN, JR.

"This is my brother."

"Oh."

"Right there."

"He's—"

"My brother."

"I'm so—"

I interrupt her with my nod. I don't ask her to touch the name. Wouldn't do that. I don't tell her about how he died, or what he was like, or any of that. Not even if she asks, which she almost never does.

"That's him, anyway," I say.

By now he's usually come back from wherever he went. Sometimes he's been with us all along, and only mentally absent. Sometimes he won't let go of her hand. I've seen guys go off and take a piss in the bushes. I know that sometimes you have to take a piss after fucking, but still. "We should get going," he'll say, and I'll lead them back to the car. I won't look at her in the mirror, even if the glass is down. When I drop them off, he usually gives me another tip, this time a bit bigger, maybe a twenty. "It's my job," I tell him.

Then I drive home. The car stays with me. It's a leasing arrangement. I park it in a garage I rent from my neighbor two doors down. So no one will mess with it. I open my door, which involves four keys, and take off my jacket and pants. My apartment isn't fit for a king, but I'm not a king, so it works out fine. Two rooms. Kitchen. Bedroom. I make a good living. Since the car is with me, I can pretty much choose my own hours, which is good. I want to get up at noon. I get up at noon. I need some extra cash. Not even need. Want. I get up at the crack of dawn, or before. I'll use the car like a cab. I've got a sign I put on top. The neighbors upstairs are usually fighting, even though it's already the morning of the next day. Why do they fight so much? I wish they wouldn't fight so much. Not for me. I can take it. But. I pour myself something strong and carry it with me to my bedroom. I go to the TV, pull the video from my bag, and put it in. I sit there on my bed, in the half darkness of the approaching morning, and I watch it all again on the screen. I watch him kiss her. I watch her kiss him back. There's a little static, but it's all pretty clear. I can see almost everything. I watch him kiss her neck, watch her crane it and intimate a moan. I'm in the television's glow. I watch him touch her breasts, her fumble with his cummerbund, him begin work at what is always an inconvenient dress. I can see out of the rear window the receding rotunda of the Capitol, and the blurred image of someone crossing the street behind us. The person is looking at the car, which means maybe he can see. Who is that? What can he see? I watch her lick her palm, and I don't know why, but that part always makes me so sad. I rewind and watch it again. I watch it again. I watch it dozens, maybe hundreds, of times. She licks her palm before taking his cock. Stop. Rewind. She licks her palm. Stop. Rewind. She licks her palm. Stop. Rewind. She licks her palm. Stop. Usually that's as far as I'll watch. Sometimes I'll make it to the end. Then I take out the video, label it with date and names, and put it on the shelf with the others, none of which I ever watch after the night itself. Jenny Barnes and Mark Fisher—Friday, May 14, 1999. Beth Baxter and David Jordan—Saturday, May 15, 1999. Mary Robinson and Casey Proctor—Tuesday, May 18, 1999. Gloria Sanders and Patrick Williamson—Thursday, May 20, 1999. Leslie Modell and Ronald Brack—Friday, May 21, 1999. Chase Merrick and Glenn Cross—Saturday, May 22, 1999. I don't watch the videos to get off. I never touch myself, if that's what you're thinking. If that's what you're thinking then you haven't understood a thing.

Iwo Jima isn't real. The island is real. The battle is real. The monument is real, too. But it's based on a staged photograph. Joe Rosenthal, the Associated Press photographer who shot it, was there when our boys captured the island. There really were those seven marines. They really did grab at the flagpole. But he couldn't snap the picture in time. So he restaged it. While the smoke still hung behind the soldiers, while their foreheads were still pelleted with sweat, he arranged them for the picture. And who knows how similar it was to what actually happened. He swore it was the same. Exactly as it was, he said, right down to whose hands were where on the flagpole. The picture won Rosenthal the Pulitzer in 1945, and was the model for the memorial, as is how we have come to remember Iwo Jima. Our memories are bound to that image, which isn't even real.

If I can go to bed at this point, I go to bed. Usually I can't. They're still fighting upstairs, I wish they would stop fighting already, and I'm just not feeling good enough to go to sleep. I'll make a bowl of tomato soup from the can. Maybe a grilled cheese. I'll drink another. Morning is coming. Should I start early? I'll start early. I've got a prom at night. Bethesda. Lynn Mitchell and Ross White. Everyone, except for my neighbors upstairs, is asleep, and I can imagine the first rays pushing over the seven marines at the memorial. I can see it. I know how the sun will reveal them, how it will make them silhouettes before illuminating them. It's cold there and it's cold here. I'll go back out to the car with a rag from the cupboard and clean the backseat.

Alvin Happens Upon the Greatest Line Ever

BY ROBERT OLEN BUTLER

THERE MUST BE a God. Now that all those nations that got together—who knows which ones?—I've never been any good in Mr. Frank's geography class—Russia's one of them and Korea's one, I think, some Korea or other—now that they've launched their nuclear missiles and we've launched ours and all the old geezer anchormen are crying at the same time—zap, zap, zap with the remote in my hand and Tom and Peter and Dan are weeping like babies right there before us, one after the other—now that all this end-of-the-world stuff everybody's been talking about till you just want to go, "Oh, shut up, you people," now that it's finally suddenly happening, here I find myself sitting on a couch right beside the hottest girl in school, right here in the church teen center, and nobody else is around but her and me. Like, I've got these parents who are probably taking the trash out now, cleaning the toilets or something, determined not to let a thing like this upset their routine. They had to drop me off for the Youths for Jesus meeting half an hour early so I wouldn't be late no matter how bad things sounded on the TV. And Jennifer Platt is sitting here right next to me, her own parents out of town somewhere, and she walked over from her house, not even knowing how things were going in the world, her being the silliest, hottest, sweetest girl God ever created. And now she sits beside me, me of all people, with my face breaking out and my hair geeking around on my head, and her long daisy-blond hair is rippling down her back and her big blue eyes are wide with terror, turned up to the TV, watching Dan Rather mopping at his eyes with a handkerchief, and she's making a little choking sound in her throat.

"Is this, like, for real?" she finally manages to say.

"Yes," I say. "It's all over, Jennifer. Life on planet Earth."

"Aren't there supposed to be horsemen or whatever?" she says.

"Horsemen?"

"Like in the Book of Revelation?"

She's looking at me now in a way she never has. She's got nobody else. Her eyes are as blue as the sky that's about to disappear for a year or so in the nuclear winter and they are still wide with how wonked-out she is. These eyes are turning to me for guidance, but I never have listened very close to the prophecies and stuff that Pastor Lynch has been trying to explain. I've been too busy watching Jennifer Platt and thinking I didn't have a shot in the world at her and praying that I was wrong. God does answer prayer. I can finally testify to that.

I say, "Nobody ever knew what that horsemen stuff meant. Now it's clear. God's brought us together to cleave unto each other." I like that *cleave*. I think I've absorbed more in this place than I realize.

Her eyes widen a little bit more. "What are you saying, Alvin?"

"I'm like the horseman."

"Pardon me?"

"To carry you away."

"You can't run from the bomb, Alvin," she says, and her voice is faint.

"I'm talking, like, in metaphors, Jen. Carry you away in the passion that God has put between a man and a woman when they, uh, cleave. Like, aren't we Adam and Eve here? Only in reverse? Like we're the last two left? See, God arranged this."

She's getting confused, but I figure that's okay. She's not saying "no" right off. I'm plugging into a thing she's been looking forward to. Maybe not with me. But I'm in the ballpark. I say, "The missiles are going to hit real soon. There's nowhere else to go. But here we are, you and me. God realizes that neither one of us wants to die a virgin."

Jennifer suddenly looks away and clamps down with her teeth on the knuckle of her right forefinger.

I can hear myself. I'm impressed. Here it is, what's going on outside, and with the White House about twenty miles from where I'm sitting—Jennifer and I are pretty much at ground zero—and I'm being cool as Harrison Ford or somebody.

Jennifer stops biting her knuckle and she looks back at me. Her eyes aren't wide anymore. They're narrow. She's suddenly pretty cool herself. I know she's considering my geekhood. This is the moment when I'm vulnerable. I'm sitting here wishing I knew more about the Bible. I maybe could find just the right passage. Something like, "Give thou to the plain man and thou shalt have riches in heaven." Which isn't bad, really. I'm thinking about quoting that and pretending it's real. But Jennifer lasers her eyes up and down my body and then she looks at the TV.

Just as she does, Dan Rather stares straight at the camera and says, in a quavery voice, "Speaking simply for this reporter, I'd suggest you go as quickly as you can to someone you love and hold them close."

Jennifer's face swings back to me. I figure Dan has given me a real boost here. This should be it. But Jennifer seems to have simply gone back to checking me out, critically. I know there's not much time.

And suddenly I have words. I cry, "Jennifer Platt, the world's coming to an end! We must have sex!"

Her face softens. Well, not softens exactly, because it's still not like soft. But the criticism is gone. The hard eyes are no longer hard. She nods very faintly and she stands up and puts her thumbs in the elastic waistband of her skirt and I can feel my Little Mister Man rising in my pants like a mushroom cloud. I can even set aside the hatred I have for my mother giving such a name as that to my dick and making it stick in my head, like, forever. All that vanishes from me. There is only Jennifer Platt, her skirt down at her ankles now and her legs long and smooth rising to her panties where her thumbs are now poised in the waistband and the very tip of me, the tip of, yes, Little Mister Man, is throbbing like crazy and I say a quick thank you to God, who is definitely in His heaven.

And now the panties descend and a sweet golden plume rises from the center of her and it is a color darker than the hair that is cascading around her face now, this gold, it is not the color of daisies but of sunlight on a white wall at the end of the day. A stopping happens inside me. I cannot breathe from the beauty of it. The beauty of the hair of her loins and also the beauty of sunlight on a wall.

She is moving, lying down on the other end of the couch, and she opens her legs and I am still struggling to draw a breath, and something else is going on inside me. The sunlight will not show itself in this world like Jennifer Platt's pubic hair ever again, not with anyone alive to see it. Jennifer's legs are open and I look at this secret place on her body and it is as pretty as her face, it is the pink of my mother's azaleas and it is pouting like a spoiled child and I love this soft place as it draws me to it, asks me to enter, and it whispers to me now of all that there is to destroy in this world, my mother's flowers and her hands that tend them and the spoiled children and the good children, and I cannot move, I feel the warmth of my tears and I am afraid.

Acknowledgments

THIS BOOK, though it has our names on the cover, was a highly collaborative effort. We'd like to thank our coworkers at *Nerve* for the big and the little things; most of the time we are too busy to tell them how much we appreciate all their support. (That goes double for our fellow editors and assistants, without whom we'd be lost.) We'd also like to single out *Nerve* poetry editor Ross Martin for introducing us to our eventual publisher, and our agent Neeti Madan for seeing it through. Thanks to our editor, Rachel Kahan, who made the process fun. But most of all, thanks to the authors collected here; your talent and achievement helped make *Nerve* the magazine we hoped it could be, and this collection something we are proud to represent. Hats off.

—*Jack Murnighan and Genevieve Field*